WRITING OUR WAY HOME

WRITING OUR WAY HOME

CONTEMPORARY STORIES BY AMERICAN JEWISH WRITERS

*EDITED BY TED SOLOTAROFF
AND NESSA RAPOPORT*

*SCHOCKEN BOOKS
NEW YORK*

Introductions and compilation copyright © 1992 by Ted
Solotaroff and Nessa Rapoport

Acknowledgments of permission to reprint previously published material may be found on pp. ix–xi.

Library of Congress Cataloging-in-Publication Data

Writing our way home: contemporary stories by American
   Jewish writers / edited by Ted Solotaroff and Nessa Rapoport.
      p. cm.
   ISBN 0-8052-4110-8
   1. American fiction—Jewish authors.   2. American fiction—20th century.   3. Jews—United   States—Fiction.
4. Short stories, American.   5. Short stories, Jewish.
I. Solotaroff, Ted, 1928–II. Rapoport, Nessa.
PS647.J4064 1992
813′.01088924—dc20   92-54105

Book design by Chris Welch
Manufactured in the United States of America

First Edition

To the memory of Eliezer Greenberg
and Wolfe Kelman, z"l

Contents

Acknowledgments

We wish to thank our many friends who made suggestions for this collection. We are particularly indebted to our editor, Bonny Fetterman, whose idea it was and who kept us on course.

Grateful acknowledgment is made to the following for permission to reprint previously published material:

Max Apple: "The Eighth Day" originally published in *Ploughshares* and included in his collection *Free Agents*, (Harper & Row, 1984). Copyright © 1983 by Max Apple. Reprinted by permission of the author c/o International Creative Management.

Saul Bellow: "Something to Remember Me By" originally published in *Esquire* Magazine, is reprinted from *Something to Remember Me By* by Saul Bellow. Copyright © 1990 by Saul Bellow. Reprinted by permission of Viking Penguin, a division of Penguin Books USA Inc.

Marsha Lee Berkman: "Deeds of Love and Rage" originally published in the *Sonora Review*. Also appeared in *Lilith* and in the anthology *Shaking Eve's Tree*, published by the Jewish Publication Society. Copyright © 1983 by Marsha Lee Berkman. Reprinted by permission of the author.

Michael Chabon: "S Angel" from *The Model World* by Michael Chabon. Copyright © 1991 by Michael Chabon. Reprinted by permission of William Morrow & Company, Inc.

E. L. Doctorow: "The Writer in the Family" from *Lives of the Poets* by E. L. Doctorow. Copyright © 1984 by E. L. Doctorow. Reprinted by permission of Random House, Inc.

Allegra Goodman: "Variant Text" from *Total Immersion* by Allegra Goodman. Copyright © 1990 by Allegra Goodman. Reprinted by permission of HarperCollins Publishers.

Mark Helprin: "North Light" from *Ellis Island and Other Stories* by Mark Helprin. Copyright © 1976, 1977, 1979, 1980, 1981 by Mark Helprin. Reprinted by permission of Delacorte Press/Seymour Lawrence, a division of Bantam Doubleday Dell Publishing Group, Inc.

Allen Hoffman: "Building Blocks" originally published in *Commentary*, May 1974. This story also appeared in *Kagan's Superfecta and Other Stories*, Abbeville Press, NY, 1981. Reprinted by permission of the author. All rights reserved.

Johanna Kaplan: "Sickness" originally published in *Other People's Lives* by Johanna Kaplan, Knopf, 1975. Copyright © 1975 by Johanna Kaplan. Reprinted by permission of Georges Borchardt, Inc. on behalf of the author.

Deirdre Levinson: "April 19, 1985" originally published in *The Threepenny Review*. Reprinted by permission of the author.

Bernard Malamud: "The Silver Crown" from *The Stories of Bernard Malamud*. Copyright © 1972, 1983 by Bernard Malamud. Reprinted by permission of Farrar, Straus & Giroux, Inc.

Daphne Merkin: "Enchantment" copyright © 1992 by Daphne Merkin. Reprinted by permission of William Morris Agency on behalf of the author.

Leonard Michaels: "Murderers" from *I Would Have Saved Them If I Could* by Leonard Michaels. Copyright © 1975 by Leonard Michaels. Reprinted by permission of Farrar, Straus & Giroux, Inc.

Cynthia Ozick: "Bloodshed" from *Bloodshed and Three Other Novellas* by Cynthia Ozick. Copyright © 1976 by Cynthia Ozick. Reprinted by permission of Alfred A. Knopf, Inc.

Grace Paley: "Zagrowsky Tells" from *Later the Same Day* by Grace Paley. Copyright © 1985 by Grace Paley. Reprinted by permission of Farrar, Straus & Giroux, Inc.

Nessa Rapoport: "The Woman Who Lost Her Names" originally published in *Lilith* Magazine. Also included in *The Woman Who Lost Her Names: Selected Writing by American Jewish Women*, Harper & Row, 1980. Copyright © 1979 by Nessa Rapoport. Reprinted by permission of the author. All rights reserved.

Robin Roger: "The Pagan Phallus" originally published in *Fire-*

TED SOLOTAROFF

The Open Community

*T*he last significant general collection of American-Jewish fiction was edited by Irving Howe in 1977. In his introduction Howe stressed the central influence of the immigrant culture, known as "Yiddishkeit," in shaping the distinctive subjects and styles that had made this fiction a significant movement in twentieth-century American letters, comparable to that of the Southern modernists. Among the similarities Howe found was that "in both instances a subculture finds its voice and its passion at exactly the moment it approaches disintegration." As such the sense of living at the end of a traditional way of life provided the writer with "an inescapable subject: the judgment, affection, and hatred they bring to bear upon the remembered world of their youth, and the costs exacted by their struggle to tear themselves away." Thus most of the stories Howe selected were set in a rapidly receding past, mainly in urban neighborhoods where few, if any, Jews live today, and dealt with conflicts in a family, a community, an individual that acculturation and pluralism have subsequently complicated or dimmed. A story like Saul Bellow's "The Old System" or Delmore Schwartz's "America! America!" or Tillie Olsen's "Tell Me a Riddle" seems today like a log that burns all the more brightly because the rest of the fire is barely smoldering or has gone out.

Though Yiddishkeit lingers on (most often, we found, in stories about old people and their discomfited children), it is inevitably thinning out into recovered memories or imagined experience of what it was like and meant to grow up Jewish in an America of momentous possibilities that was at the same time sharply divided between "us" and "them." Hence Howe surmised that the flowering of American-Jewish fiction from the 1930s through the 1960s might well prove to be another ironic wink of history, another transient staging area, like Yiddish modernism, for its own brilliant demise. As Howe wrote, without a shared past the questions and problems of Jewish identity do not yield "a thick enough sediment of felt life and shared experience to enable a new outburst of writing about American Jews."

But Howe's view overlooks certain generational distinctions and literary processes. First, the immigrant ethos was relatively speechless in English, and Yiddishkeit became a force in American fiction only after it was integrated into the dynamic of acculturation. It was the post-immigrant culture that related Wordsworth to the Rabbis, that rejected Hemingway for Kafka, that tried to play Henny Youngman off against Henry James. And the more acculturation accelerated and broadened, the more diverse became Jewish literary and intellectual life (a Bernard Malamud and a Norman Mailer, a Paul Goodman and an Irving Kristol) and the more contingent became the ties to the world of their fathers. At most, Yiddishkeit was an ingredient of the new Jewish fiction that began to appear in the 1930s and had become even more individualized and more naturalized when it broke through to full recognition twenty years later.

Howe, then, is conflating two different cultural generations that should be kept distinct in talking about the past. It makes more sense to us to speak of a post-immigrant culture that is coming to an end and a post-acculturated one that has been coming into being, along with much else that is new in our increasingly pluralistic society.

Even so there remains a kind of Jewish fixation on the past as the matrix of Jewish consciousness. Harold Rosenberg, who saw more creative possibilities than Howe does in the "open community" that American Jews now inhabit, still comes back to the idea that Jewish experience is grounded in the possibility of linking oneself "with the collective and individual experience of earlier Jews." Such has been the mind-set of Diaspora Jewry all the way back to the waters of Babylon. But what if this is no longer quite the case? What if the Jewish identification of many writers and readers alike has become grounded in post-acculturation alternatives here as in Israel, in varieties of present or recent experience, both religious and secular, that they share with other Jews and that in some cases evoke a deeper Jewish past than that of the Bronx tenements or of City College in the 1930s? What if Jewish sensibility is funded today as much by imagination as by memory?

Wishing to explore this possibility, we chose as our starting point the year 1967 because it marked a turning point in American Jewish consciousness. For 1967 was the year of the Six-Day War, which began as the darkest moment in the history of the new state of Israel, ended as the brightest, and lives on in its consequences as the most problematic. The very brevity of the war, the dramatic transformation of horrified concern to intense relief and vaulting pride, changed the way that American Jews thought not only about Israel but about themselves. As Arthur Hertzberg, Leonard Fein, and others have observed, Israel henceforth became the religion of American Jews, the transcendent object of their politics and philanthropy and pilgrimages and as such a new source of loyalty and solidarity, and in time of dogma and controversy.

The significance of Israel's peril and triumph was strengthened and amplified by other developments that impacted on the psyche of American Jewry in the 1960s. The most notable one was the emergence of the Holocaust from the darkness and silence of relative repression in the previous decade into the public light and clamor of the Eichmann trial and of its aftermath, in which the issue of the cooperation of European Jewry in its own destruction was raised by Hannah Arendt's *Eichmann in Jerusalem* and debated and soul-searched by everyone. The sedulous efficiency of the Jewish Councils and their police and the obedience of their communities that made the Final Solution so remarkably easy for the Nazis to implement threw into a glaring perspective the organized and habitual docility bred both by millennia of persecution and by the politics of two centuries of Emancipation, in which an influential few spoke for the community. This awareness was only a thought away from the timid, don't-shout-"Fire"-in-a-crowded-theater behavior of the spokesmen and rank-and-file of American Jewry during the Nazi era. So, too, the relative indifference of the Allied governments, including our own, to the Final Solution came back to mind while Israel stood alone, confronting three invading armies with their own final solution in mind. It is not fanciful to say that in destroying these armies the Israeli Defense Force also changed the political stance of Jewish memory, the open palms of "What can a Jew do?" turning into the fists of "Never Again!" which you didn't have to belong to the Jewish Defense League to clench.

With the Israeli army and its American volunteers a new type of figure has come into being: the Jew *moyen sensuel* with a gun, a role formerly reserved for the gangster, the terrorist or, more lately the tsisis-clad settler, the sports of traditional Jewish morality. What makes Mark Helprin's brief story "North Light" so potent and poignant is the light it throws on an Israeli citizen's army preparing for battle: men who were husbands, fathers, and otherwise immersed in the soft facts of life only a day before now having to summon the ferocity, poise, and solidarity that will enable them to fight and possibly survive.

American-Jewish fiction, with the exception of Philip Roth's *The Counterlife*, has been slow, and perhaps loath, to explore the more vexed subject that has been set by the occupation of the West Bank and Gaza: the morality that grows out of the barrel of a gun confronting the morality that grows out of two thousand years of oppression. Though the subject is front and center in Israeli fiction, it has been leading a furtive life in its American counterpart. One can see it at work, I think, in Cynthia Ozick's "Bloodshed." The story has been criticized, not least by Ozick herself, on the grounds that the two guns—one fake, one real—that Bleilip, the visitor to a Hasidic commune, has been hiding have no function in the story and thereby create dissonance. But one can read "Bloodshed" as dramatizing two responses to the Holocaust: the religious one, earned by the rebbe in the death camps, who brandishes the power and profundity of the Temple service of Atonement and his own spiritual intuition against the skepticism and concealed weapons of the secularist Bleilip. In Ozick's view, Bleilip's guns represent not the clenched fist of defiance but the empty hands of nihilism and blasphemy. In my view, Bleilip's stinking weapon comes out of the collective unconscious of a people who have abhorred violence but who now depend upon their mastery of it for survival and domination. Alfred Kazin tells of an incident he witnessed in Jerusalem that evokes this ambivalence. A young soldier returning from the Yom Kippur War, exhausted and still heavily armed, is approached by an old man in religious garb who shouts at him, "You're the Messiah? You?!" One can imagine much the same encounter taking place on a street in Jerusalem two thousand years ago between a warrior of the Zealots and a follower of Rabbi Yochanan ben Zakkai.

Another decisive change that took place in the 1960s was the conflict with American blacks. This was focused and fed by the struggle that broke out in New York in 1967 over the issue of local school control, pitting black militants against the American Federation of Teachers, the most powerful remnant of the waning Jewish labor movement. Formerly this movement, along with Jewish liberalism generally, had been allied with black rights and aspirations, but now the vehement rhetoric generated on both sides brought into the open the class feelings and prejudices that had long smoldered in the Northern ghettos, the one place where the Jew wasn't the underdog and remained as the most visible white presence: teachers and school officials as well as merchants, landlords, and employers.

Grace Paley's story "Zagrowsky Tells" is extremely alert to the

twists and turns of Jewish ambivalence toward blacks as the mild
but unyielding racism of the crusty old pharmacist brings down
upon him the wrath of his daughter as well as of the sixties-type
women of the community. But good fiction turns the findings of
sociology back into the questions held at a deeper level. There is a
kind of Biblical outrage in the embattled Zagrowsky, who bares
his breast, having been given a black grandson in his old age
("Tell! That opens up the congestion a little—the lungs are for
breathing, not secrets"), that evokes the suppressed racial tangle
that goes back to the dawn of Jewish history in the story of Isaac
and Ishmael.

The cultural revolution of the later 1960s initiated other currents
that were to flow through American-Jewish life in the next twenty-
five years and contribute to its sea change. Toward the end of the
1960s, a group of learned young Jews from the Boston/Brandeis
scene who were impatient with suburban Judaism began to conduct
their own services and study traditional texts together. They were
also intent on leveling the patriarchal rules that made women sec-
ond-class members of the congregation. From the beginning, they
made no distinction between the sexes in leading the prayer service,
reading from the Torah, and interpreting the text. Known as the
Boston Havurah, their intense and yet informal mode of Jewish
practice sooned fanned out to other cities on the Eastern seaboard
and across the country, creating a movement of spiritual activism
that many rabbis were to welcome within their door to vitalize their
congregation. Coming into being around the same time, spiritual
activism and feminism have been the tide and the moon for large
numbers of Jewish women, powerfully affecting their identity, kin-
ship, and creativity and bringing some of them to the forefront of
contemporary Jewish thought and art.

As Bonny Fetterman, our editor, has suggested, the Jewish revival, both religious and cultural, is related to another major change:
the presence of Israel has enabled many more Jews to be conversant
with Hebrew as a living language and culture than their forebears
were. Or, to put it another way, Yiddishkeit has not dried up and
blown away but rather is being both supplanted and to some extent
resuscitated by a nascent contemporary Jewish culture that lives

on easier and perhaps more fertile terms with religious Judaism than does the Israeli one, and seeks to draw upon its vast literary tradition.

In her share of the Introduction, Nessa Rapoport explores some of the specific creative possibilities that are open to the "Jewishly educated and culturally confident community of writers" that has been springing up all around us and is represented in this collection. Not surprisingly, most of her examples are women writers. It is worth noting that Irving Howe's collection of only fifteen years ago selected four stories by women, while in ours, they make up a small majority. This is not an outcropping of literary P.C. but rather a reflection of the general literary situation today in which women writers enjoy two distinct advantages: an accession of fresh, aggressive consciousness and an engaged audience.

Rapoport's phrase "culturally confident" also has a particular force in explaining why the American-Jewish scene is much more interesting, varied, and intense than one would have predicted twenty-five years ago. Until then it was widely assumed, given the rate of intermarriage and pace of assimilation, that American Jews were on the same road to oblivion that European Jews had been following before the Holocaust. (There were studies showing that intermarriage would have pretty much ended Jewish life in Germany by the year 2000.) But from Genesis to the emigration of Soviet Jewry, Jewish survival has worked in uncanny ways and so it has been proving in the United States and Israel. In the former, pluralism has become a fact of life, underwriting an unprecedented degree of Jewish diversity, self-expression, security, and influence. Today the varieties of Jewish experience run the gamut from the Hasidic polities of Brooklyn to the gay congregations of Greenwich Village, from neo-Orthodox yuppies to New Age kabbalists. When the Israel lobby challenges the President; or a photograph featuring a beautiful nude woman appears on the cover of *Tikkun*, a leading Jewish magazine, to illustrate a feature with the title "Sexuality After Thomas/Hill"; or English professors at Yale are prominent in the revival of Jewish learning and the publication of a best-selling version of the J Text of the Bible; or the *Forward*, the leading institution of Yiddishkeit, is published in English, you can be pretty sure there is much going on today that was not dreamt of by the immigrant culture. Jews today, rightly or wrongly, are perceived to be part of the white mainstream. Their formerly marginal position is now occupied by the people of color. Their literature now rivals the Wasp one in prestige and sales. The multicultural movement passes them by and anti-Semitism is mostly a demagogic way of attacking the power structure.

This sense of confidence, openness, and diversity is particularly evident in American-Jewish fiction. Twenty-five years ago it was pretty well dominated by Bellow, Malamud, and Roth—the Hart, Schaffner, and Marx of the industry. Though none of the later writers have yet achieved a comparable status and influence, with the possible exception of Cynthia Ozick and E. L. Doctorow, the outcropping of Jewish literary talent remains as abundant as it is varied. Its eclecticism is fostered by the developments we have been noting, both in the secular and the religious communities, that have pretty well ended the reign of the post-immigrant ethos. For a time, one could say that the fierce conflicts within this ethos—claims of the tribe and the community versus those of the individual, the pull of the past versus the push of the present—formed the central tension of American-Jewish fiction. There was a clear distinction between the writer who was a Jew and the Jew who was a writer, the former insisting on the right to explore the Jewish subject, as one did any other, by one's experience and imagination; the latter insisting that her or his experience and imagination were largely formed by and served the history and mission of the Jewish people. It was fairly easy to tell the "marginal" writers from the "authentic" ones since the protagonists of each were, broadly speaking, the antagonists of the other.

Things are no longer so clear-cut. In Allegra Goodman's story "Variant Text," high-level acculturation and intense Orthodoxy go hand-in-hand in the person of Cecil Birnbaum, Shavian scholar, *baal koreh* (presiding reader of the Torah service), and agnostic ("When you read a book, do you have to know the author to enjoy it?"). Cecil's contradictions are hardly unique in the sophisticated, observant community in Oxford whose preschool follows the principles of "Kohlberg, Piaget, the Rav Soloveichik" in inculcating "a

Torah life-style." Though modern Orthodoxy is satirized, Cecil is only lightly so. That he is a committed feminist who wears an abortion-rights pin to a Sabbath service that deeply offends him because an aliyah has been given to a man whose wife has wheeled a stroller to it, is simply part of the personal syncretism that informs his Judaism. Like his wife's hermetic higher mathematics that requires no maker, Halakhah, the formal structure of Jewish Law, is a superb creation of the human mind, though no less binding for that.

The matter-of-fact tone of "Variant Text" is as telling as its content. Like virtually all traditional codes of belief and behavior, Judaism, as Goodman shows, has been caught up in the topsy-turvy universal of change so that its permutations and encounters with modernity have tended to lighten up in the telling. Instead of the former frown of rigid defensiveness, there is the ironic crinkle of tolerance. One sees this genial mingling in Max Apple's story "The Eighth Day," in which the narrator's circumcision, the sign of the Covenant, is reenacted as a block to primal therapy and romance. In Apple's playful hands a New Age spoof ("Joan . . . was the Einstein of pseudo-science. . . . All her time was spare time except when she didn't believe in time") is deftly turned to yield an insight into Jewish humanism.

In "The Melting Pot" Lynne Sharon Schwartz moves the conflicts of acculturation through and beyond the familiar ones of the first two Jewish generations and into the polyglot tangle of cultures that America has become, particularly on the West Coast. Rita, a young immigration lawyer, is both animated and tormented by her social fluidity, the veritable "melting pot" bubbling within herself: her grandfather, the cantor, and her grandmother, the anarchist, who raised her after her Mexican mother had killed her outcast father. Renegade and orphan, she takes up with a widowed Indian scientist, a fellow exotic but one whose firm identity and caring nature live on comfortable terms with his traditions and his losses. His proposal of marriage mostly serves to point up how unattachable her mixed heritage has left her.

"The Melting Pot" takes us into the mostly unwritten, at least deeply, territory of post-acculturation, pluralism, and intermarriage where the Jewish component survives in this case as a nebulous sense of justice and compassion and a free-floating guilt that is more conducive to fantasies and nightmares than to living.

Given the welter of new social and cultural influences that are redefining America as a multi-ingredient soup rather than a melting pot, it is not surprising that the subject of Jewish identity is increasingly being set against an Israeli background. In Joanna Spiro's story "Three Thousand Years of Your History . . . Take One Year for Yourself," a young American chooses to study and work in Israel rather than follow the example of her friends who travel to more exotic places to help out and tune in. As the title itself suggests, the young narrator is trying to experience Jewish history in the one place left where it flows into the present in order to put some content into her sense of her roots, both so portentous and so meager. But despite her Hebrew classes, friendships, jobs, affairs, she fails to make contact with the buried Jew in herself; what she takes for it seems canceled rather than validated by Israel's obdurate indifference to her. Ironically enough, the meaning, or lack of it, of her experience is posed after she returns to California and is momentarily taken for black by a black male and then spurned.

It is interesting to compare this story with Nessa Rapoport's "The Woman Who Lost Her Names," which also tells of a young American woman who goes to live in Israel. But soon the similarities end, for Yosefah Peniel, née Sarah Levi, is integrated into Israeli life by her Orthodox faith and marriage to a native poet. His language and traditions do not resolve her problem of identity so much as refine it. Subtly employing form and language to orchestrate and "prove" her meaning, the narrative itself is steeped in the aggadic tradition; taking on subtle parallels to the Book of Ruth and some of its texture from the Song of Songs, Ms. Rapoport's story is closer to the meditative tales of Agnon, the great Hebrew modernist, and the early A. B. Yehoshua than it is to the norms of previous American-Jewish fiction. In the story "Orchards" by Eppie Zore'a, a similar use of Biblical allusions and overtones is implanted in a contemporary American idiom to tell the story of an Israeli couple who emigrate to America.

The Holocaust is another frequent theme in this collection, the subject that doesn't go away, the black shadow athwart Jewish memory, the communion with the "tremendum," to use the late Arthur A. Cohen's term, that perhaps most maintains the diverse Jewish population as the people of memory. The stories we have chosen, from among many, many others, deal with the half-life of the devastation that remains in the psychic marrow: infiltrating the opulence of Isaac Bashevis Singer's "A Party in Miami Beach"; mixing its reactivated screams of terror with those from Hiroshima to disrupt the moral malaise of an academic conference on genocide in Lore Segal's "The Reverse Bug"; but also providing an occasion for mother-daughter bonding in Deirdre Levinson's "April 19th, 1985."

In rescuing the Holocaust from the banality of repetitiousness, these stories from writers of diverse backgrounds provide another indication of the fresh winds of imagination that blow from various sectors of the Jewish scene. In the late 1950s, when I began to pay attention to American-Jewish fiction, I was quickly led to believe that the interesting work was being done by the "marginal" writers, that is, those who stood at a certain remove on either side of the hyphen, which enabled them to see anew and in greater complexity what more accustomed eyes took for granted or missed at the seder or the humanities staff meeting, in the dietary laws or the rules and lore of baseball. Their freedom of observation and style were typically in sharp contrast to the work of the committed Jewish writers whose essays were heavy on high-mindedness and their fiction on warmheartedness (except toward the "self-haters"!) and whose prose was typically formal or schmaltzy as though any fresh or idiomatic English was *treife*. Hence I would hardly have been prepared to read a story like Allen Hoffman's "Building Blocks," which begins with a free-wheeling account of the traditional three weeks of mourning for the Second Temple. Though the narrator comes from a family that really knows how to mourn, it is still hard for him to keep it up when Hank Aaron has hit his 700th home run or Sandy Koufax pitched another no-hitter, or to prevent counter-thoughts such as, "If the Temple had not been destroyed, what would Einstein have been, a camel driver in Beersheba? . . . If only we hadn't transgressed His Sabbath—our Sabbath. If only we had minded our own business like the Italians and Greeks and all the other short, swarthy races of antiquity. . . ." This is certainly a new tone from an Orthodox rabbi who spells God G-d; moreover, the story that follows moves with the confident economy of an accomplished writer between an Upper West Side shul and a battlefield on the Russian front in World War I to dramatize the point that in Judaism beauty and ugliness are matters of conduct rather than of objects.

At the other end of the contemporary Jewish spectrum is a story like Michael Chabon's "S Angel," which portrays a designer-label wedding reception in the Jewish Oz of Beverly Hills where acculturation has progressed to the point of becoming mutual: "even ex-cheerleaders from Ames, Iowa, and men named Lars . . . spoke with a schmoozing accent." The title, taken from the dispersed letters of a misfolded map of Los Angeles, sticks in the mind as a metaphor for a broken and vanishing history. Or there is Robin Roger's thoroughly emancipated young woman, who writes advertising copy for the Salvation Army and yearns for an uncircumsised phallus, the last vestige of the Other.

In his introduction to *Jewish-American Stories*, Howe quotes a remark of Saul Bellow's that in "the stories of the Jewish tradition, the world, and even the universe, have a human meaning. Indeed, the Jewish imagination has sometimes been found guilty of making too much of a case for us, for mankind." But this humanism has been under siege from within for some time now; and at least two of the stories we have included, Bernard Malamud's "The Silver Crown" and Leonard Michaels's "Murderers," are, for all their difference in tone and content, both subversive of the moral sentiments they would be expected to give rise to. In Michaels's story, the death of a boy voyeur is about as coldly devalued as fiction gets; and Malamud's tale of a spiritual charlatan is about as demonic.

Perhaps what most binds this eclectic collection together and gives it a characteristic Jewish thrust is the intensity of family relationships. What Walden Pond is to Thoreau or the West End of London to Henry James, a family situation is to the Jewish writer: the homestand of his or her confrontation with life as well as the repository of distinctively Jewish cultural and moral norms. For example, Bellow's own story "Something to Remember Me By" sets up two realms of death and abandonment. There is the Jewish one where the young narrator's mother is dying and which he stays away from as much as possible, knowing his future is literary and elsewhere, and the Gentile one where he encounters a dead girl, is seduced and robbed of his money and clothes, and, wearing a woman's outfit, is forced to help a drunk and his neglected daughters. What connects the two phases is the cultural contrasts between the two modes of family life and the moral point of the narrative that joins them—implicit, but all the more powerful for that: a boy who deserts his dying mother is punished not only by being abandoned himself but also by being turned into a girl. One can see that same sort of moral providence acting through the closeness of Jewish family relationships in Marsha Lee Berkman's "Deeds of Love and Rage," Grace Paley's "Zagrowsky Tells," and Adam Schwartz's study of a dysfunctional single parent and her son in "Where Is It Written?" In his four-dimensional portrayal of Kafka, Philip Roth employs the normalities of a post-immigrant family to present this profoundly enigmatic figure as a Jewish type—an example of *edelkeit,* or gentility—as well as to supply an imaginary chapter of his life that points up the inexorable intertwining of the familiar and the strange that bound Kafka's character to his work and both to his fate.

Such stories also exhibit the strand of continuity that weaves through the fabric of recent American fiction. In emphasizing new developments and possibilities we hardly wish to deny the lingering force of the post-immigrant ethos. The point of *Writing Our Way Home* is that it presents an open literary community rather than the more clearly defined and divided one that previously existed. In its fiction, the religious and the secular, the experimental and the traditional, the realistic and the surreal cohabit, and even sometimes nuzzle, more or less peaceably. At the same time there is a relatively vacant area in which we found very few stories to consider and none that met the standards of our individual tastes. This is the recent public realm.

In an era that produced a Henry Kissinger and an Ed Koch, a

Norman Podhoretz and a Noam Chomsky, a Meyer Kahane and an Ivan Boesky, a Jerry Rubin and a Jonathan Pollard, a Barbara Streisand and a Betty Friedan, an Elie Wiesel and a Paul Simon, to name but a few intriguing figures to conjure with, it is passing strange that fiction writers—and this is true of novelists as well as story writers—have steered clear of the fascinating roles and conflicts that Jews play out in contemporary society. One can, of course, view this dearth as part of the general withdrawal of interest from political, economic, social, and intellectual concerns in recent American writing, and though the point has been made many times before, it still seems worth addressing to American-Jewish writers whose European forebears in this century so frequently transposed the Jewish interest in politics and society into literature. Kafka, Canetti, Joseph Roth, Koestler, Doris Lessing, Carlos and Primo Levi, Bruno Schultz, George Konrad, Danilo Kiš, Nadine Gordimer . . . the list goes on and on. The great theme of Jewish writers in the European twentieth century has not been the Jewish family and community but rather the adventure of its progeny and their descendants in contending with the forces and issues of their time. On the other hand, the encounter of Judaism with modernity in the fiction of S. Y. Agnon and other Israeli writers provides a new continent for the traditional imagination to colonize. Now that American-Jewish fiction has achieved a comparable freedom, resourcefulness, and diversity, as reflected in this collection, the question of its further development may well rest on its ability to put the dimming concerns of the post-immigrant ethos even farther behind it and to take up those of our deep past and open present.

NESSA RAPOPORT

Summoned to the Feast

*I*n 1948, the philosopher Simon Rawidowicz published an
essay in Hebrew titled "Am ha-Holekh va-Met"—"The Ever-
Dying People." Reprinted in English in 1967, the essay contends
that "there was hardly a generation in the Diaspora period which
did not consider itself the final link in Israel's chain." The Jews
have viewed not only their tragedies as proof of their imminent
demise but their accomplishments as well. Poets and scholars from
Maimonides on, many of whom lived in what we now regard as a
golden age for Jewry, have lamented their plight as the last of their
people.

American-Jewish literary critics have been subject to the same
propensity. With the passing of the immigrant generation, the
argument runs, we American Jews have lost the status of outsiders,

marginal to mainstream society, that enabled us to write great fiction. Accepted and assimilated as we are, from whence will a vibrant American-Jewish literature emerge?

This kaddish, as Rawidowicz demonstrates, is perennially premature. The immigrant generation of Eastern European Jews that arrived here in the first decades of this century has been followed not only by three generations of native-born Americans but by succeeding waves of Jewish immigration—Syrian, Israeli, Iranian, South American, Soviet, and, once again, Eastern European. These Jews bring with them their own languages and modes of perception. Their writers will, like the immigrants who preceded them, have something to say about their communities within America, and about the tensions between their cultural inheritance and this country's.

So, too, will other kinds of Jews we are only beginning to hear from: children and grandchildren of Holocaust survivors, converts to Judaism, Sephardim, descendants of *conversos* in the American Southwest, lesbians, and gay men. Each of these groups has an idiosyncratic experience and point of view out of which imaginative writing may prosper.

The resulting literature will be new in what it represents, depicting Jews we have not yet met on the page, in predicaments and attitudes that will be fresh and distinctive. But sociology is only one ground from which to dispute the verdict of cultural extinction. There is a larger, grander reason—a literary one—that supports a belief in the ongoing flowering of Jewish letters in America. For Jews, as a covenantal community, are necessarily a literary one. We are bound together not only by our history as a people but by a history of passion for one book, a book that has sustained us as well as much of what is called "culture."

From that book, over thousands of years, and inextricably part of the way we read it, have come commentaries, arguments, parables, laws, legends, mystical meditations, poems, and songs. These writings constitute an astonishing literary civilization, which, like the best imaginative writing, exemplifies a sanctioned intoxication with language, stunning formal inventiveness, imagery made resonant by millennia of use, a dazzling range of style from the sacred to the satiric, and a relentless resistance to nostalgia, cliché, and verbal decadence.

Like fiction, this enormous body of work is interpretive, each book commenting on and responding to previous writers and their books in a widening stream from the Biblical source. At the apex of this ever-growing literature are those books that will never be surpassed or displaced: the Torah, Prophets, and Writings; the Talmud; and the praise and supplication of the daily and festival liturgies.

Over centuries our scholars developed an elaborate and sophisticated methodology of reading these texts in their quest to understand God's world, their people's destiny, and what was being asked of them. As a result, authors of Jewish interpretive writing are cited and debated on the pages of succeeding generations of commentators, even hundreds of years later, in the present tense. "Rashi says"; "Ibn Ezra claims": these writers lived nearly one thousand years ago. What greater immortality?

American-Jewish writing of the fifties and sixties transformed American letters by drawing on and legitimizing recent Jewish experience. But our fiction can equally be a dialogue with earlier Jewish books; it can retrieve the materials and structures of an august and infinitely rich imaginative tradition for art.

Such a strategy requires a Jewishly educated and culturally confident community of writers. In an era in which people are struggling to grant each ethnic tradition its cultural and moral due, we had best not mistake our material and sociological acceptance in this country for an entirely identical literary history. Judaism, manifested in its writings, is not a parochial subset of some large and vague universal tradition but rather the informing revelation of many subsequent ones in American, Anglo, Arabic, and other literary cultures. Our texts, in Hebrew, Judeo-Arabic, Yiddish, Ladino, as well as the languages we shared with our host Diaspora countries, are not reified artifacts; they are a virtually unknown body of work, rigorous and demanding, vital as long as they are read.

This anthology offers new Jewish subjects, as Ted Solotaroff demonstrates above, and newly employed Jewish literary strategies. The latter include Allegra Goodman's post-assimilationist bravura of unitalicized Hebrew; Johanna Kaplan's transformation of contemporary stereotypes of assimilation ("the Jewish prince") into authentic, organizing archetypes of Jewish mythical history ("Joseph Nasi, Joseph the prince"), as well as her dreamy leaps of verbal association that, in their midrashic technique, do not distinguish between the heroine's story in the present and the many Jewish tales that are her more real life; Daphne Merkin's juxtaposition of an Orthodox, worldly aristocracy with secular upper-class America, in syntax that ironically echoes her subject by reflecting the native German of her narrator's family; Cynthia Ozick's obsession with uniquely Jewish ideas and texts, amplified by a diction so scrupulous it seems to pay tribute to the Biblical injunction against the blurring of kinds; Robin Roger's re-creation of classic Jewish-Christian theological disputation from the funny and erotic viewpoint of a young Jewish woman; and Eppie Zore'a's effortless shuttle between contemporary and Biblical allusion, in an American-Jewish story as conditioned by Hebrew as our stories have been by Yiddish.

Having won our place in American culture, we are beginning to be confident enough to reclaim Jewish culture—and its influence on the civilizations of both West and East. It is as if our writers have taken the Talmudic exhortation about the Torah—"Turn through it and turn through it again, for everything is in it"—and applied it to the Jewish literary tradition as a resource for their work.

Over one hundred years ago, at the same time as the first massive wave of Jewish immigration arrived in the United States, a phenomenon unprecedented in history was taking place: the revival, after two thousand years, of Hebrew as a spoken language. In the Jewish year 5753, approaching the American year 2000, American-Jewish fiction is starting to reflect not only Jewish lives but Jewish letters. Today, in alliance with the creators of a flourishing Hebrew literature across the water, we are coming out of the wilderness to make culture.

WRITING OUR WAY HOME

MAX APPLE

The Eighth Day

I was always interested in myself, but I never thought I went back so far. Joan and I talked about birth almost as soon as we met. I told her I believed in the importance of early experience.

"What do you mean by early?" she asked. "Before puberty, before loss of innocence?"

"Before age five," I said.

She sized me up. I could tell it was the right answer.

She had light-blond hair that fell over one eye. I liked the way she moved her hair away to look at me with two eyes when she got serious.

"How soon before age five?" She took a deep breath before she asked me that. I decided to go the limit.

"The instant of birth," I said, though I didn't mean it and had no idea where it would lead me.

She gave me the kind of look then that men would dream about if being men didn't rush us so.

With that look Joan and I became lovers. We were in a crowded restaurant watching four large goldfish flick their tails at each other in a display across from the cash register. There was also another couple, who had introduced us.

Joan's hand snuck behind the napkin holder to rub my right index finger. With us chronology went backwards. Birth led us to love.

II

Joan was twenty-six and had devoted her adult life to knowing herself.

"Getting to know another person, especially one from the opposite gender, is fairly easy." She said this after our first night together. "Apart from reproduction it's the main function of sex. The biblical word 'to know' someone is exactly right. But nature didn't give us any such easy and direct ways to know ourselves. In fact, it's almost perverse how difficult it is to find out anything about the self."

She propped herself up on an elbow to look at me, still doing all the talking.

"You probably know more about my essential nature from this simple biological act than I learned from two years of psychoanalysis."

Joan had been through Jung, Freud, LSD, philosophy, and primitive religion. A few months before we met, she had re-experienced her own birth in primal therapy. She encouraged me to do the same. I tried and was amazed at how much early experience I seemed able to remember, with Joan and the therapist to help me. But there was a great stumbling block, one that Joan did not have. On the eighth day after my birth, according to the ancient Hebrew tradition, I had been circumcised. The circumcision and its pain seemed to have replaced in my consciousness the birth trauma. No matter how much I tried, I couldn't get back any earlier than the eighth day.

"Don't be afraid," Joan said. "Go back to birth. Think of all experience as an arch."

I thought of the golden arches of McDonald's. I focused. I howled. The therapist immersed me in warm water. Joan, already many weeks past her mother's postpartum depression, watched and coaxed. She meant well. She wanted me to share pain like an orgasm, like lovers in poems who slit their wrists together. She wanted us to be as content as trees in the rain forest. She wanted our mingling to begin in utero.

"Try," she said.

The therapist rubbed Vaseline on my temples and gripped me gently with Teflon-coated kitchen tongs. Joan shut off all the lights and played in stereo the heartbeat of a laboring mother.

For thirty seconds I held my face under water. Two rooms away a tiny flashlight glowed. The therapist squeezed my ribs until I bruised. The kitchen tongs hung from my head like antennae. But I could go back no farther than the hairs beneath the chin of the man with the blade who pulled at and then slit my tiny penis, the man who prayed and drank wine over my foreskin. I howled and I gagged.

"The birth canal," Joan and the therapist said.

"The knife," I screamed, "the blood, the tube, the pain between my legs."

Finally we gave up.

"You Hebrews," Joan said. "Your ancient totems cut you off from the centers of your being. It must explain the high density of neurosis among Jewish males."

The therapist said that the subject ought to be studied, but she didn't think anyone would give her a grant.

I was a newcomer to things like primal therapy, but Joan had been born for the speculative. She was the Einstein of pseudo-science. She knew tarot, phrenology, and metaposcopy the way other people knew about baseball or cooking. All her time was spare time except when she didn't believe in time.

When Joan could not break down those eight days between my birth and my birthright, she became, for a while, seriously anti-Semitic. She used surgical tape to hunch my penis over into a facsimile of precircumcision. She told me that smegma was probably a healthy secretion. For a week she cooked nothing but pork. I didn't mind, but I worried a little about trichinosis because she liked everything rare.

Joan had an incredible grip. Her older brother gave her a set of Charles Atlas Squeezers when she was eight. While she read, she still did twenty minutes a day with each hand. If she wanted to show off, she could close the grip exerciser with just her thumb and middle finger. The power went right up into her shoulders. She could squeeze your hand until her nipples stood upright. She won spending money arm wrestling with men in bars. She had broken bones in the hands of two people, though she tried to be careful and gentle with everyone.

I met Joan just when people were starting to bore her, all people, and she had no patience for pets either. She put up with me, at least at the beginning, because of the primal therapy. Getting me back to my birth gave her a project. When the project failed and she also tired of lacing me with pork, she told me one night to go make love to dark Jewesses named Esther or Rebecca and leave her alone.

I hit her.

"Uncharacteristic for a neurotic Jewish male," she said.

It was my first fight since grade school. Her hands were much stronger than mine. In wrestling she could have killed me, but I stayed on the balls of my feet and kept my left in her face. My reach was longer so she couldn't get me in her grip.

"I'll pull your cock off!" she screamed and rushed at me. When my jab didn't slow her, I hit her a right cross to the nose. Blood spurted down her chin. She got one hand on my shirt and ripped it so hard she sprained my neck. I hit her in the midsection and then a hard but openhanded punch to the head.

"Christ killer, cocksucker," she called me, "wife beater." She was crying. The blood and tears mingled on her madras shirt. It matched the pattern of the fabric. I dropped my arms. She rushed me and got her hands around my neck.

"I must love you," I said, "to risk my life this way."

She loosened her grip but kept her thumbs on my jugular. Her face came down on mine, making us both a bloody mess. We kissed amid the carnage. She let go, but my neck kept her fingerprints for a week.

"I'd never kill anyone I didn't love," she said. We washed each other's faces. Later she said she was glad she hadn't pulled my cock off.

After the fight we decided, mutually, to respect one another more. We agreed that the circumcision was a genuine issue. Neither of us wanted it to come between us.

"Getting to the bottom of anything is one of the great pleasures of life," Joan said. She also believed a fresh start ought to be just that, not one eight days old.

So we started fresh and I began to research my circumcision. Since my father had been dead for ten years, my mother was my only source of information. She was very reluctant to talk about it. She refused to remember the time of day or even whether it happened in the house or the hospital or the synagogue.

"All I know," she said, "is that Reb Berkowitz did it. He was the only one in town. Leave me alone with this craziness. Go swallow dope with all your friends. It's her, isn't it? To marry her in a church you need to know about your circumcision? Do what you want; at least the circumcision is one thing she can't change."

Listening in on the other line, Joan said, "They can even change sex now. To change the circumcision would be minor surgery, but that's not the point."

"Go to hell," my mother said and hung up. My mother and I had not been on good terms since I quit college. She is closer to my two brothers, who are CPAs and have an office together in New Jersey. But, to be fair to my mother, she probably wouldn't want to talk about their circumcisions either.

From the United Synagogue Yearbook which I found in the library of Temple Beth-El only a few blocks from my apartment I located three Berkowitzes. Two were clearly too young to have done me, so mine was Hyman J., listed at Congregation Adath Israel, South Bend, Indiana.

"They all have such funny names," Joan said. "If he's the one, we'll have to go to him. It may be the breakthrough you need."

"Why?" my mother begged, when I told her we were going to South Bend to investigate. "For God's sake, why?"

"Love," I said. "I love her, and we both believe it's important to know this. Love happens to you through bodies."

"I wish," my mother said, "that after eight days they could cut the love off too and then maybe you'd act normal."

South Bend was a three-hundred-mile drive. I made an appointment with the synagogue secretary to meet Hyman Berkowitz late in the afternoon. Joan and I left before dawn. She packed peanut butter sandwiches and apples. She also took along the portable tape recorder so we could get everything down exactly as Berkowitz remembered it.

"I'm not all that into primal therapy anymore," she said as we started down the interstate. "You know that this is for your sake, that even if you don't get back to the birth canal this circumcision thing is no small matter. I mean, it's almost accidental that it popped up in primal; it probably would have affected you in psychoanalysis as well. I wonder if they started circumcising before or after astrology was a very well-developed Egyptian science. Imagine taking infants and mutilating them with crude instruments."

"The instruments weren't so crude," I reminded her. "The ancient Egyptians used to do brain surgery. They invented eye shadow and embalming. How hard was it to get a knife sharp, even in the Bronze Age?"

"Don't be such a defensive Jewish boy," she said. "After all, it's your pecker they sliced, and at eight days too, some definition of the age of reason."

For people who are not especially sexual, Joan and I talk about it a lot. She has friends who are orgiasts. She has watched though never participated in group sex.

"Still," she says, "nothing shocks me like the thought of cutting the foreskin of a newborn."

III

"It's no big deal," Berkowitz tells us late that afternoon. His office is a converted lavatory. The frosted glass windows block what little daylight there still is. His desk is slightly recessed in the cavity where once a four-legged tub stood. His synagogue is a converted Victorian house. Paint is peeling from all the walls. Just off the interstate we passed an ultramodern temple.

"Ritual isn't in style these days," he tells Joan when she asks about his surroundings. "The clothing store owners and scrap dealers have put their money into the Reformed. They want to be more like the goyim."

"I'm a goy," Joan says. She raises her head proudly to display a short straight nose. Her blond hair is shoulder length.

"So what else is new?" Berkowitz laughs. "Somehow, by accident, I learned how to talk to goyim too." She asks to see his tools.

From his desk drawer he withdraws two flannel-wrapped packets. They look like place settings of sterling silver. It takes him a minute or two to undo the knots. Before us lies a long thin pearl-handled jackknife.

"It looks like a switchblade," Joan says. "Can I touch it?" He nods.

She holds the knife and examines the pearl handle for inscriptions.

"No writing?"

"Nothing," says Berkowitz. "We don't read knives."

He takes it from her and opens it. The blade is as long as a Bic pen. Even in his dark office the sharpness glows.

"All that power," she says, "just to snip at a tiny penis."

"Wrong," says Berkowitz. "For the shmekel I got another knife. This one kills chickens."

Joan looks puzzled and nauseated.

"You think a person can make a living in South Bend, Indiana, on newborn Jewish boys? You saw the temple. I've got to compete with a half dozen Jewish pediatricians who for the extra fifty bucks will say a prayer too. When I kill a chicken, there's not two cousins

who are surgeons watching every move. Chickens are my liveli-
hood. Circumcising is a hobby."

"You're cute," Joan tells him.

H. Berkowitz blushes. "Shiksas always like me. My wife worries
that someday I'll run off with a convert. You came all this way to
see my knife?" He is a little embarrassed by his question.

I try to explain my primal therapy, my failure to scream before
the eighth day.

"In my bones, in my body, all I can remember is you, the knife,
the blood."

"It's funny," Berkowitz says, "I don't remember you at all. Did
your parents make a big party, or did they pay me a little extra or
something? I don't keep records, and believe me, foreskins are
nothing to remember."

"I know you did mine."

"I'm not denying. I'm just telling you it's not so special to me to
remember it."

"Reverend," Joan says, "you may think this is all silly, but here
is a man who wants to clear his mind by reliving his birth. Circumcision is standing in the way. Won't you help him?"

"I can't put it back."

"Don't joke with us, Reverend. We came a long way. Will you
do it again?"

"Also impossible," he says. "I never leave a long enough piece
of foreskin. Maybe some of the doctors do that, but I always do a
nice clean job. Look."

He motions for me to pull out my penis. Joan also instructs me
to do so. It seems oddly appropriate in this converted bathroom.

"There," he says, admiringly. "I recognize my work. Clean,
tight, no flab."

"We don't really want you to cut it," Joan says. "He just wants
to relive the experience so that he can travel back beyond it to the
suffering of his birth. Right now your circumcision is a block in his
memory."

Berkowitz shakes his head. I zip my fly.

"You're sure you want to go back so far?"

"Not completely," I admit, but Joan gives me a look.

"Well," Berkowitz says, "in this business you get used to people making jokes, but if you want it, I'll try. It's not like you're asking me to commit a crime. There's not even a rabbinic law against pretending to circumcise someone a second time."

IV

The recircumcision takes place that night at Hyman Berkowitz's house. His wife and two children are already asleep. he asks me to try to be quiet. I am lying on his dining room table under a bright chandelier.

"I'd just as soon my wife not see this," Berkowitz says. "She's not as up to date as I am."

I am naked beneath a sheet on the hard table.

Berkowitz takes a small double-edged knife out of a torn and stained case. I can make out the remnants of his initials on the case. The instrument is nondescript stainless steel. If not for his initials, it might be mistaken for an industrial tool. I close my eyes.

"The babies," he says, "always keep their eyes open. You'd be surprised how alert they are. At eight days they already know when something's happening."

Joan puts a throw pillow from the sofa under my head.

"I'm proud of you," she whispers. "Most other men would never dare to do this. My instincts were right about you." She kisses my cheek.

Berkowitz lays down his razor.

"With babies," he says, "there's always a crowd around, at least the family. The little fellow wrapped in a blanket looks around or screams. You take off the diaper and one-two it's over." He hesitates. "With you it's like I'm a doctor. It's making me nervous, all this talking about it. I've been a mohel thirty-four years and I started slaughtering chickens four years before that. I'm almost ready for Social Security. Just baby boys, chickens, turkeys, occasionally a duck. Once someone brought me a captured deer. He was so beautiful. I looked in his eyes. I couldn't do it. The man understood. He put the deer back in his truck, drove him to the woods, and let him go. He came back later to thank me."

"You're not really going to have to do much," Joan says, "just relive the thing. Draw a drop of blood, that will be enough: one symbolic drop."

"Down there there's no drops," Berkowitz says. "It's close to arteries; the heart wants blood there. It's the way the Almighty wanted it to be."

As Berkowitz hesitates, I begin to be afraid. Not primal fear but very contemporary panic. Fear about what's happening right now, right before my eyes.

Berkowitz drinks a little of the Manischewitz wine he has poured for the blessing. He loosens his necktie. He sits down.

"I didn't have the voice to be a cantor," he says, "and for sure I wasn't smart enough to become a rabbi. Still, I wanted the religious life. I wanted some type of religious work. I'm not an immigrant, you know. I graduated from high school and junior college. I could have done lots of things. My brother is a dentist. He's almost assimilated in White Plains. He doesn't like to tell people what his older brother does.

"In English I sound like the Mafia, 'a ritual slaughterer.' " Berkowitz laughs nervously. "Every time on the forms when it says Job Description, I write 'ritual slaughterer.' I hate how it sounds."

"You've probably had second thoughts about your career right from the start," Joan says.

"Yes, I have. God's work, I tell myself, but why does God want me to slit the throats of chickens and slice the foreskins of babies? When Abraham did it, it mattered; now, why not let the pediatricians mumble the blessing, why not electrocute the chickens?"

"Do you think God wanted you to be a dentist," Joan asks, "or an insurance agent? Don't be ashamed of your work. What you do is holiness. A pediatrician is not a man of God. An electrocuted chicken is not an animal whose life has been taken seriously."

Hyman Berkowitz looks in amazement at my Joan, a twenty-six-year-old gentile woman who has already relived her own birth.

"Not everyone understands this," Berkowitz says. "Most people when they eat chicken think of the crust, the flavor, maybe of Colonel Sanders. They don't consider the life of the bird that flows through my fingers."

"You are indeed a holy man," Joan says.

Berkowitz holds my penis in his left hand. The breeze from the air conditioner makes the chandelier above me sway.

"Do it," I say.

His knife, my first memory, I suddenly think, may be the last thing I'll ever see. I feel a lot like a chicken. I already imagine that he'll hang me upside down and run off with Joan.

She'll break your hands, I struggle to tell him. You'll be out of a job. Your wife was right about you.

The words clot in my throat. I keep my eyes shut tightly.

"I can't do it," Berkowitz says. "I can't do this, even symbolically, to a full-grown male. It may not be against the law; still, I consider it an abomination."

I am so relieved I want to kiss his fingertips.

Joan looks disappointed but she, too, understands.

"A man," Hyman Berkowitz says, "is not a chicken."

I pull on my trousers and give him gladly the fifty-dollar check that was to have been his professional fee. Joan kisses his pale cheek.

The holy man, clutching his cheek, waves to us from his front porch. My past remains as secret, as mysterious, as my father's baldness. My mother in the throes of labor is a stranger I never knew. It will always be so. She is as lost to me as my foreskin. My penis feels like a blindfolded man standing before the executioner who has been saved at the last second.

"Well," Joan says, "we tried."

On the long drive home Joan falls asleep before we're out of South Bend. I cruise the turnpike, not sure of whether I'm a failure at knowing myself. At a roadside rest stop to the east of Indiana beneath a full moon, I wake Joan. Fitfully, imperfectly, we know each other.

"A man," I whisper, "is not a chicken." On the eighth day I did learn something.

SAUL BELLOW

Something to
Remember Me By

When there is too much going on, more than you can
bear, you may choose to assume that nothing in particular is happening, that your life is going round and round like a
turntable. Then one day you are aware that what you took to be a
turntable, smooth, flat, and even, was in fact a whirlpool, a vortex.
My first knowledge of the hidden work of uneventful days goes
back to February 1933. The exact date won't matter much to you.
I like to think, however, that you, my only child, will want to hear
about this hidden work. When you were a small boy you were keen
on family history. You will quickly understand that I couldn't tell
a child what I am about to tell you now. You don't talk about
deaths and vortices to a kid, not nowadays. In my time my parents

didn't hesitate to speak of death and the dying. What they seldom mentioned was sex. We've got it the other way around. My mother died when I was an adolescent. I've often told you that. What I didn't tell you was that I knew she was dying and didn't allow myself to think about it—there's your turntable.

The month was February, as I've said, adding that the exact date wouldn't matter to you. I should confess that I myself avoid fixing it. Chicago in winter, armored in gray ice, the sky low, the going heavy.

I was a high school senior, an indifferent student, generally un-popular, a background figure in the school. It was only as a high jumper that I performed in public. I had no form at all, a curious last-minute spring or convulsion put me over the bar. But this was what the school turned out to see.

Unwilling to study, I was bookish nevertheless. I was secretive about my family life. The truth is that I didn't want to talk about my mother. Besides, I had no language as yet for the oddity of my peculiar interests.

But let me get on with that significant day in the early part of February.

It began like any other winter school day in Chicago—grimly ordinary. The temperature a few degrees above zero, botanical frost shapes on the windowpane, the snow swept up in heaps, the ice gritty and the streets, block after block, bound together by the iron of the sky. A breakfast of porridge, toast, and tea. Late as usual, I stopped for a moment to look into my mother's sickroom. I bent near and said, "It's Louie, going to school." She seemed to nod. Her eyelids were brown, her face much lighter. I hurried off with my books on a strap over my shoulder.

When I came to the boulevard on the edge of the park, two small men rushed out of a doorway with rifles, wheeled around aiming upward, and fired at pigeons near the rooftop. Several birds fell straight down, and the men scooped up the soft bodies and ran indoors, dark little guys in fluttering white shirts. Depression hunt-ers and their city game. Moments before, the police car had loafed by at ten miles an hour. The men had waited it out.

This had nothing to do with me. I mention it merely because it happened. I stepped around the blood spots and crossed into the park.

To the right of the path, behind the winter lilacs, the crust of the snow was broken. In the dead black night Stephanie and I had necked there, petted, my hands under her raccoon coat, under her sweater, under her skirt, adolescents kissing without restraint. Her coonskin cap had slipped to the back of her head. She opened the musky coat to me to have me closer.

I had to run to reach the school doors before the last bell. I was on notice from the family—no trouble with teachers, no summons from the principal at a time like this. And I did observe the rules, although I despised classwork. But I spent all the money I could lay hands on at Hammersmark's Bookstore. I read *Manhattan Transfer, The Enormous Room,* and *A Portrait of the Artist.* I belonged to the Cercle Français and the Senior Discussion Club. The club's topic for this afternoon was Von Hindenburg's choice of Hitler to form a new government. But I couldn't go to meetings now, I had an after-school job. My father had insisted that I find one.

After classes, on my way to work, I stopped at home to cut myself a slice of bread and a wedge of Wisconsin cheese, and to see whether my mother might be awake. During her last days she was heavily sedated and rarely said anything. The tall, square-shouldered bottle at her bedside was filled with clear red Nembutal. The color of this fluid was always the same, as if it could tolerate no shadow. Now that she could no longer sit up to have it washed, my mother's hair was cut short. This made her face more slender, and her lips were sober. Her breathing was dry and hard, obstructed. The window shade was halfway up. It was scalloped at the bottom and had white fringes. The street ice was dark gray. Snow was piled against the trees. Their trunks had a mineral-black look. Waiting out the winter in their alligator armor they gathered coal soot.

Even when she was awake, my mother couldn't find the breath to speak. She sometimes made signs. Except for the nurse, there was nobody in the house. My father was at business, my sister had a downtown job, my brothers hustled. The eldest, Albert, clerked for a lawyer in the Loop. My brother Len had put me onto a job on the Northwestern commuter trains, and for a while I was a candy butcher, selling chocolate bars and evening papers. When my mother put a stop to this because it kept me too late, I found other work. Just now I was delivering flowers for a shop on North Avenue and riding the streetcars carrying wreaths and bouquets to all parts of the city. Behrens the florist paid me fifty cents for an afternoon; with tips I could earn as much as a dollar. That gave me time to prepare my trigonometry lesson, and, very late at night, after I had seen Stephanie, to read my books. I sat in the kitchen when everyone was sleeping, in deep silence, snowdrifts under the windows and below, the janitor's shovel rasping on the cement and clanging on the furnace door. I read banned books circulated by my classmates, political pamphlets, read *Prufrock* and *Mauberly*. I also studied arcane books too far out to discuss with anyone.

I read on the streetcars (called trolleys elsewhere). Reading shut out the sights. In fact there *were* no sights—more of the same and then more of the same. Shop fronts, garages, warehouses, narrow brick bungalows.

The city was laid out on a colossal grid, eight blocks to the mile, every fourth street a car line. The days short, the streetlights weak, the soiled snowbanks toward evening became a source of light. I carried my carfare in my mitten, where the coins mixed with lint worn away from the lining. Today I was delivering lilies to an uptown address. They were wrapped and pinned in heavy paper. Behrens, spelling out my errand for me, was pale, a narrow-faced man who wore nose glasses. Amid the flowers, he alone had no color—something like the price he paid for being human. He wasted no words: "This delivery will take an hour each way in this traffic, so it'll be your only one. I carry these people on the books, but make sure you get a signature on the bill."

I couldn't say why it was such a relief to get out of the shop, the damp, warm-earth smell, the dense mosses, the prickling cactuses, the glass iceboxes with orchids, gardenias, and sickbed roses. I preferred the brick boredom of the street, the paving stones and steel rails. I drew down the three peaks of my racing-skater's cap and hauled the clumsy package to Robey Street. When the car came panting up there was room for me on the long seat next to the door. Passengers didn't undo their buttons. They were chilled, guarded, muffled, miserable. I had reading matter with me—the remains of a book, the cover gone, the pages held together by binder's thread and flakes of glue. I carried these fifty or sixty pages in the pocket of my short sheepskin. With the one hand I had free I couldn't manage this mutilated book. And on the Broadway-Clark car, reading was out of the question. I had to protect my lilies from the balancing straphangers and people pushing toward the front.

I got down at Ainslie Street holding high the package, which had the shape of a padded kite. The apartment house I was looking for had a courtyard with iron palings. The usual lobby: a floor sinking in the middle, kernels of tile, gaps stuffed with dirt, and a panel of brass mailboxes with earpiece-mouthpieces. No voice came down when I pushed the button; instead, the lock buzzed, jarred, rattled, and I went from the cold of the outer lobby to the overheated mustiness of the inner one. On the second floor one of the two doors on the landing was open, and overshoes and galoshes and rubbers were heaped along the wall. At once I found myself in a crowd of drinkers. All the lights in the house were on, although it was a good hour before dark. Coats were piled on chairs and sofas. All whiskey in those days was bootleg, of course. Holding the flowers high, I parted the mourners. I was quasiofficial. The message went out, "Let the kid through. Go right on, buddy."

The long passageway was full, too, but the dining room was entirely empty. There, a dead girl lay in her coffin. Over her a cut-glass luster was hanging from a taped, deformed artery of wire pulled through the broken plaster. I hadn't expected to find myself looking down into a coffin.

You saw her as she was, without undertaker's makeup, a girl older than Stephanie, not so plump, thin, fair, her straight hair arranged on her dead shoulders. All buoyancy gone, a weight that counted totally on support, not so much lying as sunk in this gray rectangle. I saw what I took to be the pressure mark of fingers on her cheek. Whether she had been pretty or not was no consideration.

A stout woman (certainly the mother), wearing black, opened

the swing door from the kitchen and saw me standing over the corpse. I thought she was displeased when she made a fist signal to come forward and pulled both fists against her bosom as I passed her. She said to put the flowers on the sink, and then she pulled the pins and crackled back the paper. Big arms, thick calves, a bun of hair, her short nose thin and red. It was Behrens's practice to tie the stalks to slender green sticks. There was never any damage.

On the drainboard of the sink was a baked ham with sliced bread around the platter, a jar of French's mustard and wooden tongue depressors to spread it. I saw and I saw and I saw.

I was on my most discreet and polite behavior with the woman. I looked at the floor to spare her my commiserating face. But why should she care at all about my discreetness; how did I come into this except as a messenger and menial? If she wouldn't observe my behavior, whom was I behaving for? All she wanted was to settle the bill and send me on my way. She picked up her purse, holding it to her body as she had held her fists. "What do I owe Behrens?" she asked me.

"He said you could sign for this."

However, she wasn't going to deal in kindnesses. She said, "No." She said, "I don't want debts following me later on." She gave me a five-dollar bill, she added a tip of fifty cents, and it was I who signed the receipt, as well as I could on the enameled grooves of the sink. I folded the bill small and felt under the sheepskin coat for my watch pocket, ashamed to take money from her within sight of her dead daughter. I wasn't the object of the woman's severity, but her face somewhat frightened me. She leveled the same look at the walls, the door. I didn't figure here, however; this was no death of mine.

As if to take another reading of the girl's plain face, I looked again into the coffin on my way out. And then on the staircase I began to extract the pages from my sheepskin pocket, and in the lobby I hunted for the sentences I had read last night. Yes, here they were:

Nature cannot suffer the human form within her system of laws. When given to her charge, the human being before us is reduced to dust. Ours is the most perfect form to be found on earth. The visible world sustains

us until life leaves, and then it must utterly destroy us. Where, then, is
the world from which the human form comes?

If you swallowed some food and then died, that morsel of food
that would have nourished you in life would hasten your disintegration in death.

This meant that nature didn't make life, it only housed it.

In those days I read many such books. But the one I had read the
night before went deeper than the rest. You, my only child, are
only too familiar with my lifelong absorption in or craze for further
worlds. I used to bore you when I spoke of spirit, or pneuma, and
of a continuum between spirit and nature. You were too well
educated, respectably rational, to take stock in them. I might add,
citing a famous scholar, that what is plausible can do without
proof. I am not about to pursue this. However, there would be a
gap in what I have to tell if I were to leave out my significant book,
and this after all is a narrative, not an argument.

Anyway, I returned my pages to the pocket of my sheepskin, and
then I didn't know quite what to do. At 4:00, with no more errands, I was somehow not ready to go home. So I walked through
the snow to Argyle Street, where my brother-in-law practiced den-
tistry, thinking that we might travel home together. I prepared an
explanation for turning up at his office. "I was on the North Side
delivering flowers, saw a dead girl laid out, realized how close I was,
and came here." Why did I need to account for my innocent
behavior when it *was* innocent? Perhaps because I was always con-
templating illicit things. Because I was always being accused. Because I ran a little truck farm of deceits—but self-examination,
once so fascinating to me, has become tiresome.

My brother-in-law's office was a high, second-floor walk-up:
PHILIP HADDIS D.D.S. Three bay windows at the rounded corner of
the building gave you a full view of the street and of the lake, due
east—the jagged flats of ice floating. The office door was open, and
when I came through the tiny blind (windowless) waiting room and
didn't see Philip at the big, back-tilted dentist's chair, I thought that
he might have stepped into his lab. He was a good technician and
did most of his own work, which was a big saving. Philip wasn't

tall, but he was very big, a burly man. The sleeves of his white coat fitted tightly on his bare, thick forearms. The strength of his arms counted when it came to pulling teeth. Lots of patients were referred to him for extractions.

When he had nothing in particular to do he would sit in the chair himself, studying the *Racing Form* between the bent mantis leg of the drill, the gas flame, and the water spurting round and round in the green glass spit-sink. The cigar smell was always thick. Standing in the center of the dental cabinet was a clock under a glass bell. Four gilt weights rotated at its base. This was a gift from my mother. The view from the middle window was divided by a chain that couldn't have been much smaller than the one that stopped the British fleet on the Hudson. This held the weight of the druggist's sign—a mortar and pestle outlined in electric bulbs. There wasn't much daylight left. At noon it was poured out; by 4:00 it had drained away. From one side the banked snow was growing blue, from the other the shops were shining warmth on it.

The dentist's lab was in a cupboard. Easygoing Philip peed in the sink sometimes. It was a long trek to the toilet at the far end of the building, and the hallway was nothing but two walls—a plaster tunnel and a carpet runner edged with brass tape. Philip hated going to the end of the hall.

There was nobody in the lab, either. Philip might have been taking a cup of coffee at the soda fountain in the drugstore below. It was possible also that he was passing the time with Marchek, the doctor with whom he shared the suite of offices. The connecting door was never locked, and I had occasionally sat in Marchek's swivel chair with a gynecology book, studying the colored illustrations and storing up the Latin names.

Marchek's starred glass pane was dark, and I assumed his office to be empty, but when I went in I saw a naked woman lying on the examining table. She wasn't asleep, she seemed to be resting. Becoming aware that I was there, she stirred, and then without haste, disturbing herself as little as possible, she reached for her clothing heaped on Dr. Marchek's desk. Picking out her slip, she put it on her belly—she didn't spread it. Was she dazed, drugged?

No, she simply took her sweet time about everything, she behaved with exciting lassitude. Wires connected her nice wrists to a piece of medical apparatus on a wheeled stand.

The right thing would have been to withdraw, but it was already too late for that. Besides, the woman gave no sign that she cared one way or another. She didn't draw the slip over her breasts, she didn't even bring her thighs together. The covering hairs were parted. There were salt, acid, dark, sweet odors. These were immediately effective; I was strongly excited. There was a gloss on her forehead, an exhausted look about the eyes. I believed that I had guessed what she had been doing, but then the room was half dark, and I preferred to avoid any definite thought. Doubt seemed much better, or equivocation.

I remembered that Philip, in his offhand, lazy way, had mentioned a "research project" going on next door. Dr. Marchek was measuring the reactions of partners in the sexual act. "He takes people from the street, he hooks them up and pretends he's collecting graphs. This is for kicks, the science part is horseshit."

The naked woman, then, was an experimental subject.

I had prepared myself to tell Philip about the dead girl on Ainslie Street, but the coffin, the kitchen, the ham, the flowers were as distant from me now as the ice floes on the lake and the killing cold of the water.

"Where did you come from?" the woman said to me.

"From next door—the dentist's office."

"The doctor was about to unstrap me, and I need to get loose. Maybe you can figure out these wires."

If Marchek should be in the inner room, he wouldn't come in now that he heard voices. As the woman raised both her arms so that I could undo the buckles, her breasts swayed, and when I bent over her the odor of her upper body made me think of the frilled brown papers in a box after the chocolates had been eaten—a sweet after-smell and acrid cardboard mixed. Although I tried hard to stop it, my mother's chest mutilated by cancer surgery passed through my mind. Its gnarled scar tissue. I also called in Stephanie's closed eyes and kissing face—anything to spoil the attraction of this naked young woman. It occurred to me as I undid the clasps that instead of disconnecting her I was hooking myself. We were alone in the darkening office, and I wanted her to reach under the sheepskin and undo my belt for me.

But when her hands were free she wiped the jelly from her wrists and began to dress. She started with her bra, several times lowering her breasts into the cups, and when her arms went backward to fasten the snaps she bent far forward, as if she were passing under a low bough. The cells of my body were like bees, drunker and drunker on sexual honey (I expect that this will change the figure of Grandfather Louie, the old man remembered as this or that but never as a hive of erotic bees).

But I couldn't be blind to the woman's behavior even now. It was very broad, she laid it on. I saw her face in profile, and although it was turned downward there was no mistaking her smile. To use an expression from the Thirties, she was giving me the works. She knew I was about to fall on my face. She buttoned every small button with deliberate slowness, and her blouse had at least twenty such buttons, yet she was still bare from the waist down. Though we were so minor, she and I, a schoolboy and a floozy, we had such major instruments to play. And if we were to go further, whatever happened would never get beyond this room. It would be between the two of us and nobody would ever hear of it. Still, Marchek, that pseudoexperimenter, was probably biding his time in the next room. An old family doctor, he must have been embarrassed and angry. And at any moment, moreover, my brother-in-law Philip might come back.

When the woman slipped down from the leather table she gripped her leg and said she had pulled a muscle. She lifted one heel onto a chair and rubbed her leg, swearing under her breath and looking everywhere with swimming eyes. And then, after she had put on her skirt and fastened her stockings to the garter belt, she pushed her feet into her pumps and limped around the chair, holding it by the arm. She said, "Will you please reach my coat? Just put it over my shoulders."

She, too, wore a raccoon. As I took it from the hook I wished it had been something else. But Stephanie's coat was newer than this one and twice as heavy. The pelts had dried out, and the fur was thin. The woman was already on her way out, and stooped as I laid the coat over her back. Marchek's office had its own exit to the corridor.

At the top of the staircase, the woman asked me to help her down. I said that I would, of course, but I wanted to look once more for my brother-in-law. As she tied the woolen head scarf under her chin she smiled at me, with an Oriental wrinkling of her eyes.

Not to check in with Philip wouldn't have been right. My hope was that he would be returning, walking down the narrow corridor in his burly, sauntering, careless way. You won't remember your Uncle Philip. He had played college football, and he still had the look of a tackle, with his swelling, compact forearms. (At Soldier Field today he'd be physically insignificant; in his time, however, he was something of a strong man.)

But there was the long strip of carpet down the middle of the wall-valley, and no one was coming to rescue me. I turned back to his office. If only a patient were sitting in the chair and I could see Philip looking into his mouth, I'd be on track again, excused from taking the woman's challenge. One alternative was to tell her that Philip expected me to ride back with him to the Northwest Side. In the empty office I considered this lie, bending my head so that I wouldn't confront the clock with its soundless measured weights revolving. Then I wrote on Philip's memo pad: "Louie, passing by." I left it on the seat of the chair.

The woman had put her arms through the sleeves of the collegiate, rah-rah raccoon and was resting her fur-bundled rear on the banister. She was passing her compact mirror back and forth, and when I came out she gave the compact a snap and dropped it into her purse.

"Still the charley horse?"

"My lower back, too."

We descended, very slow, both feet on each tread. I wondered what she would do if I were to kiss her. Laugh at me, probably. We were no longer between the four walls, where anything might have happened. In the street, space was unlimited. I had no idea how far we were going, how far I would be able to go. Although she was the one claiming to be in pain, it was I who felt sick. She asked me to support her lower back with my hand, and there I discovered what an extraordinary action her hips could perform. At a party I had overheard an older woman saying to another lady, "I know how to make them burn." Hearing this was enough for me.

No special art was necessary with a boy of seventeen, not even so much as being invited to support her with my hand—to feel that intricate, erotic working of her back. I had already *seen* the woman on Marchek's examining table and had also felt the full weight of her when she leaned—when she laid her female substance on me. Moreover, she fully knew my mind. She was the thing I was thinking continually, and how often does thought find its object in circumstances like these—the object *knowing* that it has been found? The woman knew my expectations. She *was*, in the flesh, those expectations. I couldn't have sworn that she was a hooker, a tramp. She might have been an ordinary family girl with a taste for trampishness, acting loose, amusing herself with me, doing a comic sex turn as in those days people sometimes did.

"Where are we headed?"

"If you have to go, I can make it on my own," she said. "It's just Winona Street, the other side of Sheridan Road."

"No, no. I'll walk you there."

She asked whether I was still at school, pointing to the printed pages in my coat pocket.

I observed when we were passing a fruit shop (a boy of my own age emptying bushels of oranges into the lighted window) that, despite the woman's thick-cream color, her eyes were Far Eastern, black.

"You should be about seventeen," she said.

"Just."

She was wearing pumps in the snow and placed each step with care.

"What are you going to be, have you picked your profession?"

I had no use for professions. Utterly none. There were accountants and engineers in the soup lines. In the world slump, professions were useless. You were free, therefore, to make something extraordinary of yourself. I might have said, if I hadn't been excited to the point of sickness, that I didn't ride around the city on the cars to make a buck or to be useful to the family, but to take a reading of this boring, depressed, ugly, endless, rotting city. I couldn't have thought it then, but I now understand that my purpose was to interpret this place. Its power was tremendous. But so was mine. I refused absolutely to believe for a moment that people here were doing what they thought they were doing. Beneath the apparent life of these streets was their real life, beneath each face the real face, beneath each voice and its words the true tone and the real message. Of course, I wasn't about to say such things. It was beyond me at that time to say them. I was, however, a high-toned kid, "La-di-dah," my critical, satirical brother Albert called me. A high purpose in adolescence will expose you to that.

At the moment, a glamorous, sexual girl had me in tow. I couldn't guess where I was being led, nor how far, nor what she would surprise me with, nor the consequences.

"So the dentist is your brother?"

"In-law—my sister's husband. They live with us. You're asking what he's like? He's a good guy. He likes to lock his office on Friday and go to the races. He takes me to the fights. Also, at the back of the drugstore there's a poker game. . . ."

"*He* doesn't go around with books in his pocket."

"Well, no, he doesn't. He says, 'What's the use? There's too much to keep up or catch up with. You could never in a thousand years do it, so why knock yourself out?' My sister wants him to open a Loop office but that would be too much of a strain. I guess he's for inertia. He's not ready to do more than he's already doing."

"So what are you reading—what's it about?"

I didn't propose to discuss anything with her. I wasn't capable of it now. What I had in mind just then was entirely different.

But suppose I had been able to try. One does have a responsibility to answer genuine questions: "You see, miss, this is the visible world. We live in it, we breathe its air and eat its substance. When we die, however, matter goes to matter and then we're annihilated. Now, which world do we really belong to, this world of matter or another world from which matter takes its orders?"

Not many people were willing to talk about such notions. They made even Stephanie impatient. "When you die, that's it. Dead is dead," she would say. She loved a good time. And when I wouldn't take her downtown to the Oriental Theatre she didn't deny herself the company of other boys. She brought back off-color vaudeville jokes. I think the Oriental was part of a national entertainment circuit. Jimmy Savo, Lou Holtz, and Sophie Tucker played there. I was sometimes too solemn for Stephanie. When she gave imitations of Jimmy Savo singing "River, Stay Away from My Door," bringing her knees together and holding herself tight, she didn't break me up, and she was disappointed.

You would have thought that the book or book fragment in my pocket was a talisman from a fairy tale to open castle gates or carry me to mountaintops. Yet when the woman asked me what it was, I was too scattered to tell her. Remember, I still kept my hand as instructed on her lower back, tormented by that sexual grind of her movements. I was discovering what the lady at the party had meant by saying, "I know how to make them burn." So of course I was in no condition to talk to this girl about the Ego and the Will, or about the secrets of the blood. Yes, I believed that higher knowledge was shared out among all human beings. What else was there to hold us together but this force hidden behind daily consciousness? But to be coherent about it now was absolutely out of the question.

"Can't you tell me?" she said.

"I bought this for a nickel from a bargain table."

"That's how you spend your money?"

I assumed her to mean that I didn't spend it on girls.

"And the dentist is a good-natured, lazy guy," she went on. "What has he got to tell you?"

I tried to review the mental record. What did Phil Haddis say? He said that a stiff prick has no conscience. At the moment it was all I could think of. It amused Philip to talk to me. He was a chum. Where Philip was indulgent, my brother Albert, your late uncle, was harsh. He might have taught me something if he had trusted me. He was then a night-school law student clerking for Rowland, the racketeer congressman. He was Rowland's bagman, and Row-

land didn't hire him to read law but to make collections. Philip
suspected that Albert was skimming, for he dressed sharply. He
wore a derby (called, in those days, a Baltimore heater) and a
camel's hair and sharp, pointed, mafioso shoes. Toward me, Albert
was scornful. He said, "You don't understand fuck-all. You never
will."

We were approaching Winona Street, and when we got to her
building she'd have no further use for me and send me away. I'd see
no more than the flash of the glass and then stare as she let herself
in. She was already feeling in her purse for the keys. I was no longer
supporting her back, preparing instead to mutter "bye-bye," when
she surprised me with a sideward nod, inviting me to enter. I think
I had hoped (with sex-polluted hope) that she would leave me in the
street. I followed her through another tile lobby and through the
inner door. The staircase was fiercely heated by coal-fueled radiators, the skylight was wavering, and the wallpaper had come un-
stuck and was curling and bulging. I swallowed my breath. I
couldn't draw this heat into my lungs.

This had been a deluxe apartment house once, built for bankers,
brokers, and well-to-do professionals. Now it was occupied by
transients. In the big front room with its French windows there was
a crap game. In the next room people were drinking or drowsing on
the old chesterfields. The woman led me through what had once
been a private bar—some of the fittings were still in place. Then I
followed her through the kitchen—I would have gone anywhere,
no questions asked. In the kitchen there were no signs of cooking,
neither pots nor dishes. The linoleum was shredding, brown fibers
standing like hairs. She led me into a narrower corridor, parallel to
the main one. "I have what used to be a maid's room," she said.
"It's got a nice view of the alley but there is a private bathroom."

And here we were—the place wasn't much to look at. So this was
how whores operated—assuming that she was a whore: a bare
floor, a narrow cot, a chair by the window, a lopsided clothespress
against the wall. I stopped under the light fixture while she passed
behind, as if to observe me. Then she gave me a hug and a small kiss
on the cheek, more promissory than actual. Her face powder, or

perhaps it was her lipstick, had a sort of green-banana fragrance. My heart had never beaten as hard as this.

She said, "Why don't I go into the bathroom awhile and get ready while you undress and lie down in bed. You look like you were brought up neat, so lay your clothes on the chair. You don't want to drop them on the floor."

Shivering (this seemed the one cold room in the house), I began to pull off my things, beginning with the winter-wrinkled boots. The sheepskin I hung over the back of the chair. I pushed my socks into the boots and then my bare feet recoiled from the grit of the floor. I took off everything, as if to disassociate my shirt, my underthings from whatever it was that was about to happen, so that only my body could be guilty. The one thing that couldn't be excepted. When I pulled back the cover and got in I was thinking that the beds in the Bridewell would be like this. There was no pillowcase, my head lay on the ticking. What I saw on the outside was only the utility wires hung between the poles like lines on music paper, only sagging, and the glass insulators like clumps of notes. The woman had said nothing about money. Because she liked me. I couldn't believe my luck—luck with a hint of disaster. I blinded myself to the Bridewell metal cot, not meant for two. I felt also that I couldn't hold out if she kept me waiting long. And what feminine thing was she doing in there—undressing, washing, perfuming, changing?

Abruptly, she came out. She had been waiting, nothing else. She still wore the raccoon coat, even the gloves. Without looking at me she walked very quickly, almost running, and opened the window. As soon as the window shot up it let in a blast of cold air, and I stood up on the bed but it was too late to stop her. She took my clothes from the back of the chair and heaved them out. They fell into the alley. I shouted, "What are you doing!" She still refused to turn her head. As she ran away she was tying the head scarf under her chin and left the door open. I could hear her pumps beating double time in the hallway.

I couldn't run after her, could I, and show myself naked to the people in the flat? She had banked on this. When we came in, she must have given the high sign to the man she worked with, and he had been waiting in the alley. When I ran to look out, my things had already been gathered up. All I saw was the back of somebody with a bundle under his arm hurrying in the walkway between two garages. I might have picked up my boots—those she had left me—and jumped from the first-floor window, but I couldn't chase the man very far, and in a few minutes I would have wound up on Sheridan Road naked and freezing.

I had seen a drunk in his union suit, bleeding from the head after he had been rolled and beaten, staggering and yelling in the street. I didn't even have a shirt and drawers. I was as naked as the woman herself had been in the doctor's office, stripped of everything, including the five dollars I had collected for the flowers. And the sheepskin my mother had bought for me last year. Plus the book, the fragment of an untitled book, author unknown. This may have been the most serious loss of all.

Now I could think on my own about the world I really belonged to, whether it was this one or another.

I pulled down the window, and then I went to shut the door. The room didn't seem lived in, but suppose it had a tenant, and what if he were to storm in now and rough me up? Luckily there was a bolt to the door. I pushed it into its loop and then I ran around the room to see what I could find to wear. In the lopsided clothespress, nothing but wire hangers, and in the bathroom, only a cotton hand towel. I tore the blanket off the bed; if I were to slit it I might pull it over my head like a serape, but it was too thin to do me much good in freezing weather. When I pulled the chair over to the clothespress and stood on it, I found a woman's dress behind the molding, and a quilted bed jacket. In a brown paper bag there was a knitted brown tam. I had to put these things on, I had no choice.

It was now, I reckoned, about 5:00. Philip had no fixed schedule. He didn't hang around the office on the off chance that somebody might turn up with a toothache. After his last appointment he locked up and left. He didn't necessarily set out for home; he was not too keen to return to the house. If I wanted to catch him I'd have to run. In boots, dress, tam, and jacket, I made my way out of the apartment. Nobody took the slightest interest in me. More people (Philip would have called them transients) had crowded in—it was even likely that the man who had snatched up my clothes in the alley had returned, was among them. The heat in the staircase now was stifling, and the wallpaper smelled scorched, as if it were on the point of catching fire. In the street I was struck by a north wind straight from the Pole and the dress and sateen jacket counted for nothing. I was running, though, and had no time to feel it.

Philip would say, "Who was this floozy? Where did she pick you up?" Philip was unexcitable, always mild, amused by me. Anna would badger him with the example of her ambitious brothers— they hustled, they read books. You couldn't fault Philip for being pleased. I anticipated what he'd say—"Did you get in? Then at least you're not going to catch the clap." I depended on Philip now, for I had nothing, not even seven cents for carfare. I could be certain, however, that he wouldn't moralize at me, he'd set about dressing me, he'd scrounge a sweater among his neighborhood acquaintances or take me to the Salvation Army shop on Broadway if that should still be open. He'd go about this in his slow-moving, thick-necked, deliberate way. Not even dancing would speed him up, he spaced out the music to suit him when he did the fox-trot and pressed his cheek to Anna's. He wore a long, calm grin. My private term for this particular expression was Pussy-Veleerum. I saw Philip as fat but strong, strong but cozy, purring but inserting a joking comment. He gave a little suck at the corner of the mouth when he was about to make a swipe at you, and it was then that he was Pussy-Veleerum. A name it never occurred to me to speak aloud.

I sprinted past the windows of the fruit store, the delicatessen, the tailor's shop. I could count on help from Philip. My father, however, was an intolerant, hasty man. Slighter than his sons, handsome, with muscles of white marble (so they seemed to me), laying down the law. It would put him in a rage to see me like this. And it was true that I had failed to consider: my mother dying, the ground frozen, a funeral coming, the dug grave, the packet of sand from the Holy Land to be scattered on the shroud. If I were to turn up in this filthy dress, the old man, breaking under his burdens, would come down on me in a blind, Old Testament rage. I never thought of this as cruelty but as archaic right everlasting. Even Albert, who was already a Loop lawyer, had to put up with these blows—outraged, his eyes swollen and maddened, but he took it. It never occurred to us that my father was cruel, only that we had gone over the limit.

There were no lights in Philip's D.D.S. office. When I jumped up the stairs the door with its blank starred glass was locked. Frosted panes were still rare. What we had was this star-marred product for toilets and other private windows. Marchek—whom nowadays we would call a voyeur—was also, angrily, gone. I had screwed up his experiment. I tried the doors, thinking that I could spend the night on the leather examining table where the beautiful nude had lain. There also I could make telephone calls. I did have a few friends, although there were none who might help me. I couldn't have known how to explain my predicament to them. They'd think I was putting them on, that it was a practical joke—"This is Louie. A whore robbed me of my clothes and I'm stuck on the North Side without carfare. I'm wearing a dress. I lost my house keys. I can't get home."

I ran down to the drugstore to look for Philip there. He sometimes played five or six hands of poker in the druggist's back room, trying his luck before getting on the streetcar. I knew Kiyar, the druggist, by sight. He had no recollection of me—why should he have? He said, "What can I do for you, young lady?"

Did he really take me for a girl, or a tramp off the street, or a gypsy from one of the storefront fortune-teller camps? Those were now all over town. But not even a gypsy would wear this blue sateen quilted boudoir jacket instead of a coat.

"I wonder, is Phil Haddis the dentist in the back?"

"What do you want with Dr. Haddis, have you got a toothache, or what?"

"I need to see him."

The druggist was a compact little guy, and his full round bald head was painfully sensitive looking. It could pick up any degree of disturbance, I thought. Yet there was a canny glitter coming through his specs, and Kiyar had the mark of a man whose mind never would change once he had made it up. Oddly enough, he had a small mouth, baby lips. He had been on the street—how long? Forty years? In forty years you've seen it all and nobody can tell you a single thing.

"Did Dr. Haddis have an appointment with you? Are you a patient?"

He knew this was a private connection. I was no patient. "No. But if I was out here he'd want to know it. Can I talk to him one minute?"

"He isn't here."

Kiyar had walked behind the grille of the prescription counter. I mustn't lose him. If he went, what would I do next? I said, "This is important, Mr. Kiyar." He waited for me to declare myself. I wasn't about to embarrass Philip by setting off rumors. Kiyar said nothing. He may have been waiting for me to speak up. Declare myself. I assume he took pride in running a tight operation, and gave nothing away. To cut through to the man I said, "I'm in a spot. I left Dr. Haddis a note, before, but when I came back I missed him."

At once I recognized my mistake. Druggists were always being appealed to. All these pills, remedy bottles, bright lights, medicine ads drew wandering screwballs and moochers. They all said they were in bad trouble.

"You can go to the Foster Avenue station."

"The police, you mean."

I had thought of that too. I could always tell them my hard-luck story and they'd keep me until they checked it out and someone would come to fetch me. That would probably be Albert. Albert would love that. He'd say to me, "Well, aren't you the horny little bastard." He'd play up to the cops too, and amuse them.

"I'd freeze before I got to Foster Avenue," was my answer to Kiyar.

"There's always the squad car."

"Well, if Phil Haddis isn't in the back maybe he's still in the neighborhood. He doesn't always go straight home."

"Sometimes he goes over to the fights at Johnny Coulon's. It's a little early for that. You could try the speakeasy down the street, on Kenmore. It's an English basement, side entrance. You'll see a light by the fence. The guy at the slot is called Moose."

He didn't so much as offer a dime from his till. If I had said that I was in a scrape and that Phil was my sister's husband he'd proba- bly have given me carfare. But I hadn't confessed, and there was a penalty for that.

Going out, I crossed my arms over the bed jacket and opened the door with my shoulder. I might as well have been wearing nothing at all. The wind cut at my legs, and I ran. Luckily I didn't have far to go. The iron pipe with the bulb at the end of it was halfway down the block. I saw it as soon as I crossed the street. These illegal drinking parlors were easy to find, they were meant to be. The steps were cement, four or five of them bringing me down to the door. The slot came open even before I knocked and instead of the doorkeeper's eyes I saw his teeth.

"You Moose?"

"Yah. Who?"

"Kiyar sent me."

"Come on."

I felt as though I were falling into a big, warm, paved cellar. There was little to see, almost nothing. A sort of bar was set up, a few hanging fixtures, some tables from an ice cream parlor, wire- backed chairs. If you looked through the window of an English basement your eyes were at ground level. Here the glass was tarred over. There would have been nothing to see anyway: a yard, a wooden porch, a clothesline, wires, a back alley with ash heaps.

"Where did you come from, sister?" said Moose.

But Moose was a nobody here. The bartender, the one who counted, called me over and said, "What is it, sweetheart? You got a message for somebody?"

"Not exactly."

"Oh? You needed a drink so bad that you jumped out of bed and ran straight over—you couldn't stop to dress?"

"No, sir. I'm looking for somebody—Phil Haddis? The dentist?"

"There's only one customer. Is that him?"

It wasn't. My heart sank into river mud.

"It's not a drunk you're looking for?"

"No."

The drunk was on a high stool, thin legs hanging down, arms forward, and his head lay sidewise on the bar. Bottles, glasses, a beer barrel. Behind the barkeeper was a sideboard pried from the wall of an apartment. It had a long mirror—an oval laid on its side. Paper streamers curled down from the pipes.

"Do you know the dentist I'm talking about?"

"I might. Might not," said the barkeeper. He was a sloppy, long-faced giant—something of a kangaroo look about him. That was the long face in combination with the belly. He told me, "This is not a busy time. It's dinner, you know, and we're just a neighborhood speak."

It was no more than a cellar, just as the barman was no more than a Greek, huge and bored. Just as I myself, Louie, was no more than a naked male in a woman's dress. When you had named objects in this elementary way, hardly anything remained in them. The barman, on whom everything now depended, held his bare arms out at full reach and braced on his spread hands. The place smelled of yeast sprinkled with booze. He said, "You live around here?"

"No, about an hour on the streetcar."

"Say more."

"Humboldt Park is my neighborhood."

"Then you got to be a Uke, a Polack, a Scandihoof, or a Jew."

"Jew."

"I know my Chicago. And you didn't set out dressed like that. You'da frozen to death inside of ten minutes. It's for the boudoir, not winter wear. You don't have the shape of a woman, neither. The hips aren't there. Are you covering a pair of knockers? I bet not. So what's the story, are you a morphadite? Let me tell you, you got to give this Depression credit. Without it you'd never find out what kind of funny stuff is going on. But one thing I'll never believe is that you're a young girl and still got her cherry."

"You're right as far as that goes, but the rest of it is that I haven't got a cent, and I need carfare."

"Who took you, a woman?"

"Up in her room when I undressed, she grabbed my things and threw them out the window."

"Left you naked so you couldn't chase her . . . I would have grabbed her and threw her on the bed. I bet you didn't even get in."

Not even, I repeated to myself. Why didn't I push her down while she was still in her coat, as soon as we entered the room—pull up her clothes, as he would have done? Because he was born to, while I was not. I wasn't intended for it.

"So that's what happened. You got taken by a team of pros. She set you up. You were the mark. Jewish fellows aren't supposed to keep company with those bad cunts. But when you get out of your house, into the world, you want action like anybody else. So. And where did you dig up this dress with the fancy big roses? I guess you were standing with your sticker sticking out and were lucky to find anything to put on. Was she a good looker?"

Her breasts, as she lay there, kept their shape. They didn't slip sideward. The inward lines of her legs, thigh swelling toward thigh. The black crumpled hairs. Yes, a beauty, I would say.

Like the druggist, the barman saw the fun of the thing—an adolescent in a fix, the soiled dress, the rayon or sateen bed jacket. It was a lucky thing for me that business was at a standstill. If he had had customers, the barman wouldn't have given me the time of day. "In short, you got mixed up with a whore and she gave you the works."

For that matter, I had no sympathy for myself. I confessed that I had this coming, a high-minded Jewish high school boy, too high-and-mighty to be orthodox and with his eye on a special destiny. Inside the house, an archaic rule; outside, the facts of life. The facts of life were having their turn. Their first effect was ridicule. To throw my duds into the alley was the woman's joke on me. The druggist with his pain-sensitive head was all irony. And now the barman was going to get his fun out of my trouble before he, maybe, gave me the seven cents for carfare. Then I could have a full hour of shame on the streetcar. My mother, with whom I might never speak again, used to say that I had a line of pride straight down the bridge of my nose, a foolish stripe that she could see.

I had no way of anticipating what her death would signify.

The barman, having me in place, was giving me the business. And Moose ("Moosey," the Greek called him) had come away from the door so as not to miss the entertainment. The Greek's kangaroo mouth turned up at the corners. Presently his hand went up to his head and he rubbed his scalp under the black, spiky hair. Some said they drank olive oil by the glass to keep their hair so rich. "Now, give it to me again, about the dentist," said the barman.

"I came looking for him, but by now he's well on his way home."

He was then on the Broadway–Clark car, reading the Peach edition of the *Evening American*, a broad man with an innocent pout to his face, checking the race results. Anna had him dressed up as a professional man but he let the fittings—shirt, tie, buttons—go their own way. His instep was fat and swelled inside the narrow shoe she picked for him. He wore the fedora correctly. Toward the rest he admitted no obligation.

Anna cooked dinner after work, and when Philip came in my father would begin to ask, "Where's Louie?" "Oh, he's out delivering flowers," they'd tell him. But the old man was nervous about his children after dark, and if they were late he waited up for them, walking—no, trotting—up and down the long apartment. When you tried to slip in he caught you and twisted you tight by the neckband. He was small, neat, slender, a gentleman, but abrupt, not unworldly—he wasn't ignorant of vices, he had lived in Odessa and even longer in St. Petersburg—but he had no patience. The least thing might craze him. Seeing me in this dress, he'd lose his head at once. I lost *mine* when that woman showed me her snatch with all the pink layers, when she raised up her arm and asked me to disconnect the wires, when I felt her skin and her fragrance came upward.

"What's your family, what does your dad do?" asked the barman.

"His business is wood fuel for bakers' ovens. It comes by freight car from northern Michigan. Also from Birnamwood, Wisconsin. He has a yard off Lake Street, east of Halsted."

I made an effort to give the particulars. I couldn't afford to be suspected of invention now.

"I know where that is. Now that's a neighborhood just full of hookers and cathouses. You think you can tell your old man what happened to you, that you got picked up by a cutie and she stole your clothes off you?"

The effect of this question was to make me tight in the face, dim in the ears. The whole cellar grew small and distant, toylike but not for play.

"How's your old man to deal with—tough?"

"Hard," I said.

"Slaps the kids around? This time you've got it coming. What's under the dress, a pair of bloomers?"

I shook my head.

"Your behind is bare? Now you know how it feels to go around like a woman."

The Greek's great muscles were dough-colored. You wouldn't have wanted him to take a headlock on you. That's the kind of man the Organization hired, the Capone people were in charge by now. The customers would be like celluloid Kewpie dolls to him. He looked like one of those boxing kangaroos in the movies, and he could do a standing jump over the bar. Yet he enjoyed playing zany. He could curve his long mouth up at the corners like the happy face in a cartoon.

"What were you doing on the North Side?"

"Delivering flowers."

"Hustling after school but with ramming on your brain. You got a lot to learn, buddy boy. Well, enough of that. Now, Moosey, take this flashlight and see if you can scrounge up a sweater or something in the back basement for this down-on-his-luck kid. I'd be surprised if the old janitor hasn't picked the stuff over pretty good. If mice have nested in it, shake out the turds. It'll help on the trip home."

I followed Moose into the hotter half of the cellar. His flashlight picked out the laundry tubs with the hand-operated wringers mounted on them, the padlocked wooden storage bins. "Turn over some of these cardboard boxes. Mostly rags, is my guess. Dump 'em out, that's the easiest."

I emptied a couple of big cartons. Moose passed the light back and forth over the heaps. "Nothing much, like I said."

"Here's a flannel shirt," I said. I wanted to get out. The smell of heated burlap was hard to take. This was the only wearable article. I could have used a pullover or a pair of pants. We returned to the bar. As I was putting on the shirt, which revolted me (I come of finicky people whose fetish is cleanliness), the barman said, "I tell you what, you take this drunk home—this is about time for him, isn't it, Moosey?—he gets plastered here every night. See he gets home and it'll be worth half a buck to you."

"I'll do it," I said. "It all depends how far away he lives. If it's far, I'll be frozen before I get there."

"It isn't far. Winona, west of Sheridan isn't far. I'll give you the directions. This guy is a city-hall payroller. He has no special job, he works direct for the ward committeeman. He's a lush with two little girls to bring up. If he's sober enough he cooks their dinner. Probably they take more care of him than he does of them."

"I'll walk him home, if he can walk."

"First I'll take charge of his money," said the barman. "I don't want my buddy here to be rolled. I don't say you would do it, but I owe this to a customer."

Bristle-faced Moose began to empty the man's pockets—his wallet, some keys, crushed cigarettes, a red bandanna that looked foul, matchbooks, greenbacks, and change. All these were laid out on the bar.

When I look back at past moments I carry with me an apperceptive mass that ripens and perhaps distorts, mixing what is memorable with what may not be worth mentioning. Thus I see the barman with one big hand gathering in the valuable as if they were his winnings, the pot in a poker game. And then I think that if the kangaroo giant had taken this drunk on his back he might have bounded home with him in less time than it would have taken me to support him as far as the corner. But what the barman actually said was, "I got a nice escort for you, Jim."

Moose led the man back and forth to make sure his feet were operating. His swollen eyes now opened and then closed again. "McKern," Moose said, briefing me. "Southwest corner of Winona and Sheridan, the second building on the south side of the street, and it's the second floor."

"You'll be paid when you get back," said the barman.

The freeze was now so hard that the snow underfoot sounded like metal foil. Though McKern may have sobered up in the frozen street, he couldn't move very fast. Since I had to hold on to him I borrowed his gloves. He had a coat with pockets to put his hands in. I tried to keep behind him and get some shelter from the wind. That didn't work. He wasn't up to walking. I had to hold him. Instead of a desirable woman, I had a drunkard in my arms. This disgrace, you see, while my mother was surrendering to death. At about this hour, upstairs neighbors came down and relatives arrived and filled the kitchen and the dining room—a deathwatch. I should have been there, not on the far North Side. When I had earned the carfare, I'd still be an hour from home on a streetcar making four stops to the mile.

Toward the last, I was dragging McKern. I kept the street door open with my back while I pulled him into the dim lobby by the arms.

The little girls had been waiting and came down at once. They held the inner door open while I brought their daddy upstairs with a fireman's carry and laid him on his bed. The children had had plenty of practice at this. They undressed him down to the long johns and then stood silent on either side of the room. This, for them, was how things were. They took deep oddities calmly, as children generally will. I had spread his winter coat over him.

I had little sympathy for McKern, in the circumstances. I believe I can tell you why: He had passed out many times before, and he would pass out again, dozens of times before he died. Drunkenness was common and familiar, and therefore accepted, and drunks could count on acceptance and support and relied on it. Whereas if your troubles were uncommon, unfamiliar, you could count on nothing. There was a convention about drunkenness established in part by drunkards. The founding proposition was that consciousness is terrible. Its lower, impoverished forms are perhaps the worst. Flesh and blood are poor and weak, susceptible to human shock. Here my descendant will hear the voice of Grandfather Louie giving one of his sermons on higher consciousness and interrupting the story he promised to tell. You will hold him to his word, as you have every right to do.

The older girl now spoke to me. She said, "The fellow phoned and said a man was bringing Daddy home, and you'd help with supper if Daddy couldn't cook it."

"Yes. Well? . . ."

"Only you're not a man, you've got a dress on."

"It looks like it, doesn't it. Don't you worry, I'll come to the kitchen with you."

"Are you a lady?"

"What do you mean—what does it look like? All right, I'm a lady."

"You can eat with us."

"Then show me where the kitchen is."

I followed them down the corridor, narrowed by the clutter— boxes of canned groceries, soda biscuits, sardines, pop bottles. When I passed the bathroom, I slipped in for quick relief. The door had neither a hook nor a bolt, the string of the ceiling fixture had snapped off. A tiny night-light was plugged into the baseboard. I thanked God it was so dim. I put up the board while raising my skirt, and when I had begun I heard one of the children behind me. Over my shoulder I saw that it was the younger one, and as I turned my back (*everything* was happening today) I said, "Don't come in here." But she squeezed past and sat on the edge of the tub. She grinned at me. She was expecting her second teeth. Today all females were making sexual fun of me, and even the infants were looking lewd. I stopped, letting the dress fall, and said to her, "What are you laughing about?"

"If you were a girl, you'd of sat down."

The kid wanted me to understand that she knew what she had seen. She pressed her fingers over her mouth, and I turned and went to the kitchen.

There the older girl was lifting the black cast-iron skillet with

both hands. On dripping paper, the pork chops were laid out—
nearby, a mason jar of grease. I was competent enough at the gas
range, which shone with old filth. Loath to touch the pork with my
fingers, I forked the meat into the spitting fat. The chops turned my
stomach. My thought was, "I'm into it now, up to the ears." The
drunk in his bed, the dim secret toilet, the glaring tungsten twist
over the gas range, the sputtering droplets stinging the hands. The
older girl said, "There's plenty for you. Daddy won't be eating
dinner."

"No, not me. I'm not hungry," I said.

All that my upbringing held in horror geysered up, my throat
filling with it, my guts griping.

The children sat at the table, an enamel rectangle. Thick plates
and glasses, a waxed package of sliced white bread, a milk bottle,
a stick of butter, the burning fat clouding the room. The girls sat
beneath the smoke, slicing their meat. I brought salt and pepper
back from the range. They ate without conversation. My chore (my
duty) done, there was nothing to keep me. I said, "I have to go."

I looked in at McKern, who had thrown down the coat and taken
off his drawers. The parboiled face, the short nose pointed sharply,
the life signs in the throat, the broken look of his neck, the black
hair of his belly, the short cylinder between his legs ending in a
spiral of loose skin, the white shine of the shins, the tragic expression of his feet. There was a stack of pennies on his bedside table.
I helped myself to carfare but had no pocket for the coins. I opened
the hall closet feeling quickly for a coat I might borrow, a pair of
slacks. Whatever I took, Philip could return to the Greek barman
tomorrow. I pulled a trench coat from a hanger, and a pair of
trousers. For the third time I put on strangers' clothing—this is no
time to mention stripes or checks or make exquisite notations.
Escaping, desperate, I struggled into the pants on the landing, tuck-
ing in the dress, and pulled on the coat as I jumped down the stairs,
knotting tight the belt and sticking the pennies, a fistful of them,
into my pocket.

But still I went back to the alley under the woman's window to
see if her light was on, and also to look for pages. The thief or pimp
perhaps had chucked them away, or maybe they had dropped out

when he snatched the sheepskin. The windows were dark. I found nothing on the ground. You may think this obsessive crankiness, a crazy dependency on words, on printed matter. But remember, there were no redeemers in the streets, no guides, no confessors, comforters, enlighteners, communicants to turn to. You had to take teaching wherever you could find it. Under the library dome downtown, in mosaic letters, there was a message from Milton, so moving but perhaps of no utility, perhaps aggravating difficulties: A GOOD BOOK, it said, IS THE PRECIOUS LIFE'S BLOOD OF A MASTER SPIRIT.

These are the plain facts, they have to be uttered. This, remember, is the New World, and here one of its mysterious cities. I should have hurried directly, to catch a car. Instead I was in a back alley hunting pages that would in any case have blown away.

I went back to Broadway—it was very broad—and waited on a safety island. Then the car came clanging, red, swaying on its trucks, a piece of Iron Age technology, double cane seats framed in brass. Rush hour was long past. I sat by a window, homebound, with flashes of thought like tracer bullets slanting into distant darkness. Like London in wartime. What story would I tell? I wouldn't tell any. I never did. It was assumed anyway that I was lying. While I believed in honor, I did often lie. Is a life without lying conceivable? It was easier to lie than to explain myself. My father had one set of assumptions, I had another. Corresponding premises were not to be found.

I owed five dollars to Behrens. But I knew where my mother secretly hid her savings. Because I looked into all books, I had found the money in her Machzor, the prayer book for the High Holidays, the days of awe. As yet I hadn't taken anything. She had hoped until this final illness to buy passage to Europe to see her mother and her sister. When she died I would turn the money over to my father, except for ten dollars, five for the florist and the rest for Von Hugel's *Eternal Life* and *The World as Will and Idea*.

The after-dinner neighbors and cousins would be gone when I reached home. My father would be on the lookout for me. It was the rear porch door that was locked after dark. The kitchen door was off the latch. I could climb over the wooden partition. I often did that. Once you got your foot on the doorknob you could pull yourself over the top and drop to the porch without noise. Then I could see into the kitchen and slip in as soon as my patrolling father had left it. The bedroom shared by all three brothers was just off the kitchen. I could borrow my brother Len's cast-off winter coat tomorrow. I knew which closet it hung in. If my father should catch me I could expect hard blows on the top of my head, on my face, on my shoulders. But if my mother had, tonight, just died, he wouldn't hit me.

This was when the measured, reassuring, sleep-inducing turntable of days became a whirlpool, a vortex darkening toward the bottom. I had had only the anonymous pages in the pocket of my sheepskin to interpret it to me. They told me that the truth of the universe was inscribed into our very bones. That the human skeleton was itself a hieroglyph. That everything we had ever known on earth was shown to us in the first days after death. That our experience of the world was desired by the cosmos, and needed by it for its own renewal.

I do not think that these pages, if I hadn't lost them, would have persuaded me forever or made the life I led a different one.

I am writing this account, or statement, in response to an eccentric urge swelling toward me from the earth itself.

Failed my mother! That may mean, will mean, little or nothing to you, my only child, reading this document.

I myself know the power of nonpathos, in these low, devious days.

On the streetcar, heading home, I braced myself, but all my preparations caved in like sand diggings. I got down at the North Avenue stop, avoiding my reflection in the shopwindows. After a death, mirrors were immediately covered. I can't say what this pious superstition means. Will the soul of your dead be reflected in a looking glass, or is this custom a check to the vanity of the living?

I ran home, approached by the back alley, made no noise on the wooden backstairs, reached for the top of the partition, placed my foot on the white porcelain doorknob, went over the top without noise, and dropped down on our porch. I didn't follow the plan I had laid for avoiding my father. There were people sitting at the kitchen table. I went straight in. My father rose from his chair and hurried toward me. His fist was ready. I took off my tam or woolen beret and when he hit me on the head the blow filled me with gratitude. If my mother had already died, he would have embraced me instead.

Well, they're all gone now, and I have made my preparations. I haven't left a large estate, and this is why I have written this memoir, a sort of addition to your legacy.

MARSHA LEE BERKMAN

Deeds of Love and Rage

We are a troubled family. Ephraim left three months ago and Cecilia and I have had to confront each other like enemies who suddenly find themselves at the same party. Yesterday we quarreled and today, dressed in a pair of faded blue denim shorts and a yellow T-shirt that says "Foxy" in flowery iridescent letters, she moves through the house sulking. She is the only thing in motion on this hot sultry day.

My only child. . . . Her dark uncombed hair straggles around a thin face and sad thirteen-year-old eyes swollen from lack of sleep. Last night through the flimsy walls of our apartment, I heard her weeping, and this morning her whole face slumps in sorrow and rage. It is all my fault. I can see it in the frown that bridges her forehead. If only I would make concessions, try harder, her father would come back. And so we are doomed to this summer that continues to stretch endlessly before us, a time that hardly seems to be real at all but just a series of minutes, hours, days to be gotten through and endured together. How we have begun to dislike each other. By the end of summer Ephraim and I shall come to a decision for the sake of the child, but now we are still wavering back and forth. Yes, I can tell from the way her black eyes glow with a fierce fury: She is as tired of me as I am of her.

At the beginning of June Ephraim packed up his bags and took an apartment and a job on the other side of the city. He does not have enough space, he says. How foreign that word sounds on his tongue. We had begun to chip each other into little bits and pieces. Ephraim will not admit it, but sometimes I think it was the strain of the child.

As a baby she was perpetually restless and moody. She came into the world too soon, bounding feet first from the womb. I had nothing prepared. No, not even her name. I had to snatch that also without thought. She cried day and night, refusing any of the usual things, and Ephraim and I would take turns rising from our sleep, moaning with fatigue, too tired to comfort each other for this strange being who had taken over our lives.

Thirteen years and still she remains a puzzle to me, her moods flashing back and forth, a mood for every moment of the day. A look, a remark, or some dark demon within can change her in an instant. I was too old to have her. Yes, I am certain it must be that. But Ephraim is a religious man. He used to say that suffering cleanses the soul, that burdens are to be borne.

"It is a sign," he said then, clasping his heavy hands together, closing and unfolding them nervously, considering it. To Ephraim there is a purpose in the world that escapes me. There are things that we are not supposed to understand. He prefers the difficult to the simple, certain that God is testing him. He was not an easy man to live with.

This morning when Cecilia asks if her father is coming for the Sabbath, which begins at sundown, I tell her that it is hopeless.

"Your father is impossible," I blurt out in a weak moment, saying it passionately, throwing up my hands in a gesture of despair. I can hear my voice rising unpleasantly, and as soon as the words are out of my mouth, I am sorry. But it is already too late.

She turns on me. "Bitch," she says without a sound, mouthing the letters with her lips. At first I ignore her. It is far too hot to respond, to become embroiled in another one of these arguments. Anyhow, what would be the use? Let her vent her wrath on me. Let her get it out of her system, think that her father's absence is my fault. What harm can it do? But then she says it again, and this time she whispers it, but loudly enough to hear the ugly sound reverberate in the room.

"Bitch," she says a third time, growing bolder. The word explodes from her mouth, chilling me to the bone although the sun is seeping resolutely through the drapes and the room is sweltering with the heat.

"Bitch," she says again and again, unable to stop, her face contorted with rage. I feel my heart beating faster within the cage of my body, fluttering against the armor of my bones, and rising, I slap her face, so hard that it stings my hand and leaves an ugly red mark on her skin.

She runs to her room and the door slams shut. I can hear the click of her lock snapping closed, then loud sobs as she gasps for breath. I imagine her flung sideways across her bed, her hair falling wildly over the edge, beating the pillow with her tight closed fists and suddenly I am filled with pity for her and shame for myself.

Through the long hours of the morning she remains in retreat and will not come out. Finally I pound on the door and order her to open it, but the only sound is the steady whirring of a fan. Frightened that she has done something rash, racked with guilt that I have lost control, I take a hanger and, bending it, work diligently at the keyhole until at last I swing open the door.

She has stopped crying but her face is splotched with red and there is still an angry imprint where my hand crossed her cheek. She is pouting on the bed, her eyes puffy, her lower lip thrust forward. She will not even look at me. The curtains are drawn against the heat and in the dim shadowed light of the room I see

that she has strewn candy wrappers over the floor. An empty Coke
bottle sprawls on its side against the dresser. A lonely sock pro-
trudes beneath the bed. A trail of dirty clothes trace a path through
the room and end in a corner next to stacks of *True Confession*
magazines littering the rug.

"Come out," I say as calmly as I am able, swallowing hard for
what we have done to each other, what we continue to do. "We'll
make up. Everything will be all right." I try to appear more confident than I really am. "You're only hurting yourself, you know."
The words sound as hollow and meaningless as when my own
mother uttered them, and I am aware that this sort of logic will
never reach her.

"Look," I say, trying to keep my voice steady. "It has nothing
to do with you." I keep my eyes fixed firmly on her face although
she continues to stare stubbornly at the floor. "It's between your
father and me."

At last she lifts heavy lids to look up defiantly. A difficult age, I
think, and she is more difficult than most. Beneath that yellow
T-shirt with the ludicrous letters, her breasts rise as supple as ripe
fruit. Under her arms I see black prickly hair sprouting like desert
scrub. She will not let me see her naked anymore. Once I came into
the room, catching her by surprise, and saw with a shock that
triangle of womanly hair on her body. Now we stare at each other
without speaking. Suddenly overcome with remorse, I long to tell
her that I am sorry but the moment passes and instead I say nothing. I retreat and she rises mournfully to take a shower.

When I hear the water running full force, I decide to call Ephraim.
He is an engineer, capable of correcting the errors of vast machinery. Perhaps it is still possible for him to correct the errors of our
lives. I dial his number at work and he answers the phone himself,
startling me, as though he has been standing there all along, arms
crossed over his chest in a familiar posture, waiting for me to call.

"Ephraim," I begin, without bothering to ask how he is, "come
home tonight. We are eating each other alive."

"On Sunday," he says wearily, for we have been through this

before. Ephraim refuses to come on Friday for Shabbes. It is too
far he says. He is afraid that something will happen before he gets
here and he will have to travel after sundown when it is forbidden.
A thousand and one disasters pass through his mind. The car will
stall and leave him stranded. A train could have an accident, God
forbid. A bus could be hijacked on the highway (he has read of it
happening), and he will be caught as night falls and the Sabbath
descends without a prayer to stand on.

"Too late," I say. "By Sunday we'll both be dead."

"Don't worry," he answers solemnly as though he hasn't even
heard me. "I will pray for us." Suddenly I can see him standing in
the fading light, his prayer shawl draped over his shoulders, a
skullcap on his balding dome—at dawn, at dusk, in heat or cold,
swaying and rocking on the balls of his feet, summoning the God
of Israel, communing with his Maker. He is in the wrong century,
I think, the wrong life. He should have been Abraham journeying
beneath a starry sky, Moses adrift in the wilderness, Jeremiah
making his lonely vigil through the desolate city of Jerusalem.

"Ephraim, Ephraim," I plead, desperation overtaking my voice.
"Live a little! Take a chance. What harm can it do?" But he is older,
more set in his ways. I can hear him sighing and struggling with
himself.

"Yes, I'll pray," he repeats again, but he sounds exhausted, as
though what is happening to us is all too much for him.

"What good will your prayers do? What good is your God?" I
cry, aware that I am beginning to descend over the edge. Then I
decide on another tactic and this time my voice is softer, cajoling,
"Come home, Ephraim," I say, "I need you. I want you."

I can almost hear the catch in his voice, the hesitation as he
thinks it through.

"For the child, Ephraim," I persist.

"It is too difficult," he murmurs at last.

"Ah, Ephraim," I say, "*life* is difficult," but he has made up his
mind. He is firm, refusing to commit himself. "For shame," I cry,
and slam down the phone.

Tonight, tomorrow he will not even answer it. Once I let the phone ring a hundred times just to test him, knowing that he was there, swaying silently in the dark. Cecilia calls him late at night when she thinks I am asleep. I can hear her whispering about me, telling him how hard it is for us to get along, how she wishes he would come back. Now, hearing footsteps, I wonder if she has been standing there all along. I turn on the tap and quickly splash my burning face with cold water. But even so I can feel myself flushing as though she has caught me in a disreputable act. Her eyes are red and rimmed with fatigue but she has changed her clothes, and clipped her wet hair back from her forehead. Yet the place where I struck her continues to stain her cheek, forming a barrier between us. She says nothing, her face an impassive mask. Perhaps she has not heard anything after all and it is only my imagination which tortures me.

"Come," I say, trying to make the best of a bad day. "It's time to get ready for Shabbes." Before the sun sets we must clean the house, polish the silver, cook the dinner and bake the bread. In these matters Ephraim has trained her well. She obeys me silently, without a word of complaint. I uncover the dough that we prepared earlier, and we take out the bread tray and the silver candlesticks that need polishing. On the shelf next to them a sad solitary imprint marks the spot where Ephraim's wine cup stood.

She places a board on the kitchen table and her fingers move deftly over the dough, pounding and kneading it into shape, her face coloring with the heat, her eyes intent on her task. At last she twists it into thick braids to slip into the oven, pinching off a piece which she burns in an ancient ritual, closing her eyes and moving her lips in silent supplication as she has seen me do. What does she yearn for behind those sorrowful eyes? What thoughts does she think? For the past year she has suffered with nightmares that wake her up screaming in the middle of the night, as though striving to be released from some dread torment that will not leave her alone. In the morning when I come into her room I see her sheets twisted into knots, as though demons have tied them during the night.

"A stage," the doctor says, but I know better. She has always been this way. Now just more so. Sometimes I think that when I am old and defenseless, unable to take care of myself, I will have to live with her and then she will vent her stored-up rage upon my helpless body like that dough beneath her hands.

I want to say, "Tell me what you're thinking, Cecilia," but she is far away, her gaze focusing on something else, caught in a web of her own thoughts.

Yesterday to calm us both I prepared a picnic supper to take to the park. Other families were there, too, and we spread a blanket on the grass and had cold slices of roast beef and potato salad. When the ice cream man came around we bought cherry Popsicles and sat at the edge of the playground to eat them. Children were swinging, and watching them, Cecilia decided to pump her own skinny legs high over the sand boxes, soaring higher and higher until her face was filled with a strange gentle joy. Afterward, she sat very close to me and laid her head upon my shoulder, her eyes tranquil, her expression subdued. But by evening it was obvious that she was brooding. We quarreled, and later I heard her crying until I finally turned over and fell asleep.

She is still working soundlessly as the heat builds to a peak of intensity and I pause to step outside on our small balcony, where we have some hanging plants that are rapidly wilting, and two old porch chairs that Ephraim keeps meaning to paint. We are on a quiet street at the very end of a cul-de-sac, and an occasional car, coming down here by mistake, will turn around beneath our porch. But now there is not a sign of life. Across the street windows are sleepy lids, blinds and drapes closed against the broiling sun. The heat is suffocating. From next door I hear the blast of a TV, then a muffled sound as it is quickly turned down. But it is not only the heat which suffocates me. It is the knowledge of what has become of the three of us, of what we are doing to each other.

When I go back into the house Cecilia is still intent on her tasks. She raises her head and looks at me suspiciously without saying anything. The kitchen has become unbearably hot, the sun pouring through the curtains onto the linoleum floor, the futile beating of a fan on top of the refrigerator the only noise that breaks the silence. I join her and we work side by side without uttering a word.

Beads of perspiration gather on her forehead and above her upper lip, and I wonder again what she is thinking behind those inscrutable eyes.

"Cecilia," I long to say. "Let's make up, let's not fight," but something holds me back. Her mouth is pursed tightly together, her jaw clenched, and I decide not to say anything.

Instead, I open the oven and take out the bread, setting it on the counter to cool. It is dark brown, the top of the braids blackened slightly at the tips, and she glances approvingly at it. For a moment she seems about to speak, but then stops as though pride still prevents her. I season the chicken and put it in to roast. The sun continues to splash across the kitchen in waves of heat. I stop to take a bath and nap before dinner, and still we have not spoken since morning.

When I appear an hour later I see that she has spread a white cloth upon the table and set out the best dishes and silver, placing the candlesticks in the center. Over the mound of fragrant bread is a green and gold embroidered cover Cecilia made one summer at camp with the word Sabbath in Hebrew. She has changed again, this time into a clean white blouse and white shorts, and her hair is tied back with a light blue ribbon. I am wearing a long print skirt and a colorful top I bought one year in Mexico, and my hair, which is beginning to thread with gray at the sides, is pinned on top of my head with a large tortoise-shell clip.

I turn off the fan and open the windows, drawing back the curtains. For the first time in days the heat has begun to break. A cool breeze stirs the material and they flutter lightly against the screens. Before the sun is ready to disappear behind the tops of the houses like an angry red eye, I light the candles and stand before them, arms upraised to say the blessing that ushers in the day of rest. Cecilia takes her place next to me and even though my eyes are closed I can feel her hands circling the air next to mine, drawing the Sabbath closer.

"A good Shabbes," I say, forcing myself to reach out and put my arms around her shoulders, but her spine stiffens at my touch. Her body remains rigid and she averts her somber pupils from mine, her front teeth biting down hard on the middle of her lower lip.

I set the dinner on the table and then we both sit down, neither of us wanting to acknowledge Ephraim's empty place at the head of the table. Memory recalls his strong blunt hands above Cecilia's bowed head, intoning the patriarchal blessing that always brings such a strange quiet joy to her face.

In his absence I say a prayer of thanksgiving over the bread, breaking it apart with my hands, and then we eat it in thick chunks, greedily, suddenly ravenous.

"It's good," I say. "*Very* good," and she blushes with the praise, her tan cheeks turning rosy beneath the surface.

"Do you really think so?" she asks, and her expression changes as she speaks to me for the first time since morning. "You're not just saying that?"

"No. Really. It's good," I say again and I can see that she is pleased. A slight smile passes over her lips and like soldiers on a battlefield it is clear that we have decided to call a truce for the holiday.

But then, in spite of myself, I remark bitterly, "It's a pity your father couldn't be here to taste it."

For the second time that day I am sorry as soon as the words are out of my mouth. A look of pain crosses her face and her eyes linger longingly on the candles. "But he's coming Sunday, isn't he?" she asks intensely.

"Yes," I say. "Of course. On Sunday." I say it calmly this time to reassure her and perhaps myself as well. It seems to sustain the two of us, and we relax and begin to eat with relish. Gradually a strong breeze gathers outside and blows through the room, releasing us, and it appears that the weight of thirteen years does not rest as heavily on her shoulders. The muted light of the candles catches her features in an unexpected expression, and I am startled to see that it is Ephraim's face before me.

As we eat, lengthening shadows fall over the walls in ghostly shapes. Darkness enfolds us, broken only by the bright headlights flooding the living room when they come to the dead end of our apartment.

Cecilia's brow is furrowed in concentration above the slender bridge of her nose. We make desultory talk and I think how far away we are from each other. At last I set out two melons for dessert and crushed grape ices that we spoon into the hollowed centers of the fruit.

We linger for a while longer, still not speaking, and then I clear off the table while she rises to help, thrusting her arms into the soapy dishwater.

She hands me the dishes and I dry them, placing them one by one on the white counter as we work silently, the light of the candles finally sputtering to a close. The smell of burnt wax fills the air. A full moon illuminates Cecilia's slight figure and I see that the red mark on her cheek is nearly gone.

When we finish I hang up the towel to dry and our glances meet as she turns to go. How fragile she looks, how young, I think, so that I yearn to cry out to her as she disappears into the hushed darkness of the hallway. I am filled with a rush of love for her. Flesh of my flesh. Bones of my bone. Then, as though she has read my mind, suddenly she returns and standing on her tiptoes, kisses me goodnight. "Mother, I'm sorry," she says, and then just as quickly she is gone.

On Sunday Ephraim will come and perhaps things will work out after all. Who knows? But for a while at least in the stillness of this moment there is peace. At last there is peace. And tomorrow or the next day anything seems possible now, anything at all.

MICHAEL CHABON

S Angel

On the morning of his cousin's wedding, Ira performed his toilet, as he always did, with patience, hope, and ruthless punctilio. He put on his Italian wool trousers, his silk shirt, his pink socks, to which he ascribed a certain sexual felicity, and a slightly worn but still serviceable Willi Smith sports jacket. He shaved the delta of skin between his eyebrows, and took a few extra minutes to clean out the inside of his car, a battered, faintly malodorous Japanese hatchback of no character whatever. Ira never went anywhere without expecting that when he arrived he would meet the woman with whom he had been destined to fall in love. He drove across Los Angeles from Palms to Arcadia, where his cousin Sheila was being married in a synagogue Ira got lost trying to find. When he walked in late he disturbed the people sitting at the back of the shul, and his aunt Lillian, when he joined her, pinched his arm quite painfully. The congregation was dour and Conservative, and as the service dragged on Ira found himself awash in a nostalgic tedium, and he fell to wishing for irretrievable things.

At the reception that followed, in the banquet room of the old El Imperio Hotel, in Pasadena, he looked in vain for one of his more interesting young female cousins, such as Zipporah, from Berkeley, who was six feet tall and on the women's crew at Cal, or that scary one, Leah Black, who had twice in their childhood allowed Ira to see what he wanted to see. Both Ira and Sheila sprang from a rather disreputable branch of Wisemans, however, and her wedding was poorly attended by the family. All the people at Ira's table were of the groom's party, except for Ira's great-aunts, Lillian and Sophie, and Sophie's second husband, Mr. Lapidus.

"You need a new sports jacket," said Aunt Sophie.

"He needs a new *watch*," said Aunt Lillian.

Mr. Lapidus said that what Ira needed was a new barber. A lively discussion arose at table seventeen, as the older people began to complain about contemporary hair styles, with Ira's itself—there was some fancy clipperwork involved—cited frequently as an instance of their inscrutability. Ira zoned out and ate three or four pounds of the salmon carpaccio with lemon cucumber and cilantro that the waiters kept bringing around, and also a substantial number of boletus-and-goat-cheese profiteroles. He watched the orchestra members, particularly the suave-looking black tenor saxophonist with dreadlocks, and tried to imagine what they were thinking about as they blew all that corny cha-cha-cha. He watched Sheila and her new husband whispering and box-stepping and tried to imagine the same thing. She seemed pleased enough—smiling and flushed and thrilled to be wearing that dazzling dress—but she didn't look as though she were in love, as he imagined love to look. Her eye was restive, vaguely troubled, as if she were trying to remember exactly who this man was, with his arms around her waist, tipping her backward on one leg and planting a kiss on her throat.

It was as he watched Sheila and Barry walk off the dance floor that the woman in the blue dress caught Ira's eye, then looked away. She was sitting with two other women, at a table under one of the giant palm trees that stood in pots all across the banquet room, which the hotel called the Oasis Room and had decorated to suit. When Ira returned her gaze he felt a pleasant internal flush, as though he had just knocked back a shot of whiskey. The woman's expression verged a moment on nearsightedness before collapsing into a vaguely irritated scowl. Her hair was frizzy and tinted blond, her lips were thick and red but grim and disapproving, and her eyes, which might have been gray or brown, were painted to match her electric dress. Subsequent checking revealed that her body had aged better than her fading face, which nonetheless he found beautiful, and in which, in the skin at her throat and around her eyes, he thought he read strife and sad experience and a willingness to try her luck.

Ira stood and approached the woman, on the pretext of going over to the bar. As he did so he stole another long look, and eavesdropped on an instant of her conversation. Her voice was soft and just a little woeful as she addressed the woman beside her, saying something deprecating, it seemed to Ira, about lawyers' shoes. The holes in her earlobes were filled with simple gold posts. Ira swung like a comet past the table, trailing, as he supposed, a sparkling wake of lustfulness and Eau Sauvage, but she seemed not to notice him, and when he reached the bar he found, to his surprise, that he genuinely wanted a drink. His body was unpredictable and resourceful in malfunction, and he was not, as a result, much of a drinker; but it was an open bar, after all. He ordered a double shot of Sauza.

There were two men talking behind him, waiting for their drinks, and Ira edged a little closer to them, without turning around, so that he could hear better. He was a fourth-year drama student at U.C.L.A. and diligent about such valuable actorly exercises as eavesdropping, spying, and telling complicated lies to fellow-passengers on airplanes.

"That Charlotte was a class-A, top-of-the-line, capital-B-I-T bitch," said one of the men, in the silky tones of an announcer on a classical-music station. "And fucked up from her ass to her eyebrows." He had a very faint New York accent.

"Exactly, exactly," said the other, who sounded older, and well accustomed to handing out obsequious counsel to young men. "No question. You had to fire her."

"I should have done it the day it happened. Ha-ha. But instead— pow, fired in her own bed."

"Exactly. Ha-ha."

"Ira!" It was his cousin, the bride, bright and still pink from dancing. Sheila had long, kinky black hair, spectacular eyelashes, and a nose that, like Ira's, flirted dangerously, but on the whole successfully, with immenseness. He thought she looked really ter-rific, and he congratulated her wistfully. Ira and Sheila had at one time been close. Sheila hung an arm around his neck and kissed him on the cheek. Her breath blew warm in his ear. "What is that you're drinking?"

"Tequila," he said. He turned to try to get a glimpse of the men at the bar, but it was too late. They had been replaced by a couple of elderly women with empty highball glasses and giant clip-on earrings.

"Can I try?" She sipped at it and made a face. "I hope it makes you feel better than it tastes."

"It couldn't," Ira said, taking a more appreciative pull of his own.

Sheila studied his face, biting at her lip. They hadn't seen one another since the evening, over a year before, when she had taken him to see some dull and infuriating Soviet movie—"Shadow of Uzbek Love," or something like that—at U.C.L.A. She was look-ing, it seemed to him, for signs of change.

"So, are you dating anyone?" she said, and there was a glint of apprehension in her casual tone.

"Lots of people."

"Uh-huh. Do you want to meet someone?"

"No, thanks." Things had got a little wiggly, Ira now recalled, in the car on the way home from Westwood that night. Sheila drove one of those tiny Italian two-seaters capable of filling very rapidly with sexual tension, in particular at a stoplight, with Marvin Gaye coming over the radio and a pretty cousin in the driver's seat, chewing thoughtfully on a strand of hair. Ira, in a sort of art-house funk, had found himself babbling on about Marx and George Orwell and McCarthyism, and praying for green lights; and when they arrived at his place he had dashed up the steps into his apartment and locked the door behind him. He shook his head, wondering at this demureness, and drained the glass of tequila. He said, "Do you want to dance?"

They went out onto the floor and spun around a few times slowly to "I'll Never Be the Same." Sheila felt at once soft and starchy in her taffeta dress, gigantic and light as down.

"I really wish you would meet my friend Carmen," said Sheila. "She needs to meet a nice man. She lives next door to my parents in Altadena. Her husband used to beat her but now they're divorced. She has the most beautiful gray eyes."

At this Ira stiffened, and he blew the count.

"Sitting right over there under the palm tree? In the blue dress?"

"Ouch! That's my foot."

"Sorry."

"So you noticed her! Great. Go on, I., ask her to dance. She's so lonesome anymore."

The information that the older woman might actually welcome his overtures put him off, and somehow made him less certain of success. Ira tried to formulate a plausible excuse.

"She looks mean," he said. "She gave me a nasty look not five minutes ago. Oh, hey. It's Donna."

"Donna!"

Donna Furman, in a sharp gray sharkskin suit, approached and kissed the bride, first on the hand with the ring, then once on each cheek, in a gesture that struck Ira as oddly papal and totally Hollywood. Donna started to tell Sheila how beautiful she looked, but then some people with cameras came by and swept Sheila away, so Donna threw out her arms to Ira, and the cousins embraced. She wore her short hair slicked back with something that had an ozone smell, and it crackled against Ira's ear. Donna was a very distant relation, and several years older than Ira, but, as the Furmans had lived in Glassell Park, not far from Ira's family in Mount Washington, Ira had known Donna all his life, and he was glad to see her.

This feeling of gladness was not entirely justified by recent history, as Donna, a girl with a clever tongue and a scheming imagination, had grown into a charming but unreliable woman, and if Ira had stopped to consider he might, at first, have had a bone or two to pick with his fourth cousin once removed. She was a good-looking, dark-complected lesbian—way out in the open about that—with a big bust and a twelve-thousand-dollar smile. The vein of roguery that had found its purest expression in Sheila's grandfather, Milton Wiseman, a manufacturer of diet powders and placebo aphrodisiacs, ran thin but rich through Donna's character. She talked fast and took recondite drugs and told funny stories about famous people whom she claimed to know. Despite the fact that she worked for one of the big talent agencies in Culver City, in their music division, and made ten times what Ira did waiting tables and working summers at a Jewish drama camp up in Idyllwild, Donna owed Ira, at the time of this fond embrace, three hundred and twenty-five dollars.

"We ought to go out to Santa Anita tonight," Donna said, winking one of her moist brown eyes, which she had inherited from her mother, a concentration-camp survivor, a Hollywood costume designer, and a very sweet lady who had taken an overdose of sleeping pills when Donna was still a teen-ager. Donna's round, sorrowful eyes made it impossible to doubt that somewhere deep within her lay a wise and tormented soul; in her line of work they were a trump card.

"I'd love to," said Ira. "You can stake me three hundred and twenty-five bucks."

"Oh, right! I forgot about that!" Donna said, squeezing Ira's hand. "I have my checkbook in the car."

"I heard you brought a date, Donna," Ira went on, not wanting to bring out the squirrelliness in his cousin right off the bat. When Donna began to squeeze your hand it was generally a portent of fictions and false rationales. She was big on touching, which was all right with Ira. He liked being touched. "So where is the unfortunate girl?"

"Over there," Donna said, inclining her head toward Ira as
though what she was about to say were inside information capable
of toppling a regime or piling up a fortune in a single afternoon.
"At that table under the palm tree, there. With those other two
women. The tall one in the flowery thing, with the pointy nose. Her
name's Audrey."

"Does she work with you?" said Ira, happy to have an excuse to
stare openly at Carmen, seated to the right of Donna's date and
now looking back at Ira in a way that he thought could hardly be
mistaken. He wiggled his toes a few times within his lucky pink
socks. Donna's date, Audrey, waved her fingers at them. She was
pretty, with an expensive, blunt hairdo and blue eyes, although her
nose was as pointed as a marionette's.

"She lives in my building. Audrey's at the top, at the very
summit, I., of a *vast* vitamin pyramid. Like, we're talking, I don't
know, ten thousand people, from Oxnard to Norco. Here, I'll take
you over." She took hold of the sleeve of Ira's jacket, then noticed
the empty shot glass in his hand. "Hold on, let me buy you a
drink." This was said without a trace of irony. "Drinking shots?"

"Sauza. Two-story."

"A C.C.-and-water with a twist and a double Sauza," she said to
the bartender. "Tequila makes you unlucky with women."

"See that blonde Audrey is sitting beside?"

"Yeah? With the nasty mouth?"

"I'd like to be unlucky with her."

"Drink this," said Donna, handing Ira a shot glass filled to the
brim with liquid the very hue of hangover and remorse. "From
what I heard, she's a basket case, I. Bad husband. A big mess. She
keeps taking these beta-carotene tablets every time she has a Seven-
and-7, like it's some kind of post-divorce diet or I don't know."

"I think she likes me." They had started toward the table but
stopped now to convene a hasty parley on the dance floor, beneath
the front of a squat fan palm. Donna had been giving Ira sexual
advice since he was nine.

"How old are you now—twenty-one?"

"Almost."

"She's older than I am, Ira!" Donna patted herself on the chest.

"You don't want to get involved with someone so old. You want someone who still has all her delusions intact, or whatever."

Ira studied Carmen as his cousin spoke, sensing the truth in what she said. He had yet to fall in love to the degree that he felt he was capable of falling, had never written villanelles or declarations veiled in careful metaphor, nor sold his blood plasma to buy champagne or jonquils, nor haunted a mailbox or a phone booth or a certain café, nor shouted his beloved's name in the streets at three in the morning, heedless of the neighbors, and it seemed possible that to fall for a woman who had been around the block a few times might be to rob himself of many of the purely ornamental elements, the swags and antimacassars of first love. No doubt Carmen had had enough of such things. And yet it was her look of disillusion, of detachment, those stoical gray eyes in the middle of that lovely, beaten face, that most attracted him. It would be wrong to love her, he could see that; but he believed that every great love was in some measure a terrible mistake.

"Just introduce me to her, Donnie," he said, "and you don't have to pay me back."

"Pay you back what?" said Donna, lighting up her halogen smile.

Carmen *was* a basket case. The terra-cotta ashtray before her on the table, stamped with the words "EL IMPERIO," was choked with the slender butts of her cigarettes, and the lit square she held in her long, pretty fingers was trembling noticeably and spewing a huge, nervous chaos of smoke. Her gray eyes were large and moist and pink, as though she had been crying not five minutes before, and when Donna, introducing Ira, laid a hand on her shoulder, it looked as though Carmen might start in again, from the shock and the unexpected softness of this touch. All of these things might have escaped Ira's notice or been otherwise explained, but on the empty seat beside her, where Ira hoped to install himself, sat her handbag, unfastened and gaping, and one glimpse of it was enough to convince him that she was a woman out of control. Amid a blizzard of wadded florets of Kleenex, enough to decorate a small parade float, Ira spotted a miniature bottle of airline gin, a plastic

bag of jelly beans (all black ones), two unidentifiable vials of prescription medication, a crumpled and torn road map, the wreckage
of a Hershey bar, and a key chain, in the shape of a brontosaurus,
with one sad key on it. The map was bent and misfolded in such
a way that only the fragmentary words "s ANGEL," in one corner,
were legible.

"Carmen Wallace, this is my adorable little cousin Ira," Donna
said, using the hand that was not resting on Carmen's bare shoulder
to pull at Ira's cheek. "He asked to meet you."

"How do you do," said Ira, blushing badly.

"Hi," Carmen said, setting her cigarette on the indented lip of
the ashtray and extending the tips of her fingers toward Ira, who
paused a moment—channelling all of his sexual energy into the
center of his right palm—then took them. They were soft, and gone
in an instant, withdrawn as though he had burned her.

"And this is Audrey—"

"Hi, Audrey."

"—and Doreen, who's a—friend?—of the groom's."

Ira shook hands with these two and, once Carmen had moved
her appalling purse onto the floor beside her to make room for
him, soon found himself in the enviable position of being the only
man at a table of five. Doreen was wearing a bright-yellow dress
with an extremely open bodice; she had come to her friend Barry's
wedding exposing such a great deal of her remarkable chest that Ira
wondered about her motives. She was otherwise a little on the plain
side and she had a sour, horsy laugh, but she was in real estate, and
Donna and Audrey, who were thinking of buying a house together,
seemed to have a lot to say to her. There was nothing for him and
Carmen to do but speak to each other.

"Sheila says you live next door to her folks?" Ira said. Carmen
nodded, then turned her head to exhale a long jet of smoke. The
contact of their eyes was brief but he thought it had something to
it. There was about an inch and a half of Sauza left in Ira's glass and
he drained a quarter inch of it, figuring this left him with enough
to get through another five questions. He could already tell that
talking to Carmen was not going to be easy, but he considered this

an excellent omen. Easy flirtation had always struck him as an end in itself, and one that did not particularly interest him.

"Is it that big wooden house with the sort of, I don't know, those *things*, those rafters or whatever, sticking out from under all the roofs?" He spread the fingers of one hand and slid them under the other until they protruded, making a crude approximation of the overhanging eaves of a California bungalow. There was such a grand old house, to the north of Sheila's parents', that he'd always admired.

Another nod. She had a habit of opening her eyes very wide every so often, almost a tic, and Ira wondered if her contact lenses might be slipping.

"It's a Hetrick and Dewitt," she said bitterly, as though this were the most withering pair of epithets that could be applied to a house. These were the first words she had addressed to him, and in them, though he didn't know what she was talking about, he sensed a story. He took another little sip of tequila and nodded agreeably.

"You live in a Hetrick and Dewitt?" said Doreen, interrupting her conversation with Donna and Audrey to reach across Audrey's lap and tap Carmen on the arm. She looked amazed. "Which one?"

"It's the big, pretentious one on Orangeblossom, in Altadena," Carmen said, stubbing out her cigarette. She gave a very caustic sigh and then rose to her feet; she was taller than Ira had thought. Having risen to her feet rather dramatically, she now seemed uncertain of what to do next and stood wavering a little on her blue spike heels. It was clear that she felt she had been wrong to come to Sheila's wedding, but that was all she seemed able to manage, and after a moment she sank slowly back into her seat. Ira felt very sorry for her and tried to think of something she could do besides sit and look miserable. At that moment the band launched into "Night and Day," and Ira happened to look toward the table where he had left his aunts. Mr. Lapidus was pulling out Aunt Sophie's chair and taking her arm. They were going to dance.

"Carmen, would you like to dance?" Ira said, blushing, and wiggling his toes.

Her reply was no more than a whisper, and Ira wasn't sure if he'd heard it correctly, but it seemed to him that she had said, "Anything."

They walked, separately, out to the dance floor, and turned to face each other. For an awful moment they just stood, tapping their hesitant feet. But the two old people were describing a slow arc in Ira's general direction, and finally, in order to forestall any embarrassing exhortations from Mr. Lapidus, who was known for such things, Ira reached out and took Carmen by the waist and palm, and twirled her off across the wide parquet floor of the Oasis Room. It was an old-fashioned sort of tune, and there was no question of their dancing to it any way but in each other's arms.

"You're good at this," Carmen said, smiling for the first time that he could remember.

"Thanks," said Ira. He was in fact a competent dancer—his mother, preparing him for a fantastic and outmoded destiny, had taught him a handful of hokey old steps. Carmen danced beautifully, and he saw to his delight that he had somehow hit upon the precise activity to bring her, for the moment anyway, out of her beta-carotene-and-black-jelly-bean gloom. "So are you."

"I used to work at the Arthur Murray on La Cienega," she said, moving one hand a little lower on his back. "That was fifteen years ago."

This apparently wistful thought seemed to revive her accustomed gloominess a little, and she took on the faraway, hollow expression of a taxi dancer, and grew heavy in his arms. The action of her legs became overly thoughtful and accurate. Ira searched for something to talk about, to distract her with, but all of the questions he came up with had to do, at least in some respect, with *her*, and he sensed that anything on this subject might plunge her into an irrevocable sadness. At last the bubble of silence between them grew too great, and Ira pierced it helplessly.

"Where did you grow up?" he said, looking away as he spoke.

"In hotels," said Carmen, and that was that. "I don't think Sheila is happy, do you?" She coughed, and then the song came abruptly to an end. The bandleader set down his trumpet, tugged the microphone up to his mouth, and announced that in just a few short moments the cake was going to be cut.

When they returned to the table a tall, handsome man, his black hair thinning but his chin cleft and his eyes pale green, was standing behind Carmen's empty chair, leaning against it and talking to Donna, Audrey, and Doreen. He wore a fancy, European-cut worsted suit, a purple-and-sky-blue paisley necktie, a blazing white-on-white shirt, and a tiny sparkler in the lobe of his left ear. His nose was large, bigger even than Ira's, and of a complex shape, like the blade of some highly specialized tool; it dominated his face in a way that made the man himself seem dominating. The glossy fabric of his suit jacket caught and stretched across the muscles of his shoulders. When Carmen approached her place at the table he drew her chair for her. She thanked him with a happy and astonishingly carnal smile, and as she sat down he peered, with a polished audacity that made Ira wince in envy, into the scooped neck of her dress.

"Carmen, Ira," said Doreen, "this is Jeff Freebone." As Doreen introduced the handsome Mr. Freebone, all of the skin that was visible across her body colored a rich blood-orange red. Ira's hand vanished for a moment into a tanned, forehand-smashing grip. Ira looked at Donna, hoping to see at least some hint of unimpressedness in her lesbian and often cynical gaze, but his cousin had the same shining-eyed sort of *Tiger Beat* expression on her face that Doreen and Carmen—and Audrey, for that matter—had, and Ira realized that Jeff Freebone must be very, very rich.

"What's up, Ira?" he said, in a smooth, flattened-out baritone to which there clung a faint tang of New York City, and Ira recognized him, with a start, as the coarse man at the bar who had fired an unfortunate woman named Charlotte in her own bed.

"Jeff here used to work in the same office as Barry and me," Doreen told Carmen. "Now he has his own company."

"Freebone Properties," Carmen said, looking more animated than she had all afternoon. "I've seen the signs on front lawns, right?"

"Billboards," said Donna. "Ads on TV."

"How was the wedding?" Jeff wanted to know. He went around Carmen and sat down in the chair beside her, leaving Ira to stand, off to one side, glowering at his cousin Donna, who was clearly going to leave him high and dry in this. "Did they stand under that tent thing and break the mirror or whatever?"

Ira was momentarily surprised, and gratified, by this display of ignorance, since he had taken Jeff for Jewish. Then he remembered that many of Donna's Hollywood friends spoke with a schmoozing accent whether they were Jewish or not, even ex-cheerleaders from Ames, Iowa, and men named Lars.

"It was weird," Carmen declared, without elaborating—not even Jeff Freebone, apparently, could draw her out—and the degree of acquiescence this judgment received at the table shocked Ira. He turned to seek out Sheila among the hundreds of faces that filled the Oasis Room, to see if she was all right, but could not find her. There was a small crowd gathered around the cathedral cake at the far end of the room, but the bride did not seem to be among them. Weird—what had been weird about it? Was Sheila not, after all, in love with her two hours' husband? Ira tapped his foot to the music, self-conscious, and pretended to continue his search for Sheila, although in truth he was not looking at anything anymore. He was mortified by the quickness with which his love affair with the sad and beautiful woman of his dreams had been derailed, and all at once—the tequila he had drunk had begun to betray him—he came face to face with the distinct possibility that not only would he never find the one he was meant to find but that no one else ever did, either. The discussion around the table hurtled off into the imaginary and vertiginous world of real estate. Finally he had to pull a nearby chair over and sit down.

"I can get you three mil for it, sight unseen," Jeff Freebone was declaring. He leaned back in his seat and folded his hands behind his head.

"It's worth way more," said Donna, giving Carmen a poke in the ribs. "It's a work of art, Jeff."

"It's a Hetrick and Dewitt," said everyone at the table, all at once.

"You have to see it," Doreen said.

"All right then, let's see it. I drove my Rover, we can all fit. Take me to see it."

There was a moment of hesitation, during which the four women seemed to consider the dictates of decorum and the possible impli- cations of the proposed expedition to see the house that Carmen hated.

"The cake is always like sliced cardboard at these things, any- way," said Donna.

This seemed to decide them, and there followed a general scrap- ing of chairs and gathering of summer wraps.

"Aren't you coming?" said Donna, leaning over Ira—who had settled into a miserable, comfortable slouch—and whispering into his ear. The others were already making their way out of the Oasis Room. Ira scowled at her.

"Hey, come on, I. She needs a realtor, not a lover. Besides, she was way too old for you." She put her arms around his neck and kissed the top of his head. "O.K., sulk. I'll call you." Then she buttoned her sharkskin jacket and turned on one heel.

After Ira had been sitting alone at the table for several minutes, half hoping his Aunt Lillian would notice his distress and bring over a piece of cake or a petit four and a plateful of her comforting platitudes, he noticed that Carmen, not too surprisingly, had left her handbag behind. He got up from his chair and went to pick it up. For a moment he peered into it, aroused, despite himself, by the intimacy of what he was doing—like reading a woman's diary, or putting one's hand inside her empty shoe. Then he remembered his disappointment and his anger, and his fist closed around one of the vials of pills, which he quickly slipped into his pocket.

"Ira, have you seen Sheila?"

Ira dropped the purse, and whirled around. It was indeed his Aunt Lillian, but she looked very distracted and didn't seem aware of having caught Ira in the act. She kept tugging at the fringes of her wildly patterned scarf.

"Not recently," said Ira. "Why?"

Aunt Lillian explained that someone, having drunk too much, had fallen onto the train of Sheila's gown and torn it slightly; this had seemed to upset Sheila a good deal, and she had gone off somewhere, no one knew where. The bathrooms and the lobbies of the hotel had all been checked. The cake-cutting was fifteen minutes overdue.

"I'll find her," said Ira.

He went out into the high, cool lobby and crossed it several times, his heels clattering across the marble floors and his soles susurrant along the Persian carpets. He climbed a massive oak staircase to the mezzanine, where he passed through a pair of French doors that opened onto a long balcony overlooking a sparkling pool. Here he found Sheila, dropped in one corner of the terrace like a blown flower. She had taken the garland from her brow and was twirling it around and around in front of her face with the mopey fascination of a child. When she felt Ira's presence she turned, and, seeing him, broke out in a teary-eyed grin that he found very difficult to bear. He walked over to her and sat down beside her on the rough stucco deck of the balcony.

"Hi," he said.

"Are they all going nuts down there?"

"I guess. I heard about your dress. I'm really sorry."

"It's all right." She stared through the posts of the balustrade at the great red sun going down over Santa Monica. There had been a lot of rain the past few days, and the air was heartbreakingly clear. "You just feel like such a, I don't know, a big stupid puppet or something, getting pulled around."

Ira edged a little closer to his cousin, and she laid her head against his shoulder and sighed. The contact of her body was so welcome and unsurprising that it frightened him, and he began to fidget with the vial in his pocket.

"What's that?" she said, at the faint rattle.

He withdrew the little bottle and held it up to the dying light. There was no label of any kind on its side.

"I sort of stole them from your friend Carmen."

Sheila managed an offhand smile.

"Oh—how did that work out? I saw you dancing."

"She wasn't for me," said Ira. He unscrewed the cap and tipped the vial into his hand. There were only two pills left: small, pink, shaped like commas—two little pink teardrops. "Any idea what these are? Could they be beta carotene?"

Sheila shook her head and extended one hand, palm upward. At first Ira thought she wanted him to place one of the pills upon it, but she shook her head; when he took her outstretched fingers in his she nodded.

"Ira," she said in the heaviest of voices, bringing her bridal mouth toward his. Just before he kissed her he closed his eyes, brought his own hand to his mouth, and swallowed, hard.

"My darling," he said.

E. L. DOCTOROW

The Writer in the Family

*I*n 1955 my father died with his ancient mother still alive in a nursing home. The old lady was ninety and hadn't even known he was ill. Thinking the shock might kill her, my aunts told her that he had moved to Arizona for his bronchitis. To the immigrant generation of my grandmother, Arizona was the American equivalent of the Alps, it was where you went for your health. More accurately, it was where you went if you had the money. Since my father had failed in all the business enterprises of his life, this was the aspect of the news my grandmother dwelled on, that he had finally had some success. And so it came about that as we mourned him at home in our stocking feet, my grandmother was bragging to her cronies about her son's new life in the dry air of the desert.

My aunts had decided on their course of action without consult-ing us. It meant neither my mother nor my brother nor I could visit Grandma because we were supposed to have moved west too, a family, after all. My brother Harold and I didn't mind—it was always a nightmare at the old people's home, where they all sat around staring at us while we tried to make conversation with Grandma. She looked terrible, had numbers of ailments, and her mind wandered. Not seeing her was no disappointment either for my mother, who had never gotten along with the old woman and did not visit when she could have. But what was disturbing was that my aunts had acted in the manner of that side of the family of making government on everyone's behalf, the true citizens by blood and the lesser citizens by marriage. It was exactly this attitude that had tormented my mother all her married life. She claimed Jack's family had never accepted her. She had battled them for twenty-five years as an outsider.

A few weeks after the end of our ritual mourning my Aunt Frances phoned us from her home in Larchmont. Aunt Frances was the wealthier of my father's sisters. Her husband was a lawyer, and both her sons were at Amherst. She had called to say that Grandma was asking why she didn't hear from Jack. I had answered the phone. "You're the writer in the family," my aunt said. "Your father had so much faith in you. Would you mind making up something? Send it to me and I'll read it to her. She won't know the difference."

That evening, at the kitchen table, I pushed my homework aside and composed a letter. I tried to imagine my father's response to his new life. He had never been west. He had never traveled any-where. In his generation the great journey was from the working class to the professional class. He hadn't managed that either. But he loved New York, where he had been born and lived his life, and he was always discovering new things about it. He especially loved the old parts of the city below Canal Street, where he would find ships' chandlers or firms that wholesaled in spices and teas. He was a salesman for an appliance jobber with accounts all over the city. He liked to bring home rare cheeses or exotic foreign vegetables that were sold only in certain neighborhoods. Once he brought home a barometer, another time an antique ship's telescope in a wooden case with a brass snap.

"Dear Mama," I wrote. "Arizona is beautiful. The sun shines all day and the air is warm and I feel better than I have in years. The desert is not as barren as you would expect, but filled with wild-flowers and cactus plants and peculiar crooked trees that look like men holding their arms out. You can see great distances in what-ever direction you turn and to the west is a range of mountains maybe fifty miles from here, but in the morning with the sun on them you can see the snow on their crests."

My aunt called some days later and told me it was when she read this letter aloud to the old lady that the full effect of Jack's death came over her. She had to excuse herself and went out in the parking lot to cry. "I wept so," she said. "I felt such terrible longing for him. You're so right, he loved to go places, he loved life, he loved everything."

We began trying to organize our lives. My father had borrowed money against his insurance and there was very little left. Some commissions were still due but it didn't look as if his firm would honor them. There was a couple of thousand dollars in a savings bank that had to be maintained there until the estate was settled. The lawyer involved was Aunt Frances' husband and he was very proper. "The estate!" my mother muttered, gesturing as if to pull out her hair. "The estate!" She applied for a job part-time in the admissions office of the hospital where my father's terminal illness had been diagnosed, and where he had spent some months until they had sent him home to die. She knew a lot of the doctors and staff and she had learned "from bitter experience," as she told them, about the hospital routine. She was hired.

I hated that hospital, it was dark and grim and full of tortured people. I thought it was masochistic of my mother to seek out a job there, but did not tell her so.

We lived in an apartment on the corner of 175th Street and the Grand Concourse, one flight up. Three rooms. I shared the bedroom with my brother. It was jammed with furniture because when my father had required a hospital bed in the last weeks of his illness we had moved some of the living-room pieces into the bedroom and made over the living room for him. We had to navigate bookcases, beds, a gateleg table, bureaus, a record player and radio console, stacks of 78 albums, my brother's trombone and music stand, and so on. My mother continued to sleep on the convertible sofa in the living room that had been their bed before his illness. The two rooms were connected by a narrow hall made even narrower by bookcases along the wall. Off the hall were a small kitchen and dinette and a bathroom. There were lots of appliances in the kitchen—broiler, toaster, pressure cooker, counter-top dishwasher, blender—that my father had gotten through his job, at cost. A treasured phrase in our house: *at cost*. But most of these fixtures went unused because my mother did not care for them. Chromium devices with timers or gauges that required the reading of elaborate instructions were not for her. They were in part responsible for the awful clutter of our lives and now she wanted to get rid of them. "We're being buried," she said. "Who needs them!"

So we agreed to throw out or sell anything inessential. While I found boxes for the appliances and my brother tied the boxes with twine, my mother opened my father's closet and took out his clothes. He had several suits because as a salesman he needed to look his best. My mother wanted us to try on his suits to see which of them could be altered and used. My brother refused to try them on. I tried on one jacket which was too large for me. The lining inside the sleeves chilled my arms and the vaguest scent of my father's being came to me.

"This is way too big," I said.

"Don't worry," my mother said. "I had it cleaned. Would I let you wear it if I hadn't?"

It was the evening, the end of winter, and snow was coming down on the windowsill and melting as it settled. The ceiling bulb glared on a pile of my father's suits and trousers on hangers flung across the bed in the shape of a dead man. We refused to try on anything more, and my mother began to cry.

"What are you crying for?" my brother shouted. "You wanted
to get rid of things, didn't you?"

A few weeks later my aunt phoned again and said she thought it
would be necessary to have another letter from Jack. Grandma had
fallen out of her chair and bruised herself and was very depressed.

"How long does this go on?" my mother said.

"It's not so terrible," my aunt said, "for the little time left to
make things easier for her."

My mother slammed down the phone. "He can't even die when
he wants to!" she cried. "Even death comes second to Mama!
What are they afraid of, the shock will kill her? Nothing can kill
her. She's indestructible! A stake through the heart couldn't kill
her!"

When I sat down in the kitchen to write the letter I found it more
difficult than the first one. "Don't watch me," I said to my brother.
"It's hard enough."

"You don't have to do something just because someone wants
you to," Harold said. He was two years older than me and had
started at City College; but when my father became ill he had
switched to night school and gotten a job in a record store.

"Dear Mama," I wrote. "I hope you're feeling well. We're all fit
as a fiddle. The life here is good and the people are very friendly
and informal. Nobody wears suits and ties here. Just a pair of slacks
and a short-sleeved shirt. Perhaps a sweater in the evening. I have
bought into a very successful radio and record business and I'm
doing very well. You remember Jack's Electric, my old place on
Forty-third Street? Well, now it's Jack's Arizona Electric and we
have a line of television sets as well."

I sent that letter off to my Aunt Frances, and as we all knew she
would, she phoned soon after. My brother held his hand over the
mouthpiece. "It's Frances with her latest review," he said.

"Jonathan? You're a very talented young man. I just wanted to
tell you what a blessing your letter was. Her whole face lit up when
I read the part about Jack's store. That would be an excellent way
to continue."

"Well, I hope I don't have to do this anymore, Aunt Frances. It's not very honest."

Her tone changed. "Is your mother there? Let me talk to her."

"She's not here," I said.

"Tell her not to worry," my aunt said. "A poor old lady who has never wished anything but the best for her will soon die."

I did not repeat this to my mother, for whom it would have been one more in the family anthology of unforgivable remarks. But then I had to suffer it myself for the possible truth it might embody. Each side defended its position with rhetoric, but I, who wanted peace, rationalized the snubs and rebuffs each inflicted on the other, taking no stands, like my father himself.

Years ago his life had fallen into a pattern of business failures and missed opportunities. The great debate between his family on the one side, and my mother Ruth on the other, was this: who was responsible for the fact that he had not lived up to anyone's expectations?

As to the prophecies, when spring came my mother's prevailed. Grandma was still alive.

One balmy Sunday my mother and brother and I took the bus to the Beth El cemetery in New Jersey to visit my father's grave. It was situated on a slight rise. We stood looking over rolling fields embedded with monuments. Here and there processions of black cars wound their way through the lanes, or clusters of people stood at open graves. My father's grave was planted with tiny shoots of evergreen but it lacked a headstone. We had chosen one and paid for it and then the stonecutters had gone on strike. Without a headstone my father did not seem to be honorably dead. He didn't seem to me properly buried.

My mother gazed at the plot beside his, reserved for her coffin. "They were always too fine for other people," she said. "Even in the old days on Stanton Street. They put on airs. Nobody was ever good enough for them. Finally Jack himself was not good enough for them. Except to get them things wholesale. Then he was good enough for them."

"Mom, please," my brother said.

"If I had known. Before I ever met him he was tied to his mama's apron strings. And Essie's apron strings were like chains, let me tell you. We had to live where we could be near them for the Sunday visits. Every Sunday, that was my life, a visit to mamaleh. Whatever she knew I wanted, a better apartment, a stick of furniture, a summer camp for the boys, she spoke against it. You know your father, every decision had to be considered and reconsidered. And nothing changed. Nothing ever changed."

She began to cry. We sat her down on a nearby bench. My brother walked off and read the names on stones. I looked at my mother, who was crying, and I went off after my brother.

"Mom's still crying," I said. "Shouldn't we do something?"

"It's all right," he said. "It's what she came here for."

"Yes," I said, and then a sob escaped from my throat. "But I feel like crying too."

My brother Harold put his arm around me. "Look at this old black stone here," he said. "The way it's carved. You can see the changing fashion in monuments—just like everything else."

Somewhere in this time I began dreaming of my father. Not the robust father of my childhood, the handsome man with healthy pink skin and brown eyes and a mustache and the thinning hair parted in the middle. My dead father. We were taking him home from the hospital. It was understood that he had come back from death. This was amazing and joyous. On the other hand, he was terribly mysteriously damaged, or, more accurately, spoiled and unclean. He was very yellowed and debilitated by his death, and there were no guarantees that he wouldn't soon die again. He seemed aware of this and his entire personality was changed. He was angry and impatient with all of us. We were trying to help him in some way, struggling to get him home, but something prevented us, something we had to fix, a tattered suitcase that had sprung open, some mechanical thing: he had a car but it wouldn't start; or the car was made of wood; or his clothes, which had become too large for him, had caught in the door. In one version he was all bandaged and as we tried to lift him from his wheelchair into a taxi the bandage began to unroll and catch in the spokes of the wheelchair. This seemed to be some unreasonableness on his part. My mother looked on sadly and tried to get him to cooperate.

That was the dream. I shared it with no one. Once when I woke, crying out, my brother turned on the light. He wanted to know what I'd been dreaming but I pretended I didn't remember. The dream made me feel guilty. I felt guilty in the dream too because my enraged father knew we didn't want to live with him. The dream represented us taking him home, or trying to, but it was nevertheless understood by all of us that he was to live alone. He was this derelict back from death, but what we were doing was taking him to some place where he would live by himself without help from anyone until he died again.

At one point I became so fearful of this dream that I tried not to go to sleep. I tried to think of good things about my father and to remember him before his illness. He used to call me "matey." "Hello, matey," he would say when he came home from work. He always wanted us to go someplace—to the store, to the park, to a ball game. He loved to walk. When I went walking with him he would say: "Hold your shoulders back, don't slump. Hold your head up and look at the world. Walk as if you meant it!" As he strode down the street his shoulders moved from side to side, as if he was hearing some kind of cakewalk. He moved with a bounce. He was always eager to see what was around the corner.

The next request for a letter coincided with a special occasion in the house: My brother Harold had met a girl he liked and had gone out with her several times. Now she was coming to our house for dinner.

We had prepared for this for days, cleaning everything in sight, giving the house a going-over, washing the dust of disuse from the glasses and good dishes. My mother came home early from work to get the dinner going. We opened the gateleg table in the living room and brought in the kitchen chairs. My mother spread the table with a laundered white cloth and put out her silver. It was the first family occasion since my father's illness.

I liked my brother's girlfriend a lot. She was a thin girl with very straight hair and she had a terrific smile. Her presence seemed to excite the air. It was amazing to have a living breathing girl in our house. She looked around and what she said was: "Oh, I've never seen so many books!" While she and my brother sat at the table my mother was in the kitchen putting the food into serving bowls and I was going from the kitchen to the living room, kidding around like a waiter, with a white cloth over my arm and a high style of service, placing the serving dish of green beans on the table with a flourish. In the kitchen my mother's eyes were sparkling. She looked at me and nodded and mimed the words: "She's adorable!"

My brother suffered himself to be waited on. He was wary of what we might say. He kept glancing at the girl—her name was Susan—to see if we met with her approval. She worked in an insurance office and was taking courses in accounting at City College. Harold was under a terrible strain but he was excited and happy too. He had bought a bottle of Concord-grape wine to go with the roast chicken. He held up his glass and proposed a toast. My mother said: "To good health and happiness," and we all drank, even I. At that moment the phone rang and I went into the bedroom to get it.

"Jonathan? This is your Aunt Frances. How is everyone?"

"Fine, thank you."

"I want to ask one last favor of you. I need a letter from Jack. Your grandma's very ill. Do you think you can?"

"Who is it?" my mother called from the living room.

"OK, Aunt Frances," I said quickly. "I have to go now, we're eating dinner." And I hung up the phone.

"It was my friend Louie," I said, sitting back down. "He didn't know the math pages to review."

The dinner was very fine. Harold and Susan washed the dishes and by the time they were done my mother and I had folded up the gateleg table and put it back against the wall and I had swept the crumbs up with the carpet sweeper. We all sat and talked and listened to records for a while and then my brother took Susan home. The evening had gone very well.

Once when my mother wasn't home my brother had pointed out
something: the letters from Jack weren't really necessary. "What is
this ritual?" he said, holding his palms up. "Grandma is almost
totally blind, she's half deaf and crippled. Does the situation really
call for a literary composition? Does it need verisimilitude? Would
the old lady know the difference if she was read the phone book?"

"Then why did Aunt Frances ask me?"

"That is the question, Jonathan. Why did she? After all, she
could write the letter herself—what difference would it make? And
if not Frances, why not Frances' sons, the Amherst students? They
should have learned by now to write."

"But they're not Jack's sons," I said.

"That's exactly the point," my brother said. "The idea is *service*.
Dad used to bust his balls getting them things wholesale, getting
them deals on things. Frances of Westchester really needed things
at cost. And Aunt Molly. And Aunt Molly's husband, and Aunt
Molly's ex-husband. Grandma, if she needed an errand done. He
was always on the hook for something. They never thought his
time was important. They never thought every favor he got was one
he had to pay back. Appliances, records, watches, china, opera
tickets, any goddamn thing. Call Jack."

"It was a matter of pride to him to be able to do things for
them," I said. "To have connections."

"Yeah, I wonder why," my brother said. He looked out the
window.

Then suddenly it dawned on me that I was being implicated.

"You should use your head more," my brother said.

Yet I had agreed once again to write a letter from the desert and so
I did. I mailed it off to Aunt Frances. A few days later, when I came
home from school, I thought I saw her sitting in her car in front of
our house. She drove a black Buick Roadmaster, a very large clean
car with whitewall tires. It was Aunt Frances all right. She blew the
horn when she saw me. I went over and leaned in at the window.

"Hello, Jonathan," she said. "I haven't long. Can you get in the
car?"

"Mom's not home," I said. "She's working."

"I know that. I came to talk to you."

"Would you like to come upstairs?"

"I can't, I have to get back to Larchmont. Can you get in for a moment, please?"

I got in the car. My Aunt Frances was a very pretty white-haired woman, very elegant, and she wore tasteful clothes. I had always liked her and from the time I was a child she had enjoyed pointing out to everyone that I looked more like her son than Jack's. She wore white gloves and held the steering wheel and looked straight ahead as she talked, as if the car was in traffic and not sitting at the curb.

"Jonathan," she said, "there is your letter on the seat. Needless to say I didn't read it to Grandma. I'm giving it back to you and I won't ever say a word to anyone. This is just between us. I never expected cruelty from you. I never thought you were capable of doing something so deliberately cruel and perverse."

I said nothing.

"Your mother has very bitter feelings and now I see she has poisoned you with them. She has always resented the family. She is a very strong-willed, selfish person."

"No she isn't," I said.

"I wouldn't expect you to agree. She drove poor Jack crazy with her demands. She always had the highest aspirations and he could never fulfill them to her satisfaction. When he still had his store he kept your mother's brother, who drank, on salary. After the war when he began to make a little money he had to buy Ruth a mink jacket because she was so desperate to have one. He had debts to pay but she wanted a mink. He was a very special person, my brother, he should have accomplished something special, but he loved your mother and devoted his life to her. And all she ever thought about was keeping up with the Joneses."

I watched the traffic going up the Grand Concourse. A bunch of kids were waiting at the bus stop at the corner. They had put their books on the ground and were horsing around.

"I'm sorry I have to descend to this," Aunt Frances said. "I don't like talking about people this way. If I have nothing good to say about someone, I'd rather not say anything. How is Harold?"

"Fine."

"Did he help you write this marvelous letter?"

"No."

After a moment she said more softly: "How are you all getting along?"

"Fine."

"I would invite you up for Passover if I thought your mother would accept."

I didn't answer.

She turned on the engine. "I'll say good-bye now, Jonathan. Take your letter. I hope you give some time to thinking about what you've done."

That evening when my mother came home from work I saw that she wasn't as pretty as my Aunt Frances. I usually thought my mother was a good-looking woman, but I saw now that she was too heavy and that her hair was undistinguished.

"Why are you looking at me?" she said.

"I'm not."

"I learned something interesting today," my mother said. "We may be eligible for a V.A. pension because of the time your father spent in the Navy."

That took me by surprise. Nobody had ever told me my father was in the Navy.

"In World War I," she said, "he went to Webb's Naval Academy on the Harlem River. He was training to be an ensign. But the war ended and he never got his commission."

After dinner the three of us went through the closets looking for my father's papers, hoping to find some proof that could be filed with the Veterans Administration. We came up with two things, a Victory medal, which my brother said everyone got for being in the service during the Great War, and an astounding sepia photograph of my father and his shipmates on the deck of a ship. They were dressed in bell-bottoms and T-shirts and armed with mops and pails, brooms and brushes.

"I never knew this," I found myself saying. "I never knew this."

"You just don't remember," my brother said.

I was able to pick out my father. He stood at the end of the row, a thin, handsome boy with a full head of hair, a mustache, and an intelligent smiling countenance.

"He had a joke," my mother said. "They called their training ship the S.S. *Constipation* because it never moved."

Neither the picture nor the medal was proof of anything, but my brother thought a duplicate of my father's service record had to be in Washington somewhere and that it was just a matter of learning how to go about finding it.

"The pension wouldn't amount to much," my mother said. "Twenty or thirty dollars. But it would certainly help."

I took the picture of my father and his shipmates and propped it against the lamp at my bedside. I looked into his youthful face and tried to relate it to the Father I knew. I looked at the picture a long time. Only gradually did my eye connect it to the set of Great Sea Novels in the bottom shelf of the bookcase a few feet away. My father had given that set to me: it was uniformly bound in green with gilt lettering and it included works by Melville, Conrad, Victor Hugo and Captain Marryat. And lying across the top of the books, jammed in under the sagging shelf above, was his old ship's telescope in its wooden case with the brass snap.

I thought how stupid, and imperceptive, and self-centered I had been never to have understood while he was alive what my father's dream for his life had been.

On the other hand, I had written in my last letter from Arizona—the one that had so angered Aunt Frances—something that might allow me, the writer in the family, to soften my judgment of myself. I will conclude by giving the letter here in its entirety.

Dear Mama,

This will be my final letter to you since I have been told by the doctors that I am dying.

I have sold my store at a very fine profit and am sending Frances a check for five thousand dollars to be deposited in your account. My present to you, Mamaleh. Let Frances show you the passbook.

As for the nature of my ailment, the doctors haven't told me what it is, but I know that I am simply dying of the wrong life. I should never have come to the desert. It wasn't the place for me.

I have asked Ruth and the boys to have my body cremated and the ashes scattered in the ocean.

Your loving son,
Jack

ALLEGRA GOODMAN

Variant Text

Dear Aunt Ida,

Attalia is screaming under the piano. She has taken it into her head that she needs a pair of skates. Having explained that her mother and I are perfectly willing to provide our children with necessary items but unable to supply their ceaseless demand for toys, clothes, and every extravagance, the vital necessity of which is impressed on them by seven-year-old peers, I have resolved to let her scream herself to sleep. I'd say she's good for at least half an hour.

Beatrix has been exhausting herself. She is in London for the topology conference. As soon as she comes back Sunday, she will have to prepare her paper for Majorca. These conferences are always a strain and raise numerous logistical problems. Beatrix's parents, living upstairs, would seem the logical choice for baby-sitting, but they are really no longer able to control the kids—especially now that Adam can walk. Aunt Clare is out of the question.

Cecil looks fondly at the smooth black surface of his Olivetti electronic and with a grim smile flicks off the switch. If only Beatrix were home to manage the kids. She goes to a three-day conference, and they become unreasonable. Parents over forty-five should use the buddy system. He and Beatrix had made a pact to that effect when Adam was born. If either of them ran away, he or she would take the other along.

They had both thought the baby-sitting situation would be better in Oxford than it had been in Brooklyn. When Beatrix taught math at Hunter and Cecil had a class at Brooklyn College, their schedule had been much more hectic, but there was always Aunt Ida to take care of the kids. Then Beatrix got her chair at St. Ann's, and Cecil had to give up the part-time position in English at Brooklyn. He enjoyed that—the resignation letter, the packing. He feels he has made a small but significant political statement by leaving America, voting with his feet. American culture is dying. Apart from the museums and the ballet, there isn't much left of the city. It was also a relief to leave the Brooklyn shul, which rejected the books of biblical criticism he had donated in his father's memory. But above all, Cecil was making a feminist statement by following his wife to Oxford. And besides, he hadn't got along with his department.

The great domestic advantage of moving was that Beatrix's parents, the Cahens, owned this enormous Norham Gardens house right here in Oxford, and glad of the company and the cooking, they had given over the first floor to Beatrix and Cecil. It seemed ideal: two live-in baby-sitters upstairs. But naturally there were complications. The Cahens are in their late seventies; last winter Mrs. Cahen slipped on the ice and broke her arm; the cavernous house is unheatable; and as Beatrix is exhausting herself teaching her seminar and writing papers, it is Cecil who is stuck with the kids. He doesn't really mind baby-sitting within certain limits, and he enjoys replastering the ceilings and shopping for pipe fittings. But keeping up with his research is difficult. Last year, Cecil was invited to apply for a position at Leeds, but nothing came of it. Meanwhile the house and the kids are time-consuming but usually tolerable, except when Beatrix is away and Attalia decides to scream herself sick. And except for Beatrix's older sister, Clare, who has lived in the Norham Gardens house all her life. Suddenly inspired, Cecil flicks on the Olivetti and continues:

> Attalia is becoming more and more like her aunt Clare— ruining her voice with screaming, and abandoning herself to increasingly frequent rages. Unfortunately, she follows Clare in her slovenliness. Even more unfortunate, Attalia shares her aunt's lack of artistic talent.

> In the three years since we moved from New York, Clare has insisted in making life in this house intolerable. She is sullen and angry, a bad influence on both children. But perhaps we will be spared the pleasure of living en famille in this battleship with Victorian plumbing if the sale on the Brooklyn house goes through. Or at least we'll have the cash to fix up this place. It will take at least two years to rewire the house. I don't see why Mr. Cahen won't subdivide it. Most of the other Norham Gardens castles are now quite nice 20th century. . . .

Cecil gives up on the letter to his aunt in New York. He leafs through the new spring issue of *Shavian Studies*. Finally he walks to the piano, and the screams and whimpers stop. He bends down heavily under the keyboard. "Come on to bed now."

Attalia glares at her father through the strands of her slippery brown hair. She screams rather loudly for her size. Fine pair of lungs. Pity she doesn't have an ear for music. Cecil had tested both of his children early on for any signs of musical aptitude. When Attalia was two, he set her on the piano bench. She struck out at the Steinway with her fists, banging the ivory keys. Cecil had waited a few minutes and then given up.

"I'll read to you in bed," he concedes. The tired children scramble up and pad to their room. Cecil glances about for something readable. A stack of *TLS*'s balances on the sofa; the dining room table is weighted with Beatrix's mathematics, Adam's crayons, Attalia's homework (probably not done), a bunch of bananas (probably soft). "This puts me to sleep within minutes," he tells the kids. He opens *Shavian Studies*, spreading it out onto Adam's bed. "Well, well—Lewis has found a variant text of *Major Barbara*." Now both children begin to cry.

The next morning, Cecil rushes to put on his tefillin before the children wake up and the Cahens and Clare come down to be served breakfast. For a moment the house is quiet. The sun glistens on Cecil's black-framed glasses and glows red through his ears. He wraps the leather tefillin straps tightly on his arm and forehead. He knows the prayers by heart, but he reads from a pocket siddur anyway. It's more precise to read than to mumble from memory.

The kitchen stairs begin to creak as the old couple make their way down in the dark, and little shrieks escape from the children's room, where Adam is trying to comb Attalia's hair.

"Molly," Saul Cahen calls out hoarsely, "turn on the lights."

"I can't see the switch."

"Above your head."

"He's going to start a fire with this naked light bulb."

At the bottom step, a wooden door blocks the way to the kitchen. Cecil can hear the two of them pulling and twisting at the knob until the door is jammed.

"Cecil, you've locked us out!"

He shuts his eyes tightly, finishes davening, and runs down the central stairs to let them in. Saul shakes his head at his son-in-law as he helps Molly into the kitchen. She takes a seat, fanning herself with *Advances in Mathematics*, while Cecil pours the coffee. They drink only instant decaffeinated.

Attalia runs in. "Daddy, I can't go to school."

"Oh, yes you can." Cecil lifts her up and seats her at the table. Adam toddles in, with nothing on. "Pot," he says plaintively. "Pot."

After cleaning the living-room rug, Cecil makes an enormous quantity of porridge. Attalia watches morosely as her father dishes it out. She is dressed in dark green corduroy overalls and a brown and blue striped jersey. Cecil and Beatrix are nonsexist, so they dress their children in unisex clothing. Attalia's hair has never been cut. All ballerinas have long hair. Cecil takes her to ballet class every week. Even though she is the smallest girl there, Attalia is the most meticulous about the steps. She always watches her feet to make sure they are in the right places. Cecil pours each of the kids a glass of milk and a glass of orange juice. Adam drills a hole in his oatmeal with the back of his spoon and pours the juice and the milk into it together. Quite a chemist for a three-year-old, Cecil thinks. Delightful fellow.

"Cecil, why do you dress your daughter like that?" Molly's voice gathers strength at the end of her question.

"Daddy, I can't go to school," Attalia whimpers.

"She's afraid to go to school like that! You see that, Cecil? How can you send her in those work clothes?"

"It's a shame," growls Saul. "The way you send them to that school. Why do you send Adam already with the four-year-olds? He's only three years old. You're forcing them to grow up too fast. I won't say it in front of Beatrix and upset her, but now she's gone I think we should talk about this so-called gan. . . ."

The phone rings. "Adam, don't throw food!" Cecil orders as he answers it.

"Bad boy," he says, frowning; then, back into the receiver: "No, I was talking to my son. Sixty thousand dollars! That's below appraisal. I know it's in Brooklyn. The neighborhood was fine when I was there last. Just some perfectly respectable Puerto Rican fellows. Let them drink their beer on the front steps; they'll keep away the crazies. No, not the fridge. I'm shipping it. Why? Do you realize how much a new refrigerator costs? Of course, but it's too small. Frankly"—he lowers his voice—"this thing here is a piece of junk. We want the old one from New York. What do you mean, irrational? They don't make that model anymore. It would cost as much to buy a new fridge here as it would for me to ship the fridge from Brooklyn. Ben? Look, I can't explain the whole thing over long distance; this is costing you a fortune. No, I told you the house doesn't come with the fridge. Talk to you Monday. Well, I'll try a transformer. Either that or I'll rewire it."

Aunt Clare appears and prods the oatmeal with her spoon. "Burnt," she states flatly, and drops the whole pot into the sink.

"Well, we do our best," Cecil answers. But Clare is already deep in the hall closet, pulling on a black trench coat.

"Where are you going?" asks Molly. But her daughter doesn't answer. In the summers, Clare likes to work outside. She spends days in the park with her stack of Hebrew manuscripts. Cecil can't blame her; the house is a mess on the top floors, crammed with odd sunless rooms, dusty with ancient copies of the *Guardian*, old furniture, antique clothes. The Cahens don't throw things out, and they don't dust, either. Molly was never a housewife; she was a Socialist. "Clare, it's seventy degrees outside!" Molly admonishes, standing in the hallway, hands on her hips. "There are going to be patches of sun—you don't need the umbrella."

But Clare slides the thin steel point through her belt loop, and she is gone.

The gan is housed in an annex to the Oxford shul. All the money for it was given anonymously by Marv Pollack, the father of children's vitamins. The playground reminds Cecil of a hamster habitat he once saw displayed in a pet-store window. The sandbox is filled with cedar chips. Sand becomes dirty and stale and collects germs. There is no jungle gym or slide or swing set. Instead, an enormous complex of smooth wood has been built in the shape of an amino acid chain. All the classroom furniture is made out of natural woods and fibers. There are seven computer terminals, with full color capability and joysticks. The art center is decorated with laminated Chagall posters. It is here Adam finger paints, listens to Bible stories, plants pumpkin seeds, and during naptime learns deep relaxation on the futon rolled up in his cubbyhole. In the junior school, Attalia will soon be sitting in a circle of tiny chairs for Good/Bad Talk. On the blackboard, Ms. Nemirov has printed today's question:

HASHEM OR DARWIN?
YOU
DECIDE

"I can't go to school," Attalia wails. She clings to the foam seat of the Mini. Cecil pries her loose, grasping her arms and hair. "Daddy," Attalia howls, "I don't have any teeth!"

"Well, of course you don't. It's part of the human life cycle," Cecil reassures her. "If you could compose yourself, no one would notice. Right now, you're crying and looking ugly as the very devil," he tells her, quoting Higgins, "but when you're all right and quite yourself, you're what I should call attractive." Not having read *Pygmalion*, Attalia sniffles off to class.

Another father passes by, with his little girl and fat wife. Cecil looks at the heavy woman and whispers, "There but for the grace of God . . ." thinking of all the similar types his mother and her anxious friends had introduced to him. He used to call them the girls with the three D's: they were dumpy, dowdy, and devout. Beatrix is none of these things. She is lean and brilliant—and though not devout, she agreed to keep a kosher kitchen and let the kids attend the gan. Cecil does not expect more.

He himself had been brought up in a house of strict observance, exquisite baking, and strenuous but fond academic expectations. Though he does not believe in God, he remains observant. His friends find this contradictory and even hypocritical. His strict religious practice has never matched his agnostic intellectualism, his early fascination with Derrida and Paul De Man. He insists on the immutability of sacred law and at the same time savors the fluidity of secular texts. He loves one as explicit and complete, the other as open and ambiguous. And yet he refuses to smooth away this discontinuity by allowing a divine authorship of sacred work. Cecil has always enjoyed his contradictions, and still nurtures them. He finds spiritual sustenance in academic discipline and intellectual structure in the rituals of his childhood.

He was thirty-five when he married. His parents hadn't lived to see it. His friends, of course, were flabbergasted. They remembered Cecil from his Columbia days, when he refused to go to parties or talk to women. It was against his principles to attend weddings—he went to his own sister's wedding under protest, only after his mother had threatened to disinherit him. He swore he hated children, traveled to the Middle East, and enjoyed Swedish pornographic films.

He met Beatrix on a bus in Israel, and in fact had written to his father in the hospital about "the ugly woman." "She's nothing to write home about," he had written. He showed Beatrix the letter soon after their marriage, and she loved it. Cecil's father had died just before the wedding and left him the Brooklyn house. And so they spent the first years of their marriage there with the old letters and dusty furniture, the faded Schumacher drapes and the framed pictures of Cecil that had been propped up on all the tables by his mother. Cecil as a brown-eyed boy of four, Cecil on his tricycle, Cecil staring hollow-eyed through horn-rimmed glasses in his graduation picture. Cecil and Beatrix never changed anything in the house; they only added books and stacks of papers. In the evenings, Beatrix would tell Cecil about the mathematical problem she was working on. In college he had been a math major before he switched to English, and he remembered just enough to see how beautiful the schemes were. He loved the way the physicists came to Beatrix's seminars to see if they could apply her ideas to their work. But it made him strangely happy when it seemed there wasn't any real-world application for her ideas. The formal structure of Beatrix's mathematics had to be appreciated for its own sake. He's often said the same is true of halakhah.

In the schoolyard, Adam is already rolling in the cedar chips and rubbing dirt in his face and hair. The only clean thing about him is his eyes. Yes, he is a charming fellow, Cecil tells himself as he maneuvers out of the parking lot. There seems to be a bottleneck at the exit, where Margo Bettleheim is standing. Cecil reaches for the flier stuck on the windshield and peers at the bleeding purple Ditto.

TO WHOM IT MAY CONCERN:

As a specialist in Jewish early childhood education with a masters in the subject from the Hebrew University, and as a parent, I am compelled to speak out against a situation which I feel threatens the learning environment of the entire gan.

I will state flatly and unequivocally that I am appalled at the deception and irresponsibility of certain parents who have falsified official gan records and have registered their child under false pretenses. In short, by misrepresenting the age and stage of development attained by this child. Thus endangering the learning process of all involved.

It has been shown by Piaget that perceptual development and physical hand-eye-mouth coordination as well as other behavioral processes require a definite time period to develop. I am not convinced that this child has developed these skills, or that this child is ready to interact at the level of food and toy sharing interpersonal interplay required at a more mature level.

We know the preschool years to be the most significant formative experience in the educational process (Golding and Simon, 1978). Join me in protecting the future of the next generation: fill out the coupon below.

Margo Bettleheim

———Yes, I want to focus on the issue of an ordered educational process—and allow each child to develop as an organically centered and responsible member of the community.

———No, I am unconcerned with the process of development which is uniquely important to the success of the prescholastic learning environment. I am unconcerned about the interplay of persons of the same age.

Signature ——————————————————————————

Inching toward the exit in the line of cars, Cecil reads the letter and checks the space marked Yes. He signs on the dotted line: *Cecil*

Eugene Birnbaum, and he hands the form to Margo, who stands firm at her post with a mass of blond curls and two hard lines of lipstick.

He needs to go to the Bodleian, but he has to buy groceries for Shabbes first, and he can't leave them sitting in the car to melt. It's a brilliant day, a once-in-a-year summer day. Students lie out on the lawns, cadaver white, soaking up the sun. Exams are over, and a bunch of them dash across the street, chanting "Annie! Annie!" They catch her and squirt her with champagne. It makes Cecil feel old. He doesn't mind the feeling in itself, but he'd dearly love a donnish platform, an academic gown to robe his forty-seven years. All of which is trite and self-indulgent, but nonetheless true. He feels he's always watching Oxford. And it's not the punts or waltzes, the processionals, those tourist things—it's the work he misses. The place to work, the time to work, and—he doesn't complain—the notice for it. He had to apply to use the Bodleian. The registrar, with his peculiar, thin librarian's fingers, stamped his card *Unaffiliated*.

He is appalled by the prices in the Covered Market. He buys eggs, Greek olives, currants, even some frozen cranberries from America, but he rejects the outrageously expensive sole just as it is about to be rung up. "I'm not made of money," he tells the old woman behind him in line. She tisks sympathetically. New carts of vegetables are being unloaded. The market is full of exotic produce, and the prices are being driven up. They are even selling kiwifruits and orange-brown mangoes. Next thing you know, they'll put in a cappuccino bar, and gentrify this too. Grasping his carrier bag and his *Times*, Cecil makes his way to the car. A violinist is playing on the sidewalk, and Cecil drops his change in the musician's open violin case.

In the street, Ursula Quince—absurd name—and her mother thumb by without seeing him. Ursula was one of Cecil's pupils during a short tenure at the Dragon School, just after he and Beatrix arrived in England. He taught English and American poetry to the third form, which title belonged to a mass of heavy, plodding little girls with thick hair parted around their faces. They looked strikingly like their own Shetland ponies. Ursula was not the brightest in her English class. Cecil remembers particularly that just before he left, he called on her to explicate some Emily Dickinson: "I love to watch it lap the miles."

"Well, what is it *about*, Miss Quince?"

She looked up at him, affronted, then glanced around at the class, but they were busy looking invisible, so that he wouldn't interrogate them next. It was always amusing to watch these very solid girls try to disappear. They did it by opening their eyes until they looked quite empty; then they would stare ahead silently, mouths slightly ajar.

"I see," said Cecil after Ursula's eloquent silence. "I think then I'll suggest my own interpretation." And he read out again. 'I love to watch it lap the miles.' Clearly this poem is about a cat," he said, and they all nodded. "It's about a cat lapping up miles of milk." They believed this; one girl looked puzzled, but she didn't say anything. He is sure Ursula believes it to this day—if she remembers the poem.

The Cahens sit in the kitchen where he left them, and as he unpacks the groceries they start up again about the kids. This is a talent of theirs, the ability to continue nagging as if no time has passed.

"Why do you send them to that frumnik school?" Saul demands. "You want them to grow up Israelis?"

Molly stands between Cecil and the old fridge, as if to protect it. "I won't have it, Cecil," she declares. "I won't have them sent to that school with the fanatics. Beatrix won't say anything, but I will. Where my grandchildren are concerned, I'm a tiger!"

Cecil swings open the freezer box above her head and deposits the bag of cranberries. She follows him into the pantry, and Saul takes a post in the doorway. "You're taking the grandchildren away from us," he says. "You know very well that Molly and I oppose parochial education. That we've worked all our lives for the Labour party." Hand in one pocket, he stands like an orator in his gray summer suit.

"I'll tell you what they did just yesterday," says Molly. "They threw away the buns I bought Adam for his lunch. You don't know how he cried, he was so hungry."

"They were absolutely right," Cecil says. "I've told you many, many times not to buy those. They aren't kosher; don't do it again."

"They're starving him."

"Nonsense. He eats like a little pig."

"Saul," gasps Molly. "Pawns is what they are. Innocent children just sent adrift."

"Hello. Yes, this is he." Cecil speaks loudly into the telephone receiver. "Oh, Mrs. Greenberg. No. Which policy do you refer to? Yes, he is at a mature stage of development. Well, very nearly trained." He stretches the phone cord into the hall, away from the Cahens. "Listen, I'm off to the Bodleian in just a minute. We can talk after school. Concerned parents? Well, of course. In fact, I signed a statement on a related issue just this morning. Have you seen a copy? You have. Excuse me, this lies outside my field. The prereading center? Ah, Margo Bettleheim. Yes, this morning. But Adam wasn't mentioned on the form. It was a very general sort of statement. What you are saying, in layman's terms, is that my son has peed in the prereading center. And I have petitioned for his removal from the school! I see, the verb to pee is no longer used by educators. What word do you use? No, I do understand. I'm afraid I really can't. I'll talk to you this afternoon. Oh, he's extremely well adjusted. I really— Well, smack him one. Psychological scars? You don't encourage this kind of behavior, do you?"

In the cool, dim rooms of the Bodleian, Cecil muses on the hysteria of adults involved with small children. Taken in the proper perspective, one's children are really rather amusing, actually. Spread before him are his notes on Shaw's music reviews. He may have found a connection between the theory of sound that can be extrapolated from Shaw's music criticism and the form of Shaw's language theory suggested in Higgins's phonetic experiments. A subdued joy fills Cecil as he checks the originality of his idea by searching the bibliographic citations of *Shavian Studies Sound Theory*. Nothing under that heading. Music Criticism. Nothing there. Confidence rising, Cecil checks under Phonetics. He winces. There, in the column of papers on Shaw's phonetic system, is the listing: " 'Musical Intonation in Higgins' Phonetic Theory,' *Shav. Qt.* Apr. '59."

Cecil doesn't bother looking up the article. Of course, he could use it; he could write his anyway. But he's so tired of sharing topics, tunneling in the critical anthill. He wants to work on something new. The problem is, Shaw's plays themselves are old for him. He told Beatrix once, "The more I read these things, the less I see in them." Now he smiles, remembering how she laughed at this. "Absurd old thing," she laughed. "What *could* anyone do in that awful field of yours where no one knows what one's about?" She sat curled up in the enormous balding velvet chair she works in at home. "I *always* hated literature," she said. "Write and write, say what you like; there are no right answers." And she settled back among her yellow papers and the pencils that roll under the cushions of her chair. She is contented, like all good mathematicians, unconcerned with how to finish errands or what to buy for dinner. She has the comfort of being consistently disorganized. For example, she always loses things in the same place. When she thinks of it, she collects her pencils from underneath her chair, where they end up among the springs trailing out the bottom.

Junior School Principal Kineret Greenberg wears a daisy-print dress and covers her hair with matching material. "Dr. Birnbaum, as secular principal for the students four through ten, I have been delegated to ask you to withdraw your child from the gan. I think it is clear from our discussion on the phone this morning that Adam's presence at this time could disturb, or even traumatize, the classroom environment."

"My good woman," Cecil begins, but he has to stop to keep a straight face.

"It may seem a trivial matter to you," Kineret says sternly, "but an important principle is involved. The gan is an extremely selective school, and there are many children on the preschool waiting list. Margo Bettleheim, for one, is particularly anxious about her son, Moshe. Her open letter voices a legitimate concern that younger children not yet ready for the gan have been given places, while Moshe has been made to wait and thus fall behind his age group. I'm sure you agree it's only fair for Adam to wait his turn.''

"Well,'' says Cecil, "I was not aware that the school is controlled by propaganda campaigns.''

Kineret stiffens. "This school is governed by the standards of Kohlberg, Piaget, the Rav Soloveichik—''

Cecil bursts out laughing. "This is absurd! I see no reason—halakhic, psychological, or otherwise—to withdraw Adam. In fact, I see this decision as entirely his choice.''

She nods earnestly. "That is just the reply I had hoped you would make. Yes, do discuss it with your son. The discussion could play a part in your parental bonding. You know, whenever I have to speak as a teacher to a child, I try to think of the experience less as an evaluative encounter and more as an opportunity to nurture growth and understanding.''

Cecil raises his eyebrows.

"One other thing,'' Kineret adds. "Attalia's clothes. Rabbi Rothenberg is concerned about these dungarees she wears to school. I'm sure you are familiar with the whole issue of beged ish.''

"Oh, come now,'' Cecil says. "I really haven't time for this.'' He glances out the office window. The kids are waiting outside.

"No, hear me out,'' says Kineret. "The gan is working to teach Yiddishkeit, and that's a complete world picture which includes tsniustic clothes. Attalia has to wear dresses and skirts now if she is to have a healthy sexual and social identity later. Psychologically this is crucial; if she dresses like a boy, she'll never find her place within the peer group and interact normally. That's what we're working for here. We want every child at Kohlberg stage three by the end of the term. And we need help from home to achieve this. We're trying to develop a Torah life-style. . . .''

"I've been extremely patient with you,'' replies Cecil after this remarkable speech. "But I find myself overcome just now by your particular combination of self-righteousness, ignorance, and sexism.'' He nods as if to punctuate this and then walks out the door.

The Cahens always sit at the kitchen table and watch while Cecil prepares Shabbes dinner. He can't decide which is worse, Attalia and Adam underfoot, or their grandparents, who ask plaintively: "Could I trouble you for a little something in a tiny glass—very sweet?"

He lifts Adam onto the kitchen counter and says briskly, "I hear you made a fool of yourself in school today." Adam giggles and crawls into the sink, where he stands unevenly, with one foot in the drain.

"My God, he's going to maim himself," gasps Molly.

Cecil pulls Adam out of the sink and places him on the floor, where he begins to scream.

Attalia runs in from the living room. "Daddy, I have a new tooth," she shrieks. She opens her mouth and points to it.

"Congratulations," says Cecil. "I can't see anything, but I'll take your word for it."

He has to buy a new vegetable peeler. The blade on this one keeps twisting around as he peels. He holds it straight and skids it over a bent carrot. It's such an annoying situation at the gan. There would be some satisfaction in withdrawing the kids, of course. Cecil does enjoy leaving institutions. It's so cathartic. To resign, to withdraw, to speak the unspeakable, pack up, and go. And just now he's itching to tell them off, write up in detail their gross halakhic misconstruals. Beged ish! A perversion of a statute against transvestite dressing into a dictum about skirts for little girls! He piles the carrots on the cutting board and hunts up a pareve knife. Beatrix would be delighted if he yanked the kids out; she's been patient, but if they left she'd be awfully pleased. Unfortunately, so would the Cahens. And it's extremely unpleasant to contemplate living in this house, with the Cahens thinking they've won some kind of independent moral triumph. Even worse to allow a victory to Margo Bettleheim. The problem, he concludes, washing the lettuce, is that he can't seem to do anything without giving in to somebody. The Cahens or Greenberg or Bettleheim. As yet, he sees no uncompromising way to act.

He sets out the dinner on the dining-room sideboard: challot, choucroute garni (with corned beef, of course), couscous with baked egg and onions, kosher wine, and currant cake with a double measure of currants. aunt Clare wanders in, with her sheaf of papers. She looks as if she's had too much sun. "How was the park?" Cecil asks. She looks at him reproachfully and climbs the stairs to her room. She knows some extremely strange men and women in the Oxford Parks. Every once in a while she tries to bring in homeless people for the night. Cecil drives them back to their shelters—located surprisingly far away. He has them read the *Times* to him in the car. Seated at the table, Molly looks at the dinner with a veteran eye. The egg in the couscous is overbaked, the kosher wine is like vinegar, the currant cake is burned on the bottom. She looks at Cecil and says sweetly, "Could I trouble you for a piece of bread?"

The next morning, Cecil and the kids walk to shul. Attalia loves shul because she is allowed to wear the pink dress that her American aunt gave her. Beatrix is against pink. But out of courtesy to the relatives, Attalia wears it once ina while. Cecil sports an ABORTION RIGHTS button pinned to the lapel of the suit he bought after his wedding. Beatrix wants him to get a new one, but it's a perfectly good suit, and he sees no reason to buy another until this one falls apart or doesn't fit anymore. He would only buy the identical kind anyway.

They walk through the Indian quarter, past Dildunia Restaurant: "We serve not too spicy food with a smile." Adam runs ahead, and Cecil and Attalia follow, picking up his brown leather kipah. Cecil never liked the crocheted kind, and he particularly hates the ones with names and flowers worked into the borders. He's always felt it was a patriarchal custom for girls to make kippot for their boyfriends. As a young man, he would never have accepted such a gift and often wished for the chance to refuse.

"This is very bad," he says when they reach the shul. Someone is pushing strollers on Shabbat. It's shocking, really, and isn't any different than driving a vehicle or carrying, when you think about it. In fact, there are two strollers on the steps of the building. One of them is cross-stitched along the awning, M. *Bettleheim*.

Attalia stays in the cloakroom to play with the Goldman girls, while Adam follows his father into the men's section. The shul was originally designed for an egalitarian congregation that never made a go of it. Now the sanctuary is rearranged for separate seating, and there are red velvet curtains in front of the ark. But the walls are still covered with cork bulletin boards. One of the notices pinned up is Margo Bettleheim's open letter to the gan parents. Next to it is an advertisement for a cantor:

YOUNG, VIBRANT JEWISH GROUP IN HONOLULU SEEKS LIKE-MINDED LAY LEADER TO ENERGIZE HOLIDAY SERVICES.

WILL PROVIDE PLANE FARE.

WRITE TO THE BET KNESSET CONNECTION, UNITARIAN CHURCH, OLD PALI RD., HONOLULU, HAWAII, USA.

REF. REQUIRED.

MUST KNOW HEBREW!

"Good God," mutters the man standing next to Cecil.

"Oh, I quite agree—announcements like that in the sanctuary," says Cecil in sympathy. He recognizes the speaker as dark, broad-shouldered George Lewis, the very man who found the variant text of *Major Barbara* and was written up in *Shavian Studies*.

"I was not referring to the notice on the wall," Lewis replies coldly. "I was speaking of the obscene statement you are making by wearing that button on your lapel. I find it extremely offensive."

"Do you now?" Cecil glances down at his large black-and-red button. "Well, if we are to be perfectly candid, I found your little book rather offensive. I can imagine that twenty years ago, a book like yours could accrue some kind reviews and perhaps earn you a lectureship at York. But at this time, at a point when the whole question of the variant text has ceased to be an issue, when it is acknowledged—universally acknowledged, as far as I'm con-cerned—that every variant is equally valid, when the very concept of a normative, authoritative text has been discarded, I am simply at a loss to understand how your book could contribute anything to the field."

"I do not talk about these things on Shabbes," Lewis replies scornfully. "You know, I am always amazed at your lack of tact. This congregation is not a place for statements, political or otherwise. This is a holy place. A place for family. And I will say this: If you utter a word in *Shavian Studies* challenging my work, I am prepared to write a letter such as the pages of that review have never seen."

Today is Ezra Ben-Zion's Bar Mitzvah. Cecil walks to the back of the shul to congratulate Jonathan Collins, the wiry-bearded anthropology lecturer and shul gabbai who taught Ezra. "He did a fine job with Shacharit. It's nice to hear the proper consonantal values for a change, and not those twisted Hungarian and Rumanian vowels from the old-timers. I compliment you on your teaching."

"Oh, it was nothing, really," Jonathan demurs. "He's Israeli."

"Jonathan, before the Torah reading starts, I'd like to have a word with you." Cecil's compliments were merely a preamble. They duck out of the sanctuary and stand in the atrium.

"We have discussed this many times," Cecil continues, "but nothing has been done about it. You still allow Jack Bettleheim to come up to the Torah. Now, you know as well as I that he isn't shomer Shabbes. And as if that isn't enough, he flaunts it by pushing a stroller to shul."

"Well, if we must be technical, Cecil, Margo Bettleheim pushed the stroller."

Cecil is not amused: "I am not talking about technicalities."

"Why, Cecil!" Jonathan whispers, fascinated. "Do you mean to say you are talking about the principles of Jewish law as they are connected to God?"

"God has nothing to do with the problem at hand."

Jonathan looks closely at Cecil's stern face. "Oh, I see," he says slowly. "You've heard about Margo Bettleheim's open letter about Adam."

"Don't try to trivialize this," Cecil snaps impatiently. "What I am saying is that I cannot and shall not participate in a service in which men who are not shomer Shabbes receive aliyot. I thought I made my position perfectly clear when I was forced to resign from the religious practices committee and withdraw my services as baal koreh. If the situation can't be changed, I'll have to leave the service."

"But, Cecil, Jack was the Ben-Zions' choice; they chose all the aliyot for the Bar Mitzvah."

"Where is it written," Cecil says sarcastically, "that the parents of the Bar Mitzvah boy are allowed to choose a man who is not shomer Shabbes? Halakhah is halakhah."

"And God has nothing to do with this?" Jonathan chuckles. "You know, Cecil, you're what Mary Douglas used to call a primitive ritualist—the term 'primitive' meaning nothing derogatory, of course. It's quite the best thing to be, in anthropological circles. I'm sure you've read the book: *Natural Symbols*—developing character through ritual and all that. . . ."

"I found it rather diffuse, as a whole," Cecil replies witheringly. He presses on, with quiet restraint: "Now, I think it's adolescent to make a scene for its own sake. But I cannot and will not suffer a violation of Shabbat. I come here to daven and find Bettleheim's stroller at the door; I go into the sanctuary, and George Lewis threatens me and impugns my freedom of expression on reproductive rights."

"Oh, Cecil, they've got in under your shell and found your soft spots. You're a true Shavian—cool and crustacean o the surface but, underneath, seething with passion for linguistic reform and halakhic order."

Cecil turns away.

"—though I always have felt Lewis was a complete loss," Jonathan adds sympathetically. "I mean, there he is, filling up an academic post, at Wolfson, no less, with an office, a telephone, and half a secretary."

"I don't complain," Cecil says stiffly. "And please try to understand, I am not speaking out of personal or professional ambivalence. This is a matter of principle."

Jonathan coughs politely into his beard. "Dear Cecil, a matter of principle—you sound just like Margo Bettleheim." He jumps nimbly into the service, and Cecil follows more slowly. As Jonathan calls Jack Bettleheim to the Torah, Cecil folds his tallis deliberately and kneels down on his hands and knees to search under the seats for Adam.

Attalia puts on a full-scale show as they leave the social hall. Walking home, Cecil plans an addition to his letter to Aunt Ida:

> Attalia became violently attached to a certain white cake on the table and refused to leave the shul voluntarily. I explained to her that the cake was really most hideously bourgeois: It was a sticky replica of a Torah scroll formed with two jelly rolls and opened to a quite fictional passage that read:

> > Best Wishes on Your Bar Mitzvah
> > Ezra Ben-Zion

> Attalia is uninterested in our efforts to provide nutritional desserts like currant cake. Adam, however, continues to devour his dinners with gusto.

At home, Saul and Molly Cahen are waiting for Shabbes lunch in the kitchen. Cecil puts out a plate of herring, a basket of challah, and for Adam a bowl of mashed salmon. *"Pink!"* Adam screams. Carefully, he pats the salmon into his ears.

"In the mail today, Cecil, I found this." Molly waves an envelope at him. "The gan sends a list of approved and not approved summer camps for the children."

"That's fine," says Cecil. "I don't approve of any of them. They're all far too expensive. And please"—he tosses the letter back onto the pile of unopened mail—"don't talk to me about that school on Shabbes." He looks at Adam and suddenly feels quite ill. "I'm going to lie down," he tells the Cahens. "Do something with the children. Take a walk."

He must have slept for an hour by the time Clare taps on his door. She opens it a crack. "There is a strange man downstairs," she says.

"What kind of strange man?" Cecil mumbles, face crumpled against his pillow.

"He has a high-pitched laugh. Long hair. Manic eyes." This description of Jonathan from Clare—the friend of the homeless, confidante of runaways.

Jonathan jumps up from Beatrix's chair in his nimble, politic way. "Cecil, I thought I'd stop by because I feel frightful about the service. I didn't mean to make light of your problem."

"Oh, that's quite all right," says Cecil. "I don't blame you. If I'm forced to leave the shul, it will be for halakhic and not personal reasons. Have some cake."

"Well, it won't come to that, will it? You won't leave." Jonathan takes the plate, wobbling, on one hand.

"I'll have to see," says Cecil deliberately. "I've been extremely disappointed with the community here."

"But where else could you go?"

"I'll daven by myself if I have to."

"I couldn't keep it up," says Jonathan. "And I'll bet you a hundred pounds you couldn't, either. I firmly believe the religious service is a social experience. And that's not just my personal belief, it's my considered professional opinion—it's my anthropological privilege, you see, to confuse the two. Even in Albania, those last few—you never did read my book about Albania, admit it, I won't be miffed—but believe me, I watched the old dodderers for two years. The youngest was seventy-two, but they came to shul every week, the last survivors of the community, and they came out of spite. Pure ill will and competition, to show the others they'd survived another week. They were lovely; they had such appetites for life, for scandal."

Cecil looks at him sternly. "I would never go to services to gossip."

"Then why *do* you go?" Jonathan reddens a little as he asks this, but he persists. "I don't understand you, Cecil."

"Why should I have an external reason for going?" Cecil protests. "I don't go to minyan because God appears to me every morning and propels me out the door. I don't go because I long to pick up some gauntlet flung down by enemies on my doorstep with the *Times*. I go to go. I uphold halakhic principles for their own sake. I really don't see what is so hard to understand. God is for poets, as far as I'm concerned. Spiritual fulfillment and people needing people is for American daytime television, group therapy. It's for baal tshuvahs who decide to become emotionally involved with Judaism. Who come home, give their parents Art Scroll Haggadahs, and then refuse to eat anything. Now, I'm not a poet, or a baal tshuvah—"

"Oh, you can't be such a Kantian, Cecil. You can't pretend you don't need either God or gossip to keep you going. Perhaps you can do without one, but both! And I must say your doubt of God is the harder bit to believe. You simply can't think you're upholding any sort of commandments if you say you don't believe in Him. I am the Lord your God—that's the first one!"

"When you read a book," says Cecil, "do you have to know the author to enjoy it?"

"Well, what a question from you!" exclaims Jonathan. "If we didn't need to know the author, you wouldn't be in business. Isn't that your job—haggling about who wrote what and which version is the proper one to force down little children's throats in school?"

"No," says Cecil, "that's Lewis's business, not mine, as I'm sure he would tell you."

"Ah, here we are, just as I thought—back gossiping about the men from shul!"

"Jonathan, George Lewis was the example that came to mind, and nothing more. The point is that unlike Lewis, I haven't any interest in comparing the orthographical changes and the single-word excisions in two versions of a play. All the little signals these critics publish pointing to a date or an authorship—the whole question is intensely trivial. Irrelevant to the real value of the words. Why should the question of authorship suddenly become profound when applied to sacred texts?"

This last sounds flippant and sarcastic, but that is the way Cecil speaks when he is moved. What he wants to tell Jonathan is that when he studies sacred texts, he feels even more powerfully that the words themselves are enough for him; that they need no author or new interpreter. The strict beauty of the law is complete in itself, needing no stalk for support or external scaffold for restoration. How false and ill-founded the apologies for ritual are—the tracings to ancient river valley customs, the explanations of dietary and sexual laws as codes for social hygiene. And equally absurd to think each mitzvah is merely a step toward God, when so clearly the law demands obedience for itself. It is not to be used as a bargaining chip; it is no vehicle for further exaltation. But though Cecil wants to say this fully, he cannot. He can state his position, but he can't describe how passionately he holds it. It would be like telling a stranger about Beatrix and exactly how they fell in love.

The children and the Cahens were tramping about in the hall, back from their walk. Jonathan picks up Adam with the unique benignity of a man without children. "Oh, I do hope you don't pull them from the gan," he says. "You know, Cecil"—he shakes his finger—"if you really act from principle, you shouldn't let the Bettleheims and Lewis and all that ruffle you. And," he adds with mock gravity, "I for one would feel terribly let down if you left off fighting. It's a terrific show, you know, when you're in form."

That night, Cecil sits down at his Olivetti. The letter to Aunt Ida is still in the typewriter. "Most of the other Norham Gardens castles are now quite nice 20th century. . . ." Suddenly he is stricken by a terrible thought: Where will he put the refrigerator when it arrives from Brooklyn? The only clear kitchen space is in front of the door. Never mind. When Beatrix returns, she will work out the math. He will have to shop in London for that transformer on Monday. So much to do. Tickets for the Royal Ballet. The paper for Helsinki still to write. Run down for milk. The Bodleian closed. That ass Lewis.

He unrolls the letter to Aunt Ida and inserts a new piece of paper. "As an active member of the Society for Shavian Studies, I was surprised and not a little disappointed to see . . ."

"Daddy," Attalia stands sleepily in the lighted hallway. "Can I say shehechiyanu for a new tooth?"

"And while Lewis claims . . ." Cecil types.

"Daddy?"

He looks up. "I'm not really qualified to posk on that question. You'll have to ask a rabbi."

Attalia shuffles back to bed, and Cecil feels a twinge of sadness. He flicks off the typewriter and turns out the lights. He does feel bruised by Bettleheim and Greenberg at the school; he knows they want to humiliate him. And of course with Lewis it's clearly war. Never mind, he tells himself. Beatrix will be home tomorrow. It occurs to him he's been feeling sorry for himself since she left. How weak and defeated, Cecil thinks. Of course he can't resign and withdraw the kids without a fight; he can't give in on such trivial issues. Jonathan is right in that. If one cares enough for principles, one can't feel wounded by colleagues, in-laws, or even the likes of Kineret Greenberg.

He walks down the dark hall and looks in on the sleeping children. The little beasts are lovely when they're sleeping. "Attalia," he whispers, "I think it might be all right to say shehechiyanu." His words surprise him. She rolls over in her sleep, and he adds. "Or some sort of brocha. I'll look it up first thing in the morning."

MARK HELPRIN

North Light—A Recollection in the Present Tense

We are being held back. We are poised at a curve in the road on the southern ridge of a small valley. The sun shines from behind, illuminating with flawless light the moves and countermoves of several score tanks below us. For a long time, we have been absorbed in the mystery of matching the puffs of white smoke from tank cannon with the sounds that follow. The columns themselves move silently: only the great roar rising from the battle proves it not to be a dream.

A man next to me is deeply absorbed in sniffing his wrist. "What are you doing?" I ask.

"My wife," he says. "I can still smell her perfume on my wrist, and I taste the taste of her mouth. It's sweet."

We were called up this morning. The war is two days old. Now

it is afternoon, and we are being held back—even though our forces
below are greatly outnumbered. We are being held back until
nightfall, when we will have a better chance on the plain; for it is
packed with tanks, and we have only two old half-tracks. They are
loaded with guns—it is true—but they are lightly armored, they are
slow, and they present high targets. We expect to move at dusk or
just before. Then we will descend on the road into the valley and
fight amid the shadows. No one wants this: we all are terrified.

The young ones are frightened because, for most of them, this is
the first battle. But their fear is not as strong as the blood which is
rising and fills their chests with anger and strength. They have little
to lose, being, as they are, only eighteen. They look no more
frightened than members of a sports team before an important
match: it is that kind of fear, for they are responsible only to
themselves.

Married men, on the other hand, are given away by their eyes
and faces. They are saying to themselves, "I must not die; I *must not
die.*" They are remembering how they used to feel when they were
younger; and they know that they have to fight. They may be killed,
but if they don't fight they will surely be killed, because the slow
self-made fear which demands constant hesitation is the most effi-
cient of all killers. It is not the cautious who die, but the overcau-
tious. The married men are trying to strike an exact balance
between their responsibility as soldiers, their fervent desire to stay
alive, and their only hope—which is to go into battle with the
smooth, courageous, trancelike movements that will keep them out
of trouble. Soldiers who do not know how (like dancers or mountain climbers) to let their bodies think for them are very liable to
be killed. There is a flow to hard combat; it is not (as it has often
been depicted) entirely chance or entirely skill. A thousand signals
and signs speak to you, much as in music. And what a sad moment
it is when you must, for one reason or another, ignore them. The
married men fear this moment. We should have begun hours ago.
Being held back is bad luck.

"What time is it?" asks one of the young soldiers. Someone
answers him.

"Fourteen hundred." No one in the Israeli Army except high-ranking officers (colonels, generals—and we have here no colonels or generals) tells time in this fashion.

"What are you, a general?" asks the young soldier. Everyone laughs, as if this were funny, because we are scared. We should not be held back like this.

Another man, a man who is close to fifty and is worrying about his two sons who are in Sinai, keeps on looking at his watch. It is expensive and Japanese, with a black dial. He looks at it every minute to see what time it is, because he has actually forgotten. If he were asked what the time was, he would not be able to respond without checking the watch, even though he has done so fifty times in the last hour. He too is very afraid. The sun glints off the crystal and explodes in our eyes.

As younger men who badly wanted to fight, we thought we knew what courage was. Now we know that courage is the forced step of going into battle when you want anything in the world but that, when there is every reason to stay out, when you have been through all the tests, and passed them, and think that it's all over. Then the war hits like an artillery shell and you are forced to be eighteen again, but you can't be eighteen again; not with the taste of your wife's mouth in your mouth, not with the smell of her perfume on your wrists. The world turns upside down in minutes.

How hard we struggle in trying to remember the easy courage we once had. But we can't. We must either be brave in a different way, or not at all. What is that way? How can we fight like seasoned soldiers when this morning we kissed our children? There is a way, hidden in the history of war. There must be, for we can see them fighting in the valley; and, high in the air, silver specks are dueling in a dream of blue silence.

Why are we merely watching? To be restrained this way is simply not fair. A quick entrance would get the fear over with, and that would help. But, then again, in the Six Day War, we waited for weeks while the Egyptian Army built up against us. And then, after that torture, we burst out and we leapt across the desert, sprinting, full of energy and fury that kept us like dancers—nimble and absorbed—and kept us alive. That is the secret: You have to be angry. When we arrived on the ridge this morning, we were anything but angry. Now we are beginning to get angry. It is our only salvation. We are angry because we are being held back.

We swear, and kick the sides of the half-tracks. We hate the voice on our radio which keeps telling us to hold to our position. We hate that man more than we hate the enemy, for now we want engagement with the enemy. We are beginning to crave battle, and we are getting angrier, and angrier, because we know that by five o'clock we will be worn out. They should let us go now.

A young soldier who has been following the battle, through binoculars, screams. "God!" he says. "Look! Look!"

The Syrians are moving up two columns of armor that will overwhelm our men on the plain below. The sergeant gets on the radio, but from it we hear a sudden waterfall of talk. Holding the microphone in his hand, he listens with us as we discover that they know. They are demanding more air support.

"What air support?" we ask. There is no air-to-ground fighting that we can see. As we watch the Syrians approach, our hearts are full of fear for those of us below. How did our soldiers know? There must be spotters or a patrol somewhere deep in, high on a hill, like us. What air support? There are planes all over the place, but not here.

Then we feel our lungs shaking like drums. The hair on our arms and on the back of our necks stands up and we shake as flights of fighters roar over the hill. They are no more than fifty feet above us. We can feel the heat from the tailpipes, and the orange flames are blinding. The noise is superb. They come three at a time; one wave, two, three, four, five, and six. These are our pilots. The mass of the machinery flying through the air is so great and graceful that we are stunned beyond the noise. We cheer in anger and in satisfaction. It seems the best thing in the world when, as they pass the ridge (How they hug the ground; what superb pilots!) they dip their wings for our sake. They are descending into a thicket of anti-aircraft missiles and radar-directed guns—and they dip their wings for us.

Now we are hot. The married men feel as if rivers are rushing through them, crossing and crashing, for they are angry and full of energy. The sergeant depresses the lever on the microphone. He identifies himself and says, "In the name of God, we want to go in *now*. Damn you if you don't let us go in."

There is hesitation and silence on the other end. "Who is this?" they ask.

"This is Shimon."

More silence, then, "Okay, Shimon. Move! Move!"

The engines start. Now we have our own thunder. It is not even three o'clock. It is the right time; they've caught us at the right time. The soldiers are not slow in mounting the half-tracks. The sound of our roaring engines has magnetized them and they *jump* in. The young drivers race the engines, as they always do.

For a magnificent half minute, we stare into the north light, smiling. The man who tasted the sweet taste of his wife kisses his wrist. The young soldiers are no longer afraid, and the married men are in a perfect sustained fury. Because they love their wives and children, they will not think of them until the battle is over. Now we are soldiers again. The engines are deafening. No longer are we held back. We are shaking; we are crying. Now we stare into the north light, and listen to the explosions below. Now we hear the levers of the gearshifts. Now our drivers exhale and begin to drive. Now we are moving.

ALLEN HOFFMAN

Building Blocks

I arrived late for the afternoon prayers on Shivah Asar be-Tammuz. On the Seventeenth Day of the month of Tammuz, a fast day, one laments the breaching of Jerusalem's walls by Roman Legions in the final days of the Second Temple. Shivah Asar be-Tammuz is not your average fast day by any means. It kicks off the whole mourning season which runs for a full three weeks culminating in Tisha b'Av, the day the Temple itself was destroyed. This period is known, in fact, as the "Three Weeks," "*Drei Vochen*," or "*Shloshah Shavuoth*," all of which literally mean three weeks. During this period one observes customs and laws of mourning (with the exception of the intervening Sabbaths when all mourning is forbidden). One does not eat meat, drink wine, have one's hair cut, go swimming, listen to music, wear new clothes, or get married. And on the fast of Tisha b'Av one does not wear leather shoes, sit on chairs, or even study holy subjects. In other words, starting with Shivah Asar be-Tammuz you can really mourn your head off. It's not exactly a picnic, definitely not my best season and I come from a family which loves to mourn. And not just at the chapel or grave—ripping clothes, tears, stools, Kaddish, the works. Sorrow, bitterness, anguish, indulgence, sweetness—real mourning. And not just for seven days—for years. And why not? How many sensual things in life are there? But when my family mourns, we are mourning for someone—a father, a sister, an uncle. We shriek Rachel, Morris, Menachem the son of Lazar. It's all very intimate, personal. When Shivah Asar be-Tammuz comes and you mourn your head off, who is it for? The whole world! A pretty tall order. Who even knows the name of the world? Earth? Universe? Did you ever try and mourn for the whole world the week Hank Aaron hit his 700th home run? It is a confusing experience. And if the Temple had not been destroyed, what would Einstein have been, a camel driver in Beersheba? The Budapest String Quartet, olive pickers in the Galilee? It's true. Yes, and if the Temple had not been destroyed, we would not have been around for Hitler and his ovens. That's true, too. All the years of blood. If only the Jews had been good. If only we hadn't hated without cause. If only we hadn't transgressed His Sabbath—our Sabbath. If only we had minded our own business like the Italians and Greeks and all the other short, swarthy races of antiquity. What can you do? Mourn—from Shivah Asar be-Tammuz through Tisha b'Av, and who can be so certain Sandy Koufax is so happy anyway? But the man did pitch four no-hitters, so is it any wonder that I was late for *minchah*, the afternoon prayer?

Of course, I had been present for the morning prayers. At their conclusion the *minyan* attempted to find a time for *minchah*. Eight o'clock? Too soon! You can't eat till nine o'clock!! Eight-fifteen? Too late! At nine o'clock you can eat already! Eight-ten? Eight-ten? Good!

No, they couldn't start *minchah* late enough for me. My goal is always to avoid the business of the day. I was annoyed that we would have to wait so long between the afternoon and evening prayers. Waiting for a fast day to end is the deadliest, dullest waiting of all and not simply because one is hungry. That's the least of it. You want the day to end and to get back to your normal, confused life. Of course I eat when it's over. I overeat, but not because of need, rather it's the principle of the thing. Why not eat when you spent a day not eating! It places the day in perspective; you were famished. What an ordeal that was! No, it is not the eating. It is those final moments when the day is technically over, when the darkness begins to descend, the bright, harsh light relaxes and the true, luminous inner nature of the day emerges. The barest moment before the screen door slams against the frame when the agitated smidgen enters, unintimidated, unhurried, unavoidable and one is faced with the reality no architect ever envisioned: a fly is in the house. And it is His house. You are trapped. So it is between *minchah* and *ma'ariv*. When you are standing in the comfortable little wood- and book-lined room staring at the impending darkness or checking the liturgical calendar to see when it is time to pray or even wondering why your shoes get scuffed the way they do, the day rises up from the worn wood floor, comes over the heavy wooden benches and taps you on the shoulder whispering, "The night is for hiding, do you think you can hide from the day? Here I am, all twelve sun-filled hours of me." And what can you do? You turn around to face the day, all of it. So when the *minchah* prayer was finished (it went quickly since I had missed the first part) and Mr. Isaacson sat next to me at the little table in the back, I welcomed him. A few pleasant words with a charming man, a righteous man, and the day would be over. Who wanted to look Shivah Asar be-Tammuz in the eye?

He turned to me and said, "Some things come to mind, you mention Russian."

I had mentioned Russian because Mr. Isaacson is the man who makes the *minyan*. He's not the tenth man, but he is responsible for him and for seven, eight, and nine as well. In the summer it is hard to find a *minyan* and when it becomes apparent that no one is going to walk in the door, Mr. Isaacson takes his *tefillin* off and goes out to help numbers seven, eight, nine, and ten find us. He shanghais the unwary up and down Ninety-first Street. He cadges them on the corner of Broadway. He plunders other *minyans*. This last is like asking Othello to lend you his wife, but Mr. Isaacson is a hard man to say no to because what's in it for Mr. Isaacson? Is he paid for it? No, thank G-d, he has a good business. Does he have to say Kaddish? No, thank G-d, his family is fine. Does he have to run around like a *meshugeneh*? No, he could pray anywhere. Who would want to start his day by saying no to Mr. Isaacson? Not numbers seven through ten. And so when I didn't attend regularly, I wanted Mr. Isaacson to know why. Why? My wife was taking a Russian course which started quite early and I had to get the baby dressed and over to her play group. And who gives the baby a lollipop on Shabbes? Mr. Isaacson. So I understood his mentioning my mentioning Russian.

He had a distant look in his eye. He was clearly moved by the long summer fast day—waiting for the sun to set.

"I was in the Fourth Russian Army; we hadn't eaten for days. They were shelling us something terrible and then on the fourth day they told us to move forward. So we began climbing this hill. It was a big hill and we were carrying everything. They had even given me a big, heavy ammunition box to carry, too. I struggled up the hill and they told us to dig in so I dug a trench and when I finished a sergeant or an officer would say, 'You with such and such a group?' And I would say, 'No, I'm with the Fourth Russian Army,' and they would say, 'They're over there.' And I would move over there and I would start digging again. I would dig in and they would ask, 'You with such and such a group?' and I would say, 'No, I'm with the Fourth Russian Army,' and they would say, 'Oh, they're over there.' And I would move over there and dig in again and the same thing would happen. 'You with such and such a group?' 'No,' 'Go there.' It wasn't like today; you didn't ask questions. You did what they told you."

He shrugs his shoulders, *nu*, and holds his hands out palms up—what can you do? He lifts his eyes in a perplexed look. What can you do? And what could the sergeant or officer do? This man,

Mr. Isaacson of the Fourth Russian Army, is digging. He is honey-combing half of Rumania.

"I went from here to here to here." He points to various posi-tions on our table, the Rumanian hilltop, in front of us.

"Finally I found where I was supposed to be. I was digging in, it must have been near dawn because I looked down and saw water. There was a stream at the bottom of the hill. I went right down there. I didn't walk. I ran right down and threw myself in. My head and arms and everything right into the stream."

He pantomimes his immersion. He smiles: it is refreshing.

"It felt so good. We were so thirsty and tired. The others saw it, too, and they started coming down. Pretty soon the whole army was in the stream. Then they told us to get moving so everybody got up and we started marching along. I felt something under my foot, kind of unsteady, and looked down. We were walking over trenches. We were supposed to replace the garrison. We moved up and took their places and they started bombing us. It was terrible. For three days nobody moved and then in the morning they told us to attack. We went running out a little way and dug in. I started digging. They were shelling us awhile and stopped. I was so tired, I hadn't slept in several days. I guess I fell asleep. Just like that. And the next thing I knew, everybody was running over me. They had given the order to attack and I was asleep."

Mr. Isaacson laughed at this. What kind of soldier is that? The Angel of Death yells "Forward!" and he is asleep.

"So I jumped up, too, and started running. It was terrible. We were attacking north and the Germans were to the east on our flank, so they opened up their machine guns and caught us in a crossfire. We had to turn the entire army to the east."

On our table Mr. Isaacson has the entire Russian Fourth Army wheel ninety degrees to the right to face the darkening windows and the entrenched Germans.

"I saw that they had us in a crossfire and instead of going east, I got down and ran south to the other end of the battle. People were dropping and I was running low. I saw this ditch filled with dead bodies and I thought to myself, 'Moishe, men ken geharget vern,' so

I jumped in and lay down. The whole thing kept going on. After a while a Yettaslav jumped in and said, 'What are you doing?,' and I said, 'I don't know.' "

Mr. Isaacson shrugged his shoulders for both of us, the Yettaslav and me. What can you do? I asked who the man was.

"The Yettaslav was a big, strong fellow."

Mr. Isaacson straightens up and thrusts out his chest and shoulders. "He was from Yettaslav, a town near Odessa where all the men are big and strong. He said, 'Let's shoot at them,' so I took my rifle and put a bullet in and shot, but the bullet wouldn't come out, so I tried pushing it through, but I could not do it. I put another bullet in and shot and pushed. Again nothing, but that must have done it. It didn't work. I didn't know what to do, so I picked it up and gave it a *klap*."

The bullet-stuffed rifle comes crashing down on our table.

"And it broke in two. It fell apart."

We stare in astonishment and dread at the two pieces of the no-good Czarist rifle before us.

"I didn't know what to do. I looked over to the Yettaslav to see if he knew what happened, but he was right next to me shooting away. I was afraid if he saw, he might kill me. He might think I did it on purpose."

"Did he know you were Jewish?"

"Yes, he knew."

"How could he tell?"

"He was from my unit of the Fourth Russian Army. He knew me. 'Jew, dirty Jew,' he would yell and shoot me. So I leaned over the broken rifle and pretended I was shooting."

Mr. Isaacson leans over the broken rifle, resting his extended rifle-cradling arm on the *chumashim* stacked on the table. The Yettaslav and I are to the left shooting away at the Germans and can't see what is really going on—nothing. Mr. Isaacson continues to hide from us. I can only hear his voice.

"I was like this a long time. The longest time. I didn't know what to do. I was afraid to look over and see what he was doing. The whole battle was going on and I was afraid to look over at the Yettaslav. Finally, I looked over a little."

Mr. Isaacson twists only his head around for the briefest glance before returning to his hiding.

"I couldn't see anything, so I turned around again. And this time I looked."

He looks.

"And you know what? I saw the Yettaslav just sitting there. He wasn't doing nothing. Just sitting there like this."

Mr. Isaacson still using the table as the wall of the trench places one fist on top of the other and on top of the upper fist he places his chin so he sits there bent over and bemused, staring directly ahead like a stone monkey on some Asian temple frieze.

"So I sat up and said, 'Hey, are you all right?' And he didn't say anything so I reached over and touched him a little."

I feel a small tugging on my elbow.

"His head turned a little, and his hat fell off. I saw a red spot on his forehead. He was dead. He had been shot right through the head. I thought, what do you do now, and I took his gun and gave him mine. And then our sergeant came running along and jumped into the ditch. And we lay there for a long time with the whole thing going on. Along about evening it got quieter and he said, 'I wonder what's going on?' I said, 'I don't know.' And he said, 'Take a look.' So I climbed up carefully and looked around. I couldn't see anything and I jumped back down. Then he got up to take a look—nothing. And after a while he said, 'Take a look.' So I got up—nothing. I got down. Then he got up again and nothing. So we were getting up and down and nothing happened but he was a little short fellow and I guess they couldn't see him because he told me to get up again and I got shot, back in my side. It felt like somebody hit me with a strong iron rod. I bent over like this and fell back into the trench. I heard the sergeant say, '*Probalt,* finished.' "

"*Nu,*" someone calls out, "*ma'ariv.*" The evening prayer. Shivah Asar be-Tammuz is over. What! Not yet! I'm in the middle of a story. Wait a minute! But someone begins leading the evening prayer. I turn back to Mr. Isaacson, but he grabs a *siddur,* and jumps up with fervor in his eyes. He draws closer to the pipe that runs from down below and up to heaven. I hear him implore.

"He is merciful, He shall forgive iniquity, and He shall not destroy. Often He turns away his anger and shall not stir up all His wrath. Lord, save us. The King shall answer us in the day we call."

The leader calls, "Bless the Lord who is blessed."

We answer, "Blessed be the Lord who is blessed forever and ever."

And I bless the Lord who makes the evening. I glance up. Mr. Isaacson's eyes are closed as he blesses the Lord who turns the day away, Who evens the evening, Who turns His anger away and answers us in the day we call Him. Even then it is dark. Shivah Asar be-Tammuz is over, but the fast is not. Hungry supplicants rush through *ma'ariv*. For me the evening service after a fast is an anti-climax emotionally, but necessary intellectually. This service has always been a test of faith; one I rarely pass. I am purposefully, willfully patient. I thrust the day of affliction into the past in order to turn the day, bend it into experience, but the vanity of affliction rises hungrily from my stomach disintegrating concentration. Have I not done enough? Only Mr. Isaacson entreats, blesses with the fervor of the day. The day of affliction is over, but what about Mr. Isaacson? We have left him *probalt*—finished. I see him lying in a Rumanian ditch on a Russian battlefield bent and bleeding as the day turns into evening, a new day. Sorrows are never as discrete as the fasts that follow. How can they be, you can't fast forever. The service halts. No one intones the mourner's Kaddish. Everyone looks around. Are you a mourner? Are you a mourner? No familial mourners. A voice calls to the leader, *"zugt Kaddish."* A dispassionate Kaddish pours forth. The rhythm tumbles forth—the building-blocks of the universe rumbling against one another as their names are called. The roll call of cornerstones—granite of existence. So fleeting the call, so light the touch in this hurried, famished Kaddish, yet they remain granite and radiate their power when called.

It is over. We are standing. I turn to Mr. Isaacson.

"We can't leave you there, lying there like that," I joke in fear.

Fear of what? Fear of death? Fear of the day? Fear of the story? Do not give Satan an opening.

Mr. Isaacson does not hear the joke, does not feel the fear, but his eyes are open and he desires to tell the story. People turn to say goodnight. "On the way home," he explains, "I'll walk with you."

The men who are studying the *daf yomi*, the page of the day, drift toward the room with the long table and the large books. A page a day and in seven years you are finished, done.

A student of the entire Babylonian Talmud. What could be easier? What could be faster? Ah, but there is the Jerusalem Talmud! No matter, never mind. One thing at a time. And when you have completed it, what do you have? You have one. You have earned the privilege to start two. Begin again. What could be simpler?

Mr. Steimatzky approaches and asks me if I have been fasting. "You have? Good. Here!" He thrusts a strange, artificially green bag toward me.

"Take."

I peer inside the long, distended bag to see nectarines gathered in the bottom like refugees. If I hadn't fasted, they wouldn't be mine. Mr. Steimatzky is not in the catering business. I gaze at them, their green splotches all the paler and purer in the chemical green dye of the bag.

"*Nu*, take." Mr. Steimatzky has a presence, a bearing. He did not flee two countries, two worlds, learn three languages only to hand out pale nectarines in poisonous bags. He is, in fact, a diamond dealer who enfolds his natural gems in conservative custom-made shirts, soft and natural, nothing like this garish sack with its bastardized New World hybrids from Key Foods. I stand there. I am keeping a man waiting with his arm extended as if he were a beggar. A man who shuffled through the express line, eight items or less, with its clanging cash register and garish, chipped fingernails prancing madly about its keys to register the value of his own garish sack—all in a custom-made shirt—just so his fellow congregants who fasted (when you flee two worlds you only bother about the very righteous) can rejoice a little sooner. I stare at the awful color

of the bag. Who cares what color the bag is? "Though your sins be
as scarlet!" It is a matter of respect. Of generosity. Of brotherhood!
His arm is extended. Shall I refuse his kindness and take from him
his good deed instead? Shall we both return empty when we both
can draw back together filled and fulfilled; he with his *mitzvah* and
I with my nectarine?

"No thank you," I say. "I'd better wait until I get home."

He draws back his gift, offended.

"No, I'd better wait for some juice, that's easier," I remark.

What am I saying? I, who used to break the twenty-five hour
Yom Kippur fast at Glaser's Drug Store on two vanilla shakes (and
in those days they gave you the whole, cold shiny canister with its
two-plus glasses lying thick and frigid inside) and an ice-cream cone
kicker.

"I bought them for you," he entreats.

"No," I say touching my stomach apprehensively. "I'd better
not. Thanks anyway."

"Awright," he turns away hurt.

I feel embarrassed, foolish, and I owe him an apology, at least an
explanation. But how can I explain that the day isn't over, that it
is twilight and Mr. Isaacson is lying broken in a corpse-strewn
Rumanian ditch, when outside the very windows of the synagogue
Mr. Steimatzky sees darkness and inside he sees Mr. Isaacson
saying goodnight to Mr. Sobel? How can I break the fast when the
day has not turned? How can I do a good deed with nectarines when
the greatest of all *mitzvahs*, the saving of a life, lies before me? And
anyway, they aren't washed. G-d knows what is on them.

Mr. Isaacson and I are together again.

"We can't leave you like that."

We are the last in the room. I am standing prepared to stay and
listen.

"No," Mr. Isaacson motions toward the door. "Come, I'll walk
you home." He takes my arm. We are in the narrow hallway
moving toward the door.

"No, please, let me walk you home."

"No, you're hungry. I'll walk you home."

"Please, Mr. Isaacson, it's not right."

"Why?"

Why? Because he lives nearby, down the block in the other direction. Because Broadway is unpleasant and unsafe. Because I should escort you and not you, me. Because. . . .

"*Kuvid*, respect!" I cry, hoping to understand the meaning of the words, in a high croaky voice sounding and feeling like a bilingual frog, and having no more understanding than the Egyptians of the plague of those croaking reptiles. If I can't whisper the word intelligently, why do I think I can understand by yelling it?

"Respect, *kuvid!*" I cry again uselessly and doomed. But, after all, the nectarine man gave me three chances with his green bag, shall I deal more harshly with myself than Steimatzky did? What kind of respect is that? Yes, I feel like a fool screaming at Mr. Isaacson. I had hoped that when I intoned *kuvid*-respect it would be as a shofar blast up above and Gabriel would take not one, but two unwashed nectarines (in the World To Come nothing can hurt you), place them in a green Key Food fruit and vegetable bag, check them to make sure they're good ones (69¢-a-pound, not the ones in the window), staple the bag closed, and write with a heavenly fat grease pencil, "World To Come—Heavenly Reward—Pays Double." Instead, Mr. Isaacson is intimidated by my outburst and says, "All right." Now what's going to happen up there? A voice can come down at any moment and Gabriel hollers, "*Shmuck*, you yell at Isaacson who doesn't need it and you don't take a nectarine from Steimatzky who doesn't need it either. *Shmuck*, you don't know how to give and you don't know how to take." It's true Mr. Steimatzky's custom-made shirts have quite a bit of cloth in them. What can you do? Go home and eat yourself sick?

Mr. Isaacson and I descend the stone steps onto the sidewalk. We turn left toward his building. Respect!

Ninety-first Street glows pink under the high crime street lights. Cars are bumper to bumper alongside the curbs. Heavy brownstone staircases crowd down onto the quiet sidewalk. The buildings, small (a bay window, a fancy balustrade), the garbage cans few, the trees scraggly. And all is soft and close in the pellucid pink of the sodium arc. You could touch it and it wouldn't be rough. It is unreal and very intimate. Mr. Isaacson takes my arm. Behind us we hear a stammering of farewell. We turn to acknowledge Mr. Sobel's third goodnight. "*A gute nacht.*" And Mr. Sobel plunges off down the street in a stuttering motion, for every step taken, three starts.

We return to our direction, but Mr. Isaacson pauses. The mood has been broken. Mr. Sobel has limped into the night trailing shreds of Rumania, fibers of time, moans of agony. We stand exposed on Ninety-first Street. Mr. Isaacson the righteous and I.

"Let me walk you home."

"No, you live right here."

"You must be hungry."

I must be hungry. And not you? Could it be Mr. Isaacson didn't fast? The righteous? But in years he is an old man. I look at my old friend. It has been over fifty years since he turned the Little Father's weaponry into bullet-choked kindling. Why should I be disappointed that he didn't fast? Will it affect the purity of his message? Must righteousness exclude common sense? Over seventy! Until a hundred and twenty! I take his arm to guide him.

"Let me show you a little *kuvid*," I implore.

It is the night of three's. Three offerings. Three goodbys. Three weeks. Three "*kuvids.*" And in the street, my *kuvid*, my call for respect is heard and does not sound strange. And why should it? What are the upright founts channeled above us bathing the scene in a sea of pink but respect? Pellucid preventive pink: respect for the power of evil. *Kuvid* for the *ganef.* The wall has been breached; the sea enters. Arm in arm we negotiate the floodlit street. We make our way to the refuge of shadow near the corner. One tree on the block is capable of shelter. We are under it. The pinkish rays do not bounce; refuse to diffuse. Incapable of dusk, unable to dawn, how dull is their reflection. Like their inspirers, the evildoers, they leave nothing after them; powerful, but shortsighted, they wither against the simple green leaves of our shelter. And we stand in darkness. Unable to see each other, steadfastly we gaze together upon the sea of carnage. We are returned.

———

"The bugs. It must have been the bugs around my face that woke me. I was alone, lying there in the dark on my back. I knew I was injured, but I didn't know where. I checked my hands—I brought them together. No, they were all right. I felt my legs; no, it wasn't them. I felt my face; it was all right. Then I felt my stomach. It was okay, but as my arm came down from my stomach, it felt something soft and sticky on the side. I knew where I was hurt. In the side toward the back. I took my hands away. I didn't know what would be. I lay there. After a while I thought to myself, "There's no *tachlis* in this,' so I tried to get up. It hurt but I managed. I took my coat and cigarettes and a kit like kids have now and started climbing out."

"How did you know where to go?"

"I didn't, but there was a well nearby and I heard a bunch of Rumanian soldiers singing, so I thought I would go there and they could help me. I got my things together and I took a few steps. I was uneasy."

Mr. Isaacson balanced himself delicately using the darkness for support.

"But I saw I could make it, so I kept going. And when I got near, crossing a field—boom! Shells started coming in and I was knocked flat and I went out again."

In the darkness Mr. Isaacson must be shrugging his shoulders, what can you do?

"After a while, I came to again and I didn't hear any more singing. They must have left if they didn't get killed. I knew I wasn't getting anywhere in the middle of the field, so I got up again and tried walking. Same thing, I felt unsteady but I went very slowly. After a while I got to the well, but there was no one there. I took a drink. I felt a little better. I was leaning against the well and I thought I could use a smoke, so I reached for a cigarette."

"But you didn't have any."

"No, I had my cigarettes. I left my gun. What did I need that for?

I didn't feel like shooting anyone and they were lousy guns. But I took my cigarettes. So I lit it and inhaled. . . ."

I hear Mr. Isaacson inhaling and relishing the sweet smoke after crawling around for half the night like a wounded beast.

"And. . . ."

Although it is very dark, my eyes have been adjusting and I can see Mr. Isaacson. He is standing next to me, his chest uplifted inhaling the cigarette—his act of life, returning to normal. A well in a deserted field, a cigarette in the hot, summer night.

"And. . . ."

Mr. Isaacson's hands rise to his shoulders and as he exhales they choreograph in quick wavy descent consciousness sinking away, below the surface. Mr. Isaacson's head has bobbed and sunk onto his chest, his lungs empty even of smoke. We leave him there, but my Mr. Isaacson, the one I know, slips out from behind the collapsed one and tells me, "I was weak and I wasn't used to it."

He laughs. Some cigarette ad! He laughs and stops speaking. We stand there silently. The Surgeon General should have spoken to Mr. Isaacson, he could have told him. And yet, I know his daughter. I don't really know his daughter, but I have seen her. A beautiful woman, a model. Mr. Isaacson once told me with pride that she was in one of the most popular cigarette ds. You saw her everywhere. You couldn't avoid her. Was it Marlboro? Kent? What difference does it make? But there she was gaily smiling on this seesaw from the back of slick magazines, down from tall buildings, inside subway cars. Young, beautiful, refreshed, and alive! Amazing! After what a cigarette did to her father! Did she even know? Could this be what Mr. Isaacson is musing about? His daughter on that smoky seesaw and the cigarette that almost killed him? No, ridiculous! Mr. Isaacson can't be thinking of that. The righteous don't tie knots, they untie them.

"I lay there I don't know how long. I was lying there and they came around and found me."

"How did they know you were alive?"

"I guess I was moving a little or something. I had some dreams."

"Do you remember them?"

"Like it was today. Like it was now," he answers fervently.

"What were they?"

"I dreamt I was lying there worried and frightened. I didn't know what to think. It was like the world disappeared. And then my grandfather appeared, a big, handsome man with a beard. A religious man; a saintly man. I remember him very well. A good person. He was standing in front of me."

And he is standing there in front of me, too. Mr. Isaacson is straight and tall with his right arm raised and his curved but open hand rocks forward and back ever so slightly in benediction, strength, and forbearance. And Mr. Isaacson's face has become firm. Capable of joy and comfort, but now it is set firmly. We must wait for another day, it is saying. And to wait for another day we must live through this night. Benediction, strength, and forbearance. Yes we will.

"And he said to me, 'Moishe, it will be all right, don't worry.' And I knew I would be all right. I opened my eyes and I saw a figure where he had been standing. It was very dark, but I could see it had an arm extended and in the hand it held a gun. It said, '*Neyemetz* or *Rooski?*' German or Russian? Since it said *Neyemetz* or *Rooski* I thought I'd better say *Rooski*, so I said, '*Rooski.*'—'*Rooski?*'—'*Da! Rooski.*—' and he put the gun down and they came forward to help me."

"Who were they, soldiers?"

"No, they weren't soldiers. They worked for the army. For two weeks the battle was going on and the bodies were just lying there. When the battle ended, the army hired men to go around and collect the bodies and the equipment that still might be good. They were looking for the dead, but found me instead.

"They came over to me and saw that I was wounded, but by then I couldn't walk, so they took my overcoat. They gave us great, heavy overcoats, very strong, so they took that and I was lying on it like a stretcher. I couldn't keep conscious. I was going in and out and we were moving slowly. It wasn't easy for them."

Under their heavy burden—a wounded man on a Russian greatcoat without handles or rods, the rough wool tearing at tired hands fighting to maintain a grip—we pause. They came seeking death but found life and it's enough to kill them. See what happens when you don't follow orders. Hired to collect the dead, they freelanced a little and slipped a live one in on the Czar. Little Father, we heard you say dead, but look at him with your Holy Russian eyes, he's as good as dead, isn't he? Merciful Patriarch, and if he lives, you won't have other wars to swallow him alive, like a frog, a beetle? And the Czar of all the Russians, irate, all his hemophilia genes dancing a *kazatzke* in Slavic disgust, squeals, "Fools, if you wanted to take something broken, take the Holy Russian rifle Isaacson broke, and if you want to give me a present, why give me a suffering Jew? Of those I have plenty." And the human garbage collectors quake in fear, but a voice comes clapping down like a shofar from the heavens above. "These will eat nectarines in the World To Come with the righteous!" Justice! It is Gabriel. He has spoken! The nectarines are redeemed. Mr. Isaacson is saved. The day has turned. It is time to say amen.

"And so you were saved," I return in a response of faith. G-d is a faithful King.

Mr. Isaacson does not answer.

"They took you to the field hospital?"

My wife must be worried by now.

"It must have been something to know it was over."

"I woke up in the forest," Mr. Isaacson is saying. "The light was coming through the trees; it must have been dawn. they had stripped me bare. They even took my boots. I didn't have a thing. No coat, no cigarettes, nothing. They did a good job all right. They took everything."

Everything? I draw further under the tree to avoid falling nectarines. Their crash will bury Ninety-first Street, beating the high crime lights into the ground like mangled hangers writhing in darkness among fluorescent shards on a closet floor. Everything.

"*Ganovim!*" Thieves! I spit accusingly at those two who have stripped Mr. Isaacson. But Mr. Isaacson doesn't share my bitterness.

"Weren't they *ganovim?*" I ask intensely.

"No, I don't know. I guess they thought I was dead, so they left me," he says understandingly.

I feel confused and foolish. If they thought he was dead, they shouldn't have let him go. They were sent to collect the dead. That was their job! With all the Hitlers in the world, I get mad at two foolish, doddering old drunks (they must have been drunks! Weren't they goyim?). Two old drunks who tried to save a man's life and when they found that impossible, they rescued his valuables. Dust to dust was not decreed on valuables, just flesh. Yes, just flesh, but I feel something else. I feel anger. Yes, anger. Why shouldn't I feel foolish, I am angry at Mr. Isaacson. I want to ask him, Mr. Isaacson, how can you be so naive? All right, they were exhausted, they could carry you no farther, their hands raw and bloody from the unequal tug-of-war with your coat, all that may be true . . . Mr. Isaacson, hate them! Hate them as I hate them; it will do your heart a world of good. Oh, torn confusion, a world of good? I feel my heart constricting, mean and small within me. Of course, one should have a big heart. A big heart to live. A big heart like Mr. Isaacson's. And maybe, that is why he is here now. The day has turned, but what about the Three Weeks? The day has entrapped me, but what about the night? The Three Weeks have nights, and I feel the dark, invisible cords circling about me. I who would run home to supper am held by the night to a dawn. Mr. Isaacson's dawn. I cannot struggle against the unseen cords of night. I am resigned, but I am not righteous. A part of me wants to race down the street. I raise only my eyes to glance down the still street. I can see Mr. Isaacson on the prowl for our minyan. Mr. Isaacson collecting bodies all up and down Ninety-first Street, and I know what they feel when they encounter the holy collector, enmeshed in his net of righteousness. I know their torn hearts. Part screams, "Isaacson, drop dead!" But part fervently petitions, "Oh Lord, make me like Mr. Isaacson." Part pumps like mad for the subway on Broadway, but part beats with fervor, "Where are my brethren? Let us pray together, 'May-His-Great-Name-Be-Praised-For-Ever-And-Ever.'" And so a minyan is made as an IRT express slides out of the station with one fewer passenger than it would have carried. But even at that the subway car is jammed; people mashed together like the bullets in the rifle that wouldn't shoot. So where should he be? The refugee? Number ten, the minyan. I turn toward Mr. Isaacson but over his shoulder I glimpse my phantom local disappearing down Ninety-first Street. Part of me hungers for that frantic train and not for heaven where the angels remark on weekdays that the righteous can drive you crazy.

Yes, they can drive you crazy. The righteous do whatever they want with you. They control you. Who knows where his story is going? Where his tale is leading us? But his story has become my story, so I take his hand and ask, "What happened?" What happened to you? What happened to us? To all of us? And I am fearful, for I am not sure we will make it.

And we stand together under the nocturnal shade tree to discover our fate. He talks and I listen. He was discovered and carried through the deserter-filled forest on an empty gun carriage to a dressing station in an orchard where his wound was cleaned. I hear of the journey to the field hospital by wagon, too painful—by ambulance ("a real automobile"), too painful—and a roadside conference that elects to carry him all the way by stretcher. And so he arrives at the hospital in the hands of men, but fears to place his fate in their hands again after a young Jewish soldier dies under the knife. An ugly nurse begs him to consent, but he refuses. For days the world has been conspiring to destroy him, but never with his consent!

That night a Russian Orthodox priest appears in the ward and bed by bed draws near with his huge uplifted cross. Mr. Isaacson, exhausted, lifts the fringes on the corners of his garment and the priest halts. The others, he blesses with his cross, but Mr. Isaacson, he kisses.

"I got through the night all right, but the next day was bad. I couldn't keep it from hurting. No matter how I lay, no matter how I turned, it hurt. They wanted to operate, but I wouldn't let them. And how that nurse cared for me and comforted me. What a good person! But she was ugly! Ugly as sin. She cried over me and begged me to let them operate. Oh, she was good to me. What a good person. Finally, it hurt so bad, I figured it didn't make much difference, so I told her they could operate.

"The doctors had finished, so she ran to find one. I thought that was the end, but it wasn't. They opened up the wound and found a piece of shrapnel stuck between two ribs. They just took a pliers and pulled it out. It was simpler than anybody had guessed. As soon as they pulled it out, I began feeling better."

"I bet the nurse was happy, too."

"She was thrilled. How she cried over me! What a good person—ugly as sin."

Mr. Isaacson smiles, enjoying the paradox. And what did she think of Mr. Isaacson? Could she see into his heart where he called her a good person? Could she for once see her inner beauty mirrored in his eyes instead of the ugly-as-sin glances that well men unceasingly cast? Or was she herself the righteous and in her eyes Mr. Isaacson learned?

"Without her you might have been lost," I venture in appreciation of her good deed.

"Yes, and not just then," he answers.

"Another time?"

"It must have been the next day or the day after. The Germans started shelling the hospital. The bombs were falling right into the building. I thought I was going to get killed. I begged her to save me. She ran and got an officer's jacket and put it on me. And when they came running in to evacuate the officers, she shouted at them, 'He's an officer!' 'Officer?' they ask. 'Yes,' I answer, 'officer!' They look at my jacket—an officer's—and carry me right out of there as fast as they can. She saved me."

"What was her name?"

"I don't know. We just called her Nurse."

"Did you ever see her again?"

"No, a few days later they moved me farther back and I never saw her again."

"Was she Jewish?" I ask.

"I don't know," he answers. "I don't think so. I think she was Russian."

She is what she is—and that is righteous. And I am curious about the righteous. The righteous are not just nice; they are essential. Thirty-Six Righteous sustain the world. If it weren't for them the world couldn't keep going. It would stop right in the middle of no place—like a yo-yo with no more energy-feeding string to tumble down. *Kaput*—finished! And since they are righteous they are anonymous, otherwise they would never get any sleep. Anonymous, but when I come across one of them, I am curious to find out who they are. What is her name? Who is she? The righteous, it turns out, are who they are. I confess I wouldn't mind her being Jewish, but whoever she is she does her good deeds anonymously, the yo-yo spins, the world turns, and we go from year to year lurching like a blind man at noon. For at noon, the righteous can help the sightless find the path. At night we are lost. The righteous aren't cats; even they can't see in the dark. But she is not entirely anonymous. We know what she looks like. She is ugly as sin. The nectarines are served in the World To Come in an ugly green bag. Ugly as sin and never sins. Ugly? No, unscarred by beauty.

"And so you were saved," I conclude.

"Yes," he answers, "thank G-d."

And for this evening we are finished. How can we go beyond the righteous? We stand a while, quiet and reflective. Mr. Isaacson breaks the silence.

"Regards to the family."

"Thank you, regards to Mrs. Isaacson."

"Good night."

I watch Mr. Isaacson cross the street and turn to retrace my steps down Ninety-first Street past the *shtibl* staircase crowding onto the silent sidewalk. It is warm and humid. As I cross Broadway I hear a faint rumbling that might be mistaken for a distant sound from the heavens above, if beneath, the subway, hot and empty, weren't pursuing its predetermined course.

I turn onto my street and see a squat, heavy-limbed figure moving deliberately through the pink light showering down upon him. The page has been learned for the day. Why hurry? A page a day.

I am by his side.

"Are you still fasting?"

"Yes."

"They were for you."

"Yes, thank you. The Three Weeks, a very difficult period," I explain.

"Yeah, but we'll make it."

"Yes," I answer. And I open the door for the nectarine man because we'll make it, and not to—would be . . . ugly as sin.

JOHANNA KAPLAN

Sickness

*I*n books, radiators hum and sing; in my house, the radiator
howls and yelps as if a baby were locked up in it, an angry baby
who, though he cries and cries, still does not bring his mother
running. Not that she isn't longing to. But there is an older neighbor around or an aunt maybe, and her philosophy is: He's crying?
So he'll cry! And the baby in the radiator—how can he know all
this? So he sends up a last, raging yowl and I am woken up.

Here, in the brief, early whitish light, the march of neighbors has
already begun. For even though it is barely morning of my first day
home from school, the news of a sick child has shuttled through the
building like steam through the pipes, and my mother's voice rises
from the kitchen in bitterness.

"What's a doctor? He sits and sits studying long enough so that finally in one place his bathrobe wears out."

It is not a question now of tissues and aspirins, of swollen glands or a throat that won't swallow. This time it is serious: Lichtblau, the limping *Golem* with MD on his license plate, has made a housecall. Dragging one heavy foot behind the other, he has announced measles and a high fever, and in a stingy mumble as dull as the one that sends black years to the Irish kids on his new Buick in the street, he has even mentioned the possibility of hospital. But this doesn't worry me because what's a hospital? One, nurses: quick-stepping, white-clad girls whose heads are all blond and faces *shiksa*-silly. And two, doctors: bald, heavy men, sad-eyed and Jewish, who walk slowly on dragging legs, their bodies wrapped up in old maroon bathrobes, shamefully all worn away in one spot.

What would I do in a place like that? Where would I keep my glass of sweet, lukewarm tea that sits, whenever I am sick, like lightened liquid honey on a folding chair by my bed? Where would I put all my books? Where would I get my neighbor stories? As I lie back against the pillow, my room flies up before me like an airy, pastel balloon. From the window, slats of sunlight sift in, off-spinning ballerina twins to the clumsy elephant slats of the fire escape: the sun is playing a game of potsy on the linoleum. Hopping each time to a different cone of color, the sun has zoned my floor so that it's a country counter of homemade, fruit-flavored ice creams, or else great clean pails of paint from which I can choose new, sweet, custardy colors and order the painter to paint my room.

Outside, other children's feet thump off to school. Some are shouting: they just got to the corner, shoelaces dragging, and now, for spite, the light is changing. And some are crying: people with bad work habits, maybe they forgot their consent slips or their gym suits, and because it's too late now to go back, the crying buttons them into their stormcoats even tighter and their whole bodies knead with what's coming. But I am inside, I am home, and sickness is all pleasure.

"Some tremendous achievement," my mother says, and from

the kitchen her voice in anger and sourness closes in on itself till it's black, black as the telephone, a mother jungle—steamy from her tears and sour from her breath. If she listened to me, she'd be completely different, even wear nail polish, but if that's what I'm looking for, she says, what I better do is go out and get myself another mother. As it is, though, the one I have plucks pinfeathers out of a chicken, and because her fingers get clumsy and impatient instead of elegant and neat, the knife point nips them so they bleed a thin, crooked trail that maps out spongy yellow Chickenland: a bridge across the legs, a mountain pass to the wings, and all the way back through to the interior where the tiny stomach and liver lie hiding together, breathing like brothers.

"Some tremendous achievement," she tells Birdie. "To sit and sit and study and study and nowhere in the whole process is there a head that comes into it or a brain that's involved. In medical school the big expense is in bathrobes."

Birdie is puffy-brown and stuffed, the awful splendor of a Florida suntan. Her voice too is bleached—thin and hard from the sun and sandy from cigarettes. With aqua earrings, an orange dress and two orange-painted big toes that pop out from aqua open-toe shoes, Birdie is herself a sunstroke.

"Let's face it, Manya," she tells my mother. "You'll never get satisfaction. A Jewish doctor is a Jewish prince."

A Jewish prince! Joseph Nasi, Joseph the prince. . . .

The chamber was thick with incense and plush with silken pillows. In the distance a droning voice was chanting the name of Allah, summoning the faithful to prayer. But within the richly adorned room not even a palm frond dared stir, for in the center, seated upon the largest and most sumptuous silken pillow of them all, was the Sultan himself, brocade pantaloons loose about his legs and a gleaming scimitar at his waist. Behind him stood his fierce, mustachioed guards, before him veiled and scented dancing girls. All awaited his pleasure and command. Beneath the imperial turban, however, the Sultan's heavy brow was clouded and his darkened visage bespoke distress. Besides all this, he was very ugly, had a fat, puffy face as if mosquitoes couldn't keep away from him. With a soft rustle of silks, a graceful, veiled maiden appeared before him, bearing a silver tray of sweetmeats. But barely raising one languid hand, the Sultan sent her away. On hot days, sweetmeats probably made him a little nauseous. A richly garbed courtier bowed low before him.

"Sire," he said, "an emissary just arrived from the mighty King of Spain urgently begs that Your Majesty receive him." But bidding him rise, the Sultan merely looked away, saying, "I shall receive no one." A thin, hurrying Vizier flung himself at the Sultan's feet crying, "If it please Your Majesty, a messenger stands at the palace gates with a plea of grave import from Your Majesty's heroic general now engaged with the Infidel in battle far afield." The beetle-browed Sultan sighed.

Suddenly a great clatter was heard from without and finally even the fat, sitting Sultan started getting a little curious.

"What occasions this disturbance?" he demanded of his court.

"It is nothing, Your Majesty," replied a saber-bristling guardsman. "Nothing His Highness need concern himself over. It is merely a Jew."

"A *Jew?*" cried the Sultan, hastily rising from his cushions as color flooded his features. His eyes were popping, too, and probably by this time there was even a vein twitching somewhere. "A Jew? *What* Jew?"

"Merely a Jewish doctor who calls himself Joseph."

"Joseph!" The Sultan cried out with great emotion. "All praises to Allah Who has sent him to me this day. Bring Joseph to my presence immediately."

Hustled in between two armor-laden guardsmen was a slight, bearded man of modest dress and bearing and proud, intelligent eyes.

"Sire," he said, stepping forward, carefully lowering his eyes, but not bowing his head or bending his knee, for there was only One to Whom Joseph bowed. And not every other minute either because he certainly wasn't Catholic.

"O Joseph," the Sultan called out in great agitation. "What news do you bring me? What of my son, what of my ships, and what of the terrible apparition of my nightly slumbers?"

"For your son, O great Sire, I have prepared a special salve and now the lad's eye is as bright as ever it was."

"Selim," the Sultan breathed. That was his son's name in Turkish.

"Of your ships, Your Majesty. Though one was lost in a storm at sea, the cargo of all the fleet has been rescued in a foreign port by a friend and member of my faith, one Mannaseh ben Levi. Further, he has sent a message to me with the news of a worm, Your Majesty, who through his own cunning can spin silk. He offers to send to your court as many of such creatures as Your Majesty desires in the shipment with the lost cargo."

"Allah be praised!"

"Of the apparition. It was a warning to Your Majesty of the storm at sea which distressed your ships. Now that the cargo is safe, the dreaded apparition will trouble you no longer."

"O Joseph, physician to my body, my soul, and my coffers. How shall I reward you? What is it that you wish?"

"For myself, Sire, there is nothing I desire. But for my people, I ask that they may always live in peace within your walls, free to pursue their daily lives and to worship, harming no one, according to our age-old laws and beliefs."

"Granted, Joseph. Most swiftly and easily granted. But what of yourself? What do you ask for your own person?"

"Only that which is granted for my people."

"Then, Joseph, if you will not ask, I must bestow unrequested. And I, His Imperial Majesty the Sultan, name you, Joseph, a Prince of my Domain. No longer are you merely Joseph the Jewish doctor. Henceforward you are to be known as Joseph the Prince! Let cymbals sound and gongs strike!" Right in my ear: it is Birdie's Atlantic City charm bracelet sounding and gonging on the Formica table.

———

"Uh-tuh-tuh and look who's here!" she says, smiling at me, her lipsticked lips wide and bright as a sideways orange Popsicle.

Uh-tuh-tuh and look who's here. Yellow kindergarten clowns hop all over my pajamas and red spots climb through my flesh. That's who's here.

"*Ketzeleh*," says Birdie. "Are you hungry? Do you want some bread and peanut butter?" But I'm not sure what I want; my head is spinning off in a deadman's float all by itself and is strange to the rest of me—luggy limbs and scratchy skin.

"Oh, Manya," Birdie calls to my mother. "Watch how your daughter spreads the peanut butter. I love the way she does it—so perfect and so exact you'd think the knife is a paintbrush. Look how she sits there with that peanut butter like an artist."

"Some artist," my mother says. "She has no hands, she's just like me. She couldn't even tie up a goose, my father used to say about me, and that's what it is—no hands."

In the back of the *siddur*, in the Song of Songs, it says: What shall we do for our little sister, for she has no breasts? But there is nothing in it about no hands.

"Look how she makes it smooth and how she goes over and over it. By the time she's through, it's a shame to eat it."

But my mother doesn't even bother to turn around because in her opinion peanut butter and nail polish are the exact same thing: both of them made up inside the head of Howdy Doody.

Birdie has nothing against peanut butter, though. Why should she? She chews gum, plays Mah-Jongg, goes to bungalow colonies and eats Chinese food. Altogether she would be a cow but for one thing—cows get the best boys and end up with the best husbands. And this is Birdie's story: she didn't. So far did she miss in this one way that even though she has been divorced for years, she still cries to my mother in the kitchen that when she wakes up in the morning she feels that there is no taste in her, and sometimes when she stands with her shopping cart in the aisle at Daitch's, everything starts to get cold, sour, and far away. Her one son, Salem, is eighteen and goes to pharmacy school in Philadelphia: by a coincidence, an accident, the city where his father lives. Really he should be named Shalom, but from being ashamed that it was too Jewish, Birdie named him Salem and what she didn't know was that he would get called Sal—a name for an ordinary Italian hood. Still, he is very good-looking, Salem: tall, black wavy hair, and a long, rocky face like Abraham Lincoln's. Every couple of months he comes home to visit his mother, and takes back all her saved-up empty soda bottles for the deposit, pulling them along University Avenue, her shopping cart behind his long, skinny Abraham Lincoln legs all the way to Daitch's. When he's not there, I don't think she bothers about soda bottles, and anyway, when her allergies come she goes to Florida, when it's too hot in the city she goes to Monticello, in between sometimes she goes to Lakewood or Atlantic City, and for what's left she comes back to the Bronx and starts right in playing Mah-Jongg as if she were just a cow with other cows, her life the same as theirs.

"Sometimes that's what I wish for you most, Miriam," my mother tells me in the late afternoon when she sits drinking tea and her narrow, nervous face gets dreamy from the steam, and her worn-out, angry voice gets swallowed away with the heat and sweetness in the cup. "I wish you could grow up to be a cow."

But it's too late for that by now and I know it; Donna Schoenbaum, in my class in public school, is one already—and if not yet exactly a cow, then definitely a calf. Her flat, moony face tilts in the light when she raises her hand for the pass, the slow, sleepy look stays on her even in city-wide reading tests. In her father's dry-goods store, woolen underpants creep through the shelves and flannel pajamas hibernate in the window. Once, coming back from an errand for Miss Devlin, just to waste more time, I took all the barrettes and bobby pins out of my hair and stood with it just like that in the fifth-floor girls' bathroom. All of a sudden, behind me in the mirror was Donna Schoenbaum, her dirty blond hair in two fat rubber-band curls on her shoulders, her face like two wide, white, empty clouds that stand still, her eyes tiny and tight and, without her glasses, even dumber.

"Ooh, Miriam, you look just like a witch," she said with her

high, naggy, baby-cow voice. "I never saw you before with your
hair down and that's what you look like. All your long, black,
messy hair with your long, thin face and your *nose*. You look like
a witch, I swear it."

In camp once I learned a Yiddish song about a cow, a calf really,
and this the chorus of it: *donna-donna-donna-donna*, instead of *la-la-
la*. So, into her face in the mirror I said, "Donna, Donna, Donna,
Donna." A calf, all tied up, is being led off to slaughter in a wagon.
Right up above it, following along in the sky, is a bird, a swallow,
who flies back and forth, up and down, anywhere he wants while
the cow with her dumb eyes just lies staring. The wind, seeing all
this, starts laughing, keeps it up day and night, till finally the farmer
driving the wagon takes pity, looks around at that stupid-eyed,
tied-up calf, and says: Who told you to be a cow? *Donna-donna-
donna-donna*. Donna's father's store is right next door to the kosher
butcher where the huge, split bodies of killed kosher cows, hanging
on deliverymen's shoulders, wobble between the entrances of the
two stores. Sometimes the bodies stain the sidewalk.

"You even have yellow skin like a witch," Donna said. Because
I am named Miriam, my skin should be different: dark and lit
up as a crayon color, polished and sunny-olive skin like Gracie
D'Onofrio's, who has a private house with white statues and vegetables in the front and her father's exterminating business in the
basement. Gracie is the prettiest girl in my class and, except for
Marty Weintraub, the person Miss Devlin hates most. Gracie talks
all the time: on line after the bell, in the lunchroom after the
whistle, in the auditorium even in front of the principal, and in the
room when she isn't whispering, she's sending notes. "If you don't
know how to stop that tongue, I'll call your father and have him
exterminate it," is what Miss Devlin's always threatening her. But
worst of all, in Miss Devlin's opinion, is that Gracie no longer goes
to Released Time, playing hooky from her Catholic lessons. Once
on line in the Girls' Yard, in one of her after-the-bell talkings,
Gracie said, "They're all mean, and I have to get stuck with Sister
Mary Joseph, who's the meanest. All you have to do is talk once,
and she takes you downstairs and beats you."

"It's a terrible thing that your religious education can't manage to do any more for you," Miss Devlin screams at Marty Weintraub, a person who calls out and throws spitballs. "You're a rude young man, Mr. Martin Weintraub, and the Sisters would surely know what to do with a rude young man like you."

If I were in school now, the morning nearly over, where I would be, probably, is walking slowly up the back stairs on an errand for Miss Devlin. On these stairs there is a window at every half-landing, and on the higher floors the windows, through the gratings, skip the fat yellow brick of the Annex next door and fly straight to the Reservoir—the round blue beginnings of a strange little country far away from the Bronx. In the fall this little country is a colonial village settled by the Dutch: a bright, curvy shore full of tiny-roofed private houses in shapes and colors as jumbled and leaping as the changing trees, and higher than all of them, one white-topped church, sunny and placid. But in the winter, when the snow sticks to the little houses beyond the Reservoir, sealing them in long after it's become slushy in all the neighborhood streets, the little country, pale, poor, and half buried, seems even farther away—Russia. A Cossack horseman rides these backstairs windows: Anton, the custodian's helper, belted to the ledge with a pail, sits astride the sill, his stallion, and washes the windows. Pressed against the glass, his forehead is wide and empty like a Russian steppe and his cheeks are as red as my mother's were when she was a girl in Poland. From squinting in the wind, Anton's eyes get a tight, slanty, Tartar-tribesman look, and when he's working hard, his mouth curves down around a matchstick between his lips—a thin, sneering curve, practically Chmelnitski. . . .

Heavy, endless snows were falling, and throughout the bitter winter the land became a lonely, frozen waste. At night wolves howled in the dark forests and icy winds cried out through the trees. Through these trees, too, flew terrible stories: of unwary souls who ventured forth in crude wagons and were frozen to death in the deep while landowners in fur-rugged sleighs galloped by, their sleighbells jingling. In the snowbound countryside the peasants (poor farmers) could carry no wares to fairground or marketplace. And in the villages within the Jewish Pale of Settlement, families sat in their bleak, chilled houses, huddling closer together around the steaming samovar. Artisans and tradesmen, rabbis and scholars lived in these villages, and not often could they voyage abroad. For as bitter as were the Russian winters, more bitter still were the cruel and unjust restrictions placed upon them by the harsh rule of the Russian Tsar. As long as they had lived with poverty and hunger, so long had these pious, simple folk lived with fear. "O Lord," they pleaded, praying to the Almighty One with fervor and devotion, "Thou Who hast vanquished our ancient oppressors, how long must we suffer under this terrible yoke?" Thus they prayed in synagogue and study house.

In such a study house, in just such a *shtetl* (for so these villages were called), a tailor, Mottel, and his five sons sat poring over the Holy Writ as the afternoon deepened into evening. Suddenly, amidst the dull hum of men's voices chanting the Scriptures and disputing over the commentaries, a great clatter was heard at the door, soon followed by an icy blast of chill air. It was the red-bearded beadle, a lantern swaying on his arm, as he cried in a terror-filled voice, "Brothers! Brothers! Bestir yourselves! Hide! Run! Save yourselves and your sons!"

"What is it, Beadle?" asked the tailor. "A pogrom?"

"Not that," the beadle replied, his voice still shaking. "Oh, hurry, brothers, hurry! It's the Snatchers, the Tsar's kidnapers, and with them ride an army of Cossack soldiers."

"The Snatchers!" the cry went up in alarm as all hurried to their homes, for these Snatchers were the cruelest, most heartless measure the Tsar had ever devised. Eager to rid his lands of Jewish subjects, the Tsar, pretending benevolence, had offered first-class citizenship to all those Jews who would convert to Christianity. But the Jewish people remained steadfast, and the Tsar, even further angered by these "ignorant, stubborn wretches," sent out bands of kidnapers to those areas of his empire where he permitted Jews to live. The evil purpose of these kidnapers was to snatch little Jewish lads, not more than seven or eight years of age, tear them from their mothers and their homes, and send them to peasant Christian families in distant reaches of the Tsar's vast realm, where in hapless servitude they would daily be forced to go against the teachings of their faith. For twenty-five long years such captivity was theirs to endure, the latter part to be spent as unwilling conscripts in the Tsar's brutal army. By that time, gloated the ruthless Tsar, all ties with their heritage and origin would be forgotten.

As the tailor and his sons hurried through the darkened streets, fierce Cossack soldiers already crowded the pathways. Troops of burly, red-cheeked young men sat astride sturdy stallions, and the mouths of these sleek beasts foamed and steamed in the frost. A wail went up throughout the village, and from one end to the other could be heard the voice of the cobbler's widow, Teibel, crying, "Please, sirs, please! I implore you! Take pity on me! What am I but a poor, lone widow? And what is he but my one, only son and barely an infant?" But the widow's pleas were of no avail and the screaming, woebegone youth was dragged off amidst his mother's weeping.

Quickly the tailor bade all his family hide so that when the louts arrived, they would think they had happened on an empty house. But the baby, cradled in its mother's arms under the bed, began to whimper in fright when he heard the heavy, crunching footsteps stalk through the door. Frantically stuffing a cloth a bit further into the infant's mouth, the tailor's wife suddenly gasped in horror. For her sons, hiding in the yard, began to let out terrible, piteous cries: they had fallen into the hands of the snatchers. Hurriedly crawling out of her hiding place, the anguished mother clutched her youngest son to her breast and saw that the infant in her arms had gone limp and lifeless, suffocated by the tiny cloth. Late that night, peasants of the neighborhood, emboldened by drink and encouraged by the Cossack forays, swept through the miserable village, pillaging and plundering as they went.

Just as the drunken peasants are finishing off, a noise starts to come from the kitchen like a hundred toilets flushing. Ppshh, wuschsh, swishchh, it comes and goes: my mother is speaking Polish with Eva the Refugee. In Poland, my mother said, it rained constantly from Rosh Hashanah straight to Simchas Torah and rained again from Purim all the way to Pesach, and that's why when people speak Polish it sounds like a rainstorm. Not that Eva the Refugee thinks so. She comes up to see my mother when she gets the feeling that she has to speak Polish. As far as I'm concerned, if she opened up an umbrella and used a little imagination it would be just as good. But there's no one else around she can speak Polish to, not even her husband, Fritz, who's so German-looking—with his glasses that have no frames and his strange smile—that he lived underground in Germany for the whole war without anyone finding him out. What happened to Eva, though, wasn't so lucky; every time she wears a short-sleeved dress, the whole building has to see the blue number on her arm and think of the terrible life she had. When she first moved in, it was this blue number that made all the other women in the building, the cows especially, keep away from her completely, but when they found out how talented she was in gossiping, all her worries were over.

In her tiny ground-floor apartment where she lives with her husband and her fat little son, Eva sits at her window which looks out on the front court and watches everything, from early in the morning when I leave for school till very late at night when all the Mah-Jongg games are over. And these are the things she knows: what person's daughter who goes to art school and is engaged for the second time had a big fight with her boyfriend in the lobby at one in the morning, and refused to give back the ring till he tried to pull it off her finger; what very skinny woman with no children went running down to someplace in the South and came back with a baby girl that she says isn't adopted but when you take a good look into the carriage what you see is the face of a Southern *shiksa*; what boy's mother got so furious when he didn't make the SP that she went to school and tried to force the principal into telling her her son's IQ, and when he wouldn't, how this person's mother carried on so much that the principal was ready to call the police; what person's children have to go running all over the building looking for televisions to watch even though there is one in their own living room, but all it gets is snow and ghosts because this person's husband is so cheap that he won't give Rappaport a two-dollar-a-month increase for a roof antenna. There are smaller things she watches too. To my mother she says, "I didn't know your daughter was starting a new fashion with high socks—one up

and one falling down all over her ankle." And to Stuie Greenzweig's mother, "In case you never thought about it, it's possible
for a boy to walk out of the house every day at three-thirty with
Hebrew books in his hand and where his feet take him doesn't have
to be Hebrew School." So there are people who would be happier
if Eva would move, just to a different apartment.

Even Dora Rappaport, the landlord's wife, begs Eva to go into
a bigger apartment: every time she sits in her beautiful house in
Long Beach and thinks of Eva with the number on her arm in that
tiny apartment, it makes her nauseous. But Eva isn't interested. To
Rappaport and anyone else who asks, she says that she and her
husband are saving up for a house on the Island. But the truth is
that if Eva ever had to give up her ground-floor front-courtyard
window, she would have no place to put her talents.

Anyway, what Eva really wants has nothing to do with apartments or houses, it doesn't even have anything to do with watching
people from windows. What Eva really wants is a baby daughter,
and what it has to do with is the blue number on her arm. Once,
a long time ago in Europe before the Nazis came, Eva was married
to someone else, not Fritz, and had two little daughters. When the
Nazis came around and started taking people away, they told everyone that they just needed people to do work, and that they would
put all the children in special nurseries so that the mothers, who
were working, wouldn't have to be bothered. But when they got to
Eva's older sister Anzhia, who was beautiful, with long red hair,
and played the flute like a bird, she refused to be separated from
her children, and what happened to Anzhia was that she and her
three children were shot with a gun right then and there. When Eva
saw this, what she should have done is hide—quick, one, two,
three—with her two little daughters under the bed, and then be
very careful about how she stuffed cloths. But what she did do was
let her children be taken separately, and because she never saw
them again, what she would like to have now is a daughter.

What she *does* have now is a son, Stevie, who's almost five years
old, with a fat pink face, blond hair, and a tooth in the front that
got broken by Jeffrey Bugatch one time when Stevie pushed Jeffrey's baby sister Sherri off her bike and then, for good luck,

stepped on her finger. Because of his habits with younger children and because he looks so much like his father, people call out "The Nazi's here" when they see him coming, and all the mothers in the neighborhood can't wait till Stevie goes to kindergarten, where if he gets the morning session with Miss Callahan, Nazi activities will definitely be over. But that's not why Eva can't wait till he gets to school. She tells everyone around that she doesn't care how many children get into SPs, Bronx Science, or walk off with fantastic scholarships; she is convinced that as soon as the teachers in public school get a taste of her Stevie, every other smart child they ever taught will immediately drop right out of their heads. In the meantime, she dresses him in perfect clothes, and any time he goes near the sandbox or forgets to put a napkin under his ice-cream pop, she screams out, "Stevie! Stevechen! Daddy doesn't let!" If Eva were a little more perfect with her own clothes, maybe she wouldn't have a smell of so much refugee perspiring that I don't even like to stand near her. But I wouldn't get out of bed to stand near her now anyway. Right this minute, for all I know, she could be telling my mother that the reason I got sick is that there were days last week when I didn't button my top button, or that I almost never wear my gloves except when I leave in the morning. I have no way of knowing, though, because the sounds from the kitchen are still Polish. Swischhh, plishch, chwushh they go, slower and slower, so sleepy a rain that I only know it's over when I hear the bell ring.

Dr. Lichtblau's name means light blue, but the way he rings the bell is gray, heavy, and nervous. In his whole life put together, he said only one funny thing, and even *that* was only because I asked him a question. I wouldn't have asked it either, but I was sitting in his office waiting for him to fill out my medical form for camp, and all he did was stand by the window in his white coat and peek out through the venetians to see who he could catch sitting on top of his car. Outside children were skating and screaming, upstairs someone was practicing the accordion, but inside Dr. Lichtblau's ground-floor office there was such a strange, snowy quiet that I looked at the medical form and said, "What's St. Vitus Dance?"

"St. Vitus Dance, hah!" Dr. Lichtblau said to me. "With the camps your mother sends you to, the only dance you'll ever have to worry about is the Horah." And then, because I gave him a dirty look, "Not that I have anything against Zionism. I wouldn't want you to think so. As a matter of fact, and this is the truth, somehow, somewhere, distantly by marriage I'm related to David Ben-Gurion." It's not David Ben-Gurion's fault if in a big family some distant cousin somewhere goes out and marries a moron.

In my room, seeing the books on my bed, Dr. Lichtblau says, "What are you reading there—Nancy Drew?"

"No."

"What then? Sue Barton? No? What?"

What I am reading is this: It was a warm, sunny day in Düsseldorf, Germany, in the year 1809, but the gray, stuffy classroom held no hint of the lovely spring morning without. Throughout the long rows small, diligent heads were bent over the copybooks on the desks, and over the sound of busy, scratching pens only a clock ticked. Occasionally, one of the bolder, more daring lads would stealthily look about him, hoping that his raised head had not aroused the stern eye of the severe Prussian schoolmaster, for stiff, exacting discipline was the unquestioned standard of this sunless room. In the back, however, in the row closest to the windows, sat a pale, thin youth whose dark, brooding eyes turned not to his copybook but to the green, budding world beyond the window. He stared longingly, his gaze seeming to fix on a point so distant that only he could see it, and suddenly as a wave of light burst across his gentle face, he grabbed his pen and began to write furiously. But before he knew it, a dark figure was looming over him, snatching the very paper from his hand.

"Ah, and what have we here?" said the schoolmaster, lifting his pince-nez as he glared mercilessly at the dismayed youth. And as the titters of the class rose, the schoolmaster, his voice harsh and mocking, read aloud: " '*Du bist wie eine blume*—You are like a flower. So pretty, pure and sweet.' You are like a flower indeed! How dare you scribble such twaddle in my classroom? Heinrich Heine, explain yourself!"

He doesn't though, so finally I tell Dr. Lichtblau, "What I'm reading is a story with a poem inside it."

"As far as my daughter is concerned," the doctor tells my mother, "Nancy Drew is the one and only. Not that she's such a big reader, Andrea, but when it comes to Nancy Drew, she even has trouble eating if she didn't finish it."

"Andrea," my mother says very slowly, her mouth making it sound as round and ridiculous as a clown who flops around on TV shows. "She must be in Junior High by now, your daughter. How does she like it in Mount Vernon?"

"As a matter of fact, right now she's in Miami with her mother, but what their schools are like down there nobody told me."

"Such an adorable child," my mother says. "All ninety-fives in Florida-going and her mother the same in mink-wearing."

When the Lichtblaus lived in the building, before they moved to Mount Vernon, Andrea's mother used to come back from Alexander's and Loehmann's with so many packages that she had to take a taxi. These taxi-takings were counted up by Eva, but could be seen by anyone who was outside. Sometimes Andrea was in on them too, but most of the time she wasn't, because in the whole neighborhood Andrea was a girl who was famous for always being busy. Once she was busy trying to be very smart so badly that she went to the library every single day after school, looking so hard for smartness that she forgot to see if she was getting good books. Then she decided to be a brilliant pianist, and practiced "Spinning Song" day and night, till people in her father's waiting room got dizzy and complained. Then she tried to be a brilliant Girl Scout, but not many people in the building had sympathy for her cookies because they knew that where the Girl Scouts met was the Catholic church. Finally, just before she moved, she tried to be very religious, waiting around for Jewish holidays to come and crying because her mother wouldn't send her to Hebrew School.

After she moved, I saw her only once and that was in Alexander's on the Girls' Wear floor, where my mother was bending over a counter of marked-down polo shirts and picking out the ones in my size, saying, "I know it says seconds, Miriam, but they're only polo shirts and besides I can't find any imperfections." "I can," I said. "They're all ugly and how much more imperfect than that can you get?" Just as she was starting to tell me what a bitterness I made of her life, Andrea's mother, her arms so full of packages that she needed a taxi on the spot, came running over and without even bothering to say hello, immediately said, "I don't know how I'm ever going to get out of here. With all the building that they're doing and the banging and hocking, you can't get anywhere near an escalator."

"*What?*" my mother said. "You mean they're expanding again? God Almighty, I can remember when Alexander's was only a lousy little Sephardi dress shop."

"I'll never make it to the elevator with all I'm carrying," Andrea's mother said. "And even if I could find the stairs, how can I manage when I'm so loaded down?" All the time she was saying this, Mrs. Lichtblau kept going up and down on her tiptoes, looking around her in the same nervous way her husband does when he's worrying about who's standing on his car. And all of a sudden, right in the middle of Alexander's, Andrea's mother started crying. Andrea, whose hands were also all full of packages, was standing on the opposite side of the polo-shirt counter, and as soon as her mother started crying, she moved about two baby steps away from her so that she was facing me almost exactly. Except that she was taller and had different glasses, I couldn't see that there was any new and special Mount Vernon feeling about her.

"Hiya, Miriam," she said. "Are you still so smart or did you get a little dumb yet?" Especially since her mother was crying I didn't think it would be nice to tell her that anyone who could think up a question like that had to be on the dumb side herself, so I only said, "You got new glasses."

"They're not new," Andrea said. "It's just that I don't live in the disgusting Bronx any more, so you don't know what things I have."

"What things do you have?"

"A bra, for one. And as a matter of fact I needed to get a bigger one so badly that we had to come straight to Alexander's. I don't think you'll need anything like that for a couple of years at least." This immediately made me start worrying about the Song of Songs:

What shall we do for our little sister, for she has no breasts? If she were really only a *little* sister, naturally she wouldn't, but what if they were just being polite and she wasn't so little any more?

"What else do you have?" I said.

"Gorgeous underpants. And I just got a whole bunch of new ones that are even more gorgeous." Although you're not supposed to open up your packages in the middle of the store because if they see you they might think you haven't paid yet, Andrea tore open one of her top bags and pulled out a whole pile of underpants that were all exactly the same: white nylon with two bright red hearts stitched on in the middle. Holding them up nearly over her face, Andrea said, "If you think they'll run, you're all wrong. It only happens with the cheap kind." Because it seemed to me that these nylon underpants with two little hearts dancing over the crotch were the most ridiculous things I had even seen in the whole of Alexander's, I began to stare at Andrea and the underpants as she held them to her face, and suddenly I got the idea that if Andrea had underpants with two hearts embroidered on them, maybe if someone ever got a good look at her heart, they would find two little pairs of white underpants stitched on it. Though it's not exactly a medical question, it's something I still wonder about whenever I see Dr. Lichtblau and think of Andrea. But Dr. Lichtblau is not very talkative. Finally, as he's getting ready to leave, he turns to my mother and says, "She looks a lot better to me today than she did yesterday. I'm not saying that she still doesn't have the measles, but between yesterday and today there's a difference between a very severe condition and an ordinary case running its course."

"Between yesterday and today," my mother says before he's even slammed the door, "he either looked up a medical book or else called a doctor. Or who knows? With a man like him it could simply mean that he won't make any more housecalls." Still, she closes the venetian blinds as he told her to and warns me about no more reading.

"When I think of how my older sisters were blind for days and days when they had scarlet fever," my mother says. "And who ever thought they would be able to see again?"

"What I have is the measles," I tell her. "Nobody gets scarlet fever any more besides."

But she isn't listening to me; the look on her face is all Poland. "They just stayed there in the bed, all three of them together, till they couldn't walk and they couldn't move and if you looked at their faces you could see they were burning up, and if you looked at their tongues, what you saw was strawberries. I couldn't stay with them in the room any more even though it was my room, too, so I used to stand outside and watch them lying in the bedclothes. The room was so dark they thought it was always night, and they would cry out such strange things, things that didn't make any sense to me, till I started to think that everything in the room was black—the windows, the air, the bed, the blankets, and even my sisters. When they couldn't even see any more, something had to be done, so my mother decided to give them castor oil, but because of the terrible taste, they twisted and turned in the bedclothes and wouldn't take it. As sick and weak as they were, my sisters, they simply fought her off. And all day long the same thing went on till my mother became frantic. Finally, very late that night, my father came home and without saying anything, he pulled out from his pocket an orange. How he managed to get it, he never told us, all I can tell you is that it was the biggest orange I have ever seen in my life—a Jaffa orange from Palestine. Of course Palestine was nothing then—no country, no people, hardly even a place, but even at that time they had Jaffa oranges, and they were so big that just to hold it for a minute, I had to use my two hands. I can still tell you how it felt: very round with a thick, bumpy skin and a strange smell— deep and sweet and very distant, the first fruit God created on earth. My father went right in with it to my sisters and gave it to them with the castor oil, and I stood at the door and watched them eat it, and because I was foolish I stood there and wished that I could get sick too."

"Oranges get caught inside your teeth and make your fingers sticky," I tell my mother, but she doesn't answer me because I'm a prima donna and there's nothing that pleases me. She keeps standing by the window, though what she can see there I don't know; with the venetian blinds drawn, I hardly know if it's night or day. All I'm sure of is that it's after school: from downstairs you can hear Mindy Simons practicing the piano, playing "Für Elise," and Richie Lazaroff with his cheap and noisy trumpet playing "Malagueña."

Because it's so dark in my room and I can't read, I decide to tell myself my favorite story in the book, the story of Chaim Nachman Bialik, another one who sat around in school all day just staring out the window, and then after that turned out to be a poet. Not that he was like Heinrich Heine, who couldn't wait and had to rush into writing a poem the second he saw a flower. Chaim Nachman Bialik had it much worse: his dreaming in school got so bad that he practically couldn't learn how to read and because of that the rabbi used to beat him. His trouble was that every time he saw a Hebrew letter, it would look to him like a person—a man chopping wood or a woman washing clothes, and in his head he would make up stories about whatever person the letter made him think of instead of just reading the letter aloud the way it was. And not only in that way did he have it worse; his family lived in a tiny town in Russia and was very poor, and the only thing he really liked was running around in the fields outside the town. His father worked in a tavern and hated his job so much that he used to sit there reading the Talmud while he was pouring out drinks. Meanwhile, Chaim Nachman Bialik sat upstairs in his room, and when he heard the noises from the tavern—the screaming, the yelling, and the horsing around—he got terrified.

Things did not get better—his father died and he and his mother had to move to another town. When this happened, he felt so miserable that all he did was think about the field he used to run around in and wish himself back into it. Naturally, this didn't do him any good, he wasn't Mary Poppins. Besides, by this time they were even poorer. His mother tried to make some money by doing little things around in the village, but she had no luck. She used to get up so early and work so hard that every time he looked at her, her hands and face seemed so thin, weak, and tired that he was afraid she would get worn away. Because he was suffering so much, he started to spend a lot of time thinking about it, and it began to seem to him that all his mother's suffering and his own were like all the years of suffering of the Jewish people, and the more he thought about it, the whole thing from beginning to end made him sick. He wished that the Jews would snap out of it and get back to the good things they had going for them in the time of the Bible.

One day while he was sitting around dreaming as usual, he fell asleep and had a real dream. In this dream, he was in a land so strange and desolate that it could have been another planet or even the middle of the moon. All there was around him was a desert— terrible, hot, empty sands, orange-brown and wasted. Occasionally there was a squat, ugly palm tree and sometimes a rock. Vultures were screaming somewhere or maybe jackals. Above, the sun was so hard, yellow, and unending that it wore away the sky and left you with nothing to look at. After a while he realized that there were people walking through this desert—a bunch of hideous, broken-down old men. They all had beards, long cloaks, and staffs, and kept walking and walking in a slow, sickly way as if they were blind or didn't know where they were going. He tried to call to them, but they paid no attention, and when any of them came closer they were so old and disgusting, with sour phlegm on their beards, that it made him sick. The old men walked away, but the sun kept burning and draining him like a fever or a terrible sickness, and he lay stretched out in the sand helpless with thirst and with sweat. Suddenly, from the slow pull of my legs and the sweat running through my body, I realize that I've been sleeping, too, and cannot tell whether this was all the story's dream or my own. I get up and look around my bedroom, but there are no hints. Through the wall next door, Stuie and Arlene Greenzweig are watching Howdy Doody, and outside, past the venetians, the last of the sun is getting itself together over all the roof antennas in the Bronx. A thick orange globe, it floats in the sky like a bumpy Jaffa orange, a streaky golden desert, the land of Israel itself.

DEIRDRE LEVINSON

April 19th, 1985

As we enter the park this forty-second anniversary of the Warsaw Ghetto uprising, his eyes on a passing cyclist's new-fangled mount, he starts in on the evergreen topic of his next birthday, he bets we can't guess what he wants for it—talking fast against our full-throated protest that he's got ten months to go yet—he'll give us a clue, it begins with B. There was a time I would not have believed it possible for any child of mine to show himself on so grave an occasion so lightminded. But that was before I had children, before my old compulsion to raise them as living monuments to our pulverized people was foundered by the children themselves. So all I say, as we dispose ourselves for a while beside the flower-beds on the promenade, is that if it's birthdays we're talking about it had better be hers.

She will be fifteen imminently. Not a fortnight to go, but she still hasn't decided what she wants for this birthday, she says she just can't get excited about this one. For my fifteenth birthday I got new school underwear—navy-blue flannelette, with elastic at the leg— from my mother, and a Hebrew prayer-book and five bob from my father. "And a rich haul I thought it too," I add, with improving intent.

"Mercifully," the chit observes, "times have changed since those Stonehenge days. Don't tell us what you bought with the five bob, we know what you bought. Grandma told us; she's always telling us. You bought a big fat poetry-book, then you learnt all the poems in it by heart. Wonder-child!" she pinches my cheek. "My wonder-child mommy, I don't want a big fat poetry-book to learn by heart for my birthday."

"Me neither," he echoes feelingly.

"Poems you learn by heart at your age," I soldier on, "you remember for life. You'll always have them with you for company, speaking to you, sustaining you, they'll be your friends in the unfriendliest times."

He begs to differ, urging the livelier merits of a dog for company any old time. But she takes a high tone. "I'm here to tell you that I don't plan on having *poems* for friends. Whatever I do, wherever I go, there'll always be people for me to make friends with. Just regular human people, that's all, that's good enough for this human person."

Arts disqualified, letters dismissed. Just regular human people, that's all, that's good enough! How to expose this meretricious pop-culture humanism, this ass in a lion's skin, for the imposture it is?

"Now don't go taking it *personally*," she gives me a consolatory little kiss, as the two of them move off together towards the playground. "See you later, Mater. I must just go see if my babies are playing there today."

Her babies, twins, live in our building. Their mother is always telling me what a treasure, how indispensable a part of their household, our daughter is, how unfailingly reliable, understanding, sentient. "A wise one, you know what I mean, you can talk to her about anything. I call her my best friend."

You can talk to her about anything, anything uncomplicated by booklearning. Her intellectual life stops at school. She is an aficionado of the popular culture. Her ear is attuned to pop music exclusively; she has papered her room with pictures of rock stars; she has to be dragged by the hair, her gorgeous honey-brown haystack of hair, to an art museum, unless school requires it; she reads nothing, outside of her school texts, but pulp. What sort of sustenance is that to uphold her when it comes to the crunch? As for him, bless his mettlesome spirit and sociable ways, but abandon all hope of an elevated mind from that quarter. Ask him what he wants to be when he grows up, he says rich.

Here they come now, both pushing a double stroller containing the twins, whose mother hasn't waited to be asked twice. We walk briskly along the pedestrian path to the memorial stone, by the time we reach which, the small number assembled there—some old Europeans, survivors, and a handful of young people, their heirs and repositories of their story—are already singing. There are some short speeches to follow. One of the speakers urges us to remember also the gentile dissenters who died in the camps, as we salute the memory of our people who fought to the death in the Warsaw and Vilna ghettos. Then we sing a final anthem in Yiddish, and a couple of old women throw flowers over the iron railings onto the memorial stone. They give a flower each to the children. She picks up one twin, he the other, and they all drop their flowers onto the stone. Standing there with the children, I think of the nameless father briefly mentioned in an affidavit on one of the Ostland massacres. He was standing, the report relates, his young son beside him, on the edge of the mass grave they were shortly to lie in, stroking the child's head as he pointed to the sky, and seemed to explain something to him.

On our way home, retelling the scene to the children, "If you were that father, what would you be saying to your little boy?" I ask my little boy. But it isn't the father he's thinking of. "I'd be peeing in my pants," he says.

"Supposing it were you with us," before I can put my question to her, she returns it adroitly to where it belongs, "what would you say to us?"

Answer that. What would I say to them, pointing to the sky? Would there still be a sky? What to say that could have any meaning for them? I stand at the edge, she on one side, he on the other, the guns at our backs, the dead at our feet. "I'd tell you what a privilege it's been to bring you up. I'd thank you with all my heart for being the children you are," I say in a rush.

"Do you mean it, Ma?" they ask together, astonished, but no more astonished than I am. Then he says, "Can we please change the subject now, Ma? This one gives me the spookies." But the chit, leaving him to wheel the babies, holds my hand all the way home.

BERNARD MALAMUD

The Silver Crown

G ans, the father, lay dying in a hospital bed. Different doctors said different things, held different theories. There
was talk of an exploratory operation but they thought it might kill
him. One doctor said cancer.

"Of the heart," the old man said bitterly.

"It wouldn't be impossible."

The young Gans, Albert, a high school biology teacher, in the
afternoons walked the streets in sorrow. What can anybody do
about cancer? His soles wore thin with walking. He was easily
irritated; angered by the war, atom bomb, pollution, death, obviously the strain of worrying about his father's illness. To be able to
do nothing for him made him frantic. He had done nothing for him
all his life.

A female colleague, an English teacher he had slept with once, a girl who was visibly aging, advised, "If the doctors don't know, Albert, try a faith healer. Different people know different things; nobody knows everything. You can't tell about the human body."

Albert laughed mirthlessly but listened. If specialists disagree, who do you agree with? If you've tried everything, what else can you try?

One afternoon after a long walk alone, as he was about to descend the subway stairs somewhere in the Bronx, still burdened by his worries, uneasy that nothing had changed, he was accosted by a fat girl with bare meaty arms who thrust a soiled card at him that he tried to avoid. She was a stupefying sight, retarded at the very least. Fifteen, he'd say, though she looks thirty and probably has the mentality of age ten. Her skin glowed, face wet, fleshy, a small mouth open and would be forever; eyes set wide apart on the broad unfocused face, either watery green or brown, or one of each—he wasn't sure. She seemed not to mind his appraisal, gurgled faintly. Her thick hair was braided in two ropelike strands; she wore bulging cloth slippers bursting at seams and soles; a faded red skirt down to massive ankles, and a heavy brown sweater vest buttoned over blown breasts, though the weather was still hot September.

The teacher's impulse was to pass by her outthrust plump baby hand. Instead he took the card from her. Simple curiosity—once you had learned to read you read anything? Charitable impulse?

Albert recognized Yiddish and Hebrew but read in English: "Heal The Sick. Save The Dying. Make A Silver Crown."

"What kind of silver crown would that be?"

She uttered impossible noises. Depressed, he looked away. When his eyes turned to hers she ran off.

He studied the card. "Make A Silver Crown." It gave a rabbi's name and address no less: Jonas Lifschitz, close by in the neighborhood. The silver crown mystified him. He had no idea what it had to do with saving the dying but felt he ought to know. Although at first repelled by the thought, he made up his mind to visit the rabbi and felt, in a way, relieved.

The teacher hastened along the street a few blocks until he came to the address on the card, a battered synagogue in a store, Congregation Theodor Herzl, painted in large uneven white letters on the plate-glass window. The rabbi's name, in smaller, gold letters, was A. Marcus. In the doorway to the left of the store the number of the house was repeated in tin numerals, and on a card under the vacant name plate under the mezuzah appeared in pencil, "Rabbi J. Lifschitz. Retired. Consultations. Ring The Bell." The bell, when he decided to chance it, did not work—seemed dead to the touch— so Albert, his heartbeat erratic, turned the knob. The door gave easily enough and he hesitantly walked up a dark flight of narrow wooden stairs. Ascending, assailed by doubts, peering up through the gloom, he thought of turning back but at the first-floor landing compelled himself to knock loudly on the door.

"Anybody home here?"

He rapped harder, annoyed with himself for being there, engaging in the act of entrance—who would have predicted it an hour ago? The door opened a crack and that broad, badly formed face appeared. The retarded girl, squinting one bulbous eye, made noises like two eggs frying, and ducked back, slamming the door. The teacher, after momentary reflection, thrust it open in time to see her, bulky as she was, running along the long tight corridor, her body bumping the walls as she disappeared into a room at the rear.

Albert entered cautiously, with a sense of embarrassment, if not danger, warning himself to depart at once; yet stayed to peek curiously into a front room off the hallway, darkened by lowered green shades through which threadlike rivulets of light streamed. The shades resembled faded maps of ancient lands. An old gray-bearded man with thickened left eyelid, wearing a yarmulke, sat heavily asleep, a book in his lap, on a sagging armchair. Someone in the room gave off a stale odor, unless it was the armchair. As Albert stared, the old man awoke in a hurry. The small thick book on his lap fell with a thump to the floor, but instead of picking it up, he shoved it with a kick of his heel under the chair.

"So where were we?" he inquired pleasantly, a bit breathless.

The teacher removed his hat, remembered whose house he was in, and put it back on his head.

He introduced himself. "I was looking for Rabbi J. Lifschitz. Your—ah—girl let me in."

"Rabbi Lifschitz—this was my daughter Rifkele. She's not perfect, though God, who made her in His image, is Himself perfection. What this means I don't have to tell you."

His heavy eyelid went down in a wink, apparently involuntarily.

"What does it mean?" Albert asked.

"In her way she is also perfect."

"Anyway, she let me in and here I am."

"So what did you decide?"

"About what?"

"What did you decide about what we were talking about—the silver crown?"

His eyes roved as he spoke; he rubbed a nervous thumb and forefinger. Crafty type, the teacher decided. Him I have to watch myself with.

"I came here to find out about this crown you advertised," he said, "but actually we haven't talked about it or anything else. When I entered here you were sound asleep."

"At my age—" the rabbi explained with a little laugh.

"I don't mean any criticism. All I'm saying is I am a stranger to you."

"How can we be strangers if we both believe in God?"

Albert made no argument of it.

The rabbi raised the two shades and the last of daylight fell into the spacious high-ceilinged room, crowded with at least a dozen stiff-back and folding chairs, plus a broken sofa. What kind of operation is he running here? Group consultations? He dispensed rabbinic therapy? The teacher felt renewed distaste for himself for having come. On the wall hung a single oval mirror, framed in gold-plated grouping of joined metal circles, large and small; but no pictures. Despite the empty chairs, or perhaps because of them, the room seemed barren.

The teacher observed that the rabbi's trousers were a week from ragged. He was wearing an unpressed worn black suit-coat and a yellowed white shirt without a tie. His wet grayish-blue eyes were restless. Rabbi Lifschitz was a dark-faced man with brown eye pouches and smelled of old age. This was the odor. It was hard to say whether he resembled his daughter; Rifkele resembled her species.

"So sit," said the old rabbi with a light sigh. "Not on the couch, sit on a chair."

"Which in particular?"

"You have a first-class humor." Smiling absently, he pointed to two kitchen chairs and seated himself in one.

He offered a thin cigarette.

"I'm off them," the teacher explained.

"I also." The old man put the pack away. "So who is sick?" he inquired.

Albert tightened at the question, as he recalled the card he had taken from the girl: "Heal The Sick, Save The Dying."

"To come to the point, my father's in the hospital with a serious ailment. In fact he's dying."

The rabbi, nodding gravely, dug into his pants pocket for a pair of glasses, wiped them with a large soiled handkerchief, and put them on, lifting the wire earpieces over each fleshy ear.

"So we will make then a crown for him?"

"That depends. The crown is what I came here to find out about."

"What do you wish to find out?"

"I'll be frank with you." The teacher blew his nose and slowly wiped it. "My cast of mind is naturally empiric and objective—you might say non-mystical. I'm suspicious of faith healing, but I've come here, frankly, because I want to do anything possible to help my father recover his former health. To put it otherwise, I don't want anything to go untried."

"You love your father?" the rabbi clucked, a glaze of sentiment veiling his eyes.

"What I feel is obvious. My real concern right now mainly is how does the crown work. Could you be explicit about the mechanism of it all? Who wears it, for instance? Does he? Do you? Or do I have to? In other words, how does it function? And if you wouldn't mind saying, what's the principle, or rationale, behind it?

This is terra incognita for me, but I think I might be willing to take a chance if I could justify it to myself. Could I see a sample of the crown, for instance, if you have one on hand?"

The rabbi, with an absentminded start, seemed to interrupt himself about to pick his nose.

"What is the crown?" he asked, at first haughtily, then again, gently. "It's a crown, nothing else. There are crowns in Mishna, Proverbs, Kabbalah; the holy scrolls of the Torah are often protected by crowns. But this one is different, this you will understand when it does the work. It's a miracle. A sample doesn't exist. The crown has to be made individual for your father. Then his health will be restored. There are two prices—"

"Kindly explain what's supposed to cure the sickness," Albert said. "Does it work like sympathetic magic? I'm not nay-saying, you understand. I just happen to be interested in all kinds of phenomena. Is the crown supposed to draw off the illness like some kind of poultice, or what?"

"The crown is not a medicine, it is the health of your father. We offer the crown to God and God returns to your father his health. But first we got to make it the way it must be made—this I will do with my assistant, a retired jeweler. He has helped me to make a thousand crowns. Believe me, he knows silver—the right amount to the ounce according to the size you wish. Then I will say the blessings. Without the right blessings, exact to each word, the crown don't work. I don't have to tell you why. When the crown is finished your father will get better. This I will guarantee you. Let me read you some words from the mystic book."

"The Kabbalah?" the teacher asked respectfully.

"Like the Kabbalah."

The rabbi rose, went to his armchair, got slowly down on his hands and knees and withdrew the book he had shoved under the misshapen chair, a thick small volume with faded purple covers, not a word imprinted on it. The rabbi kissed the book and murmured a prayer.

"I hid it for a minute," he explained, "when you came in the room. It's a terrible thing nowadays, goyim come in your house in the middle of the day and take away that which belongs to you, if not your life itself."

"I told you right away that your daughter had let me in," Albert said in embarrassment.

"Once you mentioned I knew."

The teacher then asked, "Suppose I am a non-believer? Will the crown work if it's ordered by a person who has his doubts?"

"Doubts we all got. We doubt God and God doubts us. This is natural on account of the nature of existence. Of this kind doubts I am not afraid so long as you love your father."

"You're putting it as sort of a paradox."

"So what's so bad about a paradox?"

"My father wasn't the easiest man in the world to get along with, and neither am I for that matter, but he has been generous to me and I'd like to repay him in some way."

"God respects a grateful son. If you love your father this will go in the crown and help him to recover his health. Do you understand Hebrew?"

"Unfortunately not."

The rabbi flipped a few pages of his thick tome, peered at one closely and read aloud in Hebrew, which he then translated into English. " 'The crown is the fruit of God's grace. His grace is love of creation.' These words I will read seven times over the silver crown. This is the most important blessing."

"Fine. But what about those two prices you quoted me a minute ago?"

"This depends how quick you wish the cure."

"I want the cure to be immediate, otherwise there's no sense to the whole deal," Albert said, controlling anger. "If you're questioning my sincerity, I've already told you I'm considering this recourse even though it goes against the grain of some of my strongest convictions. I've gone out of my way to make my pros and cons absolutely clear."

"Who says no?"

The teacher became aware of Rifkele standing at the door, eating a slice of bread with lumps of butter on it. She beheld him in mild stupefaction, as though seeing him for the first time.

"Shpeter, Rifkele," the rabbi said patiently.

The girl shoved the bread into her mouth and ran ponderously down the passageway.

"Anyway, what about those two prices?" Albert asked, annoyed by the interruption. Every time Rifkele appeared his doubts of the enterprise rose before him like warriors with spears.

"We got two kinds crowns," said the rabbi. "One is for 401 and the other is 986."

"Dollars, you mean, for God's sake?—that's fantastic."

"The crown is pure silver. The client pays in silver dollars. So the silver dollars we melt—more for the large-size crown, less for the medium."

"What about the small?"

"There is no small. What good is a small crown?"

"I wouldn't know, but the assumption seems to be the bigger the better. Tell me, please, what can a 986 crown do that a 401 can't? Does the patient get better faster with the larger one? It hastens the reaction?"

The rabbi, five fingers hidden in his limp beard, assented.

"Are there any other costs?"

"Costs?"

"Over and above the quoted prices?"

"The price is the price, there is no extra. The price is for the silver and for the work and for the blessings."

"Now would you kindly tell me, assuming I decide to get involved in this deal, where I am supposed to lay my hands on 401 silver dollars? Or if I should opt for the 986 job, where can I get a pile of cartwheels of that amount? I don't suppose that any bank in the whole Bronx would keep that many silver dollars on hand nowadays. The Bronx is no longer the Wild West, Rabbi Lifschitz. But what's more to the point, isn't it true the mint isn't making silver dollars all silver any more?"

"So if they are not making we will get wholesale. If you will leave with me the cash, I will order the silver from a wholesaler, and we will save you the trouble to go to the bank. It will be the same amount of silver, only in small bars, I will weigh them on a scale in front of your eyes."

"One other question. Would you take my personal check in payment? I could give it to you right away once I've made my final decision."

"I wish I could, Mr. Gans," said the rabbi, his veined hand still nervously exploring his beard, "but it's better cash when the patient is so sick, so I can start to work right away. A check sometimes comes back, or gets lost in the bank, and this interferes with the crown."

Albert did not ask how, suspecting that a bounced check, or a lost one, wasn't the problem. No doubt some customers for crowns had stopped their checks on afterthought.

As the teacher reflected concerning his next move—should he, shouldn't he?—weighing a rational thought against a sentimental, the old rabbi sat in his chair, reading quickly in his small mystic book, his lips hastening along silently.

Albert at last got up.

"I'll decide the question once and for all night. If I go ahead and commit myself on the crown I'll bring you the cash after work tomorrow."

"Go in good health," said the rabbi. Removing his glasses he wiped both eyes with his handkerchief.

Wet or dry? thought the teacher.

As he let himself out of the downstairs door, more inclined than not toward trying the crown, he felt relieved, almost euphoric.

But by the next morning, after a difficult night, Albert's mood had about-faced. He fought gloom, irritation, felt flashes of hot and cold anger. It's throwing money away, pure and simple. I'm dealing with a clever confidence man, that's plain to me, but for some reason I am not resisting strongly. Maybe my subconscious is telling me to go along with a blowing wind and have the crown made. After that we'll see what happens—whether it rains, snows, or spring comes. Not much will happen, I suppose, but whatever does, my conscience will be in the clear.

But when he visited Rabbi Lifschitz that afternoon in the same roomful of empty chairs, though the teacher carried the required cash in his wallet, he was still uncomfortable about parting with it.

"Where do the crowns go after they are used and the patient recovers his health?" he cleverly asked the rabbi.

"I'm glad you asked me this question," said the rabbi alertly, his thick lid drooping. "They are melted, and the silver we give to the poor. A mitzvah for one makes a mitzvah for another."

"To the poor you say?"

"There are plenty poor people, Mr. Gans. Sometimes they need a crown for a sick wife or a sick child. Where will they get the silver?"

"I see what you mean—recycled, sort of, but can't a crown be reused as it is? I mean, do you permit a period of time to go by before you melt them down? Suppose a dying man who recovers gets seriously ill again at a future date?"

"For a new sickness you will need a new crown. Tomorrow the world is not the same as today, though God listens with the same ear."

"Look, Rabbi Lifschitz," Albert said impatiently, "I'll tell you frankly that I am inching toward ordering the crown, but it would make my decision a whole lot easier all around if you would let me have a quick look at one of them—it wouldn't have to be for more than five seconds—at a crown-in-progress for some other client."

"What will you see in five seconds?"

"Enough—whether the object is believable, worth the fuss and not inconsequential investment."

"Mr. Gans," replied the rabbi, "this is not a showcase business. You are not buying from me a new Chevrolet automobile. Your father lays now dying in the hospital. Do you love him? Do you wish me to make a crown that will cure him?"

The teacher's anger flared. "Don't be stupid, rabbi, I've answered that. Please don't sidetrack the real issue. You're working on my guilt so I'll suspend my perfectly reasonable doubts of the whole freaking enterprise. I won't fall for that."

They glared at each other. The rabbi's beard quivered. Albert ground his teeth.

Rifkele, in a nearby room, moaned.

The rabbi, breathing emotionally, after a moment relented.

"I will show you the crown," he sighed.

"Accept my apologies for losing my temper."

The rabbi accepted. "Now tell me please what kind of sickness your father has got."

"Ah," said Albert, "nobody is certain for sure. One day he got into bed, turned to the wall and said, 'I'm sick.' They suspected leukemia at first but the lab tests didn't confirm it."

"You talked to the doctors?"

"In droves. Till I was blue in the face. A bunch of ignoramuses," said the teacher hoarsely. "Anyway, nobody knows exactly what he has wrong with him. The theories include rare blood diseases, also a possible carcinoma of certain endocrine glands. You name it, I've heard it, with complications suggested, like Parkinson's or Addison's disease, multiple sclerosis, or something similar, alone or in combination with other sicknesses. It's a mysterious case, all in all."

"This means you will need a special crown," said the rabbi.

The teacher bridled. "What do you mean special? What will it cost?"

"The cost will be the same," the rabbi answered dryly, "but the design and the kind of blessings will be different. When you are dealing with such a mystery you got to make another one but it must be bigger."

"How would that work?"

"Like two winds that they meet in the sky. A white and a blue. The blue says, 'Not only I am blue but inside I am also purple and orange.' So the white goes away."

"If you can work it up for the same price, that's up to you."

Rabbi Lifschitz then drew down the two green window shades and shut the door, darkening the room.

"Sit," he said in the heavy dark, "I will show you the crown."

"I'm sitting."

"So sit where you are, but turn your head to the wall where is the mirror."

"But why so dark?"

"You will see light."

He heard the rabbi strike a match and it flared momentarily, casting shadows of candles and chairs amid the empty chairs in the room.

"Look now in the mirror."

"I'm looking."

"What do you see?"

"Nothing."

"Look with your eyes."

A silver candelabrum, first with three, then five, then seven burning bony candlesticks, appeared like ghostly hands with flaming fingertips in the oval mirror. The heat of it hit Albert in the face and for a moment he was stunned.

But recalling the games of his childhood, he thought, who's kidding who? It's one of those illusion things I remember from when I was a kid. In that case I'm getting the hell out of here. I can stand maybe mystery but not magic tricks or dealing with a rabbinical magician.

The candelabrum had vanished, although not its light, and he now saw the rabbi's somber face in the glass, his gaze addressing him. Albert glanced quickly around to see if anyone was standing at his shoulder, but nobody was. Where the rabbi was hiding at the moment the teacher did not know; but in the lit glass appeared his old man's lined and shrunken face, his sad eyes, compelling, inquisitive, weary, perhaps even frightened, as though they had seen more than they had cared to but were still looking.

What's this, slides or home movies? Albert sought some source of projection but saw no ray of light from wall or ceiling, nor object or image that might be reflected by the mirror.

The rabbi's eyes glowed like sun-filled clouds. A moon rose in the blue sky. The teacher dared not move, afraid to discover he was unable to. He then beheld a shining crown on the rabbi's head.

It had appeared at first like a braided mother-of-pearl turban, then had luminously become—like an intricate star in the night sky—a silver crown, constructed of bars, triangles, half-moons and crescents, spires, turrets, trees, points of spears; as though a wild storm had swept them up from the earth and flung them together in its vortex, twisted into a single glowing interlocked sculpture, a forest of disparate objects.

The sight in the ghostly mirror, a crown of rare beauty—very impressive, Albert thought—lasted no longer than five short seconds, then the reflecting glass by degrees turned dark and empty.

The shades were up. The single bulb in a frosted lily fixture on the ceiling shone harshly in the room. It was night.

The old rabbi sat, exhausted, on the broken sofa.

"So you saw it?"

"I saw something."

"You believe what you saw—the crown?"

"I believe I saw. Anyway, I'll take it."

The rabbi gazed at him blankly.

"I mean I agree to have the crown made," Albert said, having to clear his throat.

"Which size?"

"Which size was the one I saw?"

"Both sizes. This is the same design for both sizes, but there is more silver and also more blessings for the $986 size."

"But didn't you say that the design for my father's crown, because of the special nature of his illness, would have a different style, plus some special blessings?"

The rabbi nodded. "This comes also in two sizes—the $401 and $986."

The teacher hesitated a split second. "Make it the big one," he said decisively.

He had his wallet in his hand and counted out fifteen new bills—nine one hundreds, four twenties, a five, and a single—adding to $986.

Putting on his glasses, the rabbi hastily counted the money, snapping with thumb and forefinger each crisp bill as though to be sure none had stuck together. He folded the stiff paper and thrust the wad into his pants pocket.

"Could I have a receipt?"

"I would like to give you a receipt," said Rabbi Lifschitz earnestly, "but for the crowns there are no receipts. Some things are not a business."

"If money is exchanged, why not?"

"God will not allow. My father did not give receipts and also my grandfather."

"How can I prove I paid you if something goes wrong?"

"You have my word, nothing will go wrong."

"Yes, but suppose something unforeseen did," Albert insisted, "would you return the cash?"

"Here is your cash," said the rabbi, handing the teacher the packet of folded bills.

"Never mind," said Albert hastily. "Could you tell me when the crown will be ready?"

"Tomorrow night before Shabbes, the latest."

"So soon?"

"Your father is dying."

"That's right, but the crown looks like a pretty intricate piece of work to put together out of all those odd pieces."

"We will hurry."

"I wouldn't want you to rush the job in any way that would— let's say—prejudice the potency of the crown, or for that matter, in any way impair the quality of it as I saw it in the mirror—or however I saw it."

Down came the rabbi's eyelid, quickly raised without a sign of self-consciousness. "Mr. Gans, all my crowns are first-class jobs. About this you got nothing to worry about."

They then shook hands. Albert, still assailed by doubts, stepped into the corridor. He felt he did not, in essence, trust the rabbi; and suspected that Rabbi Lifschitz knew it and did not, in essence, trust him.

Rifkele, panting like a cow for a bull, let him out the front door, perfectly.

In the subway, Albert figured he would call it an investment in experience and see what came of it. Education costs money, but how else can you get it? He pictured the crown, as he had seen it, established on the rabbi's head, and then seemed to remember that as he had stared at the man's shifty face in the mirror the thickened lid of his right eye had slowly dropped into a full wink. Did he recall this in truth, or was he seeing in his mind's eye and transposing into the past something that had happened just before he left the house? What does he mean by his wink?—not only is he a fake but he kids you? Uneasy once more, the teacher clearly remembered, when he was staring into the rabbi's fish eyes in the glass, after which they had lit in visionary light, that he had fought a hunger to sleep; and the next thing there's the sight of the old boy, as though on the television screen, wearing this high-hat magic crown.

Albert, rising, cried, "Hypnosis! The bastard magician hypnotized me! He never did produce a silver crown, it's out of my imagination—I've been suckered!"

He was outraged by the knavery, hypocrisy, fat nerve of Rabbi Jonas Lifschitz. The concept of a curative crown, if he had ever for a moment believed in it, crumbled in his brain and all he could think of were 986 blackbirds flying in the sky. As three curious passengers watched, Albert bolted out of the car at the next stop, rushed up the stairs, hurried across the street, then cooled his impatient heels for twenty-two minutes till the next train clattered into the station, and he rode back to the stop near the rabbi's house. Though he banged with both fists on the door, kicked at it, "rang" the useless bell until his thumb was blistered, the boxlike wooden house, including dilapidated synagogue store, was dark, monumentally starkly still, like a gigantic, slightly tilted tombstone in a vast graveyard; and in the end unable to arouse a soul, the teacher, long past midnight, had to head home.

He awoke next morning cursing the rabbi and his own stupidity for having got involved with a faith healer. This is what happens when a man—even for a minute—surrenders his true beliefs. There are less punishing ways to help the dying. Albert considered calling the cops but had no receipt and did not want to appear that much a fool. He was tempted, for the first time in six years of teaching, to phone in sick; then take a cab to the rabbi's house and demand the return of his cash. The thought agitated him. On the other hand, suppose Rabbi Lifschitz was seriously at work assembling the crown with his helper; on which, let's say, after he had bought the silver and paid the retired jeweler for his work, he made, let's say, a hundred bucks clear profit—not so very much; and there really *was* a silver crown, and the rabbi sincerely and religiously believed it would reverse the course of his father's illness? Although nervously disturbed by his suspicions, Albert felt he had better not get the police into the act too soon, because the crown wasn't promised—didn't the old gent say—until before the Sabbath, which gave him till sunset tonight.

If he produces the thing by then, I have no case against him even if it's a piece of junk. So I better wait. But what a dope I was to order the $986 job instead of the $401. On that decision alone I lost $585.

After a distracted day's work Albert taxied to the rabbi's house and tried to rouse him, even hallooing at the blank windows facing the street; but either nobody was home or they were both hiding, the rabbi under the broken sofa, Rifkele trying to shove her bulk under a bathtub. Albert decided to wait them out. Soon the old boy would have to leave the house to step into the shul on Friday night. He would speak to him, warn him to come clean. But the sun set; dusk settled on the earth; and though the autumn stars and a sliver of moon gleamed in the sky, the house was dark, shades drawn; and no Rabbi Lifschitz emerged. Lights had gone on in the little shul, candles were lit. It occurred to Albert, with chagrin, that the rabbi might be already worshipping; he might all this time have been in the synagogue.

The teacher entered the long, brightly lit store. On yellow folding chairs scattered around the room sat a dozen men holding worn prayer books, praying. The Rabbi A. Marcus, a middle-aged man with a high voice and a short reddish beard, was dovening at the Ark, his back to the congregation.

As Albert entered and embarrassedly searched from face to face, the congregants stared at him. The old rabbi was not among them. Disappointed, the teacher withdrew.

A man sitting by the door touched his sleeve.

"Stay awhile and read with us."

"Excuse me, I'd like to but I'm looking for a friend."

"Look," said the man, "maybe you'll find him."

Albert waited across the street under a chestnut tree losing its leaves. He waited patiently—till tomorrow if he had to.

Shortly after nine the lights went out in the synagogue and the last of the worshippers left for home. The red-bearded rabbi then emerged with his key in his hand to lock the store door.

"Excuse me, rabbi," said Albert, approaching. "Are you acquainted with Rabbi Jonas Lifschitz, who lives upstairs with his daughter Rifkele—if she is his daughter?"

"He used to come here," said the rabbi with a small smile, "but since he retired he prefers a big synagogue on Mosholu Parkway, a palace."

"Will he be home soon, do you think?"

"Maybe in an hour. It's Shabbat, he must walk."

"Do you—ah—happen to know anything about his work on silver crowns?"

"What kind of silver crowns?"

"To assist the sick, the dying?"

"No," said the rabbi, locking the shul door, pocketing the key, and hurrying away.

The teacher, eating his heart, waited under the chestnut tree till past midnight, all the while urging himself to give up and go home, but unable to unstick the glue of his frustration and rage. Then shortly before 1 A.M. he saw some shadows moving and two people drifting up the shadow-encrusted street. One was the old rabbi, in a new caftan and snappy black Homburg, walking tiredly. Rifkele, in sexy yellow mini, exposing to above the big-bone knees her legs like poles, walked lightly behind him, stopping to strike her ears with her hands. A long white shawl, pulled short on the right shoulder, hung down to her left shoe.

"On my income their glad rags."

Rifkele chanted a long "Boooo" and slapped both ears with her pudgy hands to keep from hearing it.

They toiled up the ill-lit narrow staircase, the teacher trailing them.

"I came to see my crown," he told the pale, astonished rabbi, in the front room.

"The crown," the rabbi said haughtily, "is already finished. Go home and wait, your father will soon get better."

"I called the hospital before leaving my apartment, there's been no improvement."

"How can you expect so soon improvement if the doctors themselves don't know what is the sickness? You must give the crown
a little more time. God Himself has trouble to understand human
sickness."

"I came to see the thing I paid for."

"I showed you already, you saw before you ordered."

"That was an image of a facsimile, maybe, or something of the
sort. I insist on seeing the real thing, for which I paid close to one
thousand smackers."

"Listen, Mr. Gans," said the rabbi patiently, "there are some
things we are allowed to see which He lets us see them. Sometimes
I wish He didn't let us. There are other things we are not allowed
to see—Moses knew this—and one is God's face, and another is the
real crown that He makes and blesses it. A miracle is a miracle, this
is God's business."

"Don't you see it?"

"Not with my eyes."

"I don't believe a word of it, you faker, two-bit magician."

"The crown is a real crown. If you think there is magic, it is on
account those people that they insist to see it—we try to give them
an idea. For those who believe, there is no magic."

"Rifkele," the rabbi said hurriedly, "bring to Papa my book of
letters."

She left the room, after a while, a little in fright, her eyes evasive;
and returned in ten minutes, after flushing the toilet, in a shapeless
long flannel nightgown, carrying a large yellowed notebook whose
loose pages were thickly interleaved with old correspondence.

"Testimonials," said the rabbi.

Turning several loose pages, with trembling hand he extracted a
letter and read it aloud, his voice husky with emotion.

" 'Dear Rabbi Lifschitz: Since the miraculous recovery of my
mother, Mrs. Max Cohen, from her recent illness, my impulse is
to cover your bare feet with kisses. Your crown worked wonders
and I am recommending it to all my friends. Yours truly and
sincerely, (Mrs.) Esther Polatnik.'

"This is a college teacher."

He read another. " 'Dear Rabbi Lifschitz, Your $986 crown

totally and completely cured my father of cancer of the pancreas, with serious complications of the lungs, after nothing else had worked. Never before have I believed in miraculous occurrences, but from now on I will have less doubts. My thanks to you and God. Most sincerely, Daniel Schwartz.'

"A lawyer," said the rabbi.

He offered the book to Albert. "Look yourself, Mr. Gans, hundreds of letters."

Albert wouldn't touch it.

"There's only one thing I want to look at, Rabbi Lifschitz, and it's not a book of useless testimonials. I want to see my father's silver crown."

"This is impossible. I already explained to you why I can't do this. God's word is God's law."

"So if it's the law you're citing, either I see the crown in the next five minutes, or the first thing tomorrow morning I'm reporting you and your activities to the Bronx County District Attorney."

"Boooo-ooo," sang Rifkele, banging her ears.

"Shut up!" Albert said.

"Have respect," cried the rabbi. "Grubber yung!"

"I will swear out a complaint and the D.A. will shut you down, the whole freaking plant, if you don't at once return the $986 you swindled me out of."

The rabbi wavered in his tracks. "Is this the way to talk to a rabbi of God?"

"A thief is a thief."

Rifkele blubbered, squealed.

"Sha," the rabbi thickly whispered to Albert, clasping and unclasping his gray hands. "You'll frighten the neighbors. Listen to me, Mr. Gans, you saw with your eyes what it looks like the real crown. I give you my word that nobody of my whole clientele ever saw this before. I showed you for your father's sake so you would tell me to make the crown which will save him. Don't spoil now the miracle."

"Miracle," Albert bellowed, "it's a freaking fake magic, with an idiot girl for a come-on and hypnotic mirrors. I was mesmerized, suckered by you."

"Be kind," begged the rabbi, tottering as he wandered amid empty chairs. "Be merciful to an old man. Think of my poor child. Think of your father who loves you."

"He hates me, the son of a bitch, I hope he croaks."

In an explosion of silence the girl slobbered in fright.

"Aha," cried the wild-eyed rabbi, pointing a finger at God in heaven. "Murderer," he cried, aghast.

Moaning, father and daughter rushed into each other's arms, as Albert, wearing a massive, spike-laden headache, rushed down the booming stairs.

An hour later the elder Gans shut his eyes and expired.

DAPHNE MERKIN

Enchantment

I am reading aloud to my mother from Shakespeare's sonnets, trying to find one that would be appropriate to recite at her funeral.

My mother is not dying. She is a relatively robust woman, and looks younger than her sixty-three years, but she speaks of her death often and with a macabre glee. "When I am gone," she says, "I would like you to say of me that she never made mountains out of molehills." I am not sure why my mother considers this epitaph to be the highest form of tribute, and I cannot imagine that any of the mourners at her grave will understand it any better. But I know it is important to her, a link with the hearty, hiking-shoes atmosphere of her youth. "Fine," I say. Her implication, I suppose, is that all her children, finespun creatures, do just the opposite.

My mother and I are sitting on the bed in what I still think of as my room. I first shared it with two sisters, and it finally became my own during college. The room is adjacent to my mother's, and partly because of this I have had the greatest trouble leaving home. Whenever I had one of the fierce fights with her that have been a constant of our relationship ever since I can remember, I used to stand in front of her locked door and imagine my mother deep inside her bathroom, swallowing pills or reacting to my rancor by taking flight out of a window. "My mother is dead," I would think, composing the sentence formally in my head as though I were a character in a play. I saw myself freed and bereft at the same time, a figure of surpassing interest: *Who is that girl in black? I hear her mother died. So young? What a tragedy! I wonder how the children feel. They say it hit that one the hardest.* I would be watching myself being watched by others, wondering along with them what I was thinking. My imagination has always run to the vivid, although my mother is not the sort of woman to embrace personal drama. Sooner or later she always emerged from her bedroom, dry-eyed and stony.

The bed is narrow, penitential—as are all the beds my mother favors for her household. The wall I lean my back against is faintly, pleasantly cold. I note the undertow of gray that sweeps through my mother's vigilantly colored hair, and the loosened skin on her neck, beneath her strong jaw. Nothing—not these or other signs— convinces me of her mortality. The bed is tightly made up, with crisp white sheets and a slightly worn wool blanket. I was reminded of my bed in an instant when I read the description of Clarissa Dalloway's: It is the unyielding bed of someone who was meant to remain a virgin.

Now, in my own apartment, I have a double bed covered with delicately flowered sheets. Taking a great wanton leap forward, I originally ordered an even larger, queen-size bed, but when it arrived and was shoved against the wall by two surly deliverymen I immediately knew I was not up to it. I slept on top of the unwrapped mattress and box spring for a night; then I called up Bloomingdale's and told them I had made a terrible mistake, my bedroom was too small, would they please exchange the order?

Both the size of my bed and the style of linen were deliberate moves away from my mother's taste, and she sniffs at them with the same disapproval she shows toward the knickknacks that clutter my window shelves and coffee table. These knickknacks—a random assortment of pottery, small painted boxes, and the sort of oversize candles that are most often found in college-dorm rooms—are always dusty; one ceramic bowl is filled with honey drops that are so ancient and sticky they cannot be separated from one another. I apologize for these candies, making a joke of them whenever a visitor tries to dislodge one, but I have not removed them.

Over the years I have lost most of the things that have been important to me. I have a recurring dream in which all of these objects turn up again in a neat little pile: a leather-bound notebook, several watches, a stubby fountain pen with which I wrote a script full of flourishes, slips of paper on which I have scribbled crucial thoughts, a brown-and-white cashmere scarf that made me think of myself, briefly, as the mistress of an English country house. Because of, or in spite of, my tendency to lose things, I am the most intractable of hoarders. Every apartment I have lived in has become filled with magazines and slightly faulty appliances. It is a real effort of will for me to throw even used-up items out. I check the bottoms of cereal boxes for malingering flakes and dribble out the reluctant drops in milk cartons. I watch myself at these routines and recognize that they are important to me, a way of stopping up gaps. There is one tube of toothpaste that has been lying in my various medicine cabinets, untouched, for several years. The tube is cracked with age, and recently, when a friend volunteered to test it, the toothpaste squeezed out in a dried gob. "Throw it out," she said, not unreasonably.

"I might need it," I explained. "It could come in handy as a spare."

"Throw it out," she said.

I did not want her to think of me as visibly eccentric, so I threw it out. Later, after she left, I retrieved the tube from the wastebasket, and it now rests safely again on a shelf.

———

In the living room a clock chimes. "Hannah, have you done something to your hair?" my mother asks. "You look younger." My
mother watches me for signs of bloom and decay, like a plant.

"Do I?" I say, and for a moment I feel as if our roles have been
reversed—that I am old and in need of reassurance about my faded
allure. "Let me see," I say, flipping through the pages of my fat
college anthology, and begin reading a sonnet about cruelty. My
mother stares out over my head, her eyes fixed. Her eyes are a
deep-set gray-green, quite beautiful, and I sometimes pass along
compliments other people have made about them. She receives
such praise with a touching display of shyness.

" 'Be wise as thou art cruel,' " I declaim; " 'Do not press / My
tongue-tied patience with too much disdain.' " I listen to my own
voice as I read, trying to infuse it with the ripeness that I think
Shakespeare would have liked.

My mother's affection has always been unreliable, subject to
whim. One day, she sees fit to tell me that I shouldn't waste so
much money on movies. "If you do everything now," she says,
"what pleasures will be left to you when you are fifty?" The force
of her illogicality holds me, even though I know there aren't a
limited number of movies—of pleasures—in the world to use up
and after that you are left twiddling your thumbs. Then, several
days afterward, I call her late at night, in a sudden panic about my
life. "I can't anymore," I say rather desperately, although there has
been nothing terrible—no acute disappointment, no rift—to bring
on this despair. "I can't go on," I repeat. "I don't see the point. I
just want to do nothing. I want to lie on my bed for days. I can't
always be trying to accomplish something. I *could* lie on my bed,
couldn't I?"

My mother listens, or at least appears to, and this alone begins
to soothe me: I want—have always wanted—her to listen to me
forever. "It'll all be all right, Hannah," she says. "You'll see."

"And," I add out of the blue, as if this were the real sorrow, "I
never have any clothes! I'm sick of having nothing to wear!"

"Don't worry," my mother says. "I will buy you everything."

Her answer imprints itself on my mind in capital letters: "I WILL
BUY YOU EVERYTHING." The grandeur of it—the complete maternal-

ness—silences me. I want this moment to last. Never mind that it
is entirely false, that this is being said to me by the same woman
who is capable of reminding me that I owe her the five dollars she
lent me for a taxi weeks ago. Does she know what she's saying? And
how can she say such a protective thing and a day or two later, sure
enough, announce, "The trouble with you is that you're spoiled.
You think too much about yourself. If you had to sell in Wool-
worth's all day, you'd be better off." As a child, I interpreted such
vacillations as cruelty (anything else would have required an insup-
portable detachment), and to this day I tend to care most deeply
about people who can take or leave me. Such people, I've convinced myself, can be counted on in some way that precludes trust:
they will never love you or stop loving you for yourself alone.

"*That's* it," my mother says, amused by my last selection. I go
on reading, but pretty soon the poem meanders into universalisms
and no longer applies to the specific darkness in her. I skim through
a few others, trying to find one that will capture her fickle attention.
"Here's one on the tyrant Time," I announce with pedantic fervor,
and my mother is willing to listen, herself a great believer in the
power of passing hours. When I am done she says, "He was a
genius, wasn't he." Jealous of Shakespeare's momentary glory, I
explain that the phrase "the expense of spirit in a waste of shame"
refers to sexual intercourse. "I *knew* that," she says proudly, not
one to be outwitted.

In one of my bookcases is a Lucite-framed photograph of my
maternal grandfather, an Orthodox Jew, who was reading Thomas
Mann's latest novel shortly before he died, in Jerusalem. His is the
only photograph I have set out, and it is not entirely clear to me
why I have chosen him from among my many relatives. People
mistake his likeness for that of Sigmund Freud, who was a different
sort altogether. But there is a definite resemblance, in the details,
if not in the whole: the same neatly trimmed beard, narrow face,
intelligent eyes behind round wire spectacles. The fact of my grandfather's reading a secular book rather than a religious one had to be
kept a secret from some of his less broadminded friends in the

circle he belonged to. He was reputed to be a man to whom religious belief did not come easily. I suppose he is to be admired for
having adhered to the laws in spite of this, and sometimes I wonder
if the force of my grandfather's will lingers in me, and if I stray from
it unnaturally.

My mother says that people of the same generation tend to look
like each other, but I think she is pleased by her father's resemblance to Freud. She used to quote sardonic remarks she remembers her father making, but she has stopped of late, as though she
suddenly wondered at the implications.

My friends, especially the ones I retain from years back, always ask
about my mother if we haven't been in touch for a while. I could
be an astronaut now, a wielder of influence, and still they ask,
several minutes into long-distance covnersations, "How are things
with you and your mother?"

When I was much younger I would leave my mother in undrastic
ways—for weekend stays at the homes of friends and cousins. In
my family I was considered a great socialite because of these visits;
my siblings rarely ventured out. I would invariably fall in love with
the homes and mothers I was visiting, whatever form they took.
What was important was that they weren't *mine*: I could start all
over again in a living room in Queens with a mother who served
fish croquettes on glazed blue plates.

One weekend stood out in my mind for a long time as being
especially charmed. I was staying at the small and rather crowded
apartment of some cousins. The girl, who was my age, didn't like
her own mother very much, and there was, in fact, something
irascible about this woman's attitude toward her children which
wasn't that different from my mother's toward hers. Later on, I
would learn that "moodiness," as it was called, ran in my mother's
family. But then I saw only my cousin's advantages: her brothers
were far gentler than mine, and there were no sisters to contend
with. On Saturday night, after the father made the blessing over the
plaited *havdalah* candle, signifying that Shabbes was over (all the
families I visited were Orthodox ones, like mine), he drove us to an

Alexander's in a shopping center not far from their house. This was
the sort of bland excursion my family never made, and it filled me
with delight. I wandered through aisles filled with racks of clothing,
staring at ordinary skirts and blouses as though I were seeing such
things for the first time. I watched other families shopping on the
brightly lit floor around me. "How do you like that, Daddy?" said
one plump blond mother, holding up a brown suit. Something
about her tone—or it may have been her windswept look—drew
me, and I stood, staring, as her three children gathered around to
study the effect of the suit propped against their father, the most
nice-seeming of men. I tried to picture my mother calling my father
"Daddy" or our family going out as a unit to shop at a department
store. Soon after this episode—I imagine my aunt must have called
up my mother and triumphantly informed her of my desire to
come and live with them (my family was richer than most of our
relatives, and we were seen in grudgingly glamorized terms)—my
mother started referring to my "Orphan Annie act" whenever I
went away for the weekend.

"Wish them good Shabbes," she said one Friday afternoon,
standing in the front door in the usual way while I waited for the
elevator, suitcase in hand. The clamor rising from behind her—
Louisa, the maid, banging an oven shut in the kitchen, my brothers
yelping at each other upstairs—was already beginning to seem like
tender, lost music to me.

"Should I stay home?" I asked my mother tentatively.

"Don't be silly," my mother said, but I could tell she rather liked
my doubts. "You'll be back tomorrow night, Sunday morning
latest."

"Maybe I should just stay home," I said, offering my mother a
chance to declare her affection, claim me, pull me inside with
operatic attachment. Some of my friends had mothers who acted
that way, clinging to their offspring like vines. But my mother
wasn't cut from such stuff. She was German, not Eastern European,
and I had deduced from remarks made by the Polish and Hungarian
parents of my friends that *yekkes*, as people like my mother were
called, were a fatally cold bunch—aberrant, more German than
Jewish.

"Don't be silly," my mother repeated. "You're all packed." She leaned over to give me a kiss. Her muted-plaid robe smelled of perfume; I could never remember what it was called, because it was so unlikely—the name of an animal. "But do yourself a favor and don't play Orphan Annie there, O.K.? I know I'm a terrible mother, but no one else is interested."

I smiled, but I feared she was right. My longings would have to remain with me. It wasn't so much that they weren't recognized as that they seemed to be given mysteriously short shrift. The elevator cage groaned as it descended. While I chatted with Lucas, who worked the old-fashioned lever as if it were the tiller of a ship, it occurred to me once again—like a shadow I couldn't dodge—that I was stuck with what I had.

I suppose that for tenacious people like me the past is never really over: what you get left with is the tics of survival. I sit in a psychiatrist's office, where courtesy reigns, and begin my story once again. I can't separate out the feelings from the facts: My mother is the Wicked Witch, but she is also the object of desire. Someone—a nurse—once banged my head against a wall, and when I told my mother about it I remember noting, at an age when such perceptions feel less terrible than clear, that my mother's heart was not broken. But why, then, was I also made to feel special, my straight brown hair brushed by the same nurse into pigtails that were tied with bright ribbons? "Such shiny hair," my mother said. "It hangs like a curtain." My two sisters had more mediocre hair, and less attention was paid to grooming it. Years later, as soon as I could, I righted the balance: I began changing the color of my hair every six months or so to a brassy off-blond that was supposed to look, even in mid-December, as though it had got that way from the sun. And when the fashion for permanents presented itself I had the straightness of which my mother had been so proud stunned into frizzy little curls. My hair is no longer admirable, but no one recognizes me in photographs as the girl with pigtails anyway.

There are other photographs. I look at a photograph of myself as a child—a shiny, starting to yellow snapshot—and think, not for the first time, *It all started here.* I am a big-bellied three-year-old, my floppy hair not yet made a fuss of but hacked into bangs that stop, most oddly, in the middle of my forehead. I am wearing a pair of boy's striped swimming trunks and I am looking up at my mother, who is holding another baby. It is summer and I have probably just returned from a trip to the beach. My mother rarely went along; my father "needed" her at home. My father worked throughout the summer—weekends, too—except for Shabbes. On Sundays, he worked at his desk in the study, in a leather chair that creaked whenever he leaned back. At some point, I stopped thinking of this hardworking man, with his constant supply of glasses of tea, as my father; he was simply the man whom my mother, for reasons incomprehensible to me, had chosen to marry. It was easier that way.

My childhood clings to me like wet paint. It is summer and I stand in a train station, having missed the last train I can catch out to my parents' summer house before Friday evening turns into the pre-scribed inactivity of Shabbes. I call my mother from an open pay phone; anyone can eavesdrop and draw the wrong conclusions. I am crying—I am always missing trains and I have never liked the summer. It makes me melancholy, even though I tan for long hours in the sun. When I pictured my life as an adult, it never resembled this: I sit on the beach and watch other people's families, all the pails and shovels, and the husbands standing, talking to other husbands.

The handle of the phone is sticky and I am threatening to become a prostitute. "I will," I say, "you'll see," although I am a bit old to begin and am not sure how I'd go about it, in any case. I try to envision sexual encounters with a stream of strangers, and I cry even harder. "All these rules," I say to my mother, "they're killing me. There's nothing holy about them." Crowds of sweating people rush by me to trains whose departures they have clocked exactly into their schedules. Nearby, a tall black man in a large-brimmed hat smiles.

"Don't be an idiot," my mother says on the other end of the

receiver. "Nothing's so terrible. You'll come out after Shabbes."

My tears stop abruptly. "Don't be an idiot" has worked its caustic charm. I have become a person consoled by only the breeziest form of solace.

An older couple, of an experimental persuasion—types I have met only since stepping out of my family orbit—invite me to a chic beach for the day. A man walks toward us along the shore and my eyes drop to below his belly, where there is no bathing suit. Groups of women sit on towels, breasts sloping downward, pubic mounds glistening in the sun. I chat gaily with my hosts. I am as shocked as my grandfather would have been had he been dropped into the scene from out of his tree-lined Jerusalem street, where hats are still tipped in greeting by the polite and deeply nostalgic German Jews who live in the area. What surprises me is not the streak of inhibition that marks me but that I don't entirely wish to rid myself of it. I remain clothed. My bathing suit is streamlined, daring in its way, the color of champagne in a glass. I have spent some time choosing it. I stand with one hand on my hip, watching. My hosts are having an argument. "I don't like your tone," he says. "I don't like the way you sound." She is as silenced by this as though he had punched her in the jaw. My parents yell at each other in argument, and my father is not one to comment on so abstract a grievance as my mother's tone. I think of their German accents, lending a slightly martial quality to everything that is said, and of the many bathrooms in the apartment in which I grew up—the vigilance about odors and uncovered flesh. One of my brothers liked to stalk around in his underpants, which never failed to infuriate my mother—as though at any moment he would go mad and expose all. "Put a dressing gown on immediately!" she would say.

On the beach, close by, a little girl plays with the wristwatch on her father's bronzed arm, twanging the strap, laughing when he grimaces as though in pain. He is sprawled in a rickety little chair; they are both naked.

———

It is evening on a winter Sunday and I am being driven back to the city. I do not know the people in the car with me, but I assume their lives are preferable to mine. We pass emptied motel pools and I imagine the guests inside, preparing themselves for dinner. One of the two men in the car, the driver, is a lawyer. He steers with great precision, as though he were applying for the role of "Driver" in a movie. I have never learned how to drive. Everyone excuses this by saying, "Of course, you grew up in the city." When I was young, we were driven to school by Willy. He was my other grandfather's—my father's father's—chauffeur, and my sisters and I used to take turns asking him what he had eaten for dinner the night before. At eight-fifteen every weekday morning, Willy's dinner menu seemed more important than the school day ahead. I was fascinated by the glass of milk that concluded all his meals. My second-oldest sister, Rachel, used to copy the way Willy pronounced his "s"s: "A big peesh of apple pie and a tall glash of milk," she'd say grandly.

My mother has learned to drive late in life, so there is a chance for me. When I am a passenger in her car, I point out oncoming cars and stop signs. She does not pay close enough attention, although she is very skilled at last-minute maneuvers. While she concentrates on twists in the road I watch her profile—the faint freckling of her skin, the straight line of her mouth, which makes me think of a child's drawing. I know her face by heart. Sometimes I think nothing will break her spell.

LEONARD MICHAELS

Murderers

hen my uncle Moe dropped dead of a heart attack I became expert in the subway system. With a nickel I'd get to Queens, twist and zoom to Coney Island, twist again toward the George Washington Bridge—beyond which was darkness. I wanted proximity to darkness, strangeness. Who doesn't? The poor in spirit, the ignorant and frightened. My family came from Poland, then never went any place until they had heart attacks. The consummation of years in one neighborhood: a black Cadillac, corpse inside. We should have buried Uncle Moe where he shuffled away his life, in the kitchen or toilet, under the linoleum, near the coffee pot. Anyhow, they were dropping on Henry Street and Cherry Street. Blue lips. The previous winter it was cousin Charlie,

forty-five years old. Moe, Charlie, Sam, Adele—family meant a
punch in the chest, fire in the arm. I didn't want to wait for it. I
went to Harlem, the Polo Grounds, Far Rockaway, thousands of
miles on nickels, mainly underground. Tenements watched me go,
day after day, fingering nickels. One afternoon I stopped to grind
my heel against the curb. Melvin and Arnold Bloom appeared, then
Harold Cohen. Melvin said, "You step in dog shit?" Grinding was
my answer. Harold Cohen said, "The rabbi is home. I saw him on
Market Street. He was walking fast." Oily Arnold, eleven years
old, began to urge: "Let's go up to our roof." The decision waited
for me. I considered the roof, the view of industrial Brooklyn, the
Battery, ships in the river, bridges, towers, and the rabbi's apartment. "All right," I said. We didn't giggle or look to one another
for moral signals. We were running.

The blinds were up and curtains pulled, giving sunlight, wind,
birds to the rabbi's apartment—a magnificent metropolitan view.
The rabbi and his wife never took it, but in the light and air of
summer afternoons, in the eye of gull and pigeon, they were joyous. A bearded young man, and his young pink wife, sacramentally
bald. Beard and Baldy, with everything to see, looked at each other.
From a water tank on the opposite roof, higher than their windows,
we looked at them. In psycho-analysis this is "The Primal Scene."
To achieve the primal scene we crossed a ledge six inches wide. A
half-inch indentation in the brick gave us fingerholds. We dragged
bellies and groins against the brick face to a steel ladder. It went up
the side of the building, bolted into brick, and up the side of the
water tank to a slanted tin roof which caught the afternoon sun.
We sat on that roof like angels, shot through with light, derealized
in brilliance. Our sneakers sucked hot slanted metal. Palms and
fingers pressed to bone on nailheads.

The Brooklyn Navy Yard with destroyers and aircraft carriers,
the Statue of Liberty putting the sky to the torch, the dull remote
skyscrapers of Wall Street, and the Empire State Building were
among the wonders we dominated. Our view of the holy man and
his wife, on their living-room couch and floor, on the bed in their
bedroom, could not be improved. Unless we got closer. But fifty

feet across the air was right. We heard their phonograph and watched them dancing. We couldn't hear the gratifications or see pimples. We smelled nothing. We didn't want to touch.

For a while I watched them. Then I gazed beyond into shimmering nullity, gray, blue, and green murmuring over rooftops and towers. I had watched them before I could tantalize myself with this brief ocular perversion, the general cleansing nihil of a view. This was the beginning of philosophy. I indulged in ambience, in space like eons. So what if my uncle Moe was dead? I was philosophical and luxurious. I didn't even have to look at the rabbi and his wife. After all, how many times had we dissolved stickball games when the rabbi came home? How many times had we risked shameful discovery, scrambling up the ladder, exposed to their windows—if they looked. We risked life itself to achieve this eminence. I looked at the rabbi and his wife.

Today she was a blonde. Bald didn't mean no wigs. She had ten wigs, ten colors, fifty styles. She looked different, the same, and very good. A human theme in which nothing begat anything and was gorgeous. To me she was the world's lesson. Aryan yellow slipped through pins about her ears. An olive complexion mediated yellow hair and Arabic black eyes. Could one care what she really looked like? What was *really?* The minute you wondered, she looked like something else, in another wig, another style. Without the wigs she was a baldy-bean lady. Today she was a blonde. Not blonde. A blonde. The phonograph blared and her deep loops flowed Tommy Dorsey, Benny Goodman, and then the thing itself, Choo-Choo Lopez. Rumba! One, two-three. One, two-three. The rabbi stepped away to delight in blonde imagination. Twirling and individual, he stepped away snapping fingers, going high and light on his toes. A short bearded man, balls afling, cock shuddering like a springboard. Rumba! One, two-three. *Ole! Vaya,* Choo-Choo!

> *I was on my way to spend some time in Cuba.*
> *Stopped off at Miami Beach, la-la.*
> *Oh, what a rumba they teach, la-la.*
> *Way down in Miami Beach,*

> Oh, what a chroombah they teach, la-la.
> Way-down-in-Miami-Beach.

She, on the other hand, was somewhat reserved. A shift in one lush hip was total rumba. He was Mr. Life. She was dancing. He was a naked man. She was what she was in the garment of her soft, essential self. He was snapping, clapping, hopping to the beat. The beat lived in her visible music, her lovely self. Except for the wig. Also a watchband that desecrated her wrist. But it gave her a bit of the whorish. She never took it off.

Harold Cohen began a cocktail-mixer motion, masturbating with two fists. Seeing him at such hard futile work, braced only by sneakers, was terrifying. But I grinned. Out of terror, I twisted an encouraging face. Melvin Bloom kept one hand on the tin. The other knuckled the rumba numbers into the back of my head. Nodding like a defective, little Arnold Bloom chewed his lip and squealed as the rabbi and his wife smacked together. The rabbi clapped her buttocks, fingers buried in the cleft. They stood only on his legs. His back arched, knees bent, thighs thick with thrust, up, up, up. Her legs wrapped his hips, ankles crossed, hooked for constriction. "Oi, oi, oi," she cried, wig flashing left, right, tossing the Brooklyn Navy Yard, the Statue of Liberty, and the Empire State Building to hell. Arnold squealed oi, squealing rubber. His sneaker heels stabbed tin to stop his slide. Melvin said, "Idiot." Arnold's ring hooked a nailhead and the ring and ring finger remained. The hand, the arm, the rest of him, were gone.

We rumbled down the ladder. "Oi, oi, oi," she yelled. In a freak of ecstasy her eyes had rolled and caught us. The rabbi drilled to her quick and she had us. "OI, OI," she yelled above congas going clop, doom-doom, clop, doom-doom on the way to Cuba. The rabbi flew to the window, a red mouth opening in his beard: "Murderers." He couldn't know what he said. Melvin Bloom was crying. My fingers were tearing, bleeding into brick. Harold Cohen, like an adding machine, gibbered the name of God. We moved down the ledge quickly as we dared. Bongos went tocka-ti-tocka, tocka-ti-tocka. The rabbi screamed, "MELVIN BLOOM, PHILLIP

LIEBOWITZ, HAROLD COHEN, MELVIN BLOOM," as if our
names, screamed this way, naming us where we hung, smashed us
into brick.

Nothing was discussed.

The rabbi used his connections, arrangements were made. We
were sent to a camp in New Jersey. We hiked and played volleyball.
One day, apropos of nothing, Melvin came to me and said little
Arnold had been made of gold and he, Melvin, of shit. I appreciated the sentiment, but to my mind they were both made of
shit. Harold Cohen never again spoke to either of us. The counsel-
ors in the camp were World War II veterans, introspective men.
Some carried shrapnel in their bodies. One had a metal plate in his
head. Whatever you said to them they seemed to be thinking of
something else, even when they answered. But step out of line and
a plastic lanyard whistled burning notice across your ass.

At night, lying in the bunkhouse, I listened to owls. I'd never
before heard that sound, the sound of darkness, blooming, opening
inside you like a mouth.

CYNTHIA OZICK

Bloodshed

*B*leilip took a Greyhound bus out of New York and rode through icy scenes half-urban and half-countrified until he arrived at the town of the Hasidim. He had intended to walk, but his coat pockets were heavy, so he entered a loitering taxi. Though it was early on a Sunday afternoon he saw no children at all. Then he remembered that they would be in the yeshivas until the darker slant of the day. Yeshivas not yeshiva: small as the community was, it had three or four schools, and still others, separate, for the little girls. Toby and Yussel were waiting for him and waved his taxi down the lumpy road above their half-built house—it was a new town, and everything in it was new or promised: pavements, trash cans, septic tanks, newspaper stores. But just because everything was unfinished, you could sniff rawness, the opened earth meaty

and scratched up as if by big animal claws, the frozen puddles in the
basins of ditches fresh-smelling, mossy.

Toby he regarded as a convert. She was just barely a relative, a
third or fourth cousin, depending on how you counted, whether
from his mother or from his father, who were also cousins to each
other. She came from an ordinary family, not especially known for
its venturesomeness, but now she looked to him altogether uncommon, freakish: her bun was a hairpiece pinned on, over it she wore
a bandanna (a *tcheptichke*, she called it), her sleeves stopped below
her wrists, her dress was outlandishly long. With her large red face
over this costume she almost passed for some sort of peasant.
Though still self-reliant, she had become like all their women.

She served him orange juice. Bleilip, feeling his bare bald head,
wondered whether he was expected to say the blessing, whether
they would thrust a headcovering on him: he was baffled, confused,
but Yussel said, "You live your life and I'll live mine, do what you
like," so he drank it all down quickly. Relief made him thirsty, and
he drank more and more from a big can with pictures of sweating
oranges on it—some things they bought at a supermarket like all
mortals.

"So," he said to Toby, "how do you like your *shtetl?*"

She laughed and circled a finger around at the new refrigerator,
vast-shouldered, gleaming, a presence. "What a village we are! A
backwater!"

"State of mind," he said, "that's what I meant."

"Oh, state of mind. What's that?"

"Everything here feels different," was all he could say.

"We're in pieces, that's why. When the back rooms are put
together we'll seem more like a regular house."

"The carpenter," Yussel said, "works only six months a year—
we got started with him a month before he stopped. So we have to
wait."

"What does he do the rest of the year?"

"He teaches."

"He teaches?"

"He trades with Shmulka Gershons. The other half of the year

Shmulka Gershons lays pipes. Six months *Gemara* with the boys, six months on the job. Mr. Horowitz the carpenter also."

Bleilip said uncertainly, meaning to flatter, "It sounds like a wonderful system."

"It's not a *system*," Yussel said.

"Yussel goes everywhere, a commuter," Toby said: Yussel was a salesman for a paper-box manufacturer. He wore a small trimmed beard, very black, black-rimmed eyeglasses, and a vest over a rounding belly. Bleilip saw that Yussel liked him—he led him away from Toby and showed him the new hot air furnace in the cellar, the gas-fired hot water tank, the cinder blocks piled in the yard, the deep cuts above the road where the sewer pipes would go. He pointed over a little wooded crest—they could just see a bit of unpainted roof. "That's our yeshiva, the one our boys go to. It's not the toughest, they're not up to it. They weren't good enough. In the other yeshiva in the city they didn't give them enough work. Here," he said proudly, "they go from seven till half-past six."

They went back into the house by the rear door. Bleilip believed in instant rapport and yearned for closeness—he wanted to be close, close. But Yussel was impersonal, a guide, he froze Bleilip's vision. They passed through the bedrooms and again it seemed to Bleilip that Yussel was a real estate agent, a bureaucrat, a tourist office. There were a few shelves of books—holy books, nothing frivolous—but no pictures on the walls, no radio anywhere, no television set. Bleilip had brought with him, half-furtively, a snapshot of Toby taken eight or nine years before: Toby squatting on the grass at Brooklyn College, short curly hair with a barrette glinting in it, high socks and loafers, glimpse of panties, wispy blouse blurred by wind, a book with its title clear to the camera: Political Science. He offered this to Yussel: "A classmate." Yussel looked at the wall. "Why do I need an image? I have my wife right in front of me every morning." Toby held the wallet, saw, smiled, gave it back. "Another life," she said.

Bleilip reminded her, "The joke was which would be the bigger breakthrough, the woman or the Jew—" To Yussel he explained, "She used to say she would be the first lady Jewish President."

"Another life, other jokes," Toby said.

"And this life? Do you like it so much?"

"Why do you keep asking? Don't you like your own life?"

Bleilip liked his life, he liked it excessively. He felt he was part of society-at-large. He told her, without understanding why he was saying such a thing, "Here there's nothing to mock at, no jokes."

"You said we're a village," she contradicted.

"That wasn't mockery."

"It wasn't, you meant it. You think we're fanatics, primitives."

"Leave the man be," Yussel said. He had a cashier's tone, guide counting up the day's take, and Bleilip was grieved, because Yussel was a survivor, everyone in the new town, except one or two oddities like Toby, was a survivor of the deathcamps or the child of a survivor. "He's looking for something. He wants to find. He's not the first and he won't be the last." The rigid truth of this— Bleilip had thought his purposes darkly hidden—shocked him. He hated accuracy in a survivor. It was an affront. He wanted some kind of haze, a nostalgia for suffering perhaps. He resented the orange juice can, the appliances, the furnace, the sewer pipes. "He's been led to expect saints," Yussel said. "Listen, Jules," he said, "I'm not a saint and Toby's not a saint and we don't have miracles and we don't have a rebbe who works miracles."

"You have a rebbe," Bleilip said; instantly a wash of blood filled his head.

"He can't fly. What we came here for was to live a life of study. Our own way, and not to be interrupted in it."

"For the man, not the woman. You, not Toby. Toby used to be smart. Achievement goals and so forth."

"Give the mother of four sons a little credit too, it's not only college girls who build the world," Yussel said in a voice so fair-minded and humorous and obtuse that Bleilip wanted to knock him down—the first lady Jewish President of the United States had succumbed in her junior year to the zealot's private pieties, rites, idiosyncrasies. Toby was less than lucid, she was crazy to follow deviants, not in the mainstream even of their own tradition. Bleilip, who had read a little, considered these Hasidim actually christologized: everything had to go through a mediator. Of their popular romantic literature he knew the usual bits and pieces, legends, occult passions, quirks, histories—he had heard, for instance, about the holiday the Lubavitcher Hasidim celebrate on the anniversary of their master's release from prison: pretty stories in the telling, even more touching in the reading—poetry. Bleilip, a lawyer though not in practice, an ex-labor consultant, a fund-raiser by profession, a rationalist, a *misnagid* (he scarcely knew the word), purist, skeptic, enemy of fresh revelation, enemy of the Hasidim!— repelled by the sects themselves, he was nevertheless lured by their constituents. Refugees, survivors. He supposed they had a certain knowledge the unscathed could not guess at.

He said: "Toby makes her bed, she lies in it. I didn't come expecting women's rights and God knows I didn't come expecting saints."

"If not saints then martyrs," Yussel said.

Bleilip said nothing. This was not the sort of closeness he coveted—he shunned being seen into. His intention was to be a benefactor of the feelings. He glimpsed Yussel's tattoo-number (it almost seemed as if Yussel just then lifted his wrist to display it) without the compassion he had schemed for it. He had come to see a town of dead men. It spoiled Bleilip's mood that Yussel understood this.

At dusk the three of them went up to the road to watch the boys slide down the hill from the yeshiva. There was no danger: not a single car, except Bleilip's taxi, had passed through all day. The snow was a week old, it was coming on to March, the air struck like a bell-clapper, but Bleilip could smell through the cold something different from the smell of winter. Smoke of woodfire seeped into his throat from somewhere with a deep pineyness that moved him: he had a sense of farness, clarity, other lands, displaced seasons, the brooks of a village, a foreign bird piercing. The yeshiva boys came down on their shoe-soles, one foot in front of the other, lurching, falling, rolling. A pair of them tobogganed past on a garbage-can lid. The rest jostled, tumbled, squawked, their yarmulkas dropping from their heads into the snow like gumdrops, coins, black inkwells. Bleilip saw hoops of halos wheeling everywhere, and he saw their ear-curls leaping over their cheeks, and all at once he pene-

trated into what he took to be the truth of this place—the children
whirling on the hillside were false children, made of no flesh, it was
a crowd of ghosts coming down, a clamor of white smoke beat on
the road. Yussel said, "I'm on my way to *minchah*, want to come?"
Bleilip's grandfather, still a child but with an old man's pitted nose,
appeared to be flying toward him on the lid. The last light of day
split into blue rays all around them; the idea of going for evening
prayer seemed natural to him now, but Bleilip, privately elated,
self-proud, asked, "Why, do you need someone?"—because he
was remembering what he had forgotten he knew. Ten men. He
congratulated his memory, also of his grandfather's nose, thin as an
arrow—the nose, the face, the body, all gone into the earth—and
he went on piecing together his grandfather's face, tan teeth that
gave out small clicks and radiated stale farina, shapely gray half-
moon eyes with fleshy lids, eyebrows sparse as a woman's, a prickly
whiskbroom of a mustache whiter than cream. Yussel took him by
the arm: "Pessimist, joker, here we never run short, a *minyan*
always without fail, but come, anyhow you'll hear the rebbe, it's
our turn for him." Briefly behind them Bleilip saw Toby moving
into the dark of the door, trailed by two pairs of boys with golden
earlocks: he felt the shock of that sight, as if a beam of divinity had
fixed on her head, her house. But in an instant he was again humiliated by the sting of Yussel's eye—"She'll give them supper," he
said merely, "then they have homework." "You people make them
work." "Honey on the page is only for the beginning," Yussel said,
"afterward comes hard learning."

Bleilip accepted a cap for his cold-needled skull and they toiled
on the ice upward toward the schoolhouse: the rebbe gave himself
each week to a different *minyan*. When Bleilip reached for a prayer-
shawl inside a cardboard box Yussel thumbed a No at him, so he
dropped it in again. No one else paid him any attention. Through
the window the sky deepened; the shouts were gone from the hill.
Yussel handed him a *siddur*, but the alphabet was jumpy and
strange to him: it needed piecing together, like his grandfather's
visage. He stood up when the others did. Then he sat down again,
fitting his haunches into a boy's chair. It did not seem to him that
they sang out with any special fervor, as he had read the Hasidim

did, but the sounds were loud, cadenced, earnest. The leader,
unlike the others a mutterer, was the single one wearing the fringed
shawl—it made a cave for him, he looked out of it without mobility
of heart. Bleilip turned his stare here and there into the tedium—
which was the rebbe? He went after a politician's face: his analogy
was to the mayor of a town. Or a patriarch's face—the father of a
large family. They finished *minchah* and herded themselves into a
corner of the room—a long table (three planks nailed together, two
sawhorses) covered by a cloth. The cloth was grimy: print lay on it,
the backs of old *siddurim*, rubbing, shredding, the backs of the open
hands of the men. Bleilip drew himself in; he found a wooden
folding chair and wound his legs into the rungs, away from the
men. It stunned him that they were not old, but instead mainly in
the forties, plump and in their prime. Their cheeks were blooming
hillocks above their beards; some wore yarmulkas, some tall black
hats, some black hats edged with fur, some ordinary fedoras
pushed back, one a workman's cap. Their mouths especially struck
him as extraordinary—vigorous, tender, blessed. He marveled at
their mouths until it came to him that they were speaking another
language and that he could follow only a little of it: now and then
it was almost as if their words were visibly springing out of their
mouths, like flags or streamers. Whenever he understood the
words the flags whipped at him, otherwise they collapsed and
vanished with a sort of hum. Bleilip himself was a month short of
forty-two, but next to these pious men he felt like a boy; even his
shoulder-blades weakened and thinned. He made himself concentrate: he heard *azazel*, and he heard *kohen gadol*, they were knitting
something up, mixing strands of holy tongue with Yiddish. The
noise of Yiddish in his ear enfeebled him still more, like Titus's
fly—it was not an everyday language with him, except to make
cracks with, jokes, gags. . . . His dead grandfather hung from the
ceiling on a rope. Wrong, mistaken, impossible, uncharacteristic of
his grandfather!—who died old and safe in a Bronx bed, mischief-
maker, eager aged imp. The imp came to life and swung over
Bleilip's black corner. Here ghosts sat as if already in the World-to-
Come, explicating Scripture. Or whatever. Who knew? In his
grandfather's garble the Hasidim (refugees, dead men) were crying

out Temple, were crying out High Priest, and the more Bleilip
squeezed his brain toward them, the more he comprehended. Five
times on the tenth day of the seventh month, the Day of Atonement, the High Priest changes his vestments, five times he lowers
his body into the ritual bath. After the first immersion garments of
gold, after the second immersion white linen, and wearing the
white linen he confesses his sins and the sins of his household while
holding on to the horns of a bullock. Walking eastward, he goes
from the west of the altar to the north of the altar, where two goats
stand, and he casts lots for the goats: one for the Lord, one for
Azazel, and the one for the Lord is given a necklace of red wool and
will be slaughtered and its blood caught in a bowl, but first the
bullock will be slaughtered and its blood caught in a bowl; and once
more he confesses his sins and the sins of his household, and now
also the sins of the children of Aaron, this holy people. The blood
of the bullock is sprinkled eight times, both upward and downward, the blood of the goat is sprinkled eight times, then the High
Priest comes to the goat who was not slaughtered, the one for
Azazel, and now he touches it and confesses the sins of the whole
house of Israel, and utters the name of God, and pronounces the
people cleansed of sin. And Bleilip, hearing all this through the web
of a language gone stale in his marrow, was scraped to the edge of
pity and belief, he pitied the hapless goats, the unlucky bullock, but
more than this he pitied the God of Israel, whom he saw as an imp
with a pitted nose dangling on a cord from the high beams of the
Temple in Jerusalem, winking down at His tiny High Priest—now
he leaps in and out of a box of water, now he hurries in and out of
new clothes like a quick-change vaudevillian, now he sprinkles red
drops up and red drops down, and all the while Bleilip, together
with the God of the Jews, pities these toy children of Israel in the
Temple long ago. Pity upon pity. What God could take the Temple
rites seriously? What use does the King of the Universe have for
goats? What, leaning on their dirty tablecloth—no vestments, al-
tars, sacrifices—what do these survivors, exemptions, expect of
God now?

All at once Bleilip knew which was the rebbe. The man in the
work-cap, with a funny flat nose, black-haired and red-bearded, fist

on mouth, elbows sunk into his lap—a self-stabber: in all that
recitation, those calls and streamers of discourse, this blunt-nosed
man had no word: but now he stood up, scratched his chair backward, and fell into an ordinary voice. Bleilip examined him: he
looked fifty, his hands were brutish, two fingers missing, the nails
on the others absent. A pair of muscles bunched in his neck like
chains. The company did not breathe and gave him something
more than attentiveness. Bleilip reversed his view and saw that the
rebbe was their child, they gazed at him with the possessiveness of
faces seized by a crib, and he too spoke in that mode, as if he were
addressing parents, old fathers, deferential, awed, guilty. And still
he was their child, and still he owed them his guilt. He said: "And
what comes next? Next we read that the *kohen gadol* gives the goat
fated for Azazel to one of the *kohanim*, and the *kohen* takes it out
into a place all bare and wild, with a big cliff in the middle of it all,
and he cuts off a bit of the red wool they had put on it, and ties it
onto a piece of rock to mark the place, and then he drives the goat
over the edge and it spins down, down, down, and is destroyed. But
in the Temple the worship may not continue, not until it is known
that the goat is already given over to the wilderness. How can they
know this miles away in the far city? All along the way from the
wilderness to Jerusalem, poles stand up out of the ground, and on
top of every pole a man, and in the hand of every man a great shawl
to shake out, so that pole flies out a wing to pole, wing after wing,
until it comes to the notice of the *kohen gadol* in the Temple that
the goat has been dashed into the ravine. And only then can the
kohen gadol finish his readings, his invocations, his blessings, his
beseechings. In the neighborhood of Sharon often there are earth-
quakes: the *kohen gadol* says: let their homes not become their
graves. And after all this a procession, no, a parade, a celebration,
all the people follow the *kohen gadol* to his own house, he is safe out
of the Holy of Holies, their sins are atoned for, they are cleansed
and healed, and they sing how like a flower he is, a lily, like the
moon, the sun, the morning star among clouds, a dish of gold, an
olive tree. . . . That, gentlemen, is how it was in the Temple, and
how it will be again after the coming of Messiah. We learn it"—he
tapped his book—"in *Mishna Yoma, Yoma*—Targum for Day, *yom*

hakipurim, but whose is the atonement, whose is the cleansing? Does the goat for Azazel atone, does the *kohen gadol* cleanse and hallow us? No, only the Most High can cleanse, only we ourselves can atone. Rabbi Akiva reminds us: 'Who is it that makes you clean? Our Father in Heaven.' So why, gentlemen, do you suppose the Temple was even then necessary, why the goats, the bullock, the blood? Why is it necessary for all of this to be restored by Messiah? These are questions we must torment ourselves with. Which of us would slaughter an animal, not for sustenance, but for an idea? Which of us would dash an animal to its death? Which of us would not feel himself to be a sinner in doing so? Or feel the shame of Esau? You may say that those were other days, the rituals are obsolete, we are purer now, better, we do not sprinkle blood so readily. But in truth you would not say so, you would not lie. For animals we in our day substitute men. What the word Azazel means exactly is not known—we call it wilderness, some say it is hell itself, demons live there. But whatever we mean by 'wilderness,' whatever we mean by 'hell,' surely the plainest meaning is *instead of*. Wilderness instead of easeful places, hell and devils instead of plenitude, life, peace. Goat instead of man. Was there no one present in the Temple who, seeing the animals in all their majesty of health, shining hair, glinting hooves, timid nostrils, muscled like ourselves, gifted with tender eyes no different from our own, the whole fine creature trembling—was there no one there when the knife slit the fur and skin and the blood fled upward who did not feel the splendor of the living beast? Who was not in —we of the miracle of life turned to carcass? Who did not think: *how like that goat I am! The goat goes, I stay, the goat instead of me.* Who did not see in the goat led to Azazel his own destiny? Death takes us too at random, some at the altar, some over the cliff. . . . Gentlemen, we are this moment so to speak in the Temple, the Temple devoid of the Holy of Holies—when the Temple was destroyed it forsook the world, so the world itself had no recourse but to pretend to be the Temple by mockery. In the absence of Messiah there can be no *kohen gadol*, we have no authority to bless multitudes, we are not empowered, we cannot appeal except for ourselves, ourselves alone, in isolation, in futility, instead we are

like the little goats, we are assigned our lot, we are designated for
the altar or for Azazel, in either case we are meant to be cut down.
. . . O little fathers, we cannot choose, we are driven, we are not
free, we are only *instead of*: we stand *instead of*, instead of choice we
have the yoke, instead of looseness we are pointed the way to go,
instead of freedom we have the red cord around our throats, we
were in villages, they drove us into camps, we were in trains, they
drove us into showers of poison, in the absence of Messiah the
secular ones made a nation, enemies bite at it. All that we do
without Messiah is in vain. When the Temple forsook the world,
and the world presumed to mock the Temple, everyone on earth
became a goat or a bullock, he-animal or she-animal, all our prayers
are bleats and neighs on the way to a forsaken altar, a teeming
Azazel. Little fathers! How is it possible to live? When will Messiah
come? You! You! Visitor! You're looking somewhere else, who are
you not to look?"

He was addressing Bleilip—he pointed a finger without a nail.

"Who are you? Talk and look! Who!"

Bleilip spoke his own name and shook: a schoolboy in a school-
room. "I'm here with the deepest respect, Rabbi. I came out of
interest for your community."

"We are not South Sea islanders, sir, our practices are well
known since Sinai. You don't have to turn your glance. We are not
something new in the world."

"Excuse me, Rabbi, not new—unfamiliar."

"To you."

"To me," Bleilip admitted.

"Exactly my question! Who are you, what do you represent,
what are you to us?"

"A Jew. Like yourselves. One of you."

"Presumption! Atheist, devourer! For us there is the Most High,
joy, life. For us trust! But you! A moment ago I spoke your own
heart for you, *emes?*"

Bleilip knew this word: truth, true, but he was only a visitor and
did not want so much: he wanted only what he needed, a certain
piece of truth, not too big to swallow. He was afraid of choking on
more. The rebbe said, "You believe the world is in vain, *emes?*"

"I don't follow any of that, I'm not looking for theology—"

"Little fathers," said the rebbe, "everything you heard me say, everything you heard me say in a voice of despair, emanates from the liver of this man. My mouth made itself his parrot. My teeth became his beak. He fills the study-house with a black light, as if he keeps a lump of radium inside his belly. He would eat us up. Man he equates with the goats. The Temple, in memory and anticipation, he considers an abattoir. The world he regards as a graveyard. You are shocked, Mister Bleilip, that I know your kidneys, your heart? Canker! Onset of cholera! You say you don't come for 'theology,' Mister Bleilip, and yet you have a particular conception of us, *emes?* A certain idea."

Bleilip wished himself mute. He looked at Yussel, but Yussel had his eyes on his sleeve-button.

"Speak in your own language, please"—Bleilip was unable to do anything else—"and I will understand you very well. Your idea about us, please. Stand up!"

Bleilip obeyed. That he obeyed bewildered him. The crescents of faces in profile on either side of him seemed sharp as scythes. His yarmulka fell off his head but, rising, he failed to notice it—one of the men quickly clapped it back on. The stranger's palm came like a blow.

"Your idea," the rebbe insisted.

"Things I've heard," Bleilip croaked. "That in the Zohar it's written how Moses coupled with the Shekhina on Mount Sinai. That there are books to cast lots by, to tell fortunes, futures. That some Rabbis achieved levitation, hung in air without end, made babies come in barren women, healed miraculously. That there was once a Rabbi who snuffed out the Sabbath light. Things," Bleilip said, "I suppose legends."

"Did you hope to witness any of these things?"

Bleilip was silent.

"Then let me again ask. Do you credit any of these things?"

"Do you?" asked Bleilip.

Yussel intervened: "Forbidden to mock the rebbe!"

But the rebbe replied, "I do not believe in magic. That there are influences I do believe."

Bleilip felt braver. "Influences?"

"Turnings. That a man can be turned from folly, error, wrong choices. From misery, evil, private rage. From a mistaken life."

Now Bleilip viewed the rebbe; he was suspicious of such hands. The hands a horror: deformity, mutilation: caught in what machine?—and above them the worker's cap. But otherwise the man seemed simple, reasoned, balanced, after certain harmonies, sanities, the ordinary article, no mystic, a bit bossy, pedagogue, noisy preacher. Bleilip, himself a man with a profession and no schoolboy after all, again took heart. A commonplace figure. People did what he asked, nothing more complicated than this—but he had to ask. Or tell, or direct. A monarch perhaps. A community needs to be governed. A human relationship: of all words Bleilip, whose vocabulary was habitually sociological, best of all liked "relationship."

He said, "I don't have a mistaken life."

"Empty your pockets."

Bleilip stood without moving.

"Empty your pockets!"

"Rabbi, I'm not an exercise, I'm not a demonstration—"

"Despair must be earned."

"I'm not in despair," Bleilip objected.

"To be an atheist is to be in despair."

"I'm not an atheist, I'm a secularist," but even Bleilip did not know what he meant by this.

"Esau! For the third time: empty your pockets!"

Bleilip pulled the black plastic thing out and threw it on the table. Instantly all the men bent away from it.

"A certain rebbe," said the rebbe very quietly, "believed every man should carry two slips of paper in his pockets. In one pocket should be written: 'I am but dust and ashes.' In the other: 'For my sake was the world created.' This canker fills only one pocket, and with ashes." He picked up Bleilip's five-and-ten gun and said "Esau! Beast! Lion! To whom did you intend to do harm?"

"Nobody," said Bleilip out of his shame. "It isn't real. I keep it to get used to. The feel of the thing. Listen," he said, "do you think it's easy for me to carry that thing around and keep on thinking about it?"

The rebbe tried the trigger. It gave out a tin click. Then he wrapped it in his handkerchief and put it in his pocket. "We will now proceed with ma'ariv," he said. "The study hour is finished. Let us not learn more of this matter. This is Jacob's tent."

The men left the study table and took up their old places, reciting. Bleilip, humiliated (the analogy to a teacher confiscating a forbidden toy was too exact), still excited, the tremor in his groin worse, was in awe before this incident. Was it amazing chance that the rebbe had challenged the contents of his pockets, or was he a seer? At the conclusion of ma'ariv the men dispersed quickly; Bleilip recognized from Yussel's white stare that this was not the usual way. He felt like an animal they were running from. He intended to run himself—all the way to the Greyhound station— but the rebbe came to him. "You," he said (du, as if to an animal, or to a child, or to God), "the other pocket. The second one. The other side of your coat."

"What?"

"Disgorge."

So Bleilip took it out. And just as the toy gun could instantly be seen to be a toy, all tin glint, so could this one be seen for what it was: monstrous, clumsy and hard, heavy, with a scarred trigger and a barrel that smelled. Dark, no gleam. An actuality, a thing for use. Yussel moaned, dipping his head up and down. "In my house! Stood in front of my wife with it! With two!"

"With one," said the rebbe. "One is a toy and one not, so only one need be feared. It is the toy we have to fear: the incapable—"

Yussel broke in, "We should call the police, rebbe."

"Because of a toy? How they will laugh."

"But the other! This!"

"Is it capable?" the rebbe asked Bleilip.

"Loaded, you mean? Sure it's loaded."

"Loaded, you hear him?" Yussel said. "He came as a curiosity-seeker, rebbe, my wife's cousin, I had no suspicion of this—"

The rebbe said, "Go home, Yussel. Go home, little father."

"Rebbe, he can shoot—"

"How can he shoot? The instrument is in my hand."

It was. The rebbe held the gun—the real one. Again Bleilip was drawn to those hands. This time the rebbe saw. "Buchenwald," he said. "Blocks of ice, a freezing experiment. In my case only to the elbow, but others were immersed wholly and perished. The fingers left are toy fingers. That is why you have been afraid of them and have looked away."

He said all this very clearly, in a voice without an opinion.

"Don't talk to him, rebbe!"

"Little father, go home."

"And if he shoots?"

"He will not shoot."

Alone in the schoolhouse with the rebbe—how dim the bulbs, dangling on cords—Bleilip regretted that because of the dishonor of the guns. He was pleased that the rebbe had dismissed Yussel. The day (but now it was night) felt full of miracles and lucky chances. Thanks to Yussel he had gotten to the rebbe. He never supposed he would get to the rebbe himself—all his hope was only for a glimpse of the effect of the rebbe. Of influences. With these he was satisfied. He said again, "I don't have a mistaken life."

The rebbe enclosed the second gun in his handkerchief. "This one has a bad odor."

"Once I killed a pigeon with it."

"A live bird?"

"You believers," Bleilip threw out, "you'd cut up those goats all over again if you got the Temple back!"

"Sometimes," the rebbe said, "even the rebbe does not believe. My father when he was the rebbe also sometimes did not believe. It is characteristic of believers sometimes not to believe. And it is characteristic of unbelievers sometimes to believe. Even you, Mister Bleilip—even you now and then believe in the Holy One, Blessed Be He? Even you now and then apprehend the Most High?"

"No," Bleilip said; and then: "Yes."

"Then you are as bloody as anyone," the rebbe said (it was his first real opinion), and with his terrible hands put the bulging white handkerchief on the table for Bleilip to take home with him, for whatever purpose he thought he needed it.

GRACE PALEY

Zagrowsky Tells

I was standing in the park under that tree. They call it the Hanging Elm. Once upon a time it made a big improvement on all kinds of hooligans. Nowadays if, once in a while . . . No. So this woman comes up to me, a woman minus a smile. I said to my grandson, Uh oh, Emanuel. Here comes a lady, she was once a beautiful customer of mine in the pharmacy I showed you.

Emanuel says, Grandpa, who?

She looks O.K. now, but not so hot. Well, what can you do, time takes a terrible toll off the ladies.

This is her idea of a hello: Iz, what are you doing with that black child? Then she says, Who is he? Why are you holding on to him like that? She gives me a look like God in judgment. You could see it in famous paintings. Then she says, Why are you yelling at that poor kid?

What yelling? A history lesson about the park. This is a tree in guide books. How are you by the way, Miss . . . Miss . . . I was embarrassed. I forgot her name absolutely.

Well, who is he? You got him pretty scared.

Me? Don't be ridiculous. It's my grandson. Say hello, Emanuel, don't put on an act.

Emanuel shoves his hand in my pocket to be a little more glued to me. Are you going to open your mouth sonny, yes or no?

She says, Your grandson? Really, Iz, your grandson? What do you mean, your grandson?

Emanuel closes his eyes tight. Did you ever notice children get all mixed up? They don't want to hear about something, they squinch up their eyes. Many children do this.

Now listen Emanuel, I want you to tell this lady who is the smartest boy in kindergarten.

Not a word.

Goddamnit, open your eyes. It's something new with him. Tell her who is the smartest boy—he was just five, he can already read a whole book by himself.

He stands still. He's thinking. I know his little cute mind. Then he jumps up and down yelling, Me me me. He makes a little dance. His grandma calls it his smartness dance. My other ones (three children grown up for some time already) were also very smart, but they don't hold a candle to this character. Soon as I get a chance, I'm gonna bring him to the city to Hunter for gifted children; he should get a test.

But this Miss . . . Miss . . . she's not finished with us yet. She's worried. Whose kid is he? You adopt him?

Adopt? At my age? It's Cissy's kid. You know my Cissy? I see she knows something. Why not, I had a public business. No surprise.

Of course I remember Cissy. She says this, her face is a little more ironed out.

So, my Cissy, if you remember, she was a nervous girl.

I'll *bet* she was.

Is that a nice way to answer? Cissy *was* nervous . . . The nervous-
ness, to be truthful, ran in Mrs. Z.'s family. Ran? Galloped . . .
tarum tarum tarum.

When we were young I used to go over there to visit, and while
me and her brother and uncles played pinochle, in the kitchen the
three aunts would sit drinking tea. Everything was Oi! Oi! Oi!
What for? Nothing to oi about. They got husbands . . . Perfectly
fine gentlemen. One in business, two of them real professionals.
They just got in the habit somehow. So I said to Mrs. Z., one oi out
of you and it's divorce.

I remember your wife very well, this lady says. *Very* well. She
puts on the same face like before; her mouth gets small. Your wife
is a beautiful woman.

So . . . would I marry a mutt?

But she was right. My Nettie when she was young, she was very
fair, like some Polish Jews you see once in a while. Like for instance
maybe some big blond peasant made a pogrom on her great-
grandma.

So I answered her, Oh yes, very nice-looking; even now she's not
so bad, but a little bit on the grouchy side.

O.K., she makes a big sigh like I'm a hopeless case. What did
happen to Cissy?

Emanuel, go over there and play with those kids. No? No.

Well, I'll tell you, it's the genes. The genes are the most important. Environment is O.K. But the genes . . . that's where the whole
story is written down. I think the school had something to do with
it also. She's more an artist like your husband. Am I thinking of the
right guy? When she was a kid you should of seen her. She's a
nice-looking girl now, even when she has an attack. But then she
was something. The family used to go to the mountains in the
summer. We went dancing, her and me. What a dancer. People
were surprised. Sometimes we danced until 2 A.M.

I don't think that was good, she says. I wouldn't dance with my
son all night . . .

Naturally, you're a mother. But "good," who knows what's
good? Maybe a doctor. I could have been a doctor, by the way. Her
brother-in-law in business would of backed me. But then what?

You don't have the time. People call you day and night. I cured more people in a day than a doctor in a week. Many an M.D. called me, said, Zagrowsky, does it work . . . that Parke-Davis medication they put out last month, or it's a fake? I got immediate experience and I'm not too stuck up to tell.

Oh, Iz, you are, she said. She says this like she means it but it makes her sad. How do I know this? Years in a store. You observe. You watch. The customer is always right, but plenty of times you know he's wrong and also a goddamn fool.

All of a sudden I put her in a certain place. Then I said to myself, Iz, why are you standing here with this woman? I looked her straight in the face and I said, Faith? Right? Listen to me. Now you listen, because I got a question. Is it true, no matter what time you called, even if I was closing up, I came to your house with the penicillin or the tetracycline later? You lived on the fourth-floor walk-up. Your friend what's-her-name, Susan, with the three girls next door? I can see it very clear. Your face is all smeared up with crying, your kid got 105°, maybe more, burning up, you didn't want to leave him in the crib screaming, you're standing in the hall, it's dark. You were living alone, am I right? So young. Also your husband, he comes to my mind, very jumpy fellow, in and out, walking around all night. He drank? I betcha. Irish? Imagine you didn't get along so you got a divorce. Very simple. You kids knew how to live.

She doesn't even answer me. She says . . . you want to know what she says? She says, Oh shit! Then she says, Of course I remember. God, my Richie was sick! Thanks, she says, thanks, god-almighty thanks.

I was already thinking something else: The mind makes its own business. When she first came up to me, I couldn't remember. I knew her well, but where? Then out of no place, a word, her bossy face maybe, exceptionally round, which is not usual, her dark apartment, the four flights, the other girls—all once lively, young . . . you could see them walking around on a sunny day, dragging a couple kids, a carriage, a bike, beautiful girls, but tired from all day, mostly divorced, going home alone? Boyfriends? Who knows how that type lives? I had a big appreciation for them. Sometimes, five o'clock I stood in the door to see them. They were mostly the way models *should* be. I mean not skinny—round, like they were made of little cushions and bigger cushions, depending where you looked; young mothers. I hollered a few words to them, they hollered back. Especially I remember her friend Ruthy—she had two little girls with long black braids, down to here. I told her, In a couple of years, Ruthy, you'll have some beauties on your hands. You better keep an eye on them. In those days the women always answered you in a pleasant way, not afraid to smile. Like this: They said, You really think so? Thanks, Iz.

But this is all used-to-be and in that place there is not only good but bad and the main fact in regard to *this* particular lady: I did her good but to me she didn't always do so much good.

So we stood around a little. Emanuel says, Grandpa, let's go to the swings. Go yourself—it's not so far, there's kids, I see them. No, he says, and stuffs his hands in my pocket again. So don't go—Ach, what a day, I said. Buds and everything. She says, That's a catalpa tree over there. No kidding! I say. What do you call that one, doesn't have a single leaf? Locust, she says. Two locusts, I say.

Then I take a deep breath: O.K.—you still listening? Let me ask you, if I did you so much good including I saved your baby's life, how come you did *that?* You know what I'm talking about. A perfectly nice day. I look out the window of the pharmacy and I see four customers, that I seen at least two in their bathrobes crying to me in the middle of the night, Help help! They're out there with signs. ZAGROWSKY IS A RACIST. YEARS AFTER ROSA PARKS, ZAGROWSKY REFUSES TO SERVE BLACKS. It's like an etching right *here.* I point out to her my heart. I know exactly where it is.

She's naturally very uncomfortable when I tell her. Listen, she says, we were right.

I grab on to Emanuel. You?

Yes, we wrote a letter first, did you answer it? We said, Zagrowsky, come to your senses. Ruthy wrote it. We said we would like to talk to you. We tested you. At least four times, you kept Mrs. Green and Josie, our friend Josie, who was kind of Spanish black . . . she lived on the first floor in our house . . . you kept them waiting a long time till everyone ahead of them was taken care of.

Then you were very rude, I mean nasty, you can be extremely nasty, Iz. And then Josie left the store, she called you some pretty bad names. You remember?

No, I happen not to remember. There was plenty of yelling in the store. People *really* suffering; come in yelling for codeine or what to do their mother was dying. That's what I remember, not some crazy Spanish lady hollering.

But listen, she says—like all this is not in front of my eyes, like the past is only a piece of paper in the yard—you didn't finish with Cissy.

Finish? *You* almost finished my business and don't think that Cissy didn't hold it up to me. Later when she was so sick.

Then I thought, Why should I talk to this woman. I see myself: how I was standing that day how many years ago?—like an idiot behind the counter waiting for customers. Everybody is peeking in past the picket line. It's the kind of neighborhood, if they see a picket line, half don't come in. The cops say they have a right. To destroy a person's business. I was disgusted but I went into the street. After all, I knew the ladies. I tried to explain, Faith, Ruthy, Mrs. Kratt—a stranger comes into the store, naturally you have to serve the old customers first. Anyone would do the same. Also, they sent in black people, brown people, all colors, and to tell the truth I didn't like the idea my pharmacy should get the reputation of being a cut-rate place for them. They move into a neighborhood . . . I did what everyone did. Not to insult people too much, but to discourage them a little, they shouldn't feel so welcome. They could just move in because it's a nice area.

All right. A person looks at my Emanuel and says, Hey! he's not altogether from the white race, what's going on? I'll tell you what: life is going on. You have an opinion. I have an opinion. Life don't have no opinion.

I moved away from this Faith lady. I didn't like to be near her. I sat down on the bench. I'm no spring chicken. Cock-a-doodle-do, I only holler once in a while. I'm tired, I'm mostly the one in charge of our Emanuel. Mrs. Z. stays home, her legs swell up. It's a shame.

In the subway once she couldn't get off at the right stop. The door opens, she can't get up. She tried (she's a little overweight).

She says to a big guy with a notebook, a big colored fellow, Please help me get up. He says to her, You kept me down three hundred years, you can stay down another ten minutes. I asked her, Nettie, didn't you tell him we're raising a little boy brown like a coffee bean. But he's right, says Nettie, we done that. We kept them down.

We? We? My two sisters and my father were being fried up for Hitler's supper in 1944 and you say we?

Nettie sits down. Please bring me some tea. Yes, Iz, I say: *We.*

I can't even put up the water I'm so mad. You know, my Mrs., you are crazy like your three aunts, crazy like our Cissy. Your whole family put in the genes to make it for sure that she wouldn't have a chance. Nettie looks at me. She says, Ai ai. She doesn't say oi anymore. She got herself assimilated into ai . . . That's how come she also says "we" done it. Don't think this will make you an American, I said to her, that you included yourself in with Robert E. Lee. Naturally it was a joke, only what is there to laugh?

I'm tired right now. This Faith could even see I'm a little shaky. What should she do, she's thinking. But she decides the discussion ain't over so she sits down sideways. The bench is damp. It's only April.

What about Cissy? Is she all right?

It ain't your business how she is.

O.K. She starts to go.

Wait wait! Since I seen you in your nightgown a couple of times when you were a handsome young woman . . . She really gets up this time. I think she must be a woman's libber, they don't like remarks about nightgowns. Bathrobes, she didn't mind. Let her go! The hell with her . . . but she comes back. She says, Once and for all, cut it out, Iz. I really *want* to know. Is Cissy all right?

You want. She's fine. She lives with me and Nettie. She's in charge of the plants. It's an all-day job.

But why should I leave her off the hook. Oh boy, Faith, I got to say it, what you people put on me! And you want to know how Cissy is. *You!* Why? Sure. You remember you finished with the picket lines after a week or two. I don't know why. Tired? Summer maybe, you got to go away, make trouble at the beach. But I'm

stuck there. Did I have air conditioning yet? All of a sudden I see
Cissy outside. She has a sign also. She must've got the idea from
you women. A big sandwich board, she walks up and down. If
someone talks to her, she presses her mouth together.

I don't remember that, Faith says.

Of course, you were already on Long Island or Cape Cod or
someplace—the Jersey shore.

No, she says, I was not. I was not. (I see this is a big insult to her
that she should go away for the summer.)

Then I thought, Calm down, Zagrowsky. Because for a fact I
didn't want her to leave, because, since I already began to tell, I
have to tell the whole story. I'm not a person who keeps things in.
Tell! That opens up the congestion a little—the lungs are for
breathing, not secrets. My wife never tells, she coughs, coughs. All
night. Wakes up. Ai, Iz, open up the window, there's no air. You
poor woman, if you want to breathe, you got to tell.

So I said to this Faith, I'll tell you how Cissy is but you got to
hear the whole story how we suffered. I thought, O.K. Who cares!
Let her get on the phone later with the other girls. They should
know what they started.

How we took our own Cissy from here to there to the biggest
doctor—I had good contacts from the pharmacy. Dr. Francis O'-
Connel, the heavy Irishman over at the hospital, sat with me and
Mrs. Z. for two hours, a busy man. He explained that it was one of
the most great mysteries. They were ignoramuses, the most brilliant doctors were dummies in this field. But still, in my place, I
heard of this cure and that one. So we got her massaged fifty times
from head to toe, whatever someone suggested. We stuffed her
with vitamins and minerals—there was a real doctor in charge of
this idea.

If she would take the vitamins—sometimes she shut her mouth.
To her mother she said dirty words. We weren't used to it. Meanwhile, in front of my place every morning, she walks up and down.
She could of got minimum wage, she was so regular. Her afternoon
job is to follow my wife from corner to corner to tell what my wife
done wrong to her when she was a kid. Then after a couple months,
all of a sudden she starts to sing. She has a beautiful voice. She took

lessons from a well-known person. On Christmas week, in front of
the pharmacy she sings half the *Messiah* by Handel. You know it?
So that's nice, you think. Oh, that's beautiful. But where were you
you didn't notice that she don't have on a coat. You didn't see she
walks up and down, her socks are falling off? Her face and hands
are like she's the super in the cellar. She sings! she sings! Two songs
she sings the most: one is about the Gentiles will see the light and
the other is, Look! a virgin will conceive a son. My wife says, Sure,
naturally, she wishes she was a married woman just like anyone.
Baloney. She could of. She had plenty of dates. Plenty. She sings,
the idiots applaud, some skunk yells, Go, Cissy, go. What? Go
where? Some days she just hollers.

Hollers what?

Oh, I forgot about you. Hollers anything. Hollers, Racist! Hollers, He sells poison chemicals! Hollers, He's a terrible dancer, he
got three left legs! (Which isn't true, just to insult me publicly,
plain silly.) The people laugh. What'd she say? Some didn't hear so
well; hollers, You go to whores. Also not true. She met me once
with a woman actually a distant relative from Israel. Everything is
in her head. It's a garbage pail.

One day her mother says to her, Cissile, comb your hair, for
godsakes, darling. For this remark, she gives her mother a sock in
the face. I come home I see a woman not at all young with two black
eyes and a bloody nose. The doctor said, Before it's better with
your girl, it's got to be worse. That much he knew. He sent us to
a beautiful place, a hospital right at the city line—I'm not sure if it's
Westchester or the Bronx, but thank God, you could use the
subway. That's how I found out what I was saving up my money
for. I thought for retiring in Florida to walk around under the palm
trees in the middle of the week. Wrong. It was for my beautiful
Cissy, she should have a nice home with other crazy people.

So little by little, she calms down. We can visit her. She shows
us the candy store, we give her a couple of dollars; soon our life is
this way. Three times a week my wife goes, gets on the subway with
delicious foods (no sugar, they're against sugar); she brings something nice, a blouse or a kerchief—a present, you understand, to
show love; and once a week I go, but she don't want to look at me.

So close we were, like sweethearts—you can imagine how I feel.
Well, you have children so you know, little children little troubles,
big children big troubles—it's a saying in Yiddish. Maybe the
Chinese said it too.

Oh, Iz. How could it happen like that? All of a sudden. No signs?

What's with this Faith? Her eyes are full of tears. Sensitive I
suppose. I see what she's thinking. Her kids are teenagers. So far
they look O.K. but what will happen? People think of themselves.
Human nature. At least she doesn't tell me it's my wife's fault or
mine. I did something terrible! I loved my child. I know what's on
people's minds. I know psychology very well. Since this happened
to us, I read up on the whole business.

Oh, Iz . . .

She puts her hand on my knee. I look at her. Maybe she's just
a nut. Maybe she thinks I'm plain old (I almost am). Well, I said
it before. Thank God for the head. Inside the head is the only place
you got to be young when the usual place gets used up. For some
reason she gives me a kiss on the cheek. A peculiar person.

Faith, I still can't figure it out why you girls were so rotten to me.

But we were right.

Then this lady Queen of Right makes a small lecture. She don't
remember my Cissy walking up and down screaming bad language
but she remembers: After Mrs. Kendrick's big fat snotty maid
walked out with Kendrick's allergy order, I made a face and said,
Ho ho! the great lady! That's terrible? She says whenever I saw a
couple walk past on the block, a black-and-white couple, I said,
Ugh—disgusting! It shouldn't be allowed! She heard this remark
from me a few times. So? It's a matter of taste. Then she tells me
about this Josie, probably Puerto Rican, once more—the one I
didn't serve in time. Then she says, Yeah, and really, Iz, what about
Emanuel?

Don't you look at Emanuel, I said. Don't you dare. He has
nothing to do with it.

She rolls her eyes around and around a couple of times. She got
more to say. She also doesn't like how I talk to women. She says
I called Mrs. Z. a grizzly bear a few times. It's my wife, no? That I
was winking and blinking at the girls, a few pinches. A lie . . . maybe

I patted, but I never pinched. Besides, I know for a fact a couple of them loved it. She says, No. None of them liked it. Not one. They only put up with it because it wasn't time yet in history to holler. (An American-born girl has some nerve to mention history.)

But, she says, Iz, forget all that. I'm sorry you have so much trouble now. She really is sorry. But in a second she changes her mind. She's not so sorry. She takes her hand back. Her mouth makes a little O.

Emanuel climbs up on my lap. He pats my face. Don't be sad, Grandpa, he says. He can't stand if he sees a tear on a person's face. Even a stranger. If his mama gets a black look, he's smart, he doesn't go to her any more. He comes to my wife. Grandma, he says, my poor mama is very sad. My wife jumps up and runs in. Worried. Scared. Did Cissy take her pills? What's going on? Once, he went to Cissy and said, Mama, why are you crying? So this is her answer to a little boy: she stands up straight and starts to bang her head on the wall. Hard.

My mama! he screams. Lucky I was home. Since then he goes straight to his grandma for his troubles. What will happen? We're not so young. My oldest son is doing extremely well—only he lives in a very exclusive neighborhood in Rockland County. Our other boy—well, he's in his own life, he's from that generation. He went away.

She looks at me, this Faith. She can't say a word. She sits there. She opens her mouth almost. I know what she wants to know. How did Emanuel come into the story. When?

Then she says to me exactly those words. Well, where does Emanuel fit in?

He fits, he fits. Like a golden present from Nasser.

Nasser?

O.K., Egypt, not Nasser—he's from Isaac's other son, get it? A close relation. I was sitting one day thinking, Why? why? The answer: To remind us. That's the purpose of most things.

It was Abraham, she interrupts me. He had two sons, Isaac and Ishmael. God promised him he would be the father of generations; he was. But you know, she says, he wasn't such a good father to those two little boys. Not so unusual, she has to add on.

You see! That's what they make of the Bible, those women; because they got it in for men. Of *course* I meant Abraham. Abraham. Did I say Isaac? Once in a while I got to admit it, she says something true. You remember one son he sent out of the house altogether, the other he was ready to chop up if he only heard a noise in his head saying, Go! Chop!

But the question is, Where did Emanuel fit. I didn't mind telling. I wanted to tell, I explained that already.

So it begins. One day my wife goes to the administration of Cissy's hospital and she says, What kind of a place you're running here. I have just looked at my daughter. A blind person could almost see it. My daughter is pregnant. What goes on here at night? Who's the supervisor? Where is she this minute?

Pregnant? they say like they never heard of it. And they run around and the regular doctor comes and says, Yes, pregnant. Sure. You got more news? my wife says. And then: meetings with the weekly psychiatrist, the day-by-day psychologist, the nerve doctor, the social worker, the supervising nurse, the nurse's aide. My wife says, Cissy knows. She's not an idiot, only mixed up and depressed. She *knows* she has a child in her womb inside of her like a normal woman. She likes it, my wife said. She even said to her, Mama, I'm having a baby, and she gave my wife a kiss. The first kiss in a couple of years. How do you like that?

Meanwhile, they investigated thoroughly. It turns out the man is a colored fellow. One of the gardeners. But he left a couple months ago for the Coast. I could imagine what happened. Cissy always loved flowers. When she was a little girl she was planting seeds every minute and sitting all day in front of the flower pot to see the little flower cracking up the seed. So she must of watched him and watched him. He dug up the earth. He put in the seeds. She watches.

The office apologized. Apologized? An accident. The supervisor was on vacation that week. I could sue them for a million dollars. Don't think I didn't talk to a lawyer. That time, then, when I heard, I called a detective agency to find him. My plan was to kill him. I would tear him limb from limb. What to do next. They called them all in again. The psychiatrist, the psychologist, they only left out the nurse's aide.

The only hope she could live a half-normal life—not in the institutions: she must have this baby, she could carry it full term. No, I said, I can't stand it. I refuse. Out of my Cissy, who looked like a piece of gold, would come a black child. Then the psychologist says, Don't be so bigoted. What nerve! Little by little my wife figured out a good idea. O.K., well, we'll put it out for adoption. Cissy doesn't even have to see it in person.

You are laboring under a misapprehension, says the boss of the place. They talk like that. What he meant, he meant we got to take that child home with us and if we really loved Cissy . . . Then he gave us a big lecture on this baby: it's Cissy's connection to life; also, it happens she was crazy about this gardener, this son of a bitch, a black man with a green thumb.

You see I can crack a little joke because look at this pleasure. I got a little best friend here. Where I go, he goes, even when I go down to the Italian side of the park to play a little bocce with the old goats over there. They invite me if they see me in the supermarket: Hey, Iz! Tony's sick. You come on an' play, O.K.? My wife says, Take Emanuel, he should see how men play games. I take him, those old guys they also seen plenty in their day. They think I'm some kind of a do-gooder. Also, a lot of those people are ignorant. They think the Jews are a little bit colored anyways, so they don't look at him too long. He goes to the swings and they make believe they never even seen him.

I didn't mean to get off the subject. What is the subject? The subject is how we took the baby. My wife, Mrs. Z., Nettie, she plain forced me. She said, We got to take this child on us. I will move out of here into the project with Cissy and be on welfare. Iz, you better make up your mind. Her brother, a top social worker, he encouraged her, I think he's a Communist also, the way he talks the last twenty, thirty years . . .

He says: You'll live, Iz. It's a baby, after all. It's got your blood in it. Unless of course you want Cissy to rot away in that place till you're so poor they don't keep her anymore. Then they'll stuff her into Bellevue or Central Islip or something. First she's a zombie, then she's a vegetable. That's what you want, Iz?

After this conversation I get sick. I can't go to work. Meanwhile, every night Nettie cries. She don't get dressed in the morning. She walks around with a broom. Doesn't sweep up. Starts to sweep, bursts into tears. Puts a pot of soup on the stove, runs into the bedroom, lies down. Soon I think I'll have to put her away too.

I give in.

My listener says to me, Right, Iz, you did the right thing. What else could you do?

I feel like smacking her. I'm not a violent person, just very excitable, but who asked her?—Right, Iz. She sits there looking at me, nodding her head from rightness. Emanuel is finally in the playground. I see him swinging and swinging. He could swing for two hours. He likes that. He's a regular swinger.

Well, the bad part of the story is over. Now is the good part. Naming the baby. What should we name him? Little brown baby. An intermediate color. A perfect stranger.

In the maternity ward, you know where the mothers lie, with the new babies, Nettie is saying, Cissy, Cissile darling, my sweetest heart (this is how my wife talked to her, like she was made of gold—or eggshells), my darling girl, what should we name this little child?

Cissy is nursing. On her white flesh is this little black curly head. Cissy says right away: Emanuel. Immediately. When I hear this, I say, Ridiculous. Ridiculous, such a long Jewish name on a little baby. I got old uncles with such names. Then they all get called Manny. Uncle Manny. Again she says—Emanuel!

David is nice, I suggest in a kind voice. It's your grandpa's, he should rest in peace. Michael is nice too, my wife says. Joshua is beautiful. Many children have these beautiful names nowadays. They're nice modern names. People like to say them.

No, she says, Emanuel. Then she starts screaming, Emanuel Emanuel. We almost had to give her extra pills. But we were careful on account of the milk. The milk could get affected.

O.K., everyone hollered. O.K. Calm yourself, Cissy. O.K. Emanuel. Bring the birth certificate. Write it down. Put it down. Let her see it. Emanuel . . . In a few days, the rabbi came. He raised up his eyebrows a couple times. Then he did his job, which is to make the bris. In other words, a circumcision. This is done so the child will be a man in Israel. That's the expression they use. He isn't the first colored child. They tell me long ago we were mostly dark. Also, now I think of it, I wouldn't mind going over there to Israel. They say there are plenty black Jews. It's not unusual over there at all. They ought to put out more publicity on it. Because I have to think where he should live. Maybe it won't be so good for him here. Because my son, his fancy ideas . . . ach, forget it.

What about the building, your neighborhood, I mean where you live now? Are there other black people in the community?

Oh yeah, but they're very snobbish. Don't ask what they got to be so snobbish.

Because, she says, he should have friends his own color, he shouldn't have the burden of being the only one in school.

Listen, it's New York, it's not Oshkosh, Wisconsin. But she gets going, you can't stop her.

After all, she says, he should eventually know his own people. It's their life he'll have to share. I know it's a problem to you, Iz, I know, but that's the way it is. A friend of mine with the same situation moved to a more integrated neighborhood.

Is that a fact? I say, Where's that?

Oh, there are . . .

I start to tell her, Wait a minute, we live thirty-five years in this apartment. But I can't talk. I sit very quietly for a while, I think and think. I say to myself, Be like a Hindu, Iz, calm like a cucumber. But it's too much. Listen, Miss, Miss Faith—do me a favor, don't teach me.

I'm not teaching you, Iz, it's just . . .

Don't answer me every time I say something. Talking talking. It's true. What for? To whom? Why? Nettie's right. It's our business. She's telling me Emanuel's life.

You don't know nothing about it, I yell at her. Go make a picket line. Don't teach me.

She gets up and looks at me kind of scared. Take it easy, Iz.

Emanuel is coming. He hears me. He got his little worried face. She sticks out a hand to pat him, his grandpa is hollering so loud.

But I can't put up with it. Hands off, I yell. It ain't your kid. Don't lay a hand on him. And I grab his shoulder and push him through the park, past the playground and the big famous arch. She runs after me a minute. Then she sees a couple friends. Now she has what to talk about. Three, four women. They make a little bunch. They talk. They turn around, they look. One waves. Hiya, Iz.

This park is full of noise. Everybody got something to say to the next guy. Playing this music, standing on their heads, juggling—someone even brought a piano, can you believe it, some job.

I sold the store four years ago. I couldn't put in the work no more. But I wanted to show Emanuel my pharmacy, what a beautiful place it was, how it sent three children to college, saved a couple lives—imagine: one store!

I tried to be quiet for the boy. You want ice cream, Emanuel? Here's a dollar, sonny. Buy yourself a Good Humor. The man's over there. Don't forget to ask for the change. I bend down to give him a kiss. I don't like that he heard me yell at a woman and my hand is still shaking. He runs a few steps, he looks back to make sure I didn't move an inch.

I got my eye on him too. He waves a chocolate Popsicle. It's a little darker than him. Out of that crazy mob a young fellow comes up to me. He has a baby strapped on his back. That's the style now. He asks like it's an ordinary friendly question, points to Emanuel. Gosh what a cute kid. Whose is he? I don't answer. He says it again, Really some cute kid.

I just look in his face. What does he want? I should tell him the story of my life? I don't need to tell. I already told and told. So I said very loud—no one else should bother me—how come it's your business, mister? Who do you think he is? By the way, whose kid you got on your back? It don't look like you.

He says, Hey there buddy, be cool be cool. I didn't mean anything. (You met anyone lately who meant something when he opened his mouth?) While I'm hollering at him, he starts to back away. The women are gabbing in a little clutch by the statue. It's a considerable distance, lucky they got radar. They turn around sharp like birds and fly over to the man. They talk very soft. Why are you bothering this old man, he got enough trouble? Why don't you leave him alone?

The fellow says, I wasn't bothering him. I just asked him something.

Well, he thinks you're bothering him, Faith says.

Then her friend, a woman maybe forty, very angry, starts to holler, How come you don't take care of your own kid? She's crying. Are you deaf? Naturally the third woman makes a remark, doesn't want to be left out. She taps him on his jacket: I seen you around here before, buster, you better watch out. He walks away from them backwards. They start in shaking hands.

Then this Faith comes back to me with a big smile. She says, Honestly, some people are a pain, aren't they, Iz? We sure let him have it, didn't we? And she gives me one of her kisses. Say hello to Cissy—O.K.? She puts her arms around her pals. They say a few words back and forth, like cranking up a motor. Then they bust out laughing. They wave goodbye to Emanuel. Laughing. Laughing. So long, Iz . . . see you . . .

So I say, What is going on, Emanuel, could you explain to me what just happened? Did you notice anywhere a joke? This is the first time he doesn't answer me. He's writing his name on the sidewalk. EMANUEL. Emanuel in big capital letters.

And the women walk away from us. Talking. Talking.

NESSA RAPOPORT

The Woman Who Lost
Her Names

She was named after her grandmother, Sarah, a name no one
else had then because it was considered old-fashioned.
Eight days after the naming her father's brother died, and they gave
her a middle name. The brother was Yosef—Joseph—so her
mother went down to City Hall, Bureau of Births and Deaths, and
Josephine was typed in the space after Sarah. "A name with class,"
her Aunt Rosie said. Sarah hated it.

When she got to school the kindergarten teacher sent home a
note. The family read it together, sitting around the kitchen table.
"Dear Mrs. Levi, we have decided to call the child Sally for the
purpose of school as it will help integrate her and make the adjust-
ment easier."

"What's to adjust?" the brother next to her asked.

"Shah," her father said.

Her father was a gentle man, remote, inaccessible. The books that covered the tables and chairs in his small apartment were the most constant factor in his daily life, and the incongruity of raising seven Orthodox children in the enlightened secularism of the Upper West Side never penetrated his absorption in Torah. Sarah grew up next to the families of Columbia intellectuals who were already far enough from Europe to want to teach their children civilization. The girls in her class had radios, then TVs, then nose jobs and contact lenses. They grew more graceful in their affluence, and she grew a foot taller than all of them, early. There were many blond girls in her class each year, and she'd stare at their fair delicate arms whose hair was almost invisible. "Sally, how does your garden grow?" the boys would tease her in the hall, staring at her breasts, the thick dark hair covering her arms to her wrists, the wild hair that sprung from her head independent of her. She'd look down at herself, her bigness, ungainly, and think, "Peasant, you peasant," to herself and the grandmother who'd bequeathed her these outsized limbs. No one would fall in love with her.

Her mother was fierce, intense, passionately arguing, worrying about people, disdainful. "She married for money," "he could have been a scholar"—indicting these neighbors who were changing their names, selling their birthright. "Sarele," she'd suddenly gather her daughter in her arms late at night when Sarah's brothers were sleeping, "remember who you are and you'll have yourself. No matter what else you lose—" Her mother never finished the sentence. Sarah would look into her face, full of shadows, ghosts, and touch the cheek that was softer than anything. "You're a big girl, Sarah"—her mother shook herself free, always—"go to bed." Her mother would sit at the kitchen table alone, head in her hands, thinking. Once, long past midnight, Sarah saw her that way, shaking her head between her clenched fingers, and tiptoed in to say, "Mama, I understand." Her mother looked up, uncomprehending.

When she was seventeen and had given up hope she suddenly bloomed. Her hair calmed down, and a kind of beauty emerged from within her. The boys in her youth movement started to talk to her after meetings, inviting her places. First she said no, then she believed them and went gladly to rallies, campfires, lectures to raise money for the new state of Israel. She dreamed of Israel often, dancing the folk dances in the orange groves of her imagination, fighting malaria, drowning in jasmine. None of the boys touched her heart.

At school boys were thinking of college, and girls were thinking of boys. Graduation came on a hot day in June, and her parents watched her get a special award in poetry, poems she had written that no one but the teacher would ever read. "Poetry, Sarele." Her father was pleased. "My dreamer," her mother whispered. "We have a surprise for you. From Israel." The word was still strange on her mother's tongue.

Yakov Halevi was her cousin, a first cousin from Jerusalem she'd never met. He got up to greet her from the couch in her parents' living room, the room reserved for company, and she watched his thin energized frame spring forward. He was meant to be dressed in black like the rest of her cousins whose pictures she'd seen in her mother's hand, sidecurls swaying in an overseas wind. But his hair was short, startling, red, and the hair of his chest showed in his open-neck shirt. He spoke seriously, with a heavy accent, and she loved to watch the words form in his mouth before he released them. Yakov was a poet, only twenty and already known for his fervent lines. Great things were expected of him, and he carried their weight on his narrow Hebrew shoulders. Her Bible knowledge wasn't enough, and she struggled with the new language to read his book, tracing the letters of the title page, alarmed: Jerusalem Fruit, by Yakov Peniel.

"Who's Peniel?" she asked him. "Why did you change your name?"

"I didn't change it, I lost it," he laughed. "When the editor wrote to me accepting my poems, he had to ask my name, for I hadn't sent it. 'Hagidah na shmekha,' he wrote, what Yakov our forefather asked when he wrestled the angel. 'Why is it that you ask my name?' I wrote back, as the angel answered, and he published me under the name Yakov gave that place—Peniel."

"But your letters come to you in that name. How did it happen?"

He shrugged. "People wanted to meet the bright young poet,

Peniel. Then I was asked to talk, introduced that way. On the street they would say, 'That's Peniel,' and so it came to be."

"But you're the tenth generation of Jerusalem Halevis. You can't give it up, it's your name."

"Just a name," he smiled. "The soul underneath is the same, in better and worse."

She loved that humility, and the heart of Eretz Yisrael she heard pounding in his chest when he held her. He loved her and loved her America. "It's not mine," she'd insist. "I don't belong here." But he stood in the middle of New York looking up. "So big," he would cry in his foreign tongue. "So big."

He wanted to cross the country sea to sea, to marvel at mountains and chasms. She had waited so long to go home, to Israel, she could wait a little longer. Then he was her home, she became him, she loved every bone of his self, every line. The words of his mouth were her thoughts, what he touched she found worthy. It thrilled her, their sameness, and she'd wake in the mornings eager for the coming confirmations. They would say the same things at one time and reach for each other, marveling. She wasn't alone anymore, she had found a companion. When she tried to explain about the Upper West Side and the girls in her class he would say, "Every one is alone. Man is alone before God, that's our state." Hearing him say it bound her even more. She wanted to breathe his breath, use his language, and searched through his poems, word after word, for her hidden presence.

"My muse." He sorted her hair. "Sarele," saying it the old Jewish way as he'd heard his mother, also a Sarah, being called.

They knew they would marry, she floated for months on that knowledge, walking down Broadway to the rhythm of Solomon's Songs. "Sarele"—Yakov drew her to him one night—"we must talk of the name."

"It's all right. I don't mind Peniel. It's better in a way than Halevi, which is almost my name. No one would know I was married."

"It's the other name—Sarah. My mother's name. A man cannot marry a woman with his mother's name."

She turned white. "A man cannot marry?"

He noticed her face. "Oh, no, no, he can marry, but she, she must change the name."

She said in relief, "But what name? Sarah was my name."

"Do you have a middle name?"

She scowled. "Josephine."

"A *goyische* name. Josephine. So what do we do?"

She thought for a while. "I don't know. Josephine is Josie, but that's no good."

"Jozzi"—it was clumsy—"Jozzi. There isn't a Jozzi in Hebrew."

She had no suggestion.

"Wait." he told her. "Jozzi is Joseph—Yosef—is that right?"

She nodded.

"Well, then, it's Yosefah. Yosefah"—he tried it on. The Hebrew sounds spun in the air. "Yosefah." He turned her around and around till the trees flew in front of her, dizzy.

They married in spring and all summer they traveled as he fell in love with America. He loved New York City, the place where they'd started, he fingered the wheat of Midwestern fields and stood on a rock high over the ocean as if he'd discovered the water. In the evenings and as she woke up he was scribbling. Poems, letters, stories poured from his hand. She sat amazed as the papers grew and multiplied in hotel rooms, in the trunk of the car. The strange Hebrew letters leaped from the pages, keeping their secrets against her straining will. "Are you writing of me?" she wanted to know. He smiled. "They are all of you." He told her he sometimes took phrases she said and transplanted them into his work. She was grateful and mystified, peering through the foreign marks for herself, not finding resemblance.

Yearning for Israel they stayed in New York. He studied small Talmudic matters on which great things depended. She had a son, then another. The boys laughed and cried with her all day, alone in the house, surrounded by papers and books of ancient cracked binding. When he finished his doctorate they would live in Israel, and she counted the days as they lengthened to months, alone with her children and the fierceness of her desire. She was America to him, aspiring to be free, and he envied her readiness to leave such abundance behind. "It's your home," he tried to soften her, frightened by her single burning.

"It has nothing to do with me," she'd deny. He trembled in the face of seduction—the grandness of America's gestures, hundreds of plains crossed by rivers whose opposite shores were too far to see.

"We must leave," he said. "We must go."

She stopped her daydream of years and started to pack. The boat left in winter, and the grey piers of New York, city of her birth but not her death, she was sure, were left behind her, unmourned. He stood watching the gap of water widen, then turned to her and was thankful.

There were cypress and palm trees ascending, and a perfume heavier than air. Jerusalem approached them at twilight, her gold roofs and domes aching for heaven. She recognized the city as a lover, missing past time, a shock of remembrance that stirred her body like a child. The boys were crying, tired, afraid, and she sheltered them under the sleeves of her coat. "We are home."

Jerusalem was designed for the world to come more than for this one, and she washed, cleaned, shopped, scrubbed over and over again, as the dust blew in the summer and the winter wind seeped through the cracks. The boys got sick, and well, and she was sick in the morning, pregnant with the next child. Yakov laughed as he smoothed her hair. "A girl, a *maidele* next."

From America letters came. A brother was hired, her mother was sick, Aunt Rosie was worried, family troubles, her mother was sick, Papa retired, a nephew converted, her mother was dying, gone. There was no money for planes, and the pregnancy was hard, so half a world away she guarded her pain, talking to her mother in dreams about the coming daughter. Her mother, sitting now at a kitchen table that was not of the earth, holding her head in her hands. Night after night she lay on her back, her stomach a dome in her arms.

When the child was born she could hardly know, groaning in a voice unknown to herself, stuffed between Arabs and old men in this not-American hospital. Outside the war in Sinai was sending soldiers into her ward, and sending her into the hall and then home, almost before she could stand. She had borne the child alone, Yakov at the front, and when she looked down at her daughter, resting on her breast, she was full and at peace with this breathing body of her secret prayers, in love with the child, flesh of her flesh, bone of her bone, not a stranger. Yakov came home, exhausted, off for three days to see her and rejoice in his daughter. When he finally was there she stared from her bed unbelieving, two ones loved so dearly, both whole in limb. It was wondrous to her, and she ran her fingers up and down those tiny arms and legs hundreds of times. And Yakov, unmutilated, only tired, spoke to her, saying, "We must give the child a name."

"But I know the name"—and she did, waiting for him to come home from the war, reading the Book of Psalms. "She is Ayelet Hashachar: the dawn star."

Yakov smiled over her, indulgent. "This is not a name."

"This is the name," she said firmly. "Ayelet. Ayelet Hashachar, it's beautiful."

"Yes," he said gravely. "It is beautiful. But it's not the child's name. Yosefele"—the smile—"your mother."

"My mother would love the name. She would love it"—remembering her mother alone at the table dreaming her dreams long past midnight.

"Your mother was Dinsche," he told her, "and the child must be Dina. It is the Jewish way."

She looked at him, trying to find in herself some agreement, even a small accord and she'd bend to his will. But there was nothing.

"Yakov," she pleaded, "my mother won't care. I represent her. I know." Her mother holding her head in her hands. "It cannot be Dina. It can't be." Her voice was rising, new sounds that surprised her. "There's blood on that name."

She rose from the bed. "Look"—and held out the Bible, shaking, to him. "Read." She tore through the page in her haste. " 'And when Shechem the son of Hamor the Hivite, the prince of the land, saw her, he seized her and lay with her and humbled her.' "

He stood before her in silence. "Rape," she said. "You want a daughter named for a rape."

"It is out of respect," he said. "For your mother. I don't understand what you want. A *goyische* name like Diana?" he asked. "If it's better we'll call her Diana."

"Ayelet Hashachar," she whispered in mourning, swaying like a rebbe in prayer.

"So what is it?" he asked.

"I don't care what you do," came the words in that voice, the one she had heard from herself giving birth. "Do what you want," she said, turning her face to the wall.

He stroked her hair straight back from her forehead until finally she was asleep.

When the day of the naming arrived she was numb, jabbing the pins of her headcovering into her hair. She walked with her sons and her husband to the synagogue, and left them to climb the steps to the balcony for women. Below her the men were lifting the Torah, opening and closing it, dressing, undressing it, reading the day's portion. The people in the synagogue were singing quite loud, and some of the women sang, too. The women around her moved their lips to the words. She stood still. She stood in her place, the place where the mothers always sat for their children. She closed her mouth, her lips pressed together, one on top of the other, and waited to hear her daughter's name.

ROBIN ROGER

The Pagan Phallus

When Bill Gibson asked Terry Steinham if, despite being Jewish, she would be the copywriter on the Salvation Army account, she slid down in her swivel chair, hiked up her skirt, and said:

"You know I can't resist a man in uniform."

He tried to pull down the corners of his mouth.

"Get real, Steinham. What I mean is, they take their Christianity pretty seriously. Can you handle it?"

"Why not?" she asked, rummaging in her purse for an emery board. "All our clients worship something. God's as good as anything else."

"Of course, you'll have to behave yourself," he went on. "They aren't exactly wild and crazy guys."

"I bet they give great blow jobs."

"Terry!" he pleaded.

"Why else would they be called the Salivation Army?"

"Would you *please*—"

"Do you think they use the missionary position?"

"Oh, God!" gasped Bill, bolting from her office.

But at her first meeting with the Salvation Army Media Committee, she saw it was no joke. Twelve men in navy-blue uniforms sat around the conference table, hands clasped and heads bowed. Commissioner Haskell Ewart, commander of the United States Salvation Army, invited Colonel Calvert to start the meeting with a prayer.

"Lord Jesus, Our Father," he began, voice and jowls trembling in unison. Terry took a covert peek at the twelve supplicants. They each wore intense expressions, as if listening to a divine whisper. It suddenly struck her that even though she'd lived among Christians all her life, she'd never given much thought to their religion.

"Bless this committee and our endeavours, made in thy name. O Lord, bless our new envoy, Terry Steinham. . . ."

Commissioner Ewart, on her left side, nodded gravely, his chin dipping towards the silver "S" on his collar.

In fact, aside from the fact that they believed in Christ and she didn't, she had never really noticed much difference between gentiles and Jews.

"In the name of your son, who died on the cross for our sins, Christ Jesus, Amen."

"Amenamenamen," echoed the committee, lifting twelve radiant countenances. Her eyes met the Commissioner's. He gave her a reassuring smile as the committee broke into a short spurt of social chatter.

"I understand you've been to the Holy Land three times," he said, leaning towards her so she could hear over the voices.

She was momentarily confused.

"Oh—Israel. Sure."

A reverent smile softened his taut brown lips. Remembering her unholy activities with Israeli soldiers, she tried not to smirk.

"We will begin today's meeting with a discussion of a new slogan for our next fund-raising campaign."

The twelve men leaned forward, stretching their hands towards the Commissioner, offering suggestions as if they were tributes.

"Matthew 5—'Give to him who begs from you,' " called a young officer from the end of the table.

" 'Know how to give good gifts to your children.' Luke 11," called the officer directly across from her.

"I like Mark 7—'Let the children first be fed,' " a third added.

The Commissioner nodded at each of his men, listening carefully, committing to nothing. She couldn't quite fix his age. His hair was grey, but his skin was barely lined, and his jawline was crisp. As he leaned back in his swivel chair, his jacket fell open to reveal a firm, long abdomen and narrow hips.

Looking at his pants, she remembered where the difference between Christians and Jews was concealed.

"Is something funny?" the Commissioner asked her.

Her smile broadened as she shook her head. He leaned forward with a coaxing smile.

"Tell us."

"It's nothing." She laughed out loud. The twelve men began to smile, infected by her gaiety. "Just a silly thought."

"For a slogan?"

She nodded, stalling.

Twelve men crossed their hands on their laps and waited.

"What about . . . uh. . . ." She suddenly remembered the prayer she'd had to say in public school every morning. " 'Give us this day'?"

The soldiers gasped. The Commissioner's expression changed to wonder.

"Praise the Lord," said Commissioner Haskell Ewart.

Remembering the way the Commissioner had looked at her when he said "Praise the Lord," she went to a bookstore to buy herself a copy of the New Testament. A chart over the display explained which denomination adhered to which edition of the Bible. Catholics, Fundamentalists, Baptists, Episcopalians, Pentecostals, Seventh Day Adventists, Jehovah's Witnesses, Unitarians, Mormons, Greek Orthodox —her eyes rattled. There were so many Christians in the world, so many texts. In a separate box on the bottom of the chart, it read: "Jews: The Five Books of Moses."

But why was it, she wondered, that even during her most experimental phase, all her lovers had been Jewish? She ran her hand through her thick black curls as she made a mental count. Married men. Professors. Total strangers in bars. Out-of-town guests at Bar Mitzvahs. Rabbis. Schizophrenics. Not a foreskin among them.

"Excuse me, Ma'am."

A young man with a blinding smile towered over her.

"I couldn't help noticing you're looking for the Sword."

She looked around to see if he was talking to somebody else. His spotless white T-shirt, tucked into skin-tight white jeans, was cut away to reveal the kind of muscles upon which legends are built.

"No, I'm not, I'm looking for the New Testament," she answered, lifting one hand to flick her hair behind her shoulder.

"That's the Sword!" he cried, his Adam's apple leaping in his throat. "Are you just finding your way to the Sword now?"

She smiled mysteriously.

They each leaned against a shelf of books, eyeing the other. His hair fell over one eye; his lips gleamed in the light cast by his toothy grin.

"Are you free for coffee?" he asked.

A silver sword was raised on one side of the belt buckle above his fly. The leather was capped with a silver arrowhead. She suggested her place.

There was no time for interfaith dialogue.

As soon as she shut the door to her apartment, he cupped her right buttock with one hand and pulled her to him. Quickly their embrace became a game, a kind of teasing conversation. He collapsed her so she landed under him on the carpet. Acquiescing strategically, she sucked his tongue until he relaxed and slid to her side, then she pinched his inner thigh as hard as she could, pushing him over and mounting his chest. He chuckled throatily as he took advantage of his position to reach for the buttons on her shirt.

She reached for the sword.

There it was, the skin of distinction, topping off his shaft like a pink velvet toque. As if doffing its cap, it bobbed down, then up. She just stared. It looked completely different, this quivering creature, with the skin over its glans like a cover on a canary cage. She stared for so long that its pink cap dipped just slightly and he asked her if she was a virgin.

She laughed all the way to the bed.

After he left, she lay under the covers with her new Bible, flipping the pages to fan her face. A whole new world opened before her. Catholics, Fundamentalists, Baptists, Episcopalians, Pentecostals, Seventh Day Adventists, Jehovah's Witnesses, Unitarians, Evangelists, Mormons, Greek Orthodox—even Salvationists.

Commissioner Haskell Ewart, widowed young, had come to the Army a boozed-out bum, and now stood at the helm. But were his sins confined to alcohol?

Watching him conduct his meetings, make decisions, and dispatch orders with the vitality of a rising executive, Terry doubted it. Sitting opposite him at their weekly, private lunch meeting, she was certain. His handshake lingered; his compliment on her appearance was more than perfunctory. And when he bowed his head in silence before they began their meal, the private smile on his lips made her doubt that he was thinking about God.

Their conversation strayed from business. With the skills honed over countless client lunches, she lured him into discussions of his former life. Not just of the drinking, but of the needs that lay behind it: his burning desire to act, the sordid life of the stage. His pontifical veneer melted as he acted out the villains of his past: false-promising playwrights, seductive leading ladies, manipulative directors. He'd been there and back.

He had other skills. She found herself speaking of her childhood, of being a Jew in a gentile world, and the feeling of loneli-

ness—even abandonment—when her friends disappeared to celebrate their holidays. He squeezed her hand when she spoke of a
sense of unbreachable separation which she could not understand.
She was welcome among them, he assured her. She was to think of
herself as a true intimate. To prove it, he invited her to Soul's
Harbour, their spiritual retreat, where laymen—especially single
female laymen—never visited.

Driving alone in the mountains in her ancient Karmann Ghia
unnerved her, but just as the summer light was fading she came to
the gates of the mountain lodge. A brass plate on the gatepost read:
"Soul's Harbour, the Salvation Army Spiritual Retreat." Beneath
that, in smaller letters like a copyright, was their motto: "Heart to
God, hand to man." As she followed the dusty roads that switched
back and forth up the mountainside, she wondered what had possessed her to come. It was one thing to trade confidences over
lunch, another to spend the weekend together. Just what did he
mean when he said she was a true intimate? She knew that the
tremor she felt was more than the vibration of her decrepit car.

Major Brenda Trimmer, the Commissioner's secretary, led her
to her room, explaining that he was spending the evening in the
hermitage on another part of the retreat. Terry sat on her bed,
staring alternately at a picture of Jesus at the foot and a portrait of
General William Booth at the head. Booth, the Army's founder,
might have been Jewish, the Commissioner had once told her. He
had a Jewish nose. Another difference between Christians and Jews,
she thought, stretching to examine her profile in the mirror over
the dresser. She had always wanted to have her nose fixed, but her
parents drew the line of assimilation at the knife. What would have
happened if God had commanded Abraham to take the hook off
his nose instead of the skin off his dink? Haskell Ewart might be a
Jew today. She decided to find the hermitage.

The vast lawn around the lodge was spongy and deep. A dirt
path led into the trees, winding downwards to an arrangement of
rocks and boulders pointing the way. Scrambling down, she
gripped the abrasive surfaces, relishing their assertive texture. Her
palms tingled, and her toes curled inside her sneakers as she tested
for a foothold. Emerging from the rocky labyrinth, the sweat on

her collarbone cooling in the breeze, she sat and watched the stars, bright pebbles of light. Then, in a distant thicket of trees, she noticed a log cabin with a light glowing from a high, small window.

She approached quietly, rounding the front of the cabin and stepping up on the porch softly, so that she could retreat if she was intruding. In the shadow of the porch, she could see in without being seen. A fire was burning in the enormous hearth that dominated the one-room interior, and a coal-oil lamp shone on a table against one wall, illuminating the same two portraits of Jesus and William Booth that adorned her quarters. But here, on either side of the portraits were two primitive wooden gargoyles, one with eyes bulging from their sockets, the other with a long curling tongue extended from taut rectangular lips. Beneath them, on the table, were two small idols carved from the same wood: a cross-legged woman with full, round breasts topped off by bulging nipples, and beside her a man with a long slender torso supporting a phallus twice its length, his hands wound around the base as if he were wielding a bat.

The Commissioner had told her of his years in Africa, spent teaching natives to trade their impotent little idols for the omnipotent wooden cross, and as she stood staring at the unflagging phallus, she felt a sudden surge of admiration for the man and his faith. Then she saw the Commissioner approach the idols.

Out of uniform, in a hooded sweatshirt and jogging pants that hugged the curve of his buttocks, he looked like the exuberant young actor he had set out to be. He stood with his hands on his hips, in silent reverie, the dim light of the coal-oil lamp trapping a shadow in the cleft of his chin. Then he crossed his arms in front of him and pulled his sweatshirt over his head. Terry felt her heart bolt, as if a starter's gun had gone off. But she stood her ground.

What broad shoulders he had, and what smooth flesh. When he reached for the elasticized waistband of his jogging pants, she did not flinch. His buttocks were round and firm, like two smooth rocks. He kicked his pants off the ends of his feet, and did a small leap, stretching his arms up and shaking his head, as if celebrating his nakedness. Then he turrned around.

She nearly cried aloud. There was no foreskin. His prick hung

like a slack hose suspended from his pubic hair, the naked glans
shamelessly exposed. She was completely let down at the sight of
this familiar-looking pecker—just a standard kosher hot dog. Even
the pagan phallus on the table behind him had a foreskin—why
didn't he, the mighty Christian? General Booth had a Jewish nose,
and the Commissioner had a Jewish prick—what was going on?
Christian, Schmistian—they just wanted to be Jews. She turned on
her heel.

She was halfway back to the path when she heard him call her
name, and turned to find him dashing up to her, dressed in a navy
terrycloth robe.

"This is providential," he said. "I was just thinking about you
when I heard footsteps. Let me change."

He came back in his jogging clothes. They sat side by side in a
tiny shelter, looking into the darkness.

"I'm so glad we have this chance to be alone," he began. Then
a small chuckle. "The truth is, I had something in mind when I
invited you here."

She rolled her eyes in the dark. Forget it, she thought, sliding to
the far edge of her seat. No foreskin, no foreplay.

"I feel we've gotten to know each other over the past months,
and that we've opened up to each other. I know I have to you, and
I flatter myself that you have revealed something of yourself to
me."

She snorted.

"But it isn't enough. It's only a glimpse of the thing I want."

I bet, she thought.

"You have something very special, Terry," he told her, almost
in a whisper.

Yeah, and you're missing something special, she responded in
her mind.

"That longing for higher things, that gift we call faith."

"Faith?" she shrieked, jumping from the bench. "What does
faith have to do with us?"

He bowed his head and held his palms upward, as if trying to lift
the heavens.

"I would like to lead you to God."

"God?"
"God."
"God?"
"Yes, God."
She sank back down on the bench, bewildered, deflated.
"Which God?"
"The Lord is Our God. The Lord is One."
An overwhelming sense of déjà vu made her clutch her temples.
"Yes, that was the *sh'ma*," said the Commissioner. "I've studied Judaism—it is the bedrock of my faith."
"What does that make me—a chip off the old block?" She jumped from the bench, turning away from him. What presumption. What impudence. He gripped her shoulder, squeezing gently.
"I owe you an apology. That was unforgivably condescending. The truth is—." Suddenly his voice broke. "Oh, Lord," he said, his voice muffled. "I am guilty of such a shameful sin."
"Please—no." She turned to face him, putting one hand on each of his stooped shoulders. "I understand."
"It's just that I've converted pagans, but never a Jew . . . it was vain glory, pride . . . and you, you were so frank about your needs, so . . . well, I fell." He looked at her anxiously, searching her face for some kind of response. "Of course, you'll want to move off the account."
"You mean I'm just another notch on your cross?"
She clasped her hands together and held them to her lips. He wanted her soul, she wanted his . . . God, she'd been stupid. Impulsively she leaned forward and gave him a collegial kiss on the cheek.
"Forget it, Commish—it was just a miscalculation. I've made a few in my time. But can I ask you a personal question?"
"Anything," he urged her. "I have nothing to hide."
She began by asking about the foreskin on the pagan phallus.

PHILIP ROTH

"I Always Wanted You to Admire My Fasting"; or, Looking at Kafka

To the students of English 275,
University of Pennsylvania,
Fall 1972

"I always wanted you to admire my fasting," said the hunger artist. "We do admire it," said the overseer, affably. "But you shouldn't admire it," said the hunger artist. "Well then we don't admire it," said the overseer, "but why shouldn't we admire it?" "Because I have to fast, I can't help it," said the hunger artist. "What a fellow you are," said the overseer, "and why can't you help it?" "Because," said the hunger artist, lifting his head a little and speaking, with his lips pursed, as if for a kiss, right into the overseer's ear, so that no syllable might be lost, "because I couldn't find the food I liked. If I had found it, believe me, I should have made no fuss and stuffed myself like you or anyone else." These were his last words, but in his dimming eyes remained the firm though no longer proud persuasion that he was still continuing to fast.
—*"A Hunger Artist," Franz Kafka*

1

I am looking, as I write of Kafka, at the photograph taken of him at the age of forty (my age)—it is 1924, as sweet and hopeful a year as he may ever have known as a man, and the year of his death. His face is sharp and skeletal, a burrower's face: pronounced cheekbones made even more conspicuous by the absence of sideburns; the ears shaped and angled on his head like angel wings; an intense, creaturely gaze of startled composure— enormous fears, enormous control; a black towel of Levantine hair

pulled close around the skull the only sensuous feature; there is a
familiar Jewish flare in the bridge of the nose, the nose itself is long
and weighted slightly at the tip—the nose of half the Jewish boys
who were my friends in high school. Skulls chiseled like this one
were shoveled by the thousands from the ovens; had he lived, his
would have been among them, along with the skulls of his three
younger sisters. Of course it is no more horrifying to think of Franz
Kafka in Auschwitz than to think of anyone in Auschwitz—to
paraphrase Tolstoy, it is just horrifying in its own way. But he died
too soon for the holocaust. Had he lived, perhaps he would have
escaped with his good friend and great advocate Max Brod, who
eventually found refuge in Palestine, a citizen of Israel until his
death there in 1970. But *Kafka* escaping? It seems unlikely for one
so fascinated by entrapment and careers that culminate in anguished death. Still, there is Karl Rossman, his American greenhorn. Having imagined Karl's escape to America and his mixed
luck here, could not Kafka have found a way to execute an escape
for himself? The New School for Social Research in New York
becoming *his* Great Nature Theater of Oklahoma? Or perhaps
through the influence of Thomas Mann, a position in the German
department at Princeton . . . But then had Kafka lived it is not at
all certain that the books of his which Mann celebrated from *his*
refuge in New Jersey would ever have been published; eventually
Kafka might either have destroyed those manuscripts that he had
once bid Max Brod to dispose of at his death, or, at the least,
continued to keep them his secret. The Jewish refugee arriving in
America in 1938 would not then have been Mann's "religious
humorist," but a frail and bookish fifty-five-year-old bachelor, formerly a lawyer for a government insurance firm in Prague, retired
on a pension in Berlin at the time of Hitler's rise to power—an
author, yes, but of a few eccentric stories, mostly about animals,
stories no one in America had ever heard of and only a handful in
Europe had read; a homeless K., but without K.'s willfulness and
purpose, a homeless Karl, but without Karl's youthful spirit and
resilience; just a Jew lucky enough to have escaped with his life, in
his possession a suitcase containing some clothes, some family
photos, some Prague mementos, and the manuscripts, still unpub-

lished and in pieces, of *Amerika, The Trial, The Castle,* and (stranger things happen) three more fragmented novels, no less remarkable than the bizarre masterworks that he keeps to himself out of Oedipal timidity, perfectionist madness, and insatiable longings for solitude and spiritual purity.

July, 1923: Eleven months before he will die in a Vienna sanatorium, Kafka somehow finds the resolve to leave Prague and his father's home for good. Never before has he even remotely succeeded in living apart, independent of his mother, his sisters and his father, nor has he been a writer other than in those few hours when he is not working in the legal department of the Workers' Accident Insurance Office in Prague; since taking his law degree at the university, he has been by all reports the most dutiful and scrupulous of employees, though he finds the work tedious and enervating. But in June of 1923—having some months earlier been pensioned from his job because of his illness—he meets a young Jewish girl of nineteen at a seaside resort in Germany, Dora Dymant, an employee at the vacation camp of the Jewish People's Home of Berlin. Dora has left her Orthodox Polish family to make a life of her own (at half Kafka's age); she and Kafka—who has just turned forty—fall in love . . . Kafka has by now been engaged to two somewhat more conventional Jewish girls—twice to one of them—hectic, anguished engagements wrecked largely by his fears. "I am mentally incapable of marrying," he writes his father in the forty-five-page letter he gave to his mother to deliver, ". . . the moment I make up my mind to marry I can no longer sleep, my head burns day and night, life can no longer be called life." He explains why. "Marrying is barred to me," he tells his father, "because it is your domain. Sometimes I imagine the map of the world spread out and you stretched diagonally across it. And I feel as if I could consider living in only those regions that either are not covered by you or are not within your reach. And in keeping with the conception I have of your magnitude, these are not many and not very comforting regions—and marriage is not among them." The letter explaining what is wrong between this father and this son is dated November, 1919; the mother thought it best not even to deliver it, perhaps for lack of courage, probably, like the son, for lack of hope.

During the following two years Kafka attempts to wage an affair with Milena Jesenská-Pollak, an intense young woman of twenty-four who has translated a few of his stories into Czech and is most unhappily married in Vienna; his affair with Milena, conducted feverishly, but by and large through the mails, is even more demoralizing to Kafka than the fearsome engagements to the nice Jewish girls. They aroused only the paterfamilias longings that he dared not indulge, longings inhibited by his exaggerated awe of his father—"spellbound," says Brod, "in the family circle"—and the hypnotic spell of his own solitude; but the Czech Milena, impetuous, frenetic, indifferent to conventional restraints, a woman of appetite and anger, arouses more elemental yearnings and more elemental fears. According to a Prague critic, Rio Preisner, Milena was "psychopathic"; according to Margaret Buber-Neumann, who lived two years beside her in the German concentration camp where Milena died following a kidney operation in 1944, she was powerfully sane, extraordinarily humane and courageous. Milena's obituary for Kafka was the only one of consequence to appear in the Prague press; the prose is strong, so are the claims she makes for Kafka's accomplishment. She is still only in her twenties, the dead man is hardly known as a writer beyond his small circle of friends—yet Milena writes, "His knowledge of the world was exceptional and deep, and he was a deep and exceptional world in himself . . . [He had] a delicacy of feeling bordering on the miraculous and a mental clarity that was terrifyingly uncompromising, and in turn he loaded on to his illness the whole burden of his mental fear of life . . . He wrote the most important books in recent German literature." One can imagine this vibrant young woman stretched diagonally across the bed, as awesome to Kafka as his own father spread out across the map of the world. His letters to her are disjointed, unlike anything else of his in print; the word fear, frequently emphasized, appears on page after page. "We are both married, you in Vienna, I to my Fear in Prague." He yearns to lay his head upon her breast; he calls her "Mother Milena";

during at least one of their two brief rendezvous, he is hopelessly impotent. At last he has to tell her to leave him be, an edict that Milena honórs though it leaves her hollow with grief. "Do not write," Kafka tells her, "and let us not see each other; I ask you only to quietly fulfill this request of mine; only on those conditions is survival possible for me; everything else continues the process of destruction."

Then in the early summer of 1923, during a visit to his sister who is vacationing with her children by the Baltic Sea, he finds young Dora Dymant, and within a month Franz Kafka has gone off to live with her in two rooms in a suburb of Berlin, out of reach at last of the "claws" of Prague and home. How can it be? How can he, in his illness, have accomplished so swiftly and decisively the leave-taking that was so beyond him in his healthiest days? The impassioned letter-writer who could equivocate interminably about which train to catch to Vienna to meet with Milena (if he should meet with her for the weekend at all); the bourgeois suitor in the high collar, who, during his drawn-out agony of an engagement with the proper Fraulein Bauer, secretly draws up a memorandum for himself, countering the arguments "for" marriage with the arguments "against"; the poet of the ungraspable and the unresolved, whose belief in the immovable barrier separating the wish from its realization is at the heart of his excruciating visions of defeat, the Kafka whose fictions refute every easy, touching, humanish daydream of salvation and justice and fulfillment with densely imagined counter-dreams that mock all solutions and escapes—this Kafka, escapes! Overnight! K. penetrates the Castle walls—Joseph K. evades his indictment—"a breaking away from it altogether, a mode of living completely outside the jurisdiction of the court." Yes, the possibility of which Joseph K. has just a glimmering in the Cathedral, but can neither fathom nor effectuate—"not . . . some influential manipulation of the case, but . . . a circumvention of it"—Kafka realizes in the last year of his life.

Was it Dora Dymant or was it death that pointed the new way? Perhaps it could not have been one without the other. We know that the "illusory emptiness" at which K. gazed upon first entering the village and looking up through the mist and the darkness to the

Castle was no more vast and incomprehensible than was the idea of himself as husband and father to the young Kafka; but now it seems the prospect of a Dora forever, of a wife, home, and children everlasting, is no longer the terrifying, bewildering prospect it would once have been, for now "everlasting" is undoubtedly not much more than a matter of months. Yes, the dying Kafka is determined to marry, and writes to Dora's Orthodox father for his daughter's hand. But the imminent death that has resolved all contradictions and uncertainties in Kafka is the very obstacle placed in his path by the young girl's father. The request of Franz Kafka, a dying man, to bind to him in his invalidism Dora Dymant, a healthy young girl, is—denied!

If there is not one father standing in Kafka's way, there is another—and, to be sure, another beyond him. Dora's father, writes Max Brod in his biography of Kafka, "set off with [Kafka's] letter to consult the man he honored most, whose authority counted more than anything else for him, the 'Gerer Rebbe.' The rabbi read the letter, put it to one side, and said nothing more than the single syllable, 'No.' " *No.* Klamm himself could have been no more abrupt—or any more removed from the petitioner. *No.* In its harsh finality, as telling and inescapable as the curselike threat delivered by his father to Georg Bendemann, that thwarted fiancé: "Just take your bride on your arm and try getting in my way. I'll sweep her from your very side, you don't know how!" *No.* Thou shalt not have, say the fathers, and Kafka agrees that he shall not. The habit of obedience and renunciation; also his own distaste for the diseased and reverence for strength, appetite, and health. " 'Well, clear this out now!' said the overseer, and they buried the hunger artist, straw and all. Into the cage they put a young panther. Even the most insensitive felt it refreshing to see this wild creature leaping around the cage that had so long been dreary. The panther was all right. The food he liked was brought him without hesitation by the attendants; he seemed not even to miss his freedom; his noble body, furnished almost to the bursting point with all that it needed, seemed to carry freedom around with it too; somewhere in his jaws it seemed to lurk; and the joy of life streamed with such ardent passion from his throat that for the onlookers it was not easy to stand the shock of it. But they braced themselves, crowded around the cage, and did not want ever to move away." So no is no; he knew as much himself. A healthy young girl of nineteen cannot, *should* not, be given in matrimony to a sickly man twice her age, who spits up blood ("I sentence you," cries George Bendemann's father, "to death by drowning!") and shakes in his bed with fevers and chills. What sort of un-Kafka-like dream had Kafka been dreaming?

And those nine months spent with Dora have still other "Kafka-esque" elements: a fierce winter in quarters inadequately heated; the inflation that makes a pittance of his own meager pension, and sends into the streets of Berlin the hungry and needy whose sufferings, says Dora, turn Kafka "ash-gray"; and his tubercular lungs, flesh transformed and punished. Dora cares as devotedly and tenderly for the diseased writer as does Gregor Samsa's sister for her brother, the bug. Gregor's sister plays the violin so beautifully that Gregor "felt as if the way were opening before him to the unknown nourishment he craved"; he dreams, in his condition, of sending his gifted sister to the Conservatory! Dora's music is Hebrew, which she reads aloud to Kafka, and with such skill that, according to Brod, "Franz recognized her dramatic talent; on his advice and under his direction she later educated herself in the art . . ."

Only Kafka is hardly vermin to Dora Dymant, *or to himself.* Away from Prague and his father's home, Kafka, in his fortieth year, seems at last to have been delivered from the self-loathing, the self-doubt, and those guilt-ridden impulses to dependence and self-effacement that had nearly driven him mad throughout his twenties and thirties; all at once he seems to have shed the pervasive sense of hopeless despair that informs the great punitive fantasies of *The Trial*, "The Penal Colony," and "The Metamorphosis." Years earlier, in Prague, he had directed Max Brod to destroy all his papers, including three unpublished novels, upon his death; now, in Berlin, when Brod introduces him to a German publisher interested in his work, Kafka consents to the publication of a volume of four stories, and consents, says Brod, "without much need of long arguments to persuade him." With Dora to help, he diligently resumes his study of Hebrew; despite his illness and the harsh winter, he travels to the Berlin Academy for Jewish Studies to attend a series of lectures on the Talmud—a very different Kafka from the estranged melancholic who once wrote in his diary, "What have I in common with the Jews? I have hardly anything in common with myself and should stand very quietly in a corner, content that I can breathe." And to further mark the change, there is ease and happiness with a woman: with this young and adoring companion, he is playful, he is pedagogical, and one would guess, in light of his illness (*and* his happiness), he is chaste. If not a husband (such as he had striven to be to the conventional Fraulein Bauer), if not a lover (as he struggled hopelessly to be with Milena), he would seem to have become something no less miraculous in his scheme of things: a father, a kind of father to this sisterly, mothering daughter. *As Franz Kafka awoke one morning from uneasy dreams he found himself transformed in his bed into a father, a writer, and a Jew.*

"I have completed the construction of my burrow," begins the long, exquisite, and tedious story that he wrote that winter in Berlin, "and it seems to be successful. . . . Just the place where, according to my calculations, the Castle Keep should be, the soil was very loose and sandy and had literally to be hammered and pounded into a firm state to serve as a wall for the beautifully vaulted chamber. But for such tasks the only tool I possess is my forehead. So I had to run with my forehead thousands and thousands of times, for whole days and nights, against the ground, and I was glad when the blood came, for that was proof that the walls were beginning to harden; in that way, as everybody must admit, I richly paid for my Castle Keep." "The Burrow" is the story of an animal with a keen sense of peril whose life is organized around the principle of defense, and whose deepest longings are for security and serenity; with teeth and claws—*and* forehead—the burrower constructs an elaborate and ingeniously intricate system of underground chambers and corridors that are designed to afford it some peace of mind; however, while this burrow does succeed in reducing the sense of danger from without, its maintenance and protection are equally fraught with anxiety: "these anxieties are different from ordinary ones, prouder, richer in content, often long repressed, but in their destructive effects they are perhaps much the same as the anxieties that existence in the outer world gives rise to." The story (whose ending is lost) terminates with the burrower fixated upon distant subterranean noises that cause it "to assume the existence of a great beast," itself burrowing in the direction of the Castle Keep.

Another grim tale of entrapment, and of obsession so absolute that no distinction is possible between character and predicament. Yet this fiction imagined in the last "happy" months of his life is touched with a spirit of personal reconciliation and sardonic self-acceptance, with a tolerance for one's own brand of madness, that is not apparent in "The Metamorphosis"; the piercing masochistic irony of the early animal story—as of "The Judgment" and The Trial—has given way here to a critique of the self and its preoccupations that, though bordering on mockery, no longer seeks to resolve itself in images of the uttermost humiliation and defeat . . . But there is more here than a metaphor for the insanely defended ego, whose striving for invulnerability produces a defensive system that must in its turn become the object of perpetual concern—there is also a very unromantic and hard-headed fable about how and why art is made, a portrait of the artist in all his ingenuity, anxiety, isolation, dissatisfaction, relentlessness, obsessiveness, secretiveness, paranoia, and self-addiction, a portrait of the magical thinker at the end of his tether, Kafka's Prospero . . . It is an infinitely suggestive story, this story of life in a hole. For, finally, remember the proximity of Dora Dymant during the months that Kafka was at work on "The Burrow" in the two underheated rooms that was their illicit home. Certainly a dreamer like Kafka need never have entered the young girl's body for her tender presence to kindle in him a fantasy of a hidden orifice that promises "satisfied desire," "achieved ambition," and "profound slumber," but that once penetrated and in one's possession, arouses the most terrifying and heartbreaking fears of retribution and loss. "For the rest I try to unriddle the beast's plans. Is it on its wanderings, or is it working on its own burrow? If it is on its wanderings then perhaps an understanding with it might be possible. If it should really break through to the burrow I shall give it some of my stores and it will go on its way again. It will go on its way again, a fine story! Lying in my heap of earth I can naturally dream of all sorts of things, even of an understanding with the beast, though I know well enough that no such thing can happen, and that at the instant when we see each other, more, at the moment when we merely guess at each other's presence, we shall blindly bare our claws and teeth . . ."

He died of tuberculosis of the lungs and the larynx a month short of his forty-first birthday, June 3, 1924. Dora, inconsolable, whispers for days afterward, "My love, my love, my good one . . ."

2

1942. I am nine; my Hebrew school teacher, Dr. Kafka, is fifty-nine. To the little boys who must attend his "four-to-five" class each afternoon, he is known—in part because of his remote and melancholy foreignness, but largely because we vent on him our resentment at having to learn an ancient calligraphy at the very hour we should be out screaming our heads off on the ballfield—he is known as Dr. Kishka. Named, I confess, by me. His sour breath, spiced with intestinal juices by five in the afternoon, makes the Yiddish word for "insides" particularly telling, I think. Cruel, yes, but in truth I would have cut out my tongue had I ever imagined the name would become legend. A coddled child, I do not yet think of myself as persuasive, nor, quite yet, as a literary force in the world. My jokes don't hurt, how could they, I'm so adorable. And if you don't believe me, just ask my family and the teachers in school. Already at nine, one foot in Harvard, the other in the Catskills. Little Borscht Belt comic that I am outside the classroom, I amuse my friends Schlossman and Ratner on the dark walk home from Hebrew school with an imitation of Kishka, his precise and finicky professorial manner, his German accent, his cough, his gloom. "Doctor *Kishka!*" cries Schlossman, and hurls himself savagely against the newsstand that belongs to the candy store owner whom Schlossman drives just a little crazier each night. "Doctor Franz—Doctor Franz—Doctor Franz—*Kishka!*" screams Ratner, and my chubby little friend who lives upstairs from me on nothing but chocolate milk and Mallomars does not stop laughing until, as is his wont (his mother has asked me "to keep an eye on him" for just this reason), he wets his pants. Schlossman takes the occasion of Ratner's humiliation to pull the little boy's paper out of his notebook and wave it in the air—it is the assignment Dr. Kafka has just returned to us, graded; we were told to make up an alphabet of our own, out of straight lines and curved lines and dots. "That is all an alphabet is," he had explained. "That is all Hebrew is. That is all English is. Straight lines and curved lines and dots." Ratner's alphabet, for which he received a C, looks like twenty-six skulls strung in a row. I received my A for a curlicued alphabet inspired largely (as Dr. Kafka would seem to have surmised from his comment at the top of the page) by the number eight. Schlossman received an F for forgetting even to do it—and a lot he seems to care, too. He is content—he is *overjoyed*—with things as they are. Just waving a piece of paper in the air, and screaming, *"Kishka! Kishka!"* makes him deliriously happy. We should all be so lucky.

At home, alone in the glow of my goose-necked "desk" lamp (plugged after dinner into an outlet in the kitchen, my study) the vision of our refugee teacher, sticklike in a fraying three-piece blue suit, is no longer very funny—particularly after the entire beginner's Hebrew class, of which I am the most studious member, takes the name "Kishka" to its heart. My guilt awakens redemptive fantasies of heroism. I have them often about "the Jews in Europe." I must save him. If not me, who? The demonic Schlossman? The babyish Ratner? And if not now, when? For I have learned in the ensuing weeks that Dr. Kafka lives in "a room" in the house of an elderly Jewish lady on the shabby lower stretch of Avon Avenue, where the trolley still runs, and the poorest of Newark's Negroes shuffle meekly up and down the street, for all they seem to know still back in Mississippi. A *room*. And *there!* My family's apartment is no palace, but it is ours at least, so long as we pay the thirty-eight-fifty a month in rent; and though our neighbors are not rich, they refuse to be poor and they refuse to be meek. Tears of shame and sorrow in my eyes, I rush into the living room to tell my parents what I have heard (though not that I heard it during a quick game of "aces up" played a minute before class against the synagogue's rear wall—worse, played directly beneath a stained glass window embossed with the names of the dead): "My Hebrew teacher lives in a *room*."

My parents go much further than I could imagine anybody going in the real world. Invite him to dinner, my mother says. *Here?* Of course here—Friday night; I'm sure he can stand a home-cooked meal and a little pleasant company. Meanwhile my father gets on the phone to call my Aunt Rhoda, who lives with my grandmother and tends her and her potted plants in the apartment house at the corner of our street. For nearly two decades now my father has been introducing my mother's forty-year-old "baby" sister to the Jewish bachelors and widowers of New Jersey. No luck so far. Aunt Rhoda, an "interior decorator" in the dry goods department of "The Big Bear," a mammoth merchandise and produce market in industrial Elizabeth, wears falsies (this information by way of my older brother) and sheer frilly blouses, and family lore has it that she spends hours in the bathroom every day applying powders and sweeping her stiffish hair up into a dramatic pile on her head; but despite all this dash and display, she is, in my father's words, "still afraid of the facts of life." He, however, is undaunted, and administers therapy regularly and gratis: "Let 'em squeeze ya, Rhoda—it *feels* good!" I am his flesh and blood, I can reconcile myself to such scandalous talk in our kitchen—*but what will Dr. Kafka think?* Oh, but it's too late to do anything now. The massive machinery of matchmaking has been set in motion by my undiscourageable father, and the smooth engines of my proud homemaking mother's hospitality are already purring away. To throw my body into the works in an attempt to bring it all to a halt—well, I might as well try to bring down the New Jersey Bell Telephone Company by leaving our receiver off the hook. Only Dr. Kafka can save me now. But to my muttered invitation, he replies, with a formal bow that turns me scarlet—who has ever seen a person do such a thing outside of a movie house?—he replies that he would be *honored* to be my family's dinner guest. "My aunt," I rush to tell him, "will be there too." It appears that I have just said something mildly humorous; odd to see Dr. Kafka smile. Sighing, he says, "I will be delighted to meet her." Meet her? He's supposed to *marry* her. How do I warn him? And how do I warn Aunt Rhoda (a very great admirer of me and my marks) about his sour breath, his roomer's pallor, his Old World ways, so at odds with her up-to-dateness? My face feels as if it will ignite of its own—and spark the fire that will engulf the synagogue, Torah and all—when I see Dr. Kafka scrawl our address in his notebook, and beneath it, some words *in German.* "Good night, Dr. Kafka!" "Good night, and thank you, thank you." I turn to run, I go, but not fast enough: out on the street I hear Schlossman—that fiend!—announcing to my classmates who are punching one another under the lamplight down from the synagogue steps (where a card game is also in progress, organized by the Bar Mitzvah boys): "Roth invited Kishka to his *house!* To *eat!*"

Does my father do a job on Kafka! Does he make a sales pitch for familial bliss! What it means to a man to have two fine boys and a wonderful wife! Can Dr. Kafka imagine what that's like? The thrill? The satisfaction? The pride? He tells our visitor of the network of relatives on his mother's side that are joined in a "family association" of over two hundred and fifty people located in seven states, including the state of Washington! Yes, relatives even in the Far West: here are their photographs, Dr. Kafka; this is a beautiful book we published entirely on our own for five dollars a copy, pictures of every member of the family, including infants, and a family history by "Uncle" Lichtblau, the eighty-five-year-old patriarch of the clan. This is our family newsletter that is published twice a year and distributed nationwide to all the relatives. This, in the frame, is the menu from the banquet of the family association, held last year in a ballroom of the "Y" in Newark, in honor of my father's mother on her seventy-fifth birthday. My mother, Dr. Kafka learns, has served *six consecutive years* as the secretary-treasurer of the family association. My father has served a two-year term as president, as have each of his three brothers. We now have fourteen boys in the family in uniform. Philip writes a letter on V-mail stationery to five of his cousins in the Army every single month. "Religiously," my mother puts in, smoothing my hair. "I firmly believe," says my father, "that the family is the cornerstone of everything." Dr. Kafka, who has listened with close attention to my father's *spiel*, handling the various documents that have been passed to him with great delicacy and poring over them with a kind of rapt absorption that reminds me of myself over the watermarks of my stamps, now for the first time expresses himself on the subject of family; softly he says, "I agree," and inspects again the pages of our family book. "Alone," says my father, in conclusion, "alone, Dr. Kafka, is a stone." Dr. Kafka, setting the book gently upon my mother's gleaming coffee table, allows with a nod how that is so. My mother's fingers are now turning in the curls behind my ears; not that I even know it at the time, or that she does. Being stroked is my life; stroking me, my father, and my brother is hers.

My brother goes off to a Boy Scout "council" meeting, but only after my father has him stand in his neckerchief before Dr. Kafka and describe to him the skills he has mastered to earn each of his badges. I am invited to bring my stamp album into the living room and show Dr. Kafka my set of triangular stamps from Zanzibar. "Zanzibar!" says my father rapturously, as though I, not even ten, have already been there and back. My father accompanies Dr. Kafka and myself into the "sun parlor," where my tropical fish swim in the aerated, heated, and hygienic paradise I have made for them with my weekly allowance and my Hanukah *gelt*. I am encouraged to tell Dr. Kafka what I know about the temperament of the angelfish, the function of the catfish, and the family life of the black molly. I know quite a bit. "All on his own he does that," my father says to Kafka. "He gives me a lecture on one of those fish, it's seventh heaven, Dr. Kafka." "I can imagine," Kafka replies.

Back in the living room my Aunt Rhoda suddenly launches into a rather recondite monologue on "scotch plaids," designed, it would appear, only for the edification of my mother. At least she looks fixedly at my mother while she delivers it. I have not yet seen her look directly at Dr. Kafka; she did not even turn his way at dinner when he asked how many employees there were at "The Big Bear." "How would I know?" she replies, and continues conversing with my mother, something about a grocer or a butcher who would take care of her "under the counter" if she could find him nylons for his wife. It never occurs to me that she will not look at Dr. Kafka because she is shy—nobody that dolled up could, in my estimation, be shy—I can only think that she is outraged. *It's his breath. It's his accent. It's his age.* I'm wrong—it turns out to be what Aunt Rhoda calls his "superiority complex." "Sitting there, sneering at us like that," says my aunt, somewhat superior now herself. "Sneering?" repeats my father, incredulous. "Sneering and laughing, yes!" says Aunt Rhoda. My mother shrugs: "*I* didn't think he was laughing." "Oh, don't worry, by himself there he was having a very good time—*at our expense.* I know the European-type man. Underneath they think they're all lords of the manor," Rhoda says. "You know something, Rhoda?" says my father, tilting his head and pointing a finger, "I think you fell in love." "With *him?* Are you *crazy?*" "He's too quiet for Rhoda," my mother says, "I think maybe he's a little bit of a wallflower. Rhoda is a lively person, she needs lively people around her." "Wallflower? He's not a wallflower! He's a gentleman, that's all. And he's lonely," my father says assertively, glaring at my mother for coming in over his head like this *against* Kafka. My Aunt Rhoda is forty years old—it is not exactly a shipment of brand-new goods that he is trying to move. "He's a gentleman, he's an educated man, and I'll tell you something, he'd give his eye teeth to have a nice home and a wife." "Well," says my Aunt Rhoda, "let him find one then, if he's so educated. Somebody who's his equal, who he doesn't have to look down his nose at with his big sad refugee eyes!" "Yep, she's in love," my father announces, squeezing Rhoda's knee in triumph. "With him?" she cries, jumping to her feet, taffeta crackling around her like a bonfire. "With *Kafka?*" she snorts, "I wouldn't give an old man like him the time of day!"

Dr. Kafka calls and takes my Aunt Rhoda to a movie. I am astonished, both that he calls and that she goes; it seems there is more desperation in life than I have come across yet in my fish tank. Dr. Kafka takes my Aunt Rhoda to a play performed at the

"Y." Dr. Kafka eats Sunday dinner with my grandmother and my Aunt Rhoda, and at the end of the afternoon, accepts with that formal bow of his the Mason jar of barley soup that my grandmother presses him to carry back to his room with him on the No. 8 bus. Apparently he was very taken with my grandmother's jungle of potted plants—and she, as a result, with him. Together they spoke in Yiddish about gardening. One Wednesday morning, only an hour after the store has opened for the day, Dr. Kafka shows up at the dry goods department of "The Big Bear"; he tells Aunt Rhoda that he just wanted to see where she worked. That night he writes in his diary, "With the customers she is forthright and cheery, and so managerial about 'taste' that when I hear her explain to a chubby young bride why green and blue do not 'go,' I am myself ready to believe that Nature is in error and R. is correct."

One night, at ten, Dr. Kafka and Aunt Rhoda come by unexpectedly, and a small impromptu party is held in the kitchen—coffee and cake, even a thimbleful of whiskey all around, to celebrate the resumption of Aunt Rhoda's career on the stage. I have only heard tell of my aunt's theatrical ambitions. My brother says that when I was small she used to come to entertain the two of us on Sundays with her puppets—she was at that time employed by the W.P.A. to travel around New Jersey and put on puppet shows in schools and even in churches; Aunt Rhoda did all the voices, male and female, and with the help of another young girl, manipulated the manikins on their strings. Simultaneously she had been a member of the "Newark Collective Theater," a troupe organized primarily to go around to strike groups to perform *Waiting for Lefty*; everybody in Newark (as I understood it) had had high hopes that Rhoda Pilchik would go on to Broadway—everybody except my grandmother. To me this period of history is as difficult to believe in as the era of the lake-dwellers that I am studying in school; of course, people say it was once so, so I believe them, but nonetheless it is hard to grant such stories the status of the real, given the life I see around me.

Yet my father, a very avid realist, is in the kitchen, *schnapps* glass in hand, toasting Aunt Rhoda's success. She has been awarded one of the starring roles in the Russian masterpiece, *The Three Sisters*, to be performed six weeks hence by the amateur group at the Newark "Y." Everything, announces Aunt Rhoda, everything she owes to Franz, and his encouragement. One conversation—"One!" she cries gaily—and Dr. Kafka had apparently talked my grandmother out of her lifelong belief that actors are not serious human beings. And what an actor *he* is, in his own right, says Aunt Rhoda. How he had opened her eyes to the meaning of things, by reading her the famous Chekhov play—yes, read it to her from the opening line to the final curtain, all the parts, and actually left her in tears. Here Aunt Rhoda says, "Listen, listen—this is the first line of the play—it's the key to everything. Listen—I just think about what it was like that night Pop passed away, how I thought and thought what would happen, what would we all do—and, and, listen—"

"We're listening," laughs my father.

Pause; she must have walked to the center of the kitchen linoleum. She says, sounding a little surprised, " 'It's just a year ago today that father died.' "

"Shhh," warns my mother, "you'll give the little one nightmares."

I am not alone in finding my aunt "a changed person" during the ensuing weeks of rehearsal. My mother says this is just what she was like as a little girl. "Red cheeks, always those hot, red cheeks—and everything exciting, even taking a bath." "She'll calm down, don't worry," says my father, "and then he'll pop the question." "Knock on wood," says my mother. "Come on," says my father, "he knows what side his bread is buttered on—he sets foot in this house, he sees what a family is all about, and believe me, he's licking his chops. Just look at him when he sits in that club chair. This is his dream come true." "Rhoda says that in Berlin, before Hitler, he had a young girlfriend, years and years it went on, and then she left him. For somebody else. she got tired of waiting." "Don't worry," says my father, "when the time comes I'll give him a little nudge. He ain't going to live forever, either, and he knows it."

———

Then one weekend, as a respite from the "strain" of nightly re-
hearsals—which Dr. Kafka regularly visits, watching in his hat and
coat from a seat at the back of the auditorium until it is time to
accompany Aunt Rhoda home—they take a trip to Atlantic City.
Ever since he arrived on these shores Dr. Kafka has wanted to see
the famous boardwalk and the horse that dives from the high
board. But in Atlantic City something happens that I am not allowed to know about; any discussion of the subject conducted in
my presence is in Yiddish. Dr. Kafka sends Aunt Rhoda four
letters in three days. She comes to us for dinner and sits till midnight crying in our kitchen; she calls the "Y" on our phone to tell
them (weeping) that her mother is still ill and she cannot come to
rehearsal again—she may even have to drop out of the play—no,
she can't, she can't, her mother is too ill, she herself is too upset!
Good-bye! Then back to the kitchen table to cry; she wears no pink
powder and no red lipstick, and her stiff brown hair, down, is thick
and spiky as a new broom.

My brother and I listen from our bedroom, through the door
that silently he has pushed ajar.

"Have you ever?" says Aunt Rhoda, weeping. "Have you *ever*?"

"Poor soul," says my mother.

"*Who?*" I whisper to my brother. "Aunt Rhoda or—"

"Shhhh!" he says, "Shut *up*!"

In the kitchen my father grunts. "Hmm. Hmm." I hear him
getting up and walking around and sitting down again—and then
grunting. I am listening so hard that I can hear the letters being
folded and unfolded, stuck back into their envelopes and then
removed to be puzzled over one more time.

"Well?" demands Aunt Rhoda. "*Well*?"

"Well what?" answers my father.

"Well what do you want to say *now*?"

"He's *meshugeh*," admits my father. "Something is wrong with
him all right."

"But," sobs Aunt Rhoda, "no one would believe me when *I* said
it!"

"Rhody, Rhody," croons my mother in that voice I know from

those times that I have had to have stitches taken, or when I awaken
in tears, somehow on the floor beside my bed. "Rhody, don't be
hysterical, darling. It's over, kitten, it's all over."

I reach across to my brother's "twin" bed and tug on the blanket. I don't think I've ever been so confused in my life, not even
by death. The speed of things! Everything good undone in a moment! By what? "*What?*" I whisper. "*What is it?*"

My brother, the Boy Scout, smiles leeringly and with a fierce hiss
that is no answer and enough answer, addresses my bewilderment:
"Sex!"

Years later, a junior at college, I receive an envelope from home
containing Dr. Kafka's obituary, clipped from the *Jewish News*, the
tabloid of Jewish affairs that is mailed each week to the homes of
the Jews of Essex County. It is summer, the semester is over, but
I have stayed on at school, alone in my room in the town, trying
to write short stories; I am fed by a young English professor and his
wife in exchange for baby-sitting; I tell the sympathetic couple, who
are also loaning me the money for my rent, why it is I can't go
home. My tearful fights with my father are all I can talk about at
their dinner table. "Keep him away from me!" I scream at my
mother. "But, darling," she asks me, "what is going on? What is
this all about?"—the very same question with which I used to
plague my older brother, asked of me now out of the same bewilderment and innocence. "He *loves* you," she explains. But that, of
all things, seems to me to be precisely what is blocking my way.
Others are crushed by paternal criticism—I find myself oppressed
by his high opinion of me! Can it possibly be true (and can I
possibly admit) that I am coming to hate him for loving me so?
praising me so? But that makes no sense—the ingratitude! the stupidity! the contrariness! Being loved is so obviously a blessing, *the*
blessing, praise such a rare bequest; only listen late at night to my
closest friends on the literary magazine and in the drama society—
they tell horror stories of family life to rival *The Way of All Flesh*,
they return shell-shocked from vacations, drift back to school as

though from the wars. What they would give to be in my golden slippers! "What's going on?" my mother begs me to tell her; but how can I, when I can neither fully believe that this is happening to us, nor that I am the one who is making it happen. That they, who together cleared all obstructions from my path, should seem now to be my final obstruction! No wonder my rage must filter through a child's tears of shame, confusion, and loss. All that we have constructed together over the course of two century-long decades, and look how I must bring it down—in the name of this tyrannical need that I call my "independence"! Born, I am told, with the umbilical cord around my neck, it seems I will always come close to strangulation trying to deliver myself from my past into my future. . . . My mother, keeping the lines of communication open, sends a note to me at school: "We miss you"—and encloses the very brief obituary notice. Across the margin at the bottom of the clipping, she has written (in the same hand that she wrote notes to my teachers and signed my report cards, in the very same handwriting that once eased my way in the world), "Remember poor Kafka, Aunt Rhoda's beau?"

"Dr. Franz Kafka," the notice reads, "a Hebrew teacher at the Talmud Torah of the Schley Street Synagogue from 1939 to 1948, died on June 3 in the Deborah Tuberculosis Sanitorium in Browns Mills, New Jersey. Dr. Kafka had been a patient there since 1950. He was 70 years old. Dr. Kafka was born in Prague, Czechoslovakia, and was a refugee from the Nazis. He leaves no survivors."

He also leaves no books: no *Trial*, no *Castle*, no "Diaries." The dead man's papers are claimed by no one, and disappear—all except those four *"meshugeneh"* letters that are, to this day as far as I know, still somewhere in amongst the memorabilia accumulated in her dresser drawers by my spinster aunt, along with a collection of Broadway "Playbills," sales citations from "The Big Bear," and transatlantic steamship stickers.

Thus all trace of Dr. Kafka disappears. Destiny being destiny, how could it be otherwise? Does the Land Surveyor reach the Castle? Does K. escape the judgment of the Court, or Georg

Bendemann the judgment of his father? " 'Well, clear this out now!' said the overseer, and they buried the hunger artist, straw and all." No, it simply is not in the cards for Kafka ever to become *the* Kafka—why, that would be stranger even than a man turning into an insect. No one would believe it, Kafka least of all.

ADAM SCHWARTZ

Where Is It Written?

Three months before my thirteenth birthday, I persuaded my father to sue my mother for custody of me. This was in late August, near the end of a two-week visit with my father. I wrote my mother a letter informing her of my decision. I told her I knew she might be disappointed, but I wasn't rejecting her; I only wanted to spend more time with my father, to know and love him as well as I knew her. I also told her not to call me. We could discuss this when I returned home, if she wanted to.

She called the second the letter came. Phyllis, my father's wife, answered the phone. "Hold on, Sandra," she said, and held the phone out to me, her palm covering the receiver. I shook my head. Phyllis gave me an exasperated look, and told my mother I was busy. She called three more times in the next hour. I knew this was going to happen, but I was not even thirteen, and I wanted to forget how well I knew my mother. Phyllis agreed to relay her messages to me: How long should she preheat the oven for my lemon-chicken recipe? Should she run hot or cold water when scrubbing the sink with Comet? What should she do if the washing machine stopped in mid-cycle? I had typed out three pages of instructions before I left, but the calls kept coming right through dinner. Could she use ammonia on Formica surfaces? Should she use tap or distilled water in the iron? Finally, Phyllis exclaimed, "Jesus, Sandra, we're eating. He'll be home in two days." Then I watched her face darken and imagined the blast my mother was delivering: "Don't you tell me when I can talk to my own son. I'm his mother, and when I tell you to get him, you jump—understand?" Phyllis hung up the phone and sat back down at the table, her lips drawn across her face like a thin white scar. Ten seconds later the phone rang again. My father and Phyllis looked at each other. I felt like Jonah hiding in the bowels of the ship, knowing the storm above was all his fault. No one moved. "Mommy, the phone is ringing," shouted Debbie, my little stepsister. "Maybe you should answer the phone, Sam," my father said. I stood up from the table very slowly, giving myself every chance that the phone might stop ringing before I reached it.

"What's the problem, Mom? I wrote everything down."

"You little bastard! Don't bother coming home. If I never see you again I'll die happy!"

My father wasn't enthusiastic when I asked him to sue. "Lawyers? Court? Not again." My parents divorced when I was four, and the episode still bothered him. He had wanted to work things out quietly, but my mother staged a grand opera. She asked for an exorbitant amount of alimony and minimal visitation rights for my father. She accused him of being an adulterer and a wife beater. My father was a rabbi in a small town on the New Jersey shore and brought in many members of his congregation as character witnesses. My mother had no witnesses in her behalf. She lost every point she argued for.

"But, Dad," I implored, "she's driving me *crazy!*"

He and I usually didn't have a lot to say to each other, but I expected the word "crazy" to explain everything, as if I were revealing to him that we shared the same inherited trouble, like gum disease or premature balding. I pitched my case to him, describing how she moaned during meals about her haywire menstrual cycle, how she slept on the couch every night, sometimes with a cigarette still burning in her hand.

"Do you know how dangerous that is, Dad?"

He pressed his palms up his cheeks, a gesture that always led me to imagine he was trying to stretch his beard over his eyes and forehead. I envisioned him doing the same thing the day he met my mother. When I had asked her, the year before, how they came together—a far more mysterious question to me than where I had come from—she answered, "In the shower." Both were on an archaeological dig in Israel. My father, recently ordained, was covered with soap in the primitive communal shower when my mother walked in, nineteen, naked, enthusiastic about everything. Several months later they were married, but my mother was bored by the life of a rabbi's wife. She had no interest in charity work or Sisterhood meetings. She saw an analyst five times a week and signed up for courses in Sanskrit and criminology. Once she planned a lecture at the synagogue on Gurdjieff's centers of consciousness. Three people came.

I told my father I was fed up with cooking and cleaning, washing and ironing.

"I thought you liked doing housework," he said.

"Not all the time. I want to have a normal life, Dad."

He touched his beard lightly, thoughtfully. I had found the right word.

"Sometimes her boyfriends sleep over. I see them on the sofa bed when I get up in the morning."

"All right, all right."

"Dad, I'm telling you, this is an open-and-shut case. I'm old enough to live with whoever I want. That's the law."

I knew about the law from my mother. She sued everyone. Landlords, universities, car dealers, plumbers, my father. She stayed up all night researching her cases and planning her strategies. In the morning I would see her asleep on the couch, openmouthed, beneath a blanket of ashes and law books and the sheets of legal paper on which she outlined her complex and futile arguments. Years later, after I graduated from law school and returned to New Jersey, many of the older lawyers around the courthouse told me that my mother indeed had a reputation as a compulsive but extremely knowledgeable and creative litigant. "I always thought the law was a metaphysical exercise for her," one of them said to me. " 'I can sue you: therefore I exist.' "

I also learned the art of exaggeration from my mother, the art of how to invent something when the truth is boring or makes you nervous. I had seen her on the sofa bed with a man only once. The year before, she had come into my bedroom very early one morning to tell me that Sy, her sometime boyfriend, had spent the night. "You don't mind that he's here?" she asked, sitting on the side of my bed. Her weight was comforting, as were her warm, heavy, sleepy odors. I told her I didn't mind. "I slept in the other room," she said anxiously. "But I'm going to lie down next to Sy for a couple of minutes."

"All right," I said, and went back to sleep. I knew she liked Sy. She had told me that he had always wanted a boy to raise, that he was personal friends with Joe Namath, that he had a home in Florida. He bought me books, bats, tickets to ballgames. In two years he would go to jail for fraud and income tax evasion, but that morning my mother and I both believed in him. When I went into the living room, he was asleep on his side. My mother was awake, pressed up against his back with an arm around his chest. She smiled at me, as if Sy were some wonderful secret between us, something valuable she had found.

My mother's explosion of telephone calls came on Thursday night; late Sunday afternoon I took the bus from my father's house to the Port Authority. My mother usually met me inside the terminal, but I didn't see her anywhere. I called home six times in the next hour, counting twenty-three rings on the last attempt. The next local bus across the river didn't leave for two hours. I found a bench at a far end of the terminal and, sitting with my suitcase between my knees, watched everyone going home, everyone except for the panhandlers, the proselytizers, the old men sleeping against walls, teenagers who had run away.

My mother wasn't in when I arrived home. She hadn't left a note, and by ten o'clock I still hadn't heard from her. I knew what she was doing. She was letting me know how it felt to be abandoned, to suddenly be alone. I knew she would return the next day, but still I was in tears by the time I was ready for bed. My room felt like the loneliest place in the world that night, so I pulled out the sofa bed. I had never slept in the living room before, and I couldn't orient myself, couldn't gauge the black space around me.

Gradually the darkness lightened into shadows and the shadows into a dull grayness. When I could see everything in the room clearly, I began preparing for the first day of school. I kept thinking, *Now he's brushing his teeth, now he's deciding which shirt to wear, now he's pouring milk over his cereal . . .* as if, without my mother in the house, I were inhabiting someone else's life. I was all ready by six-thirty. I lay back down on the couch and watched the clock for the next hour and forty-five minutes.

At eleven thirty, during biology, the principal's secretary came to the classroom to tell me my mother had phoned. She told me I was to go right home because of an emergency. The year before, I'd been called out of class about once a month because of an "emergency" at home. Usually my mother had fought with a patient, or a married man she was seeing had stopped answering her calls, or her father had sent her another sanctimonious letter, or some judge had treated her in a cavalier manner.

I declined the secretary's offer of a ride and walked home. When I let myself into the apartment, my mother was sitting at the kitchen table. She held the letter I had written to her in one hand and was burning holes in it with her cigarette. She looked like a curious child torturing a small animal.

"I thought you saw a patient now," I finally said.

She was a psychologist, but had only four regular patients. She used her bedroom as an office, though she longed to have one in town. "Someplace beautiful," she would say. "Some place where I can really be myself."

"I canceled," she said, burning a chain of holes through my name.

"Canceled! What for? That's thirty-five dollars!"

She looked at me for the first time. "Would you please explain this, Sam?"

"I explained everything in the letter."

"Everything? Really? I can think of any number of things you didn't explain. Why you're leaving me, for instance. Can you explain that? Am I really that bad of a mother?"

"I told you I wasn't rejecting you."

"Look, Sam. Let's agree on one thing. Let's agree you're not going to treat me like I'm stupid." She said this slowly and rhythmically, as if I were the stupid one.

"Mom, I just don't want to live here anymore. That's all."

"That's all?"

"I explained. I want to live with my father."

"Tell me the last time he called."

"Maybe he doesn't call because he's afraid you'll sue if he says something you don't like over the phone."

"Oh, I see. Now it's my fault. I'm to blame because your father has no interest in you."

"I didn't say that."

"Then what are you saying? That I'm a failure as a mother?"

"No, Mom. You're not a failure. All right?"

"Then why? *Why* are you doing this to me?"

"God, Mom. I don't know! I just want to lead a normal life."

"*Normal!*" she cried. "What's not normal about the way we live?"

"Everything! The cooking, the cleaning, the shouting. Everything!"

"Who shouts?"

"You do. You're shouting now."

"Of course I am. My son tells me he doesn't want to live with me anymore. Can't I shout about that? Isn't that *normal?*"

"Mom, this conversation is retarded. I'm going back to school."

"And who asked you to cook and clean?" she shouted after me. "Not me. You love to cook. Or is that something else to blame me for?"

"Goodbye, Mom," I said, walking out the door.

"Don't come back, you lousy child! Just see how well you get along without me!"

Before I began cooking and cleaning, my clothing always came out of the wash shrunk and discolored, sending me into fits most mornings because I was embarrassed to wear wrinkled shirts to school and my mother refused to iron them.

"You iron them," she would say. "They're your shirts."

"But I don't know how!"

"Neither do I."

"Yes, you do! You're supposed to know!"

"I am? Where is it written that I'm supposed to know? Tell me! Where?"

For supper she usually boiled pouches of frozen food, and even that gave her problems. "Oh, puke!" I'd say, pursing up my face and coughing out a mouthful of half-frozen meat loaf.

Once, on her birthday, I bought her a cookbook and pleaded with her to learn some recipes.

"Oh, honey, I can't deal with recipes."

"But why?"

"Because nothing ever turns out the way it's supposed to for me."

I began with simple dishes—baked chicken and steamed vegetables, broiled lamb chops and rice. Then I moved on to lasagna, brisket in red wine sauce, curried shrimp, veal scallops with prosciutto, Grand Marnier soufflés, and poached peaches with raspberry puree. I prepared some of my most inspired meals when my mother entertained Sy.

"I don't know how you do it," she would say, anointing herself with perfume as she watched me work in the kitchen.

"It's easy, Mom. All you have to do is read the directions."

"Directions," she replied, "bore me."

———

When my first day of school ended, I returned home as usual to begin dinner. Mrs. Gutman, my mother's four-thirty patient and close friend, was sitting on the couch. She was a stout Romanian woman with a collapsing beehive of rust-colored hair held vaguely together with hundreds of bobby pins. "Hello, darlink," she greeted me, her accent falling with a thud on the "darlink." I could tell by the sad cast of her eyes that she knew all about my letter.

Mrs. Gutman had been seeing my mother longer than any other patient. Three days a week for four years she had journeyed from her apartment in Staten Island to our apartment in Bergenfield, where her fifty-minute session lasted for hours. She would call at three and four in the morning when nightmares frightened her awake. The ringing phone always exploded in my ears. I sat up in bed, my heart beating violently, as if it were connected to the phone with jumper cables. I couldn't hear my mother's words very clearly, but I would lie awake for hours listening to the dim, low murmur of her voice, a sound as comforting as the patter of rain after an electrical storm.

Mrs. Gutman was the last scheduled patient of the day because her sessions went on so long. Usually I would be preparing dinner when they finished, and Mrs. Gutman would crowd into the tiny kitchen to sample and advise. Pressing her bosom against my rib cage, she stirred, tasted, lifted covers off pots and inhaled deeply. "No, darlink. You must do like dis one," she'd say, sprinkling paprika into a stew that I had delicately seasoned and simmered for hours.

"Great! Now you've ruined it," I'd say, hurling my wooden spoon into the sink.

"No, darlink, was too bland. Taste now."

"Don't call me that. I've told you my name is Sam."

"Yes, Sam, darlink."

Later, after Mrs. Gutman had left, my mother would say, "Why do you have to be so mean to her? Because she's my friend? Is that why?"

"I've told you not to analyze me. I'm not your patient."

"You can't give me credit for my successes, can you? You know how important I am to Mrs. Gutman, but you won't give me credit for it."

"Mom, she's your patient. She shouldn't be wandering into the kitchen. It's unprofessional."

"Mrs. Gutman is one of my dearest friends."

"Well, she shouldn't be. You're her therapist. You're not supposed to be her best friend, too."

"Where is it written that I can't be both? Tell me! If Mrs. Gutman values my friendship, who are you to tell me it's wrong?"

That afternoon Mrs. Gutman stayed only for her scheduled time. When my mother came into the kitchen, I was already eating my dinner, poached turbot. She joined me at the table with peanut butter on stale white bread.

"That smells delicious," she said.

"It is."

"Can I have a taste?"

"No."

"Why not?"

"I'm seeing how well I get along without you."

"Oh, really? Who paid for that?"

I pushed my plate over to her.

"Look, honey, I'm sorry I said that. The truth is that I can't get along without you, either."

"Mom, I just want a change."

"But you don't have to leave. I can change. *I'll change.* You want me to cook? I'll learn to cook. I'll be the best cook in the world. You don't want me sleeping on the couch? I won't sleep on the couch. I'll rent an office in town. How's that? You'll never have to see any of my patients again. Just tell me what you don't like."

I was staring down at the table. Without looking up, I replied, "Mom, I've decided."

She yanked me by the elbow. "You think it's that simple? Do you think some judge is just going to send you to your father because you say you want a change?"

"Do you think there are any judges who don't know about you?"

"What is that supposed to mean?"

"I mean all the lawyers you've spent the night with."

She slapped me across the face. She had never hit me before, and she began to cry, holding her hand as if she had burned it on something.

"You're just like everyone else," she cried. "You're all the same."

I had hoped my mother would just boot me out, hurling suitcases and insults at me, and when she thought to call me back, to apologize and argue some more, I would already be ensconced at my father's house, too far away to hear a thing. But after my father sued, I barely heard her voice. At dinner she would occasionally glance up from her plate to look at me oddly, as if I were a stranger she had just found sitting at her table. If I attempted conversation, she'd either ignore me or say, "Ask your father." I felt sure her silence was purely strategic; I was certain that if I told her I was changing my mind, tears would well in her eyes, all would be forgiven, and she'd vow to change. Some nights, though, after I was in bed and she called up Mrs. Gutman, her voice sounded extremely faint, more so than usual. I kept changing the position of my head on the pillow, but I couldn't tune her in, and after a time she faded out like a voice on the radio during a long drive in the middle of the night.

At the end of September, my mother and I visited her father in Florida. He was a dentist, and we saw him twice a year to have our teeth fixed and to be reminded of things we were not supposed to do. I was not supposed to eat sweets because my teeth were low in calcium; my mother was not supposed to "use" cigarettes in public or tell anyone she was divorced. For some reason, he thought it was less embarrassing to introduce her as a widow.

"Your grandfather doesn't know about our problems," she said to me on the plane, "and I don't plan on telling him."

We always went to Florida at the wrong time—either in May or late September, when the air in New Jersey was most delicious, when the perspiration on your face was cooling as a breeze. Usually, we stayed only for two or three days, sunning by the pool of his condominium or accompanying him on the golf course for his daily 6 A.M. game. Neither my mother nor I played, but he was adamant that we come along, as if she and I might get into trouble if we were left alone. By the thirteenth hole she was desperate for a cigarette. She'd quickly light one up as my grandfather was bent over the ball. He'd catch a scent of it and stop his stroke. "Sandra, how many times have I asked you to refrain from doing that in public? Now, put it out." Once the cigarette was lit, she became calmer, drawing deeper into herself with each drag. "Sandra!" She let a long, elegant ash drop to the green.

"Sorry, Daddy," she'd say in a bored voice, as she grasped my shoulder for support and twisted the cigarette against the bottom of her shoe.

On this visit we went straight from the airport to the office. My mother's gums had ached for weeks, but she didn't have the money to see a local dentist. My grandfather ushered her into the chair and instructed her to remove her lipstick. She pressed her lips against a tissue, leaving a red O-shaped print, and then gave it to my grandfather as though she were handing over her mouth. "Sandra," he said over the hum of the drill, "have you heard from the Yoskowitzes' son?" Both his thumbs were in her mouth and she moved her head from side to side. I sat in the dental assistant's chair, where I had a direct view of the bloody saliva swirling underneath my mother's tongue. "No? Maybe he'll call when you get back. I gave your number to Jack and Ruth to give to him. He lives in Jersey City and sells hospital equipment. They showed me a copy of his tax returns, so I know for certain that he earned $81,000 last year. He thinks you're a widow, so don't say anything to disappoint him. Understand?" Her eyes widened with hurt. I wanted to do something. Unclasp the towel from around her neck, give her back her mouth, and tell her, Run, I'll meet you at the airport. "Let's just hope," he continued, "he doesn't mind that your teeth are so stained with nicotine."

She raised her hand for him to stop. "Daddy, I really don't want to hear this today. My life has been a real shit-hole lately, and I just don't want to hear this." She never glanced at me.

My grandfather held the drill in the air and looked up, like someone about to begin conducting an orchestra. "Some days," he sighed, "I'm almost relieved that Rose is gone." I watched my mother's eyes brimming with tears. When my grandfather noticed, he reached for a needle and asked if she needed more Novocain.

A month before the hearing, and two weeks before my Bar Mitzvah, I went to see a court-appointed psychologist. Florence Fein's office, in a red Victorian house, was a large room crowded with old furniture, Oriental rugs, stained glass, and antique lamps. She served me a cup of tea and then asked me what I would like to talk about. I told her I couldn't think of anything.

"Why do you think you're here?" she asked.

"Because I have an appointment."

"Perhaps you can tell me why you don't want to be here."

"Because there's nothing wrong with me."

"You don't have to have something wrong with you to come to a psychologist, Sam. Most people come here just to figure things out."

"But I don't have anything to figure out. I know I want to live with my father."

"No one is keeping you here. You're free to leave."

"Then you'll tell the judge I have to stay with my mother."

"Sam, I'm not here to penalize you for saying the wrong thing. If you really don't want to be here, I'll just write in my report that I couldn't draw any conclusions."

I was uncomfortable with Florence Fein because I knew I could never say a bad word about my mother to a stranger. For a second I wondered if my mother had anticipated this; maybe she hadn't booted me out because she knew I'd turn silent and recalcitrant with psychologists and judges.

"If I go right now, is my mother still going to have to pay for the time?"

"Why do you ask?"

"I feel bad about her spending money for nothing."

"Do you always feel bad about your mother's actions?"

"Sometimes."

"Do you think that would change if you lived with your father?"

"I don't know. . . . Don't you think people can change?"

"Of course. I wouldn't be in this business if I didn't think so."
I believed her when she said this, as if change were a reliable
commodity. I knew the word didn't hold the same meaning for my
mother. When I thought of her pleading "I can change, I'll
change!" the words sounded like *"I'm in pain, I'm in pain!"*

"Sam, you probably know that your parents' divorce was very
bitter."

"So?"

"Do you think your father has put any subtle pressure on you
to come live with him?"

"Did my mother say that?"

"Not at all. As a matter of fact, she argued that your father
wasn't all that interested in having you live with him and that you
might be deeply hurt once that became a reality for you."

"What else did she say?"

"She said she's failed at everything she's ever tried, and she
doesn't want to fail as a parent."

We looked at each other for a long two or three seconds; and in
that moment I felt the whole weight of my mother's life, as if
Florence Fein had placed in my cup a teaspoonful of matter from
a black hole, weighing millions and millions of tons.

The day before my Bar Mitzvah, my mother informed me that she
was planning on showing up. I acted surprised, but deep down I
had expected it.

"You're not religious," I argued.

She was driving me to the Port Authority.

"You know this isn't a question of religion. You just don't want
me to come. Admit it."

"But you're always saying that my father's friends are against
you. You'll have to face all of them if you come."

"And so why should they be at my son's Bar Mitzvah and not me?"

"Mom, that's not a reason to go."

"Oh, and are your reasons any better? You just want all your father's friends to think you're more your father's son. You want them to think, My, hasn't he turned out so nice and polite despite his mother."

"I told you not to analyze me! I'm not your goddamned patient!"

We entered the Lincoln Tunnel, and I was truly afraid that she might stop the car in the middle of it and order me out. We hadn't talked that way in months. But she didn't say anything until we pulled up to the bus terminal. "Talk to your father that way sometime," she said, "and see how long he lets you live with him."

That evening Phyllis fixed a traditional Sabbath meal. My father invited six couples from his congregation to join us. My mother had warned me about all of them at one time or another. They were too interested and too familiar with me, as if I were a disfigured child and they were pretending not to notice. Before we had finished the soup and melon, they asked me which subject I liked the most in school (social studies), whether I was a Yankee or a Met fan (neither—the Dodgers), whether I, too, planned on becoming a rabbi (no, a gourmet chef). Everyone gave me a pained smile. I was thinking of the last elaborate meal I'd prepared for my mother and Sy, and how I loved standing in the kitchen with her, minutes before he came to the door. My mother and the pots rattled with expectancy: would this be the man to stay with her, to adjust our haphazard course? The kitchen smelled rich with promise, as if the scent of her perfume and the odors of my cooking held the power to transform our lives, to transport us from our crowded, chaotic apartment into a large house, where we all had our own rooms, where my mother would be calm, secure, loved.

After we returned from services that evening, I told my father and Phyllis that my mother would probably show up the next morning. They looked at each other.

"Oh, Sam," my father sighed. "Couldn't you have done something?"

"No, Dad. She wants to come."

"Doesn't she know how uncomfortable this is going to be?" Phyllis said.

"Mommy, who's coming?" Debbie asked.

"Nobody, dear. Nobody."

I didn't say anything, and I went to bed feeling just like everyone else.

The next morning, I stepped up to the Torah and saw my mother sitting in a row of empty seats. She waved at me like someone in a lifeboat attempting to flag a distant ship. Everyone's eyes moved from her to me. I brought my tallis to my lips and began chanting in a language I didn't understand. From behind me, the sun beamed through a stained-glass mural. The light washed over me and the colors skated back and forth across the parchment, echoing the manic movements of my heart.

After the service, she rushed over to the receiving line and reclaimed me with a long, long embrace. She had not held or kissed me in months. Several people waiting to greet me formed an uncomfortable semicircle around us. She tightened her hold, as if I were a charm to ward off bad spirits. People began to file away. Soon we were standing alone, like two strangers who had wandered into the wrong celebration. Then Phyllis came over to tell me that the photographer was set up for a family portrait. My mother squeezed my elbow.

"You stay right here, Sam."

"We'll only be five minutes," Phyllis said impatiently. "Come, Sam."

She reached for me and my mother slapped her hand away. Phyllis looked at her hand as if she had never seen it before.

"I'm his family," my mother said. "If the photographer wants a portrait, he can come over here."

"Crazy woman," Phyllis murmured, and turned away. My mother caught her on the side of the head with her purse. Phyllis whirled around, crying "Oh! Oh!" more in disbelief than in pain. My mother lunged at her. Both women grabbed at each other's hair and face. They teetered back and forth in their high heels. I could hear nylons whispering against nylons. My father rushed over, his hand raised and his black robes billowing. I ran out.

I kept running until I reached the beach, breathless. Each gulp of the November air stung my lungs. I wrapped my tallis around my neck and walked rapidly through the sand. Then I heard my mother shout my name. I turned around. She was perhaps a hundred yards behind me, her shoes in her hands. She crossed them above her head, signaling me to stop. I walked down to the shoreline.

I recalled how she and I used to come to this same beach on winter afternoons when my parents were still married. She hated the summer crowds, but liked the remoteness of the beach in winter. Once we came with a helium balloon she had bought me at a nearby amusement park. At the shoreline she had bent down beside me and we placed our fingertips all over its shiny red surface. "We're sending a message," she said, "to your Nana Rose." I let go of the balloon, and we watched it sail up into the brilliant blue air and disappear over the ocean. She explained that when the balloon reached heaven Nana Rose would recognize our fingerprints. Perhaps I looked at her quizzically, because she then said, "Trust me, sweetie. We're already on the moon."

I watched the waves explode and dash toward me, watched the froth top my shoes, and at almost the same moment felt my socks turn to ice.

"Sam, dear, why are you standing in the water?"

She was about five feet behind me. I didn't answer or turn around.

"Honey, you'll ruin your shoes."

"Good."

"You'll catch pneumonia."

"Good."

"Won't you at least step out of the water?"

"No."

"No?"

"Maybe I want to go for a swim."

I really didn't want to swim. I just wanted to lie down in the surf and close my eyes and drift, like a toy boat or a bottle, to the other side of the ocean, washing up on the shore of a new country.

"Darling, it's too cold to swim. Wait until June. Then you can go in the water."

"Don't talk to me like that!"

"Like what, sweetie?"

"Like I'm crazy. Like I'm about to jump out a window. You're the one who's crazy, not me."

"Oh, Sam, don't criticize. Not now. Not after what I've been through. Don't be like everyone else." I turned around, ready to shout, "Why can't you be like everyone else!" Then I saw how bad she looked. One eye was half closed and her nostrils were rimmed with blood. Angry red welts laced her windpipe. She dropped to her knees and began crying noiselessly into the sand.

I was only thirteen that day, but I knew my mother would never change. She would never have a beautiful office like Florence Fein's. She would never have more than three or four patients, people like Mrs. Gutman, who were as chaotic and pained as she was. I knew she would always feel like a stranger on the planet.

Two weeks later a judge sent me to live with my father. The fight with Phyllis, and the depositions provided by nearly everyone in my father's congregation, weighed heavily against my mother. I was sullen with the judge, though he was gentle with me. Perhaps I could have said something kind about my mother, but I was only thirteen, and I didn't know that love can be as obdurate as the changes you long for. Perhaps I could have told him that after I turned around and saw her bruised face, I lifted my mother to her feet. I pressed my tallis against her bloody nose. Then I rolled it up into a tight little ball, and we trekked back up the beach together.

LYNNE SHARON SCHWARTZ

The Melting Pot

*R*ita suffers from nightmares. This morning's: she is summoned from San Francisco to New York for her grandfather's funeral, where she causes a catastrophe. She enters the chapel with her Russian-born grandmother, Sonia, on her arm, she sees the sea of men and women segregated by a carpeted aisle—solid people, bearers of durable wisdom—and her legs become immovable weights. Everything in her hardens, refusing to move towards the women's side, where she belongs. Even her teeth harden. Sonia, a scrawny, vinegary woman in perpetual haste, tries to drag her along, but Rita cannot be moved. Suddenly from the closed coffin comes a choked, rising moan almost like a tune, the voice trying to break out in protest. Rita's grandmother gasps in horror, clutches her chest, and collapses. All the mourners look at Rita and gasp in unison, like the string section opening a great symphony. One by one, they topple over in shock, both sexes heaped together, mingling. Rita's teeth clench in the dream, biting the hands that fed her.

She wakes up and holds on to Sanjay, who grunts in his sleep. The nightmares dissipate more quickly when he is there. He is a very large, smooth man and she clings to him like a rock climber. In the limbo of waking she cannot even remember which house they are in, his or hers—for they are next-door neighbors, only a wall between them for six years. They live in similar narrow row houses with luscious little flower beds in front, on a sunny San Francisco street lined with eucalyptus trees.

Sanjay, a seeker of practical solutions, thinks the ideal solution to Rita's nightmares would be for them to marry. Why should they live on opposite sides of the wall, like those silly lovers of legend? They are not children, there are no watchful parents hindering them.

"One day soon it will strike you," he says now and then in half-humorous, half-cajoling way, a man of many charms, "that it is the right thing to do. It won't happen when we are making love, but at a more trustworthy moment. Maybe after you have asked me for the fifth time to fix your dishwasher, or after I have consulted you for the ninth time on how some fourth cousin can satisfy the immigration authorities. Some very banal moment between us, and you'll suddenly know. You will want to belong to me forever."

Rita usually laughs. "You've seen too many Fred Astaire movies." But she is afraid. She doesn't want to belong to anyone forever. She has grown up watching that. And she is afraid she won't know how to fit herself in, fit with another life. She looks at their bodies, which do fit sleekly together. Parts of them are the very same color, side by side. The palms of his hands are the color of her thighs, his cheeks the color of her nipples. "What would our children be like?" she says lightly. "What would they call themselves?"

She is not really worried about possible children or what they would call themselves. She mentions it only to deflect his yearnings, because Sanjay has three children already, grown and married.

The oldest, who has gone back to India to study his roots, is Rita's age, twenty-eight. It is only natural that Sanjay's fatherliness should appeal to her, a fatherless child—that and his size and bulk, his desire to possess and protect, his willingness to fix her dishwasher and to accept the silences during which she tried to extricate herself from her history. His willingness to accept her history itself. But marrying him seems so definitive.

Now she sits up, leaning on her elbows. The room is suffused with a pre-dawn tinge of lavender. It is Sanjay's house. Of course. There are the faint smells of cumin, coriander, anise—bitter and lush. They are strongest in the kitchen but waft through the other rooms as well. Sanjay's daughter comes two afternoons a week to cook for him. She was born right here on Russian Hill, but she cooks the way her mother did. She doesn't know that her father and Rita eat her food in bed. Sanjay cannot bring himself to tell his children he sleeps with the young woman next door, although he is ready to present her as his wife.

"Why do you let her do that?" Rita asked at the beginning, three years ago. "Doesn't she have enough to do, with the baby and all?"

"I don't ask her to. She insists, ever since her mother died. She's very old-fashioned." A soulful pause. "And she's such a good cook."

"What do you cook when you're alone?"

He made a wry face. "Hamburgers. Tuna fish."

Besides the lush smell, she sees it is Sanjay's house by the shadowy bulk of the large chest of drawers, the darkened sheen of the gilded mirror above it, the glint of the framed photograph of his wife on the chest. When Rita first came to his bedroom Sanjay used to turn the photograph to the wall. As a courtesy, she assumed, for he is a man of delicate feelings, of consummate discretion; but she wasn't sure if the courtesy was directed to her or to his late wife. Now, grown familiar and cozy, he sometimes forgets. Rita has always imagined that she reminds him of his wife, that he wants her because of a resemblance. With the picture facing front, perhaps they are communing through her body.

Well, all right. Rita is used to being a link, endlessly malleable. She is used to reminding people of someone, and to being loved as a link to the true loved one. Even at work, she helps people locate their relatives, and at times she is present at the reunion and watches them embrace. When they finish embracing each other they often embrace her too, as the link. She helps them find ways to stay here. If they succeed in becoming citizens, then Rita is the bridge they pass over to their new identity.

"Immigration law!" Her grandfather, Sol, expected the worst when she started. "You'll see," he grumbled over the phone, wheezing long-distance. "You'll be always with those refugees, you'll wind up marrying one, you with your bleeding heart. And who knows where they come from, what they—"

"Enough already, Sol!" Sonia's rough voice in the background. "Enough!"

"Sometimes these people have to marry someone just to stay in this country," he explains to his granddaughter, the immigration lawyer. "They see a pretty young girl with a profession, what could be better?"

True enough. In three years Rita has had several tentative suggestions of marriage. But she tries to find those desperate souls a better way. She reminds them that they came here to be free, free, and that marriage to a stranger is no freedom. Besides, there is Sanjay.

Sanjay works all day in a laboratory, or laboratory, as he calls it; he wants to cure hemophiliacs, bleeders. (Contrary to popular notion, hemophiliacs do not bleed more intensely than most people, only longer.) Sanjay knows almost all there is to know about genes and blood. Indeed, he has the exile's air of knowing all there is to know about everything. Yet he has been here for nearly thirty years, is a citizen, and, unlike Rita's jittery clients, seems very much at home. His face has taken on a West Coast transparency. His courtly speech is sprinkled with the local argot. Still, Rita suspects, even knowing all there is to know about her, he sees her as his entryway to the land of dreams. His bridge. His American girl.

Rita's present life is, in her grandfather's view, one of disobedience (like her nightmares), but as a small child she was quite obedient. She submitted when he found her costuming paper dolls in her bedroom on a Saturday afternoon and unhooked the scissors from her thumb and forefinger, reminding her that Jews do not cut on the Sabbath. Nor do they color in coloring books, trace pictures from magazines, turn on the lights, the toaster, the radio, or the television, use the phone, cook, sew, drive. . . . The way Sol explains it, they are defined by what they are forbidden. There are things they must not eat and not wear, not do and not utter. The most constricted people are the most holy, relieved from confront-ing the daily unknown with bare instinct, for happily, every con-ceivable pattern of human event and emotion was foreseen centuries ago and the script is at hand, in old books in an old tongue. She submitted. But she was allowed to read. *A Little Prin-cess* was her favorite story, where the orphaned and hungry heroine is forced to live in a lonely freezing garret, until a kindly Indian gentleman feeds her and lights a fire in her room and finally rescues her altogether, restoring her to a life of abundance.

For the most holy people, the most holy season is fall, the most beautiful. Also the most allusive and most amenable to introspec-tion, with its amber light, its sounds of leaves scuttling, brittle as death, on the pavement, its eerie chills at sundown, and its holidays calling for renewal, guilt, atonement, remembrance, hope, and pride, one after the other in breathless succession. It is the season to think over your past deeds and ask forgiveness of anyone you might have injured, for only after asking a fellow creature's forgive-ness may you ask God's. God has a big book and keeps his ac-counts: Your fortunes in the year to come depend on your actions in the year just passed. (Karma, thinks Rita years later, when she knows Sanjay.) It is the season when Rita is required to get out of her jeans and beads and into a dress. Shoes instead of sneakers. Sweating great beads of boredom, resistance seeping from every pore to form a second skin beneath her proper clothing, she trails her grandfather to the synagogue to sit with the women in the balcony (so as not to distract the men) and listen to him sing the prayers in a language she cannot understand.

Her grandmother the atheist also conforms, sits in the women's balcony behind a curtain and fasts on the Day of Atonement, and this not merely out of obedience, like Rita. Sonia finds her identity

THE MELTING POT 289

in opposition. She conforms in order to assert her difference in the
New World, as in the Old World others asserted it for her, in the
form of ostracism and pogroms. But within the family's little con-
forming circle she has to assert her difference too, and so while her
husband is out at the synagogue she fixes herself a forbidden glass
of tea. Her wiry body moves quickly around the kitchen, as if
charged with electrical current. Snickering like a child, she raises
the steaming glass by the rim and drinks, immensely pleased with
her mischief, her high cheekbones gleaming.

"You might as well have a sandwich while you're at it," says
Rita, at eleven years old not yet required to fast, to choose between
her grandparents, obedience in bed with defiance.

A sandwich would be going too far. They destroy the evidence,
wash and dry the glass and spoon and put them away; luckily he
doesn't count the tea bags, hardly the province of a holy man.

What is the province of a holy man? God, of course. Wrong.
Rules. Sanjay could have told her that. His family's rules fill at least
as many books. Rita's grandfather loves rules, constrictions, whatever narrows the broad path of life and disciplines the meandering
spirit for its own good. The lust to submit is his ruling passion. It
is part of the covenant with God: Obey all the rules and you will
be safe. Sol takes this literally. He seeks out arcane rules to obey
and seizes upon them, appropriates them with the obsessiveness of
a Don Juan appropriating new women. Nor is that enough; his
passion requires that others obey them too. His wife. His granddaughter. For the family is the pillar of society. The family is the
society. And if a member disobeys, strays too far beyond the
pillars, he becomes an outcast. At risk in the wide world, the world
of the others. "Them."

So Rita rarely hears him speak of God. And Sonia mentions
God with contempt, as one would speak of the meanest enemy, too
mean even to contend with. "What God says I'm not interested
in!" she shouts bitterly when Sol nags her back onto the little path
of submission. "I'm interested in what people do right here on
earth!" Alone together, Sonia and Rita never tire of cataloguing the
discrepancies between God's reputation and his manifest deeds.
They, obey in their hearts? It is to laugh. And laugh they do,

showing their perfect teeth, as enduring as rocks. Of course they are women, their minds fixed on the specific. Perhaps they cannot grasp the broader scheme of things.

"What would be sins?" Rita asks her grandfather, thinking of Sonia's tea.

He pats his soft paunch thoughtfully with both hands. "Lying to your grandparents. Thinking wicked thoughts. Being unkind to people."

This sounds fairly mild. She tries to enumerate her greater sins but can think of none that any God worthy of the name would take notice of. With a new assassination almost yearly, the portraits of the dead promptly appearing on the walls at school, can God care that she listens to the Supremes on a Saturday afternoon, she and the radio muffled under a blanket? She asks her grandmother about sins but Sonia waves her arm dismissively, an arc of contempt scything the air. Rita infers that God, rather than mortals, has a lot to answer for, though she doesn't know what in particular is on her grandmother's mind besides the general wretchedness abounding. Poor people ride to Washington on mules. Long-haired students in Chicago get beaten by police. Rita passes the time in the balcony constructing cases against God on their behalf. Her father was a lawyer, she has managed to glean; she invokes his help. The cases are very good, watertight, with evidence starting from Abraham; no, Abel. But no matter what the jury decides, God remains. That is his nature, she gathers, to be there watching and judging, always alert for a misstep, but not helping.

Light is coming in at the window, a Pacific coast autumn light, creamy, soft-edged. As it slides up his face, Sanjay wakes, and Rita tells him about her bad dream, for she cannot shake it. She tells him how in the dream her father's father, the most obedient servant of his Lord, is taken, even so. How his obedience did not shield him in the end, and how she, by her disobedience rooted in a certain juxtaposition of genes, causes a shocking event, rivaling the one that convulsed the family twenty-six years ago.

"Heredity," says Sanjay sleepily, "doesn't work that way. You make too much of it." He has exchanged the faith in karma for the science of genetics. And he wants to help. He wants her to turn around and live facing front. Odd, since he comes from a country imprisoned in history, while she is the young West Coast lawyer. Sometimes it seems they have changed places.

"And don't you make much of it? Don't you tell me you get glimpses of your father's face in the mirror when you shave, but with a peeled, American expression? I feel my mother when I brush my hair. In the texture of the hair."

"That's different. You can inherit hair but not destinies."

He sounds so sure. . . . "I think in the dream he was trying to sing. Did I ever tell you that my grandfather used to sing in the synagogue?"

"I thought your mother was the singer."

"Her too. That was a different kind of song. He ran the store all week, but on Saturday mornings he was a cantor, he led the prayers. Then when I was about seventeen, he had some minor surgery in his throat and he never sang again."

"Why, what happened?"

"Nothing. He was afraid."

"Of what?"

"Well that's exactly it. Something cosmic. That his head might burst, I don't know. It was just too risky. The absurd thing was, he had the operation to restore his voice. We never heard him sing again. So what do you make of a man who loves to sing and sings for the glory of God, then refuses to sing out of fear?"

"In his hear the still sings. He sings, Safe, safe." Sanjay composes a little tune on the word.

Rita smiles. "I thought immigrants always sang, Free, free."

"Not always. We"—he means his brother and himself, who came here to be educated and returned home only to visit—"we sing, Away, away. New, new." He yawns, and then, in a lower key, "Guilt, guilt."

All the indigenous American tunes, thinks Rita. But she is still smiling. He has a way of making heavy things feel lighter. He has a mild grace that buoys him through life. Maybe she should marry him after all. She is so malleable an American, she could become anyone with ease. And it would be a way to live; it would be safe, safe. She might even let her hair grow long and smooth it down with coconut oil, start frying wheat cakes and clarifying butter and stepping delicately down the hills of San Francisco as Sanjay's wife did, holding up her long skirts.

That was how Rita first saw them, the Indian gentleman and his wife. It was the day of her graduation from college, which her grandparents flew west to attend. Afterwards, she took them across the bay to San Francisco, to show them her new apartment. For she was staying on. Through a friend, she had found a summer job in a Spanish record store, and in the fall she would start law school.

While Sonia tore through the rooms like a high wind, Sol stood at the front window, holding the curtain to one side and peering out as though he were in a hostile country, a place you could get yourself killed. Though not much of a traveler, he had been here once before, briefly.

"Who are your neighbors?" he asks, gesturing with his chin.

"I don't know. Which ones?" Rita comes over to peer out too.

It is an Indian couple, the man tall and broad, with heavy eyebrows and longish hair, dressed impeccably, even a bit flamboyantly, in a light gray suit. Rita likes the suit and likes his walk, stately, meditative, achieving a look that is both scholarly and debonair. By his side is a slight woman in a green and gold sari, holding his arm. Her head is lowered, so Rita can barely see her face. She holds the sari up skillfully, climbing the hill.

"I guess they're an Indian couple."

"Indians?" Her grandfather's voice rises. Bows and arrows?

"From India. You know, Gandhi, Nehru, no eating cows. That's what the women wear."

"I know what India is. I read the papers too, Rita. I'm not as ignorant as you think."

"Sorry, Papa."

"How do they live? Nice?"

She shrugs. "I guess so."

"Yes. They're not the same as the colored."

"Oh, Papa, don't start."

The Indian couple is moving unusually slowly, their heads cast

down. They look like a devoted pair; they walk in step, rhythmically. As they turn into the front yard next door, to the left, he
swings the gate open for her.

Much later, when Rita tells Sanjay about the first time she saw
him, he says they might have been coming from the doctor; it was
the month when his wife had some tests. The tests said yes, but it
would probably not get really bad till the end.

It is strange, Rita thinks now, that she was with her grandfather
when she first saw Sanjay.

A scene from one of Rita's silences: Her great-uncle Peter, her
grandfather's twin brother, is a philanthropic dentist—he fills the
cavities of Orthodox Jewish orphans for free. Also he checks Rita's
teeth. Her grandmother drives her to his office for a checkup every
six months, on a Sunday morning. The tiny waiting room is
crowded with old people—fifty years old at least; where are the
orphans of legend? They wait in the little waiting room which
smells of dental supplies—sweet, medicinal, like wintergreen—
until all the paying customers have had their turns, which may take
an entire Sunday morning. Rita and Sonia share many qualities of
temperament, notably the impatience gene. They wait with diffi-
culty. Though they like to talk, they find no solace in the small talk
that accompanies waiting. They leaf through magazines, they go to
the superbly clean bathroom smelling of mouthwash, they pace the
tiny waiting room. Sonia, unable to be confined, goes out to walk
around the block. Rita cannot take such liberties since it's her
mouth waiting to be examined, and her uncle might take a notion
to sneak her in between the creaky patients. Her grandmother
walks fast, round and round the block; Rita imagines her tense,
bony body crackling like November twigs. Sonia's short auburn
hair is alive in the breeze, and her fierce mind works on the fabric
of the past, ripping stitches, patching.

At last it is Rita's turn. Her great-uncle, bald and moon-faced,
rotund in his sparkling white jacket, round-collared like a priest's,
beckons, the outstretched hand making a swift fluttering motion,
giving the impression that she has been dilatory, that she has kept

him waiting. He greets her using a Hebrew name that no one ever
uses. She feels he is talking to some invisible person in the room.
"What a pretty complexion," he says, in a way that suggests perhaps it is not, a consoling way. And, "What strong white teeth!"
In a stage whisper, over her head: "She must get those from her
mother."

"I have strong white teeth too," Sonia says with savage energy.
"When have you ever had to fix anything in my mouth?"

Sonia dislikes her brother-in-law passionately. All the dislike she
cannot expend on her husband she transfers to his twin brother.
Peter and Sol are cautious people, supremely timid in the face of
life. Yet they came to the New World as infants and know only by
hearsay what they escaped. Sonia, who came later, remembers, and
finds their timidities an indulgence. Her family are extravagant-
tempered Russians whom Russians never accepted as such, which
is why they journeyed so far. Genetically defiant people with hy-
peractive brains, willful, angry, ebullient. Their bones snap, the
veins in their temples throb. There is nothing they cannot feel
passionate about, and so they lavish huge and frightful energies on
life and live long, propelled by their exuberant indignation. Rita is
fascinated by them and bored by her grandfather's docile family.
She sees the two sides of the family as opposing teams, opposing
stances towards life. When she is older she sees her grandparents
in an incessant game of running bases: they throw the ball back and
forth—the ball is truth, how to live—and she, Rita, must run
between them, pulled now to the safety of rules and traditions, now
back to the thrills of defiance and pride.

Once she is in the funny chair, Peter gives her avuncular rides up
and down, chattering affectionately, almost too affectionately, as if
he is trying extra hard. There are whispered words with her grandmother, exchanges Rita doesn't grasp except that Sonia wants none
of his proffered commiseration. "You can't trust one of them, not
one," he mumbles. "That's the way it is, that's the way it will
always be."

"Shh, shh," Sonia hushes him in disgust. "Just do her teeth, no
speeches." Sonia always sticks up for her; with crackling Sonia she
is utterly safe.

"Such beautiful dark hair." He does seem to like her, in the brief time he has available. Yet he calls her by the wrong name, which you do not do to someone you like. That's not who I am, Rita wants to cry out, but there is something peculiar and mysterious about who she is that keeps her silent, openmouthed like an idiot. She sometimes gets glimmerings of losses below the surface, like sunken jewels that divers plunge and grope for in vain. They might be memories of a different climate, or the feel of an embrace, or a voice, feelings so fleeting and intangible she can hardly call them memories. But they have been with her since she can remember— wispy vapors of another way she might once have been, another mode of feeling the world, as believers in reincarnation sense their past lives.

That's not who I am, she wants to cry out, but she can offer no more, she knows nothing more, and anyway he is all frothing joviality and patter, while his hands nimbly prepare the instruments. Rita is enthralled by the rows of false teeth lined up on the cabinet, pink gums and ivory teeth, the many different shapes waiting like orphans to be adopted, for mouths to come by and take them in, ready to be pressed into service chewing and forming the dental consonants. Unspoken words and stories are hiding in the teeth.

"So. Are you going to play Queen Esther this year?"

"No." She rinses and spits. "The teacher said I should be Vashti."

"Well, Vashti is good too. She was very beautiful."

"She gets killed in the beginning. I was Vashti last year."

"Finished?" asks Sonia impatiently.

Fortunately Rita's teeth are excellent, she can be disposed of in five minutes. Rocks, he says every time. She has rocks in her head. And he tells her that her teeth, like her grandmother's, will last a lifetime. Good news. Sharp and hard, they bite, they grip, grind, gnash, and clench. They make the words come out clear. Sonia grinds her teeth all night, Sol remarks at breakfast. Good, Rita thinks. They will be useful in times of stress. They will help her chew hard things and grind them down, make them fit for swallowing.

———

When Sanjay's wife died, Rita paid a neighborly call, as her grand-father taught her to do. Solomon was conscientious about visiting the bereaved. He would enter their houses with no greeting (that was the rule), seat himself in a corner, open a book, and pray as though he were alone in the room and the universe, which in a sense he was, for all around him people continued to speak, eat, and even make merry as survivors will.

The rules behind her, no book to guide her, Rita brings a rich, fruity cake to Sanjay and greets him. They have exchanged greet-ings on the street, she has inquired with concern about his wife, but she has never been in his house before. She notices he has some Indian things—a big brass tray, a lacquered vase with an array of peacock feathers, and several photos of Allahabad, his home town, a very holy place, he tells her, where two holy rivers meet. One photo shows masses of people, the tops of heads, mostly, bathing in a holy river banked by two fantastical buildings, castles out of a tale of chivalry. Otherwise it is a San Francisco kind of house—airy, with thriving plants and colorful pillows. It smells spicy.

They become friends. They go to an occasional movie, a restau-rant. He asks her advice about relatives who need green cards. She asks if he can fix her dishwasher. She loves the way he moves, his great weight treading softly, the smooth sound of his voice and the way after all these years he keeps pronouncing certain words in the British fashion—"dance," "record," "laboratory"—his slow, very inquisitive eyes and hard mouth.

Finally, after several months of decorous behavior they meet by chance on the street one evening and get to talking. Something feels different. Ripe. His eyes and his speech are slower, more judicious than usual, almost ponderous. He asks her into his house and she smells the sharp spices. He gives her some stuffed chappattis his daughter brought over that morning; he insists on warming them in the oven first. Delicious. The bread is important; it is, she understands, part of the seduction. Standing very erect, shoulders squared, like a man about to deliver a speech, he says, "Well, Rita, I have never courted an American young woman before, so you'll have to forgive my . . . ineptness. But it seems time, to me. And you? Will you?" She nods. He looks so safe.

Upstairs, the furniture in the bedroom is weighty, built for the ages. It reminds her of the furniture in her grandparents' apartment. Married furniture. The first thing Sanjay does is turn his wife's photograph to the wall.

Rita lets herself be undressed. "Oh. Oh," he says, touching her. When he takes her in his arms she feels an immense relief—at last!—as if she has been freezing for years and suddenly a fur coat is thrown over her, the kind of coat shown in photos of Russian winters, and she realizes she has wanted him from the moment she saw him from the window three years ago, looking out with her grandfather. She can feel his immense relief too, but that, she imagines, is because he has not held anyone in his arms in months. Oh God, she hopes it will not be . . . like that.

No, he is in no hurry. He proves to know a lot about women. Maybe in a past incarnation he was a woman—she can almost believe it. Also, from the way he touches her, she feels how he must have loved his wife. She wonders if she feels like his wife, if maybe all women feel alike, after a certain point. In his arms, Rita forgets who she is. She could almost be his wife. And then she falls immediately asleep.

When she wakes, the bedside lamp is on and Sanjay is weeping into the pillow. He looks up and sees her watching.

"I'm sorry. Forgive me." He stops abruptly.

Is this all she will ever be, a link to the beloved dead?

"Really, I'm terribly sorry, Rita. I thought you were sleeping."

"It's all right, Sanjay, it's all right." What else can she say?

She does not sleep much that night but watches him sleep. For hours, it seems. She has shielded herself so far, but now it envelops her like a shower of gold threads, of red powder, and she sees that love is the greatest defiance of all. She is afraid of it.

She has to leave early, go home to the other side of the wall and change, pick up her cap and gown. She is graduating from law school that very day. Sanjay says he wants to be there, so she gives him a ticket—she has them to spare since her grandparents are not flying out this time. Sol's heart is too irregular.

Just before she leaves to take her place in the line, he slips her a tiny candy wrapped in silver paper. "For luck."

She starts to unwrap it.

"No, no. You eat the paper too."

She trusts him infinitely. She eats the paper. Silver, sweet, delicious. Bits of it stick in her teeth, making the taste linger.

When he announces months later that he loves her and wants to marry her, that he has thought it over and waited to speak until he was quite sure, she takes the information skeptically.

"Why? Can't you believe that I loved her and now I love you?"

"I don't know."

"You must have loved other people. I don't think about them."

"But I haven't."

"Maybe, maybe not. You do love me, though," Sanjay says. "I know. Must I see a problem in that, perhaps?" This is comical, she thinks, this interrogation. He can be so matter-of-fact, even imperious. There is a sliver of amusement in his eyes, too. Whatever he is, she loves.

"I never felt this before. I don't know what to make of it."

"Come now. You must have. American girls . . ."

"I was busy with other things."

"What things?"

She can't tell him how she spent her college years. It's too crazy. Not yet, anyway. So instead she says something hurtful. "You're too old for me."

He seems impervious, tilts his head carelessly. "That can't be helped. And anyway, you don't really mind."

It's true, she doesn't. Quite the contrary.

Rita and Sanjay find that their backgrounds have a number of things in common. A preponderance of rules for proper behavior is one, especially rules about not consorting—eating or sleeping—with members of another caste. This, like pioneers, they have both

left behind. Arranged marriages is another. This one does not seem
so far behind.

"So you never really knew her before you were married?"

"We knew each other, but not in the way that you mean. The
families met several times. We spoke. It's not really so preposter-
ous. The idea is that you come to love each other. We trust in
proximity to breed love."

Rita frowns. He is still trusting.

"It sounds very unromantic, I know. But it doesn't exclude
romance of a kind."

"Does it work? I mean, for most people?"

"Well, more than you'd expect. Some love each other with a
good will kind of love. Some even have passionate love. But there
are other ways to love besides those, more ways than are recognized
here. You can love someone simply because she's yours, part of
you. You've accepted each other and you don't question it. My
parents were like that. Are still like that."

"And what about you? What kind of love was it?"

He closes his eyes. The pain of loss, regret? Or merely impatience. "Why do you keep asking? You know the answer."

She knows. The goodwill kind, the passionate kind, the totally
accepting kind. Often, those first three years, she saw them walking
arm in arm down the street, their steps falling together in rhythm.
Belonging.

"You were lucky. Did she know, the first night, what she was
supposed to do?"

"Not precisely. She was a very sheltered girl."

"But you knew, I presume?"

Sanjay takes a deep breath and his face begins a little perform-
ance—his face has a great repertoire of expressions. His eyes roll,
his forehead wrinkles, his lips curl. "What do you think?"

"Was she appalled?"

"No."

Rita would like to know, in graphic detail, exactly how Sanjay
made it clear what was expected. She is not a voyeur by nature;
rather, she is mystified by the transmutations of love—how indif-

ference turns into love, love into indifference and even worse. But
it is useless to ask. He doesn't tell. It must be too precious. Yes,
because he does love to tell stories about his parents, his brothers
and sisters and cousins. She has heard comic stories about bicycles
capsized in the mud and a flirtatious widowed aunt, stories of
school pranks and festival antics, and painful stories about a baby
sister who died of diphtheria on the day Gandhi was shot. But no
stories about his wife.

"I know what you're thinking. But people can love more than
once, Rita. After all . . ."

"I know, I know." Yet she knows only in the abstract. She feels
generally ignorant on the subject. She thinks that what she saw,
growing up, was not love but a species of belonging.

Her grandparents' marriage took place in 1927 and was also
arranged, though not as strictly as Sanjay's. The couple was introduced; they took several walks together over the Brooklyn Bridge;
they went to a few movies and even to an opera, *Madame Butterfly*.
This was all quite ordinary. But the wedding itself was extraordinary. The father of the groom had collapsed and died two days
before. No matter; the rules say ceremonies must take place as
scheduled, like Broadway shows. And the bride did not refuse; she
had not yet learned how. But she had her doubts, surely, Rita
thinks. For it is hard to imagine the Sonia she knows being so
compliant. Surely she must have been astounded, felt that such a
beginning did not augur well and maybe she had better pull out
before it was too late? But it was already too late.

"Can you picture that wedding?" she queries Sanjay.

"Well, quiet, I'd imagine. Very quiet."

No doubt. A dearth of dancing, the musicians laboring to rouse
an unappreciative crowd. Rita's various aunts and uncles, disguised
as young people, gathered around linen-covered tables, eating
sweetbreads and drinking sweet wine while salt streams down their
faces. The children fretful and confused—no one is urging delica-
cies on them or swinging them through the air. Her own father not
yet an outcast, not even born, a gleam, as they say, in his father's
very gleaming eye. As her grandparents toast their life together, the
groom weeps under the harshness of his own discipline. He can

barely drink and cannot eat. He does not need to eat. Self-pity and self-satisfaction are his feast—for this ordeal will make him a better person, bring him favor in the eyes of his God. What kind of eyes could they be?

Very quickly the couple has an indissoluble connection, a son. Sonia's first decade of marriage is a depression, then comes the war.

Throughout their married life there are many changes in the world. The maps of Europe, Africa, and Asia change drastically. There are immense shifts of population, new technologies, cures for diseases; wonders and horrors as usual. The twentieth century. But—and she has to admire his tenacity—Rita's grandfather's world remains the world he grew up in, a small world left over from the youth of the century, a bit cramped and crowded, like a room to which new pieces are added but from which nothing is ever thrown away, a thoroughly benign and safe world, according to his stories—for he is, yes, a storyteller, with a magnetic eye, bluest of blues, and a magnetic voice.

"Our house was the place where all immigrants stopped first," he says. "And no matter how crowded we were, when they opened the door, whoever came in I welcomed them with open arms. I was only a child. But I felt the call of blood."

Open arms. He lives, Rita comes to understand, by appropria- tion. He takes in, processes, categorizes, labels, and provides a commentary. To have any act unexplained or unexcused, anyone left out of the scheme, can put the world in an imbalanced state, as taunting and intolerable as an unresolved chord in his singer's ear.

So he narrates the fortunes of each arrival, one by one: loves, travels, business ventures, progeny. And in his stories—long, highly dramatized, and gripping—never a harsh word is spoken between sister and brother, parent and child, husband and wife, only happy grateful immigrants making good in the promised land, learning the customs and the lingo. He has an instinctive way of skimming over pain or crisis, a lighting mostly on moments of epiphany when generosity and breadth of spirit are revealed, mo- ments when virtue triumphs over self-interest. What everyone fled from is never mentioned above a whisper, and never at all in the presence of "them," the others, the ones who can never be trusted,

302 Lynne Sharon Schwartz

who pursue and destroy. The moral is always the same: The family is the pillar of society. There are no distinctions when it comes to family. A cousin? "Like my own brother!" (A granddaughter? "Like my own daughter!") And when a member strays beyond the pillars he becomes an outcast. Formerly appropriated, now vomited up.

Since Sol's stories extol righteousness, Rita asks why, then, he and his brother don't go out, this minute, and work for civil rights and for an end to the war in Vietnam. If they fled from the draft on one continent, shouldn't they protest it on another? Sol listens because she is a clever speaker, and when she becomes too annoying he waves her away like a mosquito. Her uncle the dentist points out that all the boys in the immediate neighborhood are going to college, not Asia. Once, her great-aunt, the dentist's wife, loses patience. "Protest, protest!" she mocks, eyeing Rita as she would a stranger who has jumped the line at the bakery. "She should be glad she has a roof over her head."

What could it mean? Rita knows her parents are . . . well . . . dead, it must be. The subject is taboo. It is as if she is Sol's and Sonia's child. This is her roof, isn't it? Her grandfather tells his sister-in-law to shut her big mouth. Sonia goes further and throws her out of the house, and the incident is closed. Everyone goes to bed with a headache.

Undaunted, at fourteen years old Rita thinks she too can appropriate the world, make it over to fit her vision. Not all immigrants are so well assimilated, she finds out. She feels for those beyond the pillars, maybe because she is darker than any Jew she knows and has never had a chance to play Queen Esther. With an adolescent's passion to convert, she wants her grandfather to feel for them too, and to agree that breadth of spirit does not mean obeying the most rules but scorning them all, except for the rules of the heart. She wants him to thrill to the uneven rhythms of heroic outcasts, anarchists: "I might have lived out my life talking at street corners, to scorning men. I might have died unmarked, unknown, a failure. Now we are not a failure. This is our career and our triumph. Never in our full life could we hope to do so much work for tolerance, for justice, for man's understanding of man as we do now by

accident. Our words—our lives—our pains—nothing! The taking
of our lives—lives of a good shoemaker and a poor fish-peddler—
all! That last moment belongs to us—that agony is our triumph!"
She finds this in a book about famous trials of the century, and
shivers with passion.

But Solomon hears it impassively, and in response, launches into
one of his own speeches—clears his throat and prepares his oratori-
cal voice. "Ours, Rita, is a religion of ethics. A man's devotion to
God is shown in how he treats his fellow man, beginning with his
own—his children, his grandchildren"—he smiles fondly, justly
pleased with himself on this score—"his neighbors." (Sonia puts
down the skirt she is hemming, tosses aside her glasses and stalks
out of the room.) "In other words, *mamaleh*, charity begins at
home."

Very well, and where is home? Everywhere, she lectures him in
turn. He calls her a bleeding heart. Whatever he cannot appropriate, whatever refuses to go down and be assimilated—outsiders,
heinous deeds, gross improprieties—he ignores, which means it
ceases to exist.

He has been unable to appropriate, for instance, his son's marriage to a Mexican immigrant, which took place in far-off San
Francisco, California, in 1955. This Rita learns through piecing
together family whispers. If Sol had had his way, ostracism—the
tool of his enemies—would not have sufficed; according to the
rules, his son would have been interred in absentia and mourned
for a week, and neighbors would have visited him and Sonia while
they sat on wooden boxes, wearing bedroom slippers, with the
mirrors in the house covered by bed sheets. But he didn't have his
way. Sonia refused to do it. It was the beginning of her refusals.

That her mother was Mexican is one of four or five facts Rita
knows about her. Her name was Carmen. She was a singer—
strangely enough, like Rita's grandfather, but singing a different
kind of song. Rita would like to know what kind of love her
parents had and how they came to marry, but she never will. It was
certainly not arranged.

———

Rita's dream foresees her grandfather's funeral because he is not well, Sanjay suggests reasonably. Perhaps; she shrugs. She is not really seeking explanations. It is certainly true that Sol's fears have caught up with him, and that there are not enough rules to cover them adequately. Once sturdy, he has become in old age what he calls "nervous." He sees death coming, and his nervous system is in a twit. He has spells of weakness, shortness of breath, panic; all activities have to be gauged in advance as to how taxing they will be and the chance of mishaps. He monitors his vital signs with loving care, as solicitous of himself as a mother. The path has narrowed till on the vast new continent there is hardly room to place one foot in front of the other. Safe, safe. Rita hates the way he lives. She wants him to get up and do something—sing, pray, sell sportswear, anything but pave the way for death, be the advance man.

But for safety he must keep himself as confined as possible, especially since Rita and Sonia have slipped out of his control. He would not be so "nervous," he claims, if he could oversee what they were doing at all times. Of course, this cannot be. Rita is far away, doing God knows what and with whom, and Sonia has to manage the store. Sonia began to elude him long ago anyhow. For the first three decades of their marriage she obeyed, and then something happened. It was as if she had sealed up her disobedience the way pioneer women canned fruits and vegetables for a later season, and then she broke it out in abundance, jar after jar releasing its briny fumes. Years ago, members of the congregation reported that they saw the cantor's wife, her granddaughter beside her, driving his car on the Sabbath, a cigarette in her invincible teeth! Where could they be going? There was even talk of replacing him, but it came to nothing—they pitied him, first his great tragedy with his son and now unable to control his family.

Sonia, once tame, has reverted to the ways of her family. Anarchists, though not the grand kind. No, they fit very well into the elastic New World. Except that they argue passionately with the clerks of bureaucracies, they walk on the grass, they refuse to wait on lines, they smoke in nonsmoking areas, they open doors labeled authorized personnel only, they zip through traffic jams on the shoulders of roads or in lanes blocked off by orange stanchions. It is part of their passion, their brand of civil disobedience. Sol is horrified and Rita is amused, even though these are gestures only, to show they will not take the law from anyone, for they know who the lawgivers are. Clay like all the rest. They obey what they like, laws unto themselves. They are in fact (some of them, at any rate) lawyers. They came here in installments, three boys and three girls from Kiev. The girls became seamstresses, the boys lawyers. The girls went to factories, to sit on a cushion and sew a fine seam, while the boys were sent to school—the New World not so unlike the Old in that regard.

Three dressmakers make three lawyers: stitch, stitch. The dressmakers live in small apartments in Jewish ghettos with their husbands, small businessmen like Rita's grandfather, while their brothers prosper in modern assimilated suburbs. Then in 1959, the only child—a son—of one of the girls is stabbed to death in far-off San Francisco, California. That is truly lawless. The family, convulsed, will grieve in unison. That is not the kind of lawlessness, the kind of anarchy they intended, no, never, never! His mother will stop recognizing the world, any world, New, Old, all the same to her.

The family fears she may never return to the realm of the living. Days go by while she sits on a hard kitchen chair with her eyes fixed on nothing. She will not change her clothing or eat or sleep. When spoken to she will not respond, or else shakes her head, or at the most says, "Not now." It seems she is waiting for something, someone. Perhaps she is remembering how she refused to mourn her son when he married out of his faith—was it for this, so she could mourn him now?

Meanwhile her husband, accompanied by his twin brother the dentist, will fly out to the unknown western territories to settle his son's affairs and see that justice is done—a most adventurous trip, which he would not undertake for any other reason, but shock has made him a father again. The former outcast as a corpse is unobjectionable. And what, of all things, will he discover in the shadow of the Golden Gate but a child! Just two years old. If he had known, maybe . . . The child has been staying with her maternal uncle and his wife (her mother being in no condition to take care of her), but really, it is very difficult. They own a bar, a nightclub, actually—he is the bartender, his wife the waitress. (And there Rita's mother sang her Spanish songs. A vision in sequins? A floozy? She will never know.) No place for a baby. Without a moment's hesitation, Solomon transcends himself (possibly for the baby's blue eyes, which reflect his own), to perform the one daring act of his life—he takes her back. He takes her in. It is an act that could speak best for itself, but he cannot resist the ready phrase, a Jewish Polonius.

"It was the call of blood," he explains to Sonia as he enters carrying the child on one arm, suitcase and briefcase dangling from the other. She stares at him in the stupor that has become her mode of existence. Nothing surprises her. "Here," he says more naturally, holding out his burden like an offering. "Better take her to the bathroom. Her name is Rita." He thrusts her at Sonia. "Take a look at her eyes. Like skies."

A good name, Rita. It can derive from either set of genes. And there are plenty of dark Jews, her grandfather will declaim, presenting her to the family and the neighbors, the little bilingual prodigy. Yemenites. Ethiopians. The sons of Ham. Anyway, she is not all that dark. Some regular Jews are swarthy. Anyway, there she is, and her grandmother takes her to the bathroom, feeds her, clothes her, and low, a miracle sprung from tragedy, Sonia returns to life like Sarah in Genesis, fertilized in old age. Soon the neighborhood women start coming back to the house for fittings. They stand stiffly, only their mouths moving, as she pins folds of fabric around them, the pins stuck in her tough teeth. Rita plays with dolls at their feet, and not all her dolls are blonde. One is quite dark, with glossy black hair—Sonia understands the demands of a pluralistic society. That doll is not Rita's best baby, however. Her best baby is a blue-eyed blonde she calls Nita, to rhyme. The clients fuss over her, how cute, how bright, congratulate her grandmother on this unexpected boon, but their tone is very odd, not utterly pure. Ambiguous, like Rita.

For Sonia, though, there is no ambiguity. She accepts their good-will with nonchalance—the pains in her mouth make it hard to speak in any case—and in their presence ignores Rita. When they

leave she clasps her close, then talks, talks, low and fast like someone who has saved up words over a lifetime. She talks as if she is
talking to herself—much of it a small child can hardly understand.
So many things that she thinks and feels, but not the one thing. Of
Rita's parents she never speaks, but she returns to life, and best of
all, learns to drive. She neglects the housework that exasperates
her, and together they breeze through the tangled city like tourists.
Even when Rita is a big schoolgirl, she will wait for her and greet
her at the door at three-fifteen: "Let's take a ride, okay?"

They ride through exotic neighborhoods of Greeks, Asians,
blacks, Hispanics, Russians—there they eat pirogen and caviar and
borscht. A passionately discontented woman, angular and veiny,
Sonia is most content at the wheel of the dark green Pontiac. A
born voyager. Short, straight-backed, she sits on a pillow and
stretches her neck like a swan to peruse the traffic. Her driving style
is aggressive, arrogant, anarchic. And Rita by her side is her natural
passenger. Nothing can shock or frighten her, so thoroughly does
she trust her grandmother, so closely are they twined, having accepted each other on first sight with no questions asked, like Sanjay's parents—neither the U-turns in tunnels nor the sprinting
across intersections nor the sparring with buses and trucks. Sonia
is omnipotent, fearless. Queen of the Road. Defying the rules
about the Sabbath, she takes Rita to, of all places, the beach, where
in all kinds of weather they wet their feet in the surf and build sand
castles and Sonia tells stories—not morality tales like Sol's but true
stories without morals—of what lies across the openness of the
Atlantic, and she tells Rita that they came here to be free, free.

Now Rita longs for those forbidden afternoons at the edge of the
Atlantic. Like a child, she would like to incorporate her grandmother, swallow her, as her grandfather lived by appropriating.
Appropriation is the tactic of the lost and the scared. Oh, if only
Rita could swallow her whole, if only she would go down, she
could have Sonia forever with her. Safe at last. Then she would
never clutch her heart and die as in the nightmare, leaving Rita
standing alone, severed.

———

While Sanjay and Rita are watching a Fred Astaire and Ginger Rogers movie on television one evening, her phone rings. Rita speaks to her friend who still works in the Spanish record store in the Mission district. When she hangs up she says, "I've just been invited to a wedding. Rosalia's brother Luis. Would you like to come?"

"I never knew you could speak Spanish like that." They have been lovers for almost a year.

"Oh. Well, I need it, you know, for my clients."

"But you speak it like a native. I thought you were only two years old . . ."

"I learned when I was in college. Do you want to go to the wedding? It'll be fun. Lots of music and dancing."

"Sure."

She sits down and touches his hand. "I used to go out with her brother, years ago. He's very nice. Gentle, you know, like Rosalia. I'm glad he's getting married."

"You never mentioned it before."

"Well, it was nothing, really. We were kids. There's no way it should bother you."

"It doesn't. Only I sometimes realize I know so little about you. You tell me so little."

Sanjay develops an interest in her past loves. Like her curiosity about his wife, his is not lascivious in nature. Rather, he wants coherent social history. What has her life been all about? And generically, what are young American women's lives all about? A question that has never occupied him before.

She is not a typical case, Rita tries to explain. But it's a matter of optics, of the precision of the lens. To a fifty-year-old naturalized Indian widower, she is representative enough. He wants his American girl, Rita thinks. And he wants the real thing.

"Did you ever sleep with any of your clients?"

"No! Anyway, by the time I had clients I already knew you."

"Well, what about at law school?"

"One student." She grins, teasing. "One professor."

"A professor!"

"Is there any more paratha?"

Sanjay reaches for the plate on the floor. "Yes, but they're cold by now."

All during these absurd conversations they eat his daughter's food. Rita feels funny about that, but Sanjay says nonsense, his daughter made it to be enjoyed. Food is for whoever is hungry.

"I don't mind them cold. Thanks. You'll be relieved to know I wasn't in his class at the time."

"But a law professor. A jurist! He must have been so much older."

"He was seven years older, Sanjay. What about you?"

"I may be old, but at least I'm pure!" He laughs loud belly laughs. His whole body shakes. The bed shakes. Rita feels safe, wrapped up warm in his laughter. He is so domesticated, so easy to entertain. Pure: he says he never knew any women besides his wife. Before he was married, two prostitutes. They don't count.

"We'd better start at the beginning. What about in college?"

"This is getting very silly. Stop."

"Aha! Now we're getting somewhere."

"Just Luis, for a while."

"Why a Chicano?"

"Why not? Now stop. Really. It's annoying."

"Because there's something you're not telling me. Why won't you marry me? You're footloose. Then you'd know where you belong."

The Indian gentleman next door wants to rescue the poor orphan girl, give her food and warm clothes and light a fire in her garret. And she would not be cast out if she married him, as her father was. It's thirty years later. And it's Rita. What can you expect? They are prepared for almost anything from her. They believe in nature, not nurture, and she believes with them.

But she has never told anyone. She shakes her head.

"Is it terrible?" Sanjay asks. He is not fooling around anymore. She sees his age in the set of his face. His lips are parted. His cheeks are sagging in a kind of resigned expectation.

"Yes."

He hands her more stuffed bread. "Well, eat something while you tell me, then." To her surprise, his eyes, however old and

sympathetic, have turned lustful. He is waiting to hear about a
frenzied, tragic love affair. Rita stares right into them as she speaks.

She was seventeen. There was talk in the house about where she
would be sent to college. Oh, how she kept them young, kept them
abreast of things. She said to her grandmother in the kitchen,
making the fish for Friday night, "You have to tell me now. Or I'll
go away forever, I swear it."

"Big shot!" Sonia says, her fingers plunged deep in the bowl of
chopped fish. "Where will you go? And with what?"

"There's always a way for a girl to make a living, Grandma. This
is 1974, after all," and she smirks brazenly. "I know plenty of
places I can stay."

A look of doom streaks over Sonia's face, and it is not so much
prostitution she is thinking of as certain types of irregular living
conditions: dope fiends, drifters, hippies, pads. Rita is bad enough
already, with her ideas, her gypsy clothes, her unexplained forays
into Manhattan, her odd-looking inky newspapers, the closely
typed petitions she brings home indefatigably for them to sign; but
at least she sleeps in her bed every night and takes showers. . . . At
the same time, the vision of such irregularity holds a fascination for
her grandmother, Rita can tell. She sees enticement seasoning the
horror in her eyes, orange flecks against the green. Sonia might
have tried it herself if she hadn't been so tired, sewing in the
factory. Sometimes she even signs the petitions, after Sol goes to
bed.

"You're not going anywhere," Sonia says confidently, blinking
away her enticement, slapping the fish into ovals, and she shoves
the bowl in Rita's direction for help. "Just to college like all your
cousins."

"But I'm not the same as them. I have a right to know what I am,
don't I? All these years you would never answer me. But I'm not
a child anymore. It's my life."

There is something different, this time, in the way she says it, or
maybe Sonia is simply worn down—Sol will be going to the hospital for his throat operation very soon; there have been doctors'

appointments, consultations; he lays down the law in an ever hoarser voice. "You can't ask this of me!" she groans, but they both understand she means the opposite. Rita waits, her hands growing cold in the bowl of fish. She forms an oval and places it in the baking pan.

"They were separated. They never could get along. I knew. I used to speak to him all the time. No one could stop me from using the phone." She looks at Rita curiously. "I even knew about you."

"What about me?"

"That they had you! But I didn't tell him. That's what he wanted, not to know anything. Like he was dead. So let him not know, I thought." Sonia sits silent, not moving, a hostile witness in the box.

"So?"

She sighs as though she had hoped for a reprieve, that this much would be enough. "So he went over there to get something. They had an argument."

"And?"

She wipes her hands carefully on a dish towel. Then she takes the towel and holds it up to her face, covering her face. Her words come muffled through the towel. "She stabbed him."

"She what?"

"With a knife." She weeps behind the towel.

Rita is weirdly calm. Of all the scenes she has invented, never anything like this. Much more romantic, her visions were. Lost at sea. Activists kidnapped by the Klan. Wasting disease. Cult suicide. Yes, her nights have been busy, but all wrong. "I don't believe it."

"Don't, then. You asked. You pestered me for years."

"It's not possible. He must have been stronger than her."

"But he didn't have the knife," she wails. "Oh, my baby." Shoulders heaving, towel over her face.

Suddenly Rita cannot bear that towel anymore and snatches it away. Her grandmother's hollowed face is wet and blotched and smells of fish. "No. That can't be the whole story. He must have attacked her first."

Sonia gives the maddest laugh, a witch's cackle. "He? The gentlest boy who ever breathed?"

Rita could almost laugh too. Their child, gentle! But she also knows they do not attack. A picture is coming into focus, a kitchen, a hysterical woman who looks like an older version of herself, waving a bread knife; a pale man trying to wrest it from her. But she's too quick, too fierce. . . . Oh God, already she's becoming a type, a caricature. Leave her be. Leave that room altogether, before it gets bloody. . . . What about the baby . . . ? The baby is in another room, mercifully sleeping, yes. Go back, try again, try it in the living room. The scene has endless possibilities, bloody ones, Rita could labor over it for years. Give up the rest of her life to screening it every possible way: He said . . . No, she said . . . She grabbed . . . No, he . . .

"Wasn't there a trial? Didn't the facts come out at the trial? I bet she was a battered wife." Yes, lately even juries have learned to sympathize. Her poor mother, black and blue? Sonia looks baf- fled—this is beyond her imaginings. "I'll find out the truth," Rita shouts. "I'll visit her in jail." Where she languishes, thinking only of her lost baby.

"She's not in jail."

"No?"

"Finished. Six years and out. Good behavior! Rita, everyone said it, even her brother, what kind of woman she was, how she treated him so terrible. He was a good man, the brother. He wrote us a letter about . . . I felt sorry for him."

The outrage. She killed Rita's gentle father and she walks the streets free. "She never looked for me?" Now, now, she feels tears. This is the real outrage. Sonia feels it too.

"We wouldn't have given you up anyway. You were my reason to go on living. Two years I waited to see you." She covers her face again, this time with her hand and only for an instant. "And then I got you for good." As she gazes at Rita, her brow, for once, is calm. "You're just like him."

Me! thinks Rita, with my murderer's face? It must be a torment to have me around, reminding everyone. And what is just like him? They never say. Now more than ever she wants so badly to see him, it is almost like a sexual longing—she will die, just shrink and evaporate, if she cannot see him, touch him. She does not recognize the feeling till much later, though, when she knows Sanjay.

("When I know you," she says. "When I know you.")

For her mother Rita does not long—she feels she has her already, in her bones, her blood, the coarseness of her hair. In some essential, inescapable way, she carries her around.

"Why did they get married?" she whispers to Sonia. Why does anyone?

"Ha!" Sonia is recovered now, is getting back to her work. She must know these spasms of grief intimately after so many years, the way people know their attacks of epilepsy or asthma—the shape of their parabolas, and the intensity. She must have learned how to assimilate them into her days and proceed. It strikes Rita that she has never seen her grandmother idle. From dawn onwards Sonia scurries about, shopping, cooking, sewing, driving. Then at ten o'clock she falls exhausted into her old stuffed chair in the living room to read novels under a solitary lamp, while Sol calls every ten minutes, "Come to bed already!"

"Why did they have me?"

"Come on with the fish, Rita. It'll be midnight at this rate before we eat."

There is only one place she wants to go to college: Berkeley. Her grandfather is sure it is because they have the most hippies there. Her grandmother knows better, but in the end Rita gets her way. They are old and weary, no match for her in her new wisdom. For what scope and vision she suddenly possesses! Now she understands why her grandfather cleaves to the rules and her grandmother cleaves to him, all the while raging against God and driving like a maniac. She understands why the family, those stolidly decent people, look at her with a blend of pity and suspicion—it's not the color she is, no, it's that at any moment she may show her true colors. . . . She understands so much, it feels at night as if her head will burst with understanding and with blood. Only the one thing she wants to understand she doesn't.

She will find her and make her tell how it was. How to think about it. Until she knows, between her and the rest of the world is a wall of blood, ever fresh, never clotting, and she will never cross it into a life.

Her mother must have been a Catholic; as a girl she must have knelt and confessed to puny childish sins—lying, being unkind, thinking wicked thoughts. Maybe the Christ in her village church dripped with crimson paint and so she got used to spilled blood, it didn't seem alien and horrifying. It doesn't to Sanjay; he is used to handling it, but what does it tell him?

("Stop torturing yourself. It's only a physical substance, a liquid. It carries things, but not the kinds of things you mean. Don't tell me I traveled halfway across the world to find a mystic."

He's getting to sound like a Jew, thinks Rita. They are changing places.)

When she goes away to school her grandparents are afraid she will become a hippie, a druggie, but instead she spends her free time in San Francisco, the Mission district, where the Mexicans and Chicanos live, looking and waiting. A deranged sort of looking— she doesn't really want to find. She wants to be found. She learns Spanish—relearns—and it nestles lovingly in her mouth. Her tongue wraps around the syllables like a lover returning from exile to embrace his beloved, feeling the familiar contours. People say she sounds like a native speaker. She learns it so she can ask around for her, but she never asks. She doesn't even know her mother's name. Carmen, yes, but not her last name. Useless to ask for her own last name. Her mother does not seem one of the family. She would not have kept it.

("How did you expect to find her? What did you think you were doing?" Sanjay is incredulous. The Rita he knows is so sane, so sensible, aside from the nightmares. So presentable. It would be his pleasure to bring her home to meet his family, once they had gotten used to the idea of a half-Jewish, half-Mexican American lawyer twenty-two years younger.)

What did she think she was doing? Wandering around the Mission looking for a woman who looked like her, who would be looking in turn for a girl like Rita. Only the woman isn't looking. She has never looked. Luncheonettes, candy stores, bars—Rita can't get to like the food she buys as her excuse for being there, heavy and beany, maybe because for her it is the food of despair. She reads the names of singers on posters outside cafés, she reads the personal ads in newspapers, she even studies the names along-side doorbells in dingy, flaking old buildings. Crazy, she knows it. No explanation or story could change the fact. Like God in the trials she staged as a child, it remains: One lives having killed the other. It would be the same fact if the roles were reversed.

Nothing ever happens except some men try to pick her up, and once her pocket is picked in a movie line, and she makes friends with a girl who works in a record store and goes out with her brother for a few months. Rita is drawn by the easy friendliness of the family. She sees a life there that she might retreat into, but she would have to tell so many lies, and even so she would never fit in, never feel quite right. By what right is she anywhere, she the most contingent of contingencies, a superfluous mystery? So she breaks it off. And with that, the quest breaks off as well. Enough. She is worn out, like a soldier after battle, like a battleground in the night. For a month, over Christmas vacation of her junior year, she goes home to do nothing but sleep, grinding her teeth.

When Sonia asks anxiously what she plans to do after college, she says she will apply to law school. Because she is tired of her obsessions, tired of the parents she can't remember and who have left her this hard inheritance to swallow, tired of breaking her teeth on it. However hard she gnaws, the mystery won't crack. World without end, she is two years old, and in the next room is some kind of dreadful racket going on that will not let her sleep, some kind of screeching not at all like the singing she is used to, and maybe it is all a bad dream, but the next thing she knows she is in an airplane with two strange men who are interchangeable and who weep, and it is a miserable trip, she wets her pants, she throws up.

"Rita, Rita." Sanjay takes her in his arms. "Lie down and rest. Give it up."

Lying there, Rita wonders once again who she would be had she been left with her aunt and uncle in the bar. Maybe then her mother would have rushed to her when she got out of jail, like a doe flying to her fawn, and sheltered her and told her . . . every-thing. Or would she have done as the mother eel, who flees to the

other end of the world and leaves its young behind, groping in
slime? Maybe she could have become a nightclub singer too? But
she has no voice—she would probably work in a store like Rosalia.
Or go off to New York to search for her father's family, who would
appear exotic and a little alluring. She might speak English with a
rippling musical accent and move and dress and feel about the
world in a different way. She could be almost anyone, and anywhere. Even now, there are times when she thinks of her name and
who it stands for, and it feels like looking in a mirror and seeing a
blank sheet, the sheet covering a mirror in a house of the bereaved.
But she is this, and here, this person in Sanjay's arms.

She thought he would be horrified, repelled by her. Instead he
has fallen asleep holding her, his arm draped across her middle like
a sash. She watches him sleep for a while, then gets up and tiptoes
around the bedroom. She takes a good look at the photograph of
his wife. Yes, there is a certain resemblance. The result of nature,
history, the migrations of people, and love.

It is strange that with all the hours she has spent in this bedroom
she has never poked around. She opens the dresser drawers, one
after another, but all she sees are Sanjay's socks and underwear and
handkerchiefs neatly and predictably folded. Then, on a shelf in the
closet she finds a pile of saris, also neatly folded, all colors, generous, deep colors, gold threads running through the fabrics. She
chooses a red one, the bridal color. But she can't figure out how to
get it on right. It is fun, this dressing up; she did it as a child. Vashti.
Finally she gets the sari on in a makeshift fashion, not the way
Sanjay's wife used to wear it. In the bottom drawer of the night
table she finds little jars of powders—red, amber, green, blue—and
she plays with them, dabs them on her hands, puts some green on
her eyelids. She has seen women with a spot of red in the center of
the forehead, but she is not sure what it means, maybe a symbol of
Hindu caste or rank; she doesn't dare do it. She appraises herself
in the mirror. Queen Esther, at last. Behind her in the mirror she
sees Sanjay roll over and open his eyes. He blinks and the color
drains away, leaving him yellowish.

"Rita? What are you doing?"

"How do I look?"

"That's not how it goes. Don't, anyway. Take it off. It's not right."

She steps to the edge of the bed, presenting herself. "Fix it. You must know how it goes. You must have seen it done a million times."

"I don't. Do you know how to tie a tie?"

She tries to dab some red powder on him, but he moves out of reach. He won't play. "Please, Rita. Stop."

She yanks off the red sari, the bridal color, rolls it into a ball, and weeps into it.

"But I love you," he protests, a frightening look of middle-aged acceptance on his face. He does not show any shock at what she has told him—that is what is frightening. Will time do that to her too, and then what will she have left? "I do, Rita." If she didn't know him, his smile might seem simpleminded. "You don't have to masquerade for me to love you."

But she cannot believe it. It costs so much.

LORE SEGAL

The Reverse Bug

"Let's get the announcements out of the way," said Ilka, the teacher, to her foreigners in Conversational English for Adults. "Tomorrow evening the institute is holding a symposium. Ahmed," she asked the Turkish student with the magnificently drooping mustache, who also wore the institute's janitorial keys hooked to his belt, "where are they holding the symposium?"

"In the New Theatre," said Ahmed.

"The theme," said the teacher, "is 'Should there be a statute of limitations on genocide?' with a wine-and-cheese reception—"

"In the lounge," said Ahmed.

"To which you are all invited. Now," Ilka said in the bright voice of a hostess trying to make a sluggish dinner party go, "what shall we talk about? Doesn't do me a bit of good, I know, to ask you all to come forward and sit in a nice cozy clump. Who would like to start us off? Tell us a story, somebody. We love stories. Tell the class how you came to America."

The teacher looked determinedly past the hand, the arm, with which Gerti Gruner stirred the air—death, taxes, and Thursdays, Gerti Gruner in the front row center. Ilka's eye passed over Paulino, who sat in the last row, with his back to the wall. Matsue, a pleasant, older Japanese from the university's engineering department, smiled at Ilka and shook his head, meaning "Please, not me!" Matsue was sitting in his usual place by the window, but Ilka had to orient herself as to the whereabouts of Izmira, the Cypriot doctor, who always left two empty rows between herself and Ahmed, the Turk. Today it was Juan, the Basque, who sat in the rightmost corner, and Eduardo, the Spaniard from Madrid, in the leftmost.

Ilka looked around for someone too shy to self-start who might enjoy talking if called upon, but Gerti's hand stabbed the air immediately underneath Ilka's chin, so she said, "Gerti wants to start. Go, Gerti. When did you come to the United States?"

"In last June," said Gerti.

Ilka corrected her, and said, "Tell the class where you came from, and, everybody, please speak in whole sentences."

Gerti said, "I have lived before in Uruguay."

"We would say, '*Before that I lived*,' " said Ilka, and Gerti said, "And *before that* in Vienna."

Gerti's story bore a family likeness to the teacher's own superannuated, indigestible history of being sent out of Hitler's Europe as a little girl.

Gerti said, "In the Vienna train station has my father told to me . . ."

"*Told me*."

"*Told me* that so soon as I am coming to Montevideo . . ."

Ilka said, "As soon as I *come*, or more colloquially, *get* to Montevideo . . ."

Gerti said, "*Get* to Montevideo, I should tell to all the people . . ."

Ilka corrected her. Gerti said, "*Tell* all the people to bring my

father out from Vienna before come the Nazis and put him in
concentration camp.''

Ilka said, "In 'the' or 'a' concentration camp."

"Also my mother," said Gerti, "and my Opa, and my Oma, and
my Onkel Peter, and the twins, Hedi and Albert. My father has
told, 'Tell to the foster mother, "Go, please, with me, to the
American Consulate." ' "

"My father went to the American Consulate," said Paulino, and
everybody turned and looked at him. Paulino's voice had not been
heard in class since the first Thursday, when Ilka had got her
students to go around the room and introduce themselves to one
another. Paulino had said that his name was Paulino Patillo and
that he was born in Bolivia. Ilka was charmed to realize it was
Danny Kaye of whom Paulino reminded her—fair, curly, middle-
aged, smiling. He came punctually every Thursday. Was he a very
sweet or a very simple man?

Ilka said, "Paulino will tell us his story after Gerti has finished.
How old were you when you left Europe?" Ilka asked, to reactivate
Gerti, who said, "Eight years," but she and the rest of the class, and
the teacher herself, were watching Paulino put his right hand inside
the left breast pocket of his jacket, withdraw an envelope, turn it
upside down, and shake out onto the desk before him a pile of
news clippings. Some looked sharp and new, some frayed and
yellow; some seemed to be single paragraphs, others the length of
several columns.

"You got to Montevideo . . ." Ilka prompted Gerti.

"And my foster mother has fetched me from the ship. I said,
'Hello, and will you please bring out from Vienna my father before
come the Nazis and put him in—*a* concentration camp!' " Gerti
said triumphantly.

Paulino had brought the envelope close to his eyes and was
looking inside. He inserted a forefinger, loosened something that
was stuck, and shook out a last clipping. It broke at the fold when
Paulino flattened it onto the desk top. Paulino brushed away the
several paper crumbs before beginning to read: "La Paz, September
19."

"Paulino," said Ilka, "you must wait till Gerti is finished."

But Paulino read, "Señora Pilar Patillo has reported the disappearance of her husband, Claudio Patillo, after a visit to the American Consulate in La Paz on September 15."

"Gerti, go on," said Ilka.

"The foster mother has said, 'When comes home the Uncle from the office, we will ask.' I said, 'And bring out, please, also my mother, my Opa, my Oma, my Onkel Peter . . .' "

Paulino read, "A spokesman for the American Consulate contacted in La Paz states categorically that no record exists of a visit from Señor Patillo within the last two months. . . ."

"Paulino, you really *have* to wait your turn," Ilka said.

Gerti said, " 'Also the twins.' The foster mother has made such a desperate face with her lips."

Paulino read, "Nor does the consular calendar for September show any appointment made with Señor Patillo. Inquiries are said to be under way with the Consulate at Sucre." And Paulino folded his column of newsprint and returned it to the envelope.

"O.K., thank you, Paulino," Ilka said.

Gerti said, "When the foster father has come home, he said, 'We will see, tomorrow,' and I said, 'And will you go, please, with me, to the American Consulate?' and the foster father has made a face."

Paulino was flattening the second column of newsprint on his desk. He read, "New York, December 12 . . ."

"*Paulino*," said Ilka, and caught Matsue's eye. He was looking expressly at her. He shook his head ever so slightly and with his right hand, palm down, he patted the air three times. In the intelligible language of charade with which humankind frustrated God at Babel, Matsue was saying, "Calm down, Ilka. Let Paulino finish. Nothing you can do will stop him." Ilka was grateful to Matsue.

"A spokesman for the Israeli Mission to the United Nations," read Paulino, "denies a report that Claudio Patillo, missing after a visit to the American Consulate in La Paz since September 15, is en route to Israel. . . ." Paulino finished reading this column also, folded it into the envelope, and unfolded the next column. "U.P.I., January 30. The car of Pilar Patillo, wife of Claudio Patillo, who was reported missing from La Paz last September, has been found at the bottom of a ravine in the eastern Andes. It is not known

whether any bodies were found inside the wreck," Paulino read
with the blind forward motion of a tank that receives no message
from any sound or movement in the world outside. The students
had stopped looking at Paulino; they were not looking at the
teacher. They looked into their laps. Paulino read one column after
the other, returning each to his envelope before he took the next,
and when he had read and returned the last, and returned the
envelope to his breast pocket, he leaned his back against the wall
and turned to the teacher his sweet, habitual smile of expectant
participation.

Gerti said, "In that same night have I woken up . . ."

"That night I *woke* up," the teacher helplessly said.

"*Woke* up," Gerti Gruner said, "and I have thought, What if it
is even now, this exact minute, that one Nazi is knocking at the
door, and I am here lying not telling to anybody anything, and I
have stood up and gone into the bedroom where were sleeping the
foster mother and father. Next morning has the foster mother gone
with me to the refugee committee, and they found for me a different foster family."

"Your turn, Matsue," Ilka said. "How, when, and why did you
come to the States? We're all here to help you!" Matsue's written
English was flawless, but he spoke with an accent that was almost
impenetrable. His contribution to class conversation always involved a communal interpretative act.

"Aisutudieddu attoza unibashite innu munhen," Matsue said.

A couple of stabs and Eduardo, the madrileño, got it: "You
studied at the university in Munich!"

"You studied acoustics?" ventured Izmira, the Cypriot doctor.

"The war trapped you in Germany?" proposed Ahmed, the
Turk.

"You have been working in the ovens," suggested Gerti, the
Viennese.

"Acoustic ovens?" marvelled Ilka. "Do you mean stoves?
Ranges?"

No, what Matsue meant was that he had got his first job with a
Munich firm employed in soundproofing the Dachau ovens so that
what went on inside could not be heard on the outside. "I made the

tapes," said Matsue. "Tapes?" they asked him. They figured out that Matsue had returned to Japan in 1946. He had collected Hiroshima "tapes." He had been brought to Washington as an acoustical consultant to the Kennedy Center, and had come to Connecticut to design the sound system of the New Theatre at Concordance University, where he subsequently accepted a research appointment in the department of engineering. He was now returning home, having finished his work—Ilka thought he said—on the reverse bug.

Ilka said, "I thought, ha ha, you said 'the reverse bug'!"

"The reverse bug" was what everybody understood Matsue to say that he had said. With his right hand he performed a row of air loops, and, pointing at the wall behind the teacher's desk, asked for, and received, her O.K. to explain himself in writing on the blackboard.

Chalk in hand, he was eloquent on the subject of the regular bug, which can be introduced into a room to relay to those outside what those inside want them not to hear. A sophisticated modern bug, explained Matsue, was impossible to locate and deactivate. Buildings had had to be taken apart in order to rid them of alien listening devices. The reverse bug, equally impossible to locate and deactivate, was a device whereby those outside were able to relay *into* a room what those inside would prefer not to have to hear.

"And how would such a device be used?" Ilka asked him.

Matsue was understood to say that it could be useful in certain situations to certain consulates, and Paulino said, "My father went to the American Consulate," and put his hand into his breast pocket. Here Ilka stood up, and, though there was still a good fifteen minutes of class time, said, "So! I will see you all next Thursday. Everybody—be thinking of subjects you would like to talk about. Don't forget the symposium tomorrow evening!" She walked quickly out the door.

Ilka entered the New Theatre late and was glad to see Matsue sitting on the aisle in the second row from the back with an empty seat beside him. The platform people were already settling into their places. On the right, an exquisite golden-skinned Latin man was talking, in a way people talk to people they have known a long time, with a heavy, rumpled man, whom Ilka pegged as Israeli. "Look at the thin man on the left," Ilka said to Matsue. "He has to be from Washington. Only a Washingtonian's hair gets to be that particular white color." Matsue laughed. Ilka asked him if he knew who the woman with the oversized glasses and the white hair straight to the shoulders might be, and Matsue said something that Ilka did not understand. The rest of the panelists were institute people, Ilka's colleagues—little Joe Bernstine from philosophy, Yvette Gordot, a mathematician, and Leslie Shakespere, an Englishman, the institute's new director, who sat in the moderator's chair.

Leslie Shakespere had the soft weight of a man who likes to eat and the fine head of a man who thinks. It had not as yet occurred to Ilka that she was in love with Leslie. She watched him fussing with the microphone. "Why do we need this?" she could read Leslie's lips saying. "Since when do we use microphones in the New Theatre?" Now he quieted the hall with a grateful welcome for this fine attendance at a discussion of one of our generation's unmanageable questions—the application of justice in an era of genocides.

Here Rabbi Shlomo Grossman rose from the floor and wished to take exception to the plural formulation: "All killings are not murders; all murders are not 'genocides.' "

Leslie said, "Shlomo, could you hold your remarks until question time?"

Rabbi Grossman said, "Remarks? Is that what I'm making? Remarks! The death of six million—is it in the realm of a question?"

Leslie said, "I give you my word that there will be room for the full expression of what you want to say when we open the discussion to the floor." Rabbi Grossman acceded to the evident desire of the friends sitting near him that he should sit down.

Director Leslie Shakespere gave the briefest of accounts of the combined federal and private funding that had enabled the Concordance Institute to invite these very distinguished panelists to take part in the institute's Genocide Project. "The institute, as you know, has a long-standing tradition of 'debriefings,' in which the

participants in a project that is winding down sum up their thinking
for the members of the institute, the university, and the public. But
this evening's panel has agreed, by way of an experiment, to talk in
an informal way of our notions, of the history of the interest each
of us brings to this question—problem—at the point of entry. I
want us to interest ourselves in the *nature of inquiry*: Will we come
out of this project with our original notions reinforced? Modified?
Made over?

"I imagine that this inquiry will range somewhere between the
legal concept of a statute of limitations that specifies the time
within which human law must respond to a specific crime, and the
Biblical concept of the visitation of punishment of the sins of the
fathers upon the children. One famous version plays itself out in
the 'Oresteia,' where a crime is punished by an act that is itself a
crime and punishable, and so on, down the generations. Enough.
Let me introduce our panel, whom it will be our very great pleasure
to have among us in the coming months."

The white-haired man turned out to be the West German ex-
mayor of Obernpest, Dieter Dobelmann. Ilka felt the prompt con-
viction that she had known all along—that one could tell from a
mile—that that mouth, that jaw, had to be German. Leslie dwelled
on Dobelmann's persuasive anti-Nazi credentials. The woman with
the glasses was on loan to the institute from Georgetown University. ("The white hair! You see!" Ilka whispered to Matsue, who
laughed.) She was Jerusalem-born Shulamit Gershon, professor of
international law, and longtime adviser to Israel's ongoing project
to identify Nazi war criminals and bring them to trial. The rumpled
man was the English theologian William B. Thayer. The Latin
really was a Latin—Sebastian Maderiaga, who was taking time off
from his consulate in New York. Leslie squeezed his eyes to see
past the stage lights into the well of the New Theatre. There was a
rustle of people turning to locate the voice that had said, "My
father went to the American Consulate," but it said nothing further
and the audience settled back. Leslie introduced Yvette and Joe, the
institute's own fellows assigned to Genocide.

Ilka and Matsue leaned forward, watching Paulino across the
aisle. Paulino was withdrawing the envelope from his breast

pocket. "Without a desk?" whispered Ilka anxiously. Paulino up-
turned the envelope onto the slope of his lap. The young student
sitting beside him got on his knees to retrieve the sliding batch of
newsprint and held onto it while Paulino arranged his coat across
his thighs to create a surface.

"My own puzzle," said Leslie, "with which I would like to puzzle
our panel, is this: Where do I, where do we all, get these feelings
of moral malaise when wrong goes unpunished and right goes
unrewarded?"

Paulino had brought his first newspaper column up to his eyes
and read, "La Paz, September 19. Señora Pilar Patillo has reported
the disappearance of her husband, Claudio Patillo . . ."

"Where," Leslie was saying, "does the human mind derive its
expectation of a set of consequences for which it finds no evidence
whatsoever in nature or in history, or in looking around its own
autobiography? . . . Could I *please* ask for quiet from the floor until
we open the discussion?" Leslie was once again peering out into the
hall.

The audience turned and looked at Paulino reading, "Nor does
the consular calendar for September show any appointment . . ."
Shulamit Gershon leaned toward Leslie and spoke to him for several moments while Paulino read, "A spokesman for the Israeli
Mission to the United Nations denies a report . . ."

It was after several attempts to persuade him to stop that Leslie
said, "Ahmed? Is Ahmed in the hall? Ahmed, would you be good
enough to remove the unquiet gentleman as gently as necessary
force will allow. Take him to my office, please, and I will meet with
him after the symposium."

Everybody watched Ahmed walk up the aisle with a large and
sheepish-looking student. The two lifted the unresisting Paulino
out of his seat by the armpits. They carried him reading, "The car
of Pilar Patillo, wife of Claudio Patillo . . ."—backward, out the
door.

The action had something about it of the classic comedy routine.
There was a cackling, then the relief of general laughter. Leslie
relaxed and sat back, understanding that it would require some
moments to get the evening back on track, but the cackling did not

stop. Leslie said, "Please." He waited. He cocked his head and listened: it was more like a hiccupping that straightened and elongated into a sound drawn on a single breath. Leslie looked at the panel. The panel looked. The audience looked all around. Leslie bent his ear down to the microphone. It did him no good to turn the button off and on, to put his hand over the mouthpiece, to bend down as if to look it in the eye. "Anybody know—is the sound here centrally controlled?" he asked. The noise was growing incrementally. Members of the audience drew their heads back and down into their shoulders. It came to them—it became impossible to not know—that it was not laughter to which they were listening but somebody yelling. Somewhere there was a person, and the person was screaming.

Ilka looked at Matsue, whose eyes were closed. He looked an old man.

The screaming stopped. The relief was spectacular, but lasted only for that same unnaturally long moment in which a howling child, having finally exhausted its strength, is fetching up new breath from some deepest source for a new onslaught. The howl resumed at a volume that was too great for the small theatre; the human ear could not accommodate it. People experienced a physical distress. They put their hands over their ears.

Leslie had risen. He said, "I'm going to suggest an alteration in the order of this evening's proceedings. Why don't we clear the hall—everybody, please, move into the lounge, have some wine, have some cheese while we locate the source of the trouble."

Quickly, while people were moving along their rows, Ilka popped out into the aisle and collected the trail of Paulino's news clippings. The young student who had sat next to Paulino found and handed her the envelope.

Ilka walked down the hall in the direction of Leslie Shakespere's office, diagnosing in herself an inappropriate excitement at having it in her power to throw light.

Ilka looked into Leslie's office. Paulino sat on a hard chair with his back to the door, shaking his head violently from side to side.

Leslie stood facing him. He and Ahmed and all the panelists, who had disposed themselves about Leslie's office, were screwing their eyes up as if wanting very badly to close every bodily opening through which unwanted information is able to enter. The intervening wall had somewhat modified the volume, but not the variety—length, pitch, and pattern—of the sounds that continually altered as in response to a new and continually changing cause.

Leslie said, "We know this stuff goes on whether we are hearing it or not, but this . . ." He saw Ilka at the door and said, "Mr. Patillo is your student, no? He refuses to tell us how to locate the screaming unless they release his father."

Ilka said, *"Paulino? Does Paulino say* he 'refuses'?"

Leslie said to Paulino, "Will you please tell us how to find the source of this noise so we can shut it off?"

Paulino shook his head and said, "It is my father screaming."

Ilka followed the direction of Leslie's eye. Maderiaga was perched with a helpless elegance on the corner of Leslie's desk, speaking Spanish into the telephone. Through the open door that led into a little outer office, Ilka saw Shulamit Gershon hang up the phone. She came back in and said, "Patillo is the name this young man's father adopted from his Bolivian wife. He's Klaus Herrmann, who headed the German Census Bureau. After the Anschluss they sent him to Vienna to put together the registry of Jewish names and addresses. Then on to Budapest, and so on. After the war we traced him to La Paz. I think he got into trouble with some mines or weapons deals. We put him on the back burner when it turned out the Bolivians were after him as well."

Now Maderiaga hung up and said, "Hasn't he been the busy little man! My office is going to check if it's the Gonzales people who got him for expropriating somebody's tin mine, or the R.R.N. If they suspect Patillo of connection with the helicopter crash that killed President Barrientos, they'll have more or less killed him."

"It is my father screaming," said Paulino.

"It's got nothing to do with his father," said Ilka. While Matsue was explaining the reverse bug on the blackboard the previous evening, Ilka had grasped the principle. It disintegrated as she was explaining it to Leslie. She was distracted, moreover, by a retro-spective image: Last night, hurrying down the corridor, Ilka had turned her head and must have seen, since she was now able to recollect, young Ahmed and Matsue moving away together down the hall. If Ilka had thought them a curious couple, the thought, having nothing to feed on, had died before her lively wish to maneuver Gerti and Paulino into one elevator just as the doors were closing, so she could come down in the other.

Now Ilka asked Ahmed, "Where did you and Matsue go after class last night?"

Ahmed said, "He wanted to come into the New Theatre."

Leslie said, "Ahmed, forgive me for ordering you around all evening, but will you go and find me Matsue and bring him here to my office?"

"He has gone," said Ahmed. "I saw him leave by the front door with a suitcase on wheels."

"He is going home," said Ilka. "Matsue has finished his job."

Paulino said, "It is my father screaming."

"No, it's not, Paulino," said Ilka. "Those screams are from Dachau and they are from Hiroshima."

"It is my father," said Paulino, "and my mother."

Leslie asked Ilka to come with him to the airport. They caught up with Matsue queuing, with only five passengers ahead of him, to enter the gangway to his plane.

Ilka said, "Matsue, you're not going away without telling us how to shut the thing off!"

Matsue said, "Itto dozunotto shattoffu."

Ilka and Leslie said, "Excuse me?"

With the hand that was not holding his boarding pass, Matsue performed a charade of turning a faucet and he shook his head. Ilka and Leslie understood him to be saying, "It does not shut off." Matsue stepped out of the line, kissed Ilka on the cheek, stepped back, and passed through the door.

———

When Concordance Institute takes hold of a situation, it deals humanely with it. Leslie found funds to pay a private sanitarium to evaluate Paulino. Back at the New Theatre, the police, a bomb squad, and a private acoustics company from Washington set themselves to locate the source of the screaming.

Leslie looked haggard. His colleagues worried when their director, a sensible man, continued to blame the microphone after the microphone had been removed and the screaming continued. The sound seemed not to be going to loop back to any familiar beginning, so that the hearers might have become familiar—might, in a manner of speaking, have made friends—with one particular roar or screech, but to be going on to perpetually new and fresh howls of pain.

Neither the Japanese Embassy in Washington nor the American Embassy in Tokyo had got anywhere with the tracers sent out to locate Matsue. Leslie called in a technician. "Look into the wiring!" he said, and saw in the man's eyes that look experts wear when they have explained something and the layman says what he said in the beginning all over again. The expert had another go. he talked to Leslie about the nature of the sound wave; he talked about cross-Atlantic phone calls and about the electric guitar. Leslie said, "Could you look *inside* the wiring?"

Leslie fired the first team of acoustical experts, found another company, and asked them to check inside the wiring. The new man reported back to Leslie: He thought they might start by taking down the stage portion of the theatre. If the sound people worked closely with the demolition people, they might be able to avoid having to mess with the body of the hall.

The phone call that Maderiaga had made on the night of the symposium had, in the meantime, set in motion a series of official acts that were bringing to America—to Concordance—Paulino Patillo's father, Claudio/Klaus Patillo/Herrmann. The old man was eighty-nine, missing an eye by an act of man and a lung by an act of God. On the plane he suffered a collapse and was rushed from the airport straight to Concordance University's Medical Center.

Rabbi Grossman walked into Leslie's office and said, "Am I hearing things? You've approved a house, on this campus, for the accomplice of the genocide of Austrian and Hungarian Jewry?"

"And a private nurse!" said Leslie.

"Are you out of your mind?" asked Rabbi Grossman.

"Practically. Yes," said Leslie.

"You look terrible," said Shlomo Grossman, and sat down.

"What," Leslie said, "am I the hell to do with an old Nazi who is postoperative, whose son is in the sanitarium, who doesn't know a soul, doesn't have a dime, doesn't have a roof over his head?"

"Send him home to Germany," shouted Shlomo.

"I tried. Dobelmann says they won't recognize Claudio Patillo as one of their nationals."

"So send him to his comeuppance in Israel!"

"Shulamit says they're no longer interested, Shlomo! They have other things on hand!"

"Put him back on the plane and turn it around."

"For another round of screaming? Shlomo!" cried Leslie, and put his hands over his ears against the noise that, issuing out of the dismembered building materials piled in back of the institute, blanketed the countryside for miles around, made its way down every street of the small university town, into every back yard, and filtered in through Leslie's closed and shuttered windows. "Shlomo," Leslie said, "come over tonight. I promise Eliza will cook you something you can eat. I want you, and I want Ilka—and we'll see who all else—to help me think this thing through."

"We . . . I," said Leslie that night, "need to understand how the scream of Dachau is the same, and how it is a different scream from the scream of Hiroshima. And after that I need to learn how to listen to the selfsame sound that rises out of the Hell in which the torturer is getting what he's got coming. . . ."

His wife called, "Leslie, can you come and talk to Ahmed?"

Leslie went out and came back in carrying his coat. A couple of young punks with an agenda of their own had broken into Patillo/ Herrmann's new American house. They had gagged the nurse and tied her and Klaus up in the new American bathroom. Here Ilka began to laugh. Leslie buttoned his coat and said, "I'm sorry, but I have to go on over. Ilka. Shlomo, please, I leave for Washington tomorrow, early, to talk to the Superfund people. While I'm there I want to get a Scream Project funded. Ilka? Ilka, what is it?" But Ilka was helplessly giggling and could not answer him. Leslie said, "What I need is for you two to please sit down, here and now, and come up with a formulation I can take with me to present to Arts and Humanities."

The Superfund granted Concordance an allowance, for scream disposal, and the dismembered stage of the New Theatre was loaded onto a flatbed truck and driven west. The population along Route 90 and all the way down to Arizona came out into the street, eyes squeezed together, heads pulled back and down into shoulders. They buried the thing fifteen feet under, well away from the highway, and let the desert howl.

ISAAC BASHEVIS SINGER

A Party in Miami Beach

*M*y friend the humorist Reuben Kazarsky called me on the telephone in my apartment in Miami Beach and asked, "Menashe, for the first time in your life, do you want to perform a *mitzvah?*"

"Me a *mitzvah?*" I countered. "What kind of word is that—Hebrew? Aramaic? Chinese? You know I don't do *mitzvahs*, particularly here in Florida."

"Menashe, it's not a plain *mitzvah*. The man is a multimillionaire. A few months ago, he lost his whole family in a car accident—a wife, a daughter, a son-in-law and a baby grandchild of two. He is completely broken. He has built here in Miami Beach, in Hollywood and in Fort Lauderdale maybe a dozen condominiums and rental houses. He is a devoted reader of yours. He wants to make a party for you, and if you don't want a party, he simple wants to meet you. He comes from somewhere around your area— Lublin or how do you call it? To this day, he speaks a broken English. He came here from the camps without a stitch to his back, but within fifteen years, he became a millionaire. How they manage this I'll never know. It's an instinct like for a hen to lay eggs or for you to scribble novels."

"Thanks a lot for the compliment. What can come out from this *mitzvah?*"

"In the other world, a huge portion of the leviathan and a Platonic affair with Sarah, daughter of Tovim. On this lousy planet, he's liable to sell you a condominium at half price. He is loaded and he's been left without heirs. He wants to write his memoirs and for you to edit them. He has a bad heart; they've implanted a pace-maker. He goes to mediums or they come to him."

"When does he want to meet me?"

"It could even be tomorrow. He'll pick you up in his Cadillac."

At five the next afternoon, my house phone began to buzz and the Irish doorman announced that a gentleman was waiting down-stairs. I rode down in the elevator and saw a tiny man in a yellow shirt, green trousers and violet shoes with gilt buckles. The sparse hair remaining around his bald pate was the color of silver, but the round face reminded me of a red apple. A long cigar thrust out of the tiny mouth. He held out a small, damp palm, pressed my hand once, twice, three times, then said, in a piping voice:

"This is a pleasure and an honor! My name is Max Flederbush."

At the same time, he studied me with smiling brown eyes that were too big for his size—womanly eyes. The chauffeur opened the door to a huge Cadillac and we got in. The seat was upholstered in red plush and was as soft as a down pillow. As I sank down into it, Max Flederbush pressed a button and the window rolled down. He spat out his cigar, pressed the button again and the window closed.

He said, "I'm allowed to smoke about as much as I'm allowed to eat pork on Yom Kippur, but habit is a powerful force. It says somewhere that a habit is second nature. Does this come from the Gemara? The Midrash? Or is it simply a proverb?"

"I really don't know."

"How can that be? You're supposed to know everything. I have a Talmudic concordance, but it's in New York, not here. I'll phone my friend Rabbi Stempel and ask him to look it up. I have three apartments—one here in Miami, one in New York and one in Tel Aviv—and my library is scattered all over. I look for a volume here and it turns out to be in Israel. Luckily, there is such a thing as a telephone, so one can call. I have a friend in Tel Aviv, a professor at Bar-Ilan University, who stays at my place—for free, naturally—and it's easier to call Tel Aviv than New York or even someone right here in Miami. It goes through a little moon, a Sputnik or whatever. Yes, a satellite. I forget words. I put things down and I don't remember where. Our mutual friend, Reuben Kazarsky, no doubt told you what happened to me. One minute I had a family, the next—I was left as bereft as Job. Job was apparently still young and God rewarded him with new daughters, new camels and new asses, but I'm too old for such blessings. I'm sick, too. Each day that I live is a miracle from heaven. I have to guard myself with every bite. The doctor does allow me a nip of whiskey, but only a drop. My wife and daughter wanted to take me along on that ride, but I wasn't in the mood. It actually happened right here in Miami. They were going to Disney World. Suddenly, a truck came up driven by some drunk and it shattered my world. The drunk lost both of his legs. Do you believe in Special Providence?"

"I don't know how to answer you."

"According to your writings, it seems you do believe."

"Somewhere deep inside, I do."

"Had you lived through what I have, you'd grow firm in your beliefs. Well, but that's how man is—he believes and he doubts."

The Cadillac had pulled up and a parking attendant had taken it over. We walked inside a lobby that reminded me of a Hollywood supercolossal production—rugs, mirrors, lamps, paintings. The apartment was in the same vein. The rugs felt as soft as the upholstery in the car. The paintings were all abstract. I stopped before one that reminded me of a Warsaw rubbish bin on the eve of a holiday when the garbage lay heaped in huge piles. I asked Mr. Flederbush what and by whom this was, and he replied:

"Trash like the other trash. Pissako or some other bluffer."

"Who is this Pissako?"

Out of somewhere materialized Reuben Kazarsky, who said, "That's what he calls Picasso."

"What's the difference? They're all fakers," Max Flederbush said. "My wife, may she rest in peace, was the expert, not me."

Kazarsky winked at me and smiled. He had been my friend even back in Poland. He had written a half-dozen Yiddish comedies, but they had all failed. He had published a collection of vignettes, but the critics had torn it to shreds and he had stopped writing. He had come to America in 1939 and later had married a widow 20 years older than he. The widow died and Kazarsky inherited her money. He hung around rich people. He dyed his hair and dressed in corduroy jackets and hand-painted ties. He declared his love to every woman from 15 to 75. Kazarsky was in his 60s, but he looked no more than 50. He let his hair grow long and wore side whiskers. His black eyes reflected the mockery and abnegation of one who has broken with everything and everybody. In the cafeteria on the Lower East Side, he excelled at mimicking writers, rabbis and party leaders. He boasted of his talents as a sponger. Reuben Kazarsky suffered from hypochondria and because he was by nature a sexual philanthropist, he had convinced himself that he was impotent. We were friends, but he had never introduced me to his benefactors. It seemed that Max Flederbush had insisted that Reuben bring us together. He now complained to me:

"Where do you hide yourself? I've asked Reuben again and again to get us together, but according to him, you were always in Europe, in Israel or who knows where. All of a sudden, it comes out that you're in Miami Beach. I'm in such a state that I can't be alone for a minute. The moment I'm alone, I'm overcome by a gloom that's worse than madness. This fine apartment you see here turns suddenly into a funeral parlor. Sometimes I think that the real heroes aren't those who get medals in wartime but the bachelors who live out their years alone."

"Do you have a bathroom in this palace?" I asked.

"More than one, more than two, more than three," Max answered. He took my arm and led me to a bathroom that bedazzled me by its size and elegance. The lid of the toilet seat was transparent, set with semiprecious stones and a two-dollar bill implanted within it. Facing the mirror hung a picture of a little boy urinating in an arc while a little girl looked on admiringly. When I lifted the toilet-seat lid, music began to play. After a while, I stepped out onto the balcony that looked directly out to sea. The rays of the setting sun scampered over the waves. Gulls still hunted for fish. Far off in the distance, on the edge of the horizon, a ship swayed. On the beach, I spotted some animal that from my vantage point, 16 floors high, appeared like a calf or a huge dog. But it couldn't be a dog and what would a calf be doing in Miami Beach? Suddenly, the shape straightened up and turned out to be a woman in a long bathrobe digging for clams in the sand.

After a while, Kazarsky joined me on the balcony. He said, "That's Miami. It wasn't he but his wife who chased after all these trinkets. She was the businesslady and the boss at home. On the other hand, he isn't quite the idle dreamer he pretends to be. He has an uncanny knack for making money. They dealt in everything—buildings, lots, stocks, diamonds, and eventually she got involved in art, too. When he said buy, she bought; and when he said sell, she sold. When she showed him a painting, he'd glance at it, spit and say, 'It's junk, they'll snatch it out of your hands. Buy!' Whatever they touched turned to money. They flew to Israel, established Yeshivas and donated prizes toward all kinds of endeavors—cultural, religious. Naturally, they wrote it all off in taxes. Their daughter, that pampered brat, was half-crazy. Any complex you can find in Freud, Jung and Adler, she had it. She was born in a DP camp in Germany. Her parents wanted her to marry a chief rabbi or an Israeli prime minister. But she fell in love with a gentile, an archaeology professor with a wife and five children. His wife wouldn't divorce him and she had to be bought off with a quarter-million-dollar settlement and a fantastic alimony besides. Four weeks after the wedding, the professor left to dig for a new Peking man. he drank like a fish. It was he who was drunk, not the truck driver. Come, you'll soon see something!"

Kazarsky opened the door to the living room and it was filled with people. In one day, Max Flederbush had managed to arrange

a party. Not all the guests could fit into the large living room.
Kazarsky and Max Flederbush led me from room to room and the
party was going on all over. Within minutes, maybe 200 people had
gathered, mostly women. It was a fashion show of jewelry, dresses,
pants, caftans, hairdos, shoes, bags, make-up, as well as men's
jackets, shirts and ties. Spotlights illuminated every painting. Waiters served drinks. Black and white maids offered trays of hors
d'oeuvres.

In all this commotion, I could scarcely hear what was being said
to me. The compliments started, the handshakes and the kisses. A
stout lady seized me around and pressed me to her enormous
bosom. She shouted into my ear, "I read you! I come from the
towns you describe. My grandfather came here from Ishishok. He
was a wagon driver there and here in America, he went into the
freight business. If my parents wanted to say something I wouldn't
understand, they spoke Yiddish, and that's how I learned a little of
the language."

I caught a glimpse of myself in the mirror. My face was smeared
with lipstick. Even as I stood there, trying to wipe it off, I received
all kinds of proposals. A cantor offered to set one of my stories to
music. A musician demanded I adapt an opera libretto from one of
my novels. A president of an adult-education program invited me
to speak a year hence at his synagogue. I would be given a plaque.
A young man with hair down to his shoulders asked that I recom-
mend a publisher, or at least an agent, to him. He declared, "I *must*
create. This is a physical need with me."

One minute all the rooms were full, the next—all the guests were
gone, leaving only Reuben Kazarsky and myself. Just as quickly and
efficiently, the help cleaned up the leftover food and half-drunk
cocktails, dumped all the ashtrays and replaced all the chairs in
their rightful places. I had never before witnessed such perfection.
Out of somewhere, Max Flederbush dug out a white tie with gold
polka dots and put it on.

He said, "Time for dinner."

"I ate so much I haven't the least appetite," I said.

"You must have dinner with us. I reserved a table at the best
restaurant in Miami."

After a while, the three of us, Max Flederbush, Reuben Kazarsky and I, got into the Cadillac and the same chauffeur drove us. Night had fallen and I no longer saw nor tried to determine where I was being taken. We drove for only a few minutes and pulled up in front of a hotel resplendent with lights and uniformed attendants. One opened the car door ceremoniously, a second fawningly opened the glass front door. The lobby of this hotel wasn't merely supercolossal but supersupercolossal—complete to light effects, tropical plants in huge planters, vases, sculptures, a parrot in a cage. We were escorted into a nearly dark hall and greeted by a headwaiter who was expecting us and led us to our reserved table. He bowed and scraped, seemingly overcome with joy that we had arrived safely. Soon, another individual came up. Both men wore tuxedos, patent-leather shoes, bow ties and ruffled shirts. They looked to me like twins. They spoke with foreign accents that I suspected weren't genuine. A lengthy discussion evolved concerning our choice of foods and drinks. When the two heard I was a vegetarian, they looked at each other in chagrin, but only for a second. Soon they assured me they would serve me the best dish a vegetarian had ever tasted. One took our orders and the other wrote them down. Max Flederbush announced in his broken English that he really wasn't hungry, but if something tempting could be dredged up for him, he was prepared to give it a try. He interjected Yiddish expressions, but the two waiters apparently understood him. He gave precise instructions on how to roast his fish and prepare his vegetables. He specified spices and seasonings. Reuben Kazarsky ordered a steak and what I was to get, which in plain English was a fruit salad with cottage cheese.

When the two men finally left, Max Flederbush said, "There were times if you would have told me I'd be sitting in such a place eating such food, I would have considered it a joke. I had one fantasy—one time before I died to get enough dry bread to fill me. Suddenly, I'm a rich man, alas, and people dance attendance on me. Well, but flesh and blood isn't fated to enjoy any rest. The angels in heaven are jealous, Satan is the accuser and the Almighty is easily convinced. He nurses a longtime resentment against us Jews. He still can't forgive the fact that our great-great-grandfathers worshiped the golden calf. Let's have our picture taken."

A man with a camera materialized. "Smile!" he ordered us.

Max Flederbush tried to smile. One eye laughed, the other cried. Reuben Kazarsky began to twinkle. I didn't even make the effort. The photographer said he was going to develop the film and that he'd be back in three quarters of an hour.

Max Flederbush asked, "What was I talking about, eh? Yes, I live in apparent luxury, but a woe upon this luxury. As rich and as elegant the house is, it's also a Gehenna. I'll tell you something; in a certain sense, it's worse here than in the camps. There, at least, we all hoped. A hundred times a day we comforted ourselves with the fact that the Hitler madness couldn't go on for long. When we heard the sound of an airplane, we thought the invasion had started. We were all young then and our whole lives were before us. Rarely did anyone commit suicide. Here, hundreds of people sit, waiting for death. A week doesn't go by that someone doesn't give up the ghost. They're all rich. The men have accumulated fortunes, turned worlds upside down, maybe swindled to get there. Now they don't know what to do with their money. They're all on diets. There is no one to dress for. Outside of the financial page in the newspaper, they read nothing. As soon as they finish their breakfasts, they start playing cards. Can you play cards forever? They have to, or die from boredom. When they get tired of play-ing, they start slandering one another. Bitter feuds are waged. Today they elect a president, the next day they try to impeach him. If he decides to move a chair in the lobby, a revolution breaks out. There is one touch of consolation for them—the mail. An hour before the postman is due, the lobby is crowded. They stand with their keys in hand, waiting like for the Messiah. If the postman is late, a hubbub erupts. If one opens his mailbox and it's empty, he starts to grope and burrow inside, trying to create something out of thin air. They are all past seventy-two and they receive checks from Social Security. If the check doesn't come on time, they worry about it more than those who need it for bread. They're always suspicious of the mailman. Before they mail a letter, they shake the cover three times. The women mumble incantations.

"It says somewhere in the Book of Morals that if man will remember his dying day, he won't sin. Here you can as much forget about death as you can forget to breathe. Today I meet someone by the swimming pool and we chat. Tomorrow I hear he's in the other world. The moment a man or a woman dies, the widow or widower starts right in looking for a new mate. They can barely sit out the shivah. Often, they marry from the same building. Yesterday they maligned the other with every curse in the book, today they're husband and wife. They make a party and try to dance on their shaky legs. The wills and insurance policies are speedily rewritten and the game begins anew. A month or two don't go by and the bridegroom is in the hospital. The heart, the kidneys, the prostate.

"I'm not ashamed before you—I'm every bit as silly as they are, but I'm not such a fool as to look for another wife. I neither can nor do I want to. I have a doctor here. He's a firm believer in the benefits of walking and I take a walk each day after breakfast. On the way back, I stop at the Bache brokerage house. I open the door and there they sit, the oldsters, staring at the ticker, watching their stocks jump around like imps. They know full well that they won't make use of these stocks. It's all to leave in the inheritance, and their children and grandchildren are often as rich as they are. But if a stock goes up, they grow optimistic and buy more of it.

"Our friend Reuben wants me to write my memoirs, I have a story to tell, yes I do. I went through not only one Gehenna but ten. This very person who sits here beside you sipping champagne spent three quarters of a year behind a cellar wall, waiting for death. I wasn't the only one—there were six of us men there and one woman. I know what you're going to ask. A man is only a man, even on the brink of the grave. She couldn't live with all six of us, but she did live with two—her husband and her lover—and she satisfied the others as best as she could. If there had been a machine to record what went on there, the things that were said and the dreams that were played out, your greatest writers would be made to look like dunces by comparison. In such circumstances, the souls strip themselves bare and no one has yet adequately described a naked soul. The *szmalcowniks*, the informers, knew about us and they had to be constantly bribed. We each had a little money or some valuable objects and as long as they lasted, we kept buying pieces of life. It came to it that these informers brought us bread, cheese, whatever was available—everything for ten times the actual price.

"Yes, I could describe all this in pure facts, but to give it flavor requires the pen of a genius. Besides, one forgets. If you would ask me now what these men were called, I'll be damned if I could tell you. But the woman's name was Hilda. One of the men was called Edek, Edek Saperstein, and the other—Sigmunt, but Sigmunt what? When I lie in bed and can't sleep, it all comes back as vivid as if it would have happened yesterday. Not everything, mind you.

"Yes, memoirs. But who needs them? There are hundreds of such books written by simple people, not writers. They send them to me and I send them a check. But I can't read them. Each one of these books is poison, and how much poison can a person swallow? Why is it taking so long for my fish? It's probably still swimming in the ocean. And your fruit salad first has to be planted. I'll give you a rule to follow—when you go into a restaurant and it's dark, know that this is only to deceive. The headwaiter is one of the Polish children of Israel, but he poses as a native Frenchman. He might even be a refugee himself. When you come here, you have to sit and wait for your meal, so that later on the bill won't seem too excessive. I'm neither a writer nor a philosopher, but I lie awake half the nights and when you can't sleep, the brain churns like a mill. The wildest notions come to me. Ah, here is the photographer! A fast worker. Well, let's have a look!"

The photographer handed each of us two photos in color and we sat there quietly studying them.

Max Flederbush asked me, "Why did you come out looking so frightened? That you write about ghosts, this I know. But you look here as if you'd seen a real ghost. If you did, I want to know about it."

"I hear you go to séances," I said.

"Eh? I go. Or, to put it more accurately—they come to me. This is all bluff, too, but I *want* to be fooled. The woman turns off the lights and starts talking, allegedly in my wife's voice. I'm not such a dummy, but I listen. Here they come with our food, the Miami *szmalcowniks*."

The door opened and the headwaiter came in leading three men.

All I could see in the darkness was that one was short and fat, with a square head of white hair that sat directly on his broad shoulders, and with an enormous belly. He wore a pink shirt and red trousers. The two others were taller and slimmer. When the headwaiter pointed to our table, the heavy-set man broke away from the others, came toward us and shouted in a deep voice:

"Mr. Flederbush!"

Max Flederbush jumped up from his seat.

"Mr. Albeginni!"

They began to heap praises upon each other. Albeginni spoke in broken English with an Italian accent.

Max Flederbush said, "Mr. Albeginni, you know my good friend, Kazarsky, here. And this man is a writer, a Yiddish writer. He writes everything in Yiddish. I was told that you understand Yiddish!"

Albeginni interrupted him. "*A gezunt oyf dein kepele . . . Hock nisht kein tcheinik . . . A gut boychik . . .* My parents lived on Rivington Street and all my friends spoke Yiddish. On Sabbath, they invited me for gefilte fish, *cholent*, kugel. Who do you write for—the papers?"

"He writes books."

"Books, eh? Good! We need books, too. My son-in-law has three rooms full of books. He knows French, German. He's a foot doctor, but he first had to study math, philosophy and all the rest. Welcome! Welcome! I've got to get back to my friends, but later on we'll—"

He held out a heavy, sweaty hand to me. He breathed asthmatically and smelled of alcohol and hair tonic. The words rumbled out deep and grating from his throat. After he left, Max said:

"You know who he is? One of the Family."

"Family?"

"You don't know who the Family is? Oh! You've remained a greenhorn! The Mafia. Half Miami Beach belongs to them. Don't laugh, but they keep order here. Uncle Sam has saddled himself with a million laws that, instead of protecting the people, protect the criminal. When I was a boy studying about Sodom in cheder, I couldn't understand how a whole city or a whole country could become corrupt. Lately, I've begun to understand. Sodom had a constitution and our nephew, Lot, and the other lawyers reworked it so that right became wrong and wrong—right. Mr. Albeginni actually lives in my building. When the tragedy struck me, he sent me a bouquet of flowers so big it couldn't fit through the door."

"Tell me about the cellar where you sat with the other men and the only woman," I said.

"Eh? I thought that this would intrigue you. I talked to one of the writers about my memoirs and when I told him about this, he said. 'God forbid! You must leave this part out. Martyrdom and sex don't mix. You must write only good things about them.' That's the reason I lost the urge for the memoirs. The Jews in Poland were people, not angels. They were flesh and blood just like you and me. We suffered, but we were men with manly desires. One of the five was her husband. Sigmunt. This Sigmunt was in contact with the *szmalcowniks*. He had all kinds of dealings with them. He had two revolvers and we resolved that if it looked like we were about to fall into murderers' hands, we would kill as many of them as possible, then put an end to our own lives. It was one of our illusions. When it comes down to it, you can't manage things so exactly. Sigmunt had been a sergeant in the Polish army in 1920. He had volunteered for Pilsudski's legion. He got a medal for marksmanship. Later on, he owned a garage and imported automobile parts. A giant, six foot tall or more. One of the *szmalcowniks* had once worked for him. If I was to tell you how it came about that we all ended up together in that cellar, we'd have to sit here till morning. His wife, Hilda, was a decent woman. She swore that she had been faithful to him throughout their marriage. Now, I will tell you who her lover was. No one but yours truly. She was 17 years older than me and could have been my mother. She treated me like a mother, too. 'The child,' that's what she called me. The child this and the child that. Her husband was insanely jealous. He warned us he'd kill us both if we started anything. He threatened to castrate me. He could have easily done it, too. But gradually, she wore him down. How this came about you could neither describe nor write, even if you possessed the talent of a Tolstoy or a Zeromski. She persuaded him, hypnotized him like Delilah did Samson. I didn't want any part of it. The other four men were furious with me. I wasn't up to it, either. I had become impotent. What it means to spend 24 hours out of the day locked in a cold, damp cellar in the company of five men and one woman, words cannot describe. We had to cast off all shame. At night we barely had enough room to stretch our legs. From sitting in one place, we developed constipation. We had to do everything in front of witnesses and this is an anguish Satan himself couldn't endure. We had to become cynical. We had to speak in coarse terms to conceal our shame. It was then I discovered that profanity has its purpose. I have to take a little drink. So . . . *L'chayim!*

"Yes, it didn't come easy. First she had to break down his resistance, then she had to revive my lust. We did it when he was asleep, or he only pretended. Two of the group had turned to homosexuality. The whole shame of being human emerged there. If man is formed in God's image, I don't envy God . . .

"We endured all the degradation one can only imagine, but we never lost hope. Later, we left the cellar and went off, each his own way. The murderers captured Sigmunt and tortured him to death. His wife—my mistress, so to say—made her way to Russia, married some refugee there, then died of cancer in Israel. One of the other four is now a rich man in Brooklyn. He became a penitent, of all things, and he gives money to the Bobow rabbi or to some other rabbi. What happened to the other three, I don't know. If they lived, I would have heard from them. That writer I mentioned— he's a kind of critic—claims that our literature has to concentrate only on holiness and martyrdom. What nonsense! Foolish lies!"

"Write the whole truth," I said.

"First of all, I don't know how. Secondly, I would be stoned. I generally am unable to write. As soon as I pick up a pen, I get a pain in the wrist. I become drowsy, too. I'd rather read what you write. At times, It seems to me you're stealing my thoughts.

"I shouldn't say this, but I'll say it anyway. Miami Beach is full of widows and when they heard that I'm alone, the phone calls and the visits started. They haven't stopped yet. A man alone and something of a millionaire, besides! I've become such a success I'm literally ashamed before myself. I'd like to cling to another person.

Between another's funeral and your own, you still want to snatch a bit of that swinish material called pleasure. But the women are not for me. Some *yenta* came to me and complained, 'I don't want to go around like my mother with a guilt complex. I want to take everything from life I can, even more than I can.' I said to her, 'The trouble is, one cannot . . .' With men and women, it's like with Jacob and Esau: When one rises, the other falls. When the females turn so wanton, the men become like frightened virgins. It's just like the prophet said, 'Seven women shall take hold of one man.' What will come of all this, eh? What, for instance, will the writers write about in five hundred years?"

"Essentially, about the same things as today," I replied.

"Well, and what about in a thousand years? In ten thousand years? It's scary to think the human species will last so long. How will Miami Beach look then? How much will a condominium cost?"

"Miami Beach will be under water," Reuben Kazarsky said, "and a condominium with one bedroom for the fish will cost five trillion dollars."

"And what will be in New York? In Paris? In Moscow? Will there still be Jews?"

"There'll be only Jews," Kazarsky said.

"What kind of Jews?"

"Crazy Jews, just like you."

Translated from the Yiddish by Joseph Singer

JOANNA SPIRO

Three Thousand Years of Your History . . . Take One Year for Yourself

T he same summer Rachel flew from Los Angeles to Tel Aviv, her college friends flew elsewhere. One went to India to slow the birthrate; one, to Indonesia to quicken food production. Leonard, her closest friend, took the year she took and went to Bangkok, to Beijing, illegally to Laos. He went away looking to be embraced, and laid himself in gentle, welcoming hands, and wrote back fluid, infatuated phrases of ease: an air-conditioned taxi in a humid Thai summer, a warm Japanese bath, an opium haze equal to infinite orgasm. Leonard went to the far east to lose and find himself, to resign and regain himself, to decipher the code of ideograms that might lead the way on. Rachel went to Israel, seeking initiation into the strange and holy language she was supposed to understand, but could not; to decipher the code that might lead the way on, or back, or on.

COME SEE FOR YOURSELF

Israel in summer seethed with movement. The streets staged a dance of dark, bright bodies; the buses were packed with moving forms and spoken words. Dirty green army clothes and the slash lines of guns punctuated the masses on buses and sidewalks. Everywhere Rachel saw bared skin the tan color of her own—shoulders, chests, calves, backs, sandaled feet.

She went first to the city of Haifa to study Hebrew at the university on Mt. Carmel. She rode the buses from place to place, from mountaintop to city center to the port itself, hearing everywhere the conversations in rapid, dense Hebrew which reflected her back to herself stupid, dumb. Rachel's Hebrew teacher at the university, an employee of the Jewish Agency, who believed that all children of Israel, Rachel somehow included, should return to Israel, seemed to think Hebrew was properly Rachel's mother tongue. This country is your country, this language your language, she had said to Rachel, but Rachel was a child in this country, an idiot in this language.

Mornings Rachel drew letters and words, phrases and paragraphs, in present, in past, in future. After class she would go to the Haifa beaches with the twin girls from New Jersey. They took the bus down the mountain and hitched to the shore. Rachel let the two with their matching bare brown shoulders point their index fingers into the street fishing for a ride. At the beach she sat on her towel on the hot sand under the Biblical sun beating down on crowds of undressed browning bodies. The lifeguard yelled through a megaphone at wayward children who were out too far. Hebrew Rachel by now could understand: Little girl, come back.

Today on the way back to the university a young man and a young woman boarded the bus and sat in the seat in front of hers. The boy wore a grey t-shirt, stretched at the neck so a span of the skin of his back showed. The girl wore a too-big sweater, possibly his, with a few of her long red curling hairs caught in the weave. The moment they were in the seat he fell into her lap and she bowed her body over his, as if they could not bear the pain of boarding the bus, the separation of passing through the narrow door, down the narrow aisle. The boy could not be much younger than army-age. Rachel, in the isolation of her own bus-seat, could not have been a colder stranger to the two in front, to the bus, to the state itself, and the more so for the heat of Israelis toward one another. For each other, heated love, heated hatred, and for the foreigner, the American, unseamed indifference, except for an aloof hand extended to collect the green dollars.

As the bus passed through the narrow back streets of Haifa, Rachel saw the Arab men selling stinking fish, the Arab women sweeping the dirt from back steps, From their bitter mouths Rachel imagined she heard the words of the travel poster parroted: "Welcome to the holy land." The guard at the university entrance stopped an Arab boy to search through his bags of books and food, while Rachel passed undisturbed, her bag unexamined. The privilege of rulers: she was not likely to be carrying a bomb, not likely to be carrying in her heart a passion for retribution. Here having a home was like having an arm, and having it threatened, or having it taken. Rachel, standing on land torn from hand to violent hand from generation to generation, felt herself as nonchalant a floater as any American, rootless and unconcerned, at home in any Mc-Donald's, as happy or as unhappy in any of twenty interchangeable cities across the vast sprawl of a continent. By naming her its own Israel bestowed on her the shame of victims—the inconceivable slaughter—and at the same time made hers the bloody hands of the victor. She was neither; she was both. Her people: she walked away from them and they ran after; she approached them and they fled. Rich American, diaspora Jew, woman without birthright, Jew bearing the mark of death: she was none of these things, and all of them only when wrongly named, claimed and pointed at from all directions, falsely, greedily, damningly.

She met Matthew, a midwestern American with a face as smooth, as blank as an egg, studying Arabic in Haifa. Why was he here? He would not say, or he would say anything—to become a historian, to work for the CIA. He had acquired his fluency in Hebrew from his last girlfriend; now, he told Rachel, he was looking for an Arab girl to sleep with. He was unreadable, unplaceable; he was always searched and questioned before boarding El Al flights to the States. But Rachel wanted to be he; so clean, so foreign, so immune to connection. To sleep with a woman he didn't love to acquire the commodity of her language; to live in a country he didn't love; to stockpile knowledge and later barter it for a professorship. Rachel felt adulterous, living in Israel, and cursed with an incapacity for fidelity. Whatever Matthew's hidden and convoluted reasons for staying here, they seemed simpler than her own.

Each weekend the tall ugly dormitory emptied all Friday afternoon as the students went home for the Sabbath. On these Friday afternoons Rachel stood by her window, watching the traffic along the pathway to the bus stop, feeling the heat of her narrow room. At night she lay in the isolation of her narrow bed in the emptied building, and felt herself a tiny ember of consciousness in a wide and growing darkness, and understood how very near to empty the room was.

One weekend toward the end of the summer term an Australian, also studying Hebrew at the university, took Rachel to Kibbutz Beit Shemesh to visit his brother who had moved permanently to Israel with his young family. The brother said cheerfully to Rachel that he was very happy, and simply resigned to speaking like a retarded eight-year-old for a while. His six-year-old daughter already spoke Hebrew as easily as any of the children. In the small neat white kibbutz apartment he said earnestly to Rachel that it had nothing to do with God, but that she would find that she had a soul and that that soul was at home in Israel.

After the Sabbath had ended, when the buses began to run again, Rachel found a seat on the bus back to Jerusalem. She tried to give it to a boy of about thirteen who stood in the aisle holding a baby, but he wouldn't take it. Instead he passed the crying baby, warm and dimly conscious, to Rachel. The plump body seemed to grow bigger under her hands with each passing moment. The woman in the seat beside Rachel turned to her and reached out her arms, and they stretched the small girl across their two laps, where she slept robustly all the way back to the central bus station. Rachel sat, her sister by the window, her brother in the aisle, her child in her lap: for the timeless, sleepy, hypnotic moment of the busride, family restored, God above, home regained.

REACH FOR THE SKY

In late September, possessed of a tiny fluency in Hebrew, Rachel left Haifa for Kibbutz Rosh Hanikra, which lay on the Mediterranean just at the border with Lebanon. The kibbutz grew corn and citrus fruits and maintained a restaurant frequented by Israeli soldiers and the U.N. forces in Lebanon. For her first weeks there she worked in the restaurant, clearing tables, looking out over the blue of the Mediterranean. She could not stop looking into the blue, nor could she see how color so intense could be so quotidian for the soldiers and kibbutz members, for the U.N. men speaking all languages, gleaming white, gleaming black but all sitting around the same tables, drinking the same beer, reaching the same volume of drunken and combative voices. Each afternoon party of Austrians, of Africans, formed its own circular world, in which each face looked only as far as the other round faces around the table, never seeing the sea. There Rachel heard for the first time the argument that she must kiss someone because tomorrow he might die. It was a common line among the passing Israeli soldiers if a good one and after a while not difficult to disregard, as after a while it became harder to see what was so blue in the blue of the sea. Laughing faces above guns passed on jeeps; the soldiers beckoned to her when she walked in the street and called, come on, are you going to Lebanon? Your gun, said the soldier Rachel had agreed to sit beside, to drink coffee with, is for the three years you are in the army your wife. You sleep with it, you eat with it, your hand never leaves it. He stroked the metal length of it. He took her for a ride on a borrowed motorcycle. He insisted on buying her an ice cream before they started off so that one hand was occupied holding the stick of the melting sweet and Rachel, her cheek against the gun across his back, had only the other with which to hold tentatively onto the edge of the little windshield, because holding onto the soldier, she felt, was more dangerous than falling off. Then that one too passed over the border, and there were only faces of soldiers, explosions on the other side, sirens at night, the enemy unseen and named only as terrorists, but terror was everywhere; mundane, a dilute fear of what might seep into the kibbutz at night, or come over the hill, or show its face in the car you caught a ride in. The kibbutz sat right on the border, right on the edge: and this was only one of the four guarded borders facing four hostile nations.

A special unit of the army was stationed on the kibbutz; after their army term they went to establish new kibbutzes on the borders. When Rachel began working the dining hall she met Mimi, a member of this unit. Mimi had been working dining hall detail for months, and Rachel was surprised: in Israel where men and women alike trained for the sacred and national duty of the army, wasn't this rather tame work? Mimi scoffed, and Rachel came to see that to Mimi this was preferable to serving coffee to men in some army office or sitting with other girls in the entrance to the Haifa subway listlessly glancing into commuters' bags as if for bombs. Rachel and Mimi washed pots and potatoes together for a while. Mimi looked after Rachel when she contracted what was called shilshul. Rachel lay on her cot coming to know her own unnourished body, which could not work, could not think, could barely rise from the bed to go drink water, to go expel its last attempt to consume and assimilate some form of sustenance. It was a fast, of a sort, resulting, Rachel gathered, from some evil residue on the fat fruit of unmatched beauty she had picked in the orchard and consumed without waiting, without washing. The bitterness of nausea seemed to prove to Rachel that the foreign fruit of Israel could not nourish, could only poison her. But Mimi brought her through, from water to broth to bread, and when Rachel could happily eat again, Mimi brought her home for Shabbat, to the other extreme of the continuum Rachel had stepped onto with her days of sick starvation.

The town was Shlomi, a "development town." This, Rachel

came to understand, meant large numbers of Sephardic immigrants had come here from Morocco, from Yemen, and were artificially settled in cheap apartment blocks, artificially provided with industry, labor. Now, twenty years later, the walls of the apartments were crumbling, the artificial industries had died natural deaths, and there was no money. But there was plenty of family. Though Mimi and Rachel arrived in a pouring rainstorm late on Friday afternoon, a little crowd of people hurried through the flooded street, coming home from everywhere to this nowhere town so as to be home for Shabbat. Mimi's parents spoke very little English, but Rachel did not find their Hebrew difficult, because the phrases addressed to her ran from Eat, to Take, to Take more, to Take another. First there were the sandwiches, the moment they got inside and dried off a little and pushed through the low crowd of little brothers. Then the ice cream. Then, an hour later, the dinner: the soup, the bread, the fish, the chicken, the beef, the wines, the salads, the cakes, the second round of ice cream. Then tea and cookies. Finally Mimi took Rachel through the misty streets full of people going visiting to visit two schoolfriends, one after the other—young women her age, newly married, and therefore exempt from army service. Both friends had dark quiet husbands, one newly employed, one newly unemployed; one had a dark-eyed yelling new baby. Both had baked for the Sabbath. Both served tea and cake. That night, beside Mimi in her bed, beneath the intricately woven scarves from Morocco Mimi had hung on the wall, Rachel dreamed of proffered platters of chicken which she tried in vain to decline. On Saturday night when the buses started running again Mimi and Rachel returned to the kibbutz, holding the four bags which Mimi's mother had placed in each of their four hands, bags of fruit and cookies and rolls and meats. Though Mimi cooked for the whole kibbutz, she hardly ever partook of what the kibbutz produced. She lived from Saturday to Saturday out of her mother's bags of sustenance.

Rachel began to work in the garden of children, as it was called, where she met Judy, another American who could speak Hebrew. Judy had dark eyes, a storm of loose black curls, white skin, a small stateliness. Before they had offered her the work in the children's

house Judy had chosen always to work in the citrus groves, climbing into the treetops among the sharp and jagged branches to pluck
the fruits. But she was interested in children—in Jewish children,
in Arab children, in finding a way to heal the wounds, because she
wanted to live here, and wanted to live here in peace. Judy wanted
to live in the profound peace of prayer, which it seemed could be
reached only through politics. Work was over in midafternoon,
and in early evening Rachel and Judy would meet again in the
dining hall and cut platefuls of cucumbers and tomatoes and pep-
pers and onions and talk. Of prayer, and of a war, which was never
far from Judy's sight. The infinite black fact of the war in Europe
seemed to Judy to endow Israel with sense, with natural meaning.
Though Rachel could see the black edge of the war, it could not for
her as for Judy throw national politics into relief in such a way as
to make them make sense. Judy had come to Israel to complete
what her parents had begun. Both her parents had survived the
years of the second world war, and had come out of Europe, having
lost mothers, fathers, all family, all sense of peace, and had come
to Palestine, not yet adults, utterly alone. Each had left Palestine to
go to school in America, where they had met, had married, had
accidentally prospered, had settled, had stayed. Judy, born in affluence, in peacetime, knew America's fat calm for a thin layer of
deception overlying malignancy and preferred Israel, where the
threat could be seen, shot at, spoken to, settled with, someday,
maybe. Judy spoke of her mother as a child: tiny, skeleton-thin,
hidden in attic after attic after damp cellar in a French farmhouse,
in the Italian alps, in a convent in Rome. Judy's presence was for
Rachel in that foreign place such a comfort, her beauty such a light;
only now did Rachel begin to see with any clarity what the murder
of the Jews in Europe had taken from her, and might have taken.

She received letters from her friends abroad: they reported feeling drawn in, assimilated, members of villages and participants in
culture as they never had in America. Leonard wrote from Beijing:
"I want to become part of the huge family of China. I went to the
Great Wall; I felt that the wall was built by my own ancestors, that
the ancient stones are the stones of my own ancient past." But
Rachel became more and more foreign. On the kibbutz no one

spoke English to her; on buses and in the streets no one recognized her as American. Her Hebrew was quick now, her skin and hair dark; but the more others thought her Israeli, the more she knew she was not. She was not America's, she was not Israel's, she was of no place. But standing over the Mediterranean, a moment. Handing a long ear of abandoned edible corn to a child of the kibbutz in a field where black birds were rising from thick-planted stalks of corn just before the vegetable fountain thrown by the combine moving toward them in unreal grace—the spray of corn-matter rising between blue of sky and blue of sea, and the small sea of children around her, moving toward the machine in fascination, away from the machine in fear—a white, rising, unspeakable joy.

MASADA: A DEAD SEA AND A LIVING HISTORY

Masada must be hiked up briskly just before sunrise, for full effect. Masada, where these days those entering the Israeli army underwent their initiation, Masada, the last holdout of the Jews; Masada, of the long siege; Masada, site of the mass suicide. The parallels were lost on no one who stood in the state of Israel where it perched on the edge of the Mediterranean as precarious as any who might want to drive it off the earth and into the sea could desire. But take parallel lines and twist them in space, say never again, or say you have built the third temple in the image of a state. Stand on the site of the death of the last of the Israelites and know that they persist. Take the ashes of millions and write a declaration to house them, a constitution to govern them: and claim that you have made sense out of an insanity of death.

Step after step, upwards and up, and the fortress really very peaceful, and the rising sun bright peace. The day before she had been in Jerusalem, speaking with a former American who had made the ascent. His Hebrew was excellent; his *reish* came right from the throat. His enthusiasm was like a well of life, he seemed to feed on the contradictions, on the energy generated by the conflict of the religious and the secular, the Arab and the Jew, the pro-peace and the pro-killing factions. Rachel, unlike him, felt the battling forces

cancel each other out into a profound nullity, and felt in the streets
of Jerusalem at times that she could hardly raise her head to think
anymore over the din of the fighting without and the fighting
within. Daniel, the new Israeli, gave talks to American students
sometimes on behalf of the Jewish Agency. He was a success, a
good example. To Rachel he said: Israel is a country reborn. Israel
is a miracle of resurrection. He used Amos Oz's metaphor: the
diaspora is a museum case for dead and dusty artifacts of ancient
Jewish culture. In Israel you make your own history rather than
venerating relics. Yes, things are difficult, and Israel is under scru-
tiny: two olive trees uprooted on the West Bank make the front
pages of the world's papers, when how many in Iran and Iraq have
to die to merit a page six mention? That is because Israel is real life,
Israel is center stage. Israel is a focus of world attention . . . Israel
is a miracle of rebirth. Thrive on tension, breathe electricity, mus-
ter all your strength to bring to the struggle of creating your nation
as you want it: if you want justice, come forward and make it; if you
want to see the peace, come forward and write it.

Rachel granted the electricity, the excitement, the thrill of the
edge. She recognized the fascination; more than that, the fascination had lodged itself in a deep place in her heart. In a dark place
of her heart: the fascination of Israel was neighbor to the fascination of the kitchen knife, of the mushroom cloud, of the parachute
or the noose. For Israel was a country on the edge of death.

COME MEET THE FAMILY. STUDY THE ROOTS OF YOUR
PEOPLE.

On the eve of the New Year Rachel had two propositions for
lodgings. She had come to Jerusalem for the holiday. Baruch Levine, ex-American, man with a mission, would have her sleep in the
women's annex of his hostel for wayward American Jews. She had
slept there last night, on a mattress among other young American
women who were in Jerusalem for the holiday, sampling the holiday cooking, the religious fervor, the rhetoric of the Orthodox

populations of the holy city. And this afternoon she had met a French Jew and officer of the Israeli army who had another proposition for where she might spend the night. Rachel walked with him with his rifle between them to the Arab quarter of the old city where he ordered tea with nana for her, speaking to the vendor in Arabic. He spoke to her in curvaceous French, in poor English, in rapid army Hebrew. Despite her years of high school French, Rachel understood the constituent remarks of the attempted seduction best in Hebrew. He told her about his childhood, about his decision to come to the Israeli army rather then be drafted into the French, about how after a time he had grown accustomed to killing people. As they walked back through the Jewish quarter toward Baruch Levine's he pointed out to her a hole in the paving where a grenade had gone off a few days before—things always heated up around the high holy days. The Arabs hate the Jews and the Jews hate the Arabs: a little refrain to repeat to yourself as you walk the narrow streets of the old city. They walked through the market where the Arab merchants called plaintively, angrily, for Rachel's American dollars, and she wondered in which of the world's nations the cold steel of her soldier's rifle had been forged, and saw Israel filthy with blood.

Baruch Levine gave what lessons he could—a crash course in holy law for any student who happened his way, attracted by the idea of Shabbat dinner in real Jerusalem, or by stories of Levine's magnetism and his strange crusade, or by an inner pull toward some true path they believed Levine could guide them onto. Any could come and eat Levine's food, but only after washing the hands thrice in prayer and repeating the blessing over the bread, syllable for foreign syllable, after Levine. On the holy day, when the other women in the hostel were napping, Rachel was sitting in the kitchen writing a letter to Leonard about these crazy Orthodox when Levine's loud voice ordered from behind her, "STOP WRITING." It was forbidden. So Rachel put away her pen, and left the hostel. She led little of her life, she knew, to Levine's specifications, and Levine knew in his heated heart that he was living by the law of God. At least in this country, Rachel thought, seeing her French soldier, the lips that spoke and committed impurities to her, upon her, on holy days, were Jewish lips. If that to Levine was any satisfaction.

The Western Wall was lit by colored floodlights; crowds of tourists and worshippers covered the flat plain of the enclosure. The men prayed at the men's two-thirds of the wall, the women at the women's third. Little men in uniform scurried among the tourists, trying to make them stop taking photographs, stop writing: trying to enforce the laws of the covenant with God. Baruch Levine pursued the same project in his own manner. He stood on a crate, a few hundred feet from the wall, surrounded by a crowd of student visitors and the resident disciples who guided students to families in all parts of Jerusalem. He set up visits for the second ritual dinner of the New Year, like an auctioneer: one spot with a Hasidic family in the Jewish quarter, I need one taker, you, and Rachel was led off to a white apartment in the heart of the old city to dine with a fat ex-American come to Jerusalem to be holy and his docile, bovine wife, obedient and pregnant, come from England to marry this man God, Rachel thought, only knew why. The wife cooked, served, and tended to the two tiny noisy children; the husband officiated, doled out the words of God at intervals from his prayer book, and held forth for Rachel's benefit on how things were. Women were born to bear children, and when their minds were twisted, when they were brainwashed into believing they were meant for other things, they became sick. He looked at her with pity. It's biology, he said, and passed his haggard wife the apples dipped in honey for double sweetness in the year to come.

But in a quiet back alley of the Jewish quarter, late that night, after leaving the dinner, Rachel met another young man, in Orthodox dress, but miraculously willing to look at her, to speak to her, who explained that women were closer to God, and were therefore excused from the elaborate and difficult process of prayer and ritual by which men had to reach toward God. Women were naturally what men had to labor to become: gentle, pious, dedicated to their families. Rachel thought for a long time afterwards of this man's

delicate face and generous interpretation, but knew that his generosity was a breach of the law. The law said to be of God could not
be understood otherwise: women were excused from their duties
to God because such callings were liable to interfere with the services they were obligated to provide to their husbands.

Judy joined Rachel in Jerusalem for Yom Kippur. They stayed in
the apartment of an American friend of Judy's. On the morning of
the day of atonement Rachel was awakened by a strange heat coming to her from the other side of the pull-out bed: Judy's body,
burning. They went to morning services. Judy picked up a non-
standard prayer book, the last one left, and the irregularity, combined with the fever, despite her familiarity with the prayers, kept
her from following the service. She stood in the waves of prayed
words, lost. Scraping a tear from her cheek with her long sleeve, she
said to Rachel softly, "I can't pray." Rachel felt then for the first
time a barrier fall away from between them, for although she could
often barely see to make her way in Judy's world, she understood,
at least, what it was to be unable to pray.

On the eve of Simchas Torah, Rachel and Judy followed Judy's
friend along the stony paths of the ancient center to the one non-
Orthodox place of worship in the old city, where women could
stand beside men and say the old words. Rachel peered into the
doorways of the Orthodox rooms, standing in the chill evening,
watching the black coated men holding their sons in the air, singing
and rejoicing over the book which kept their wives and the sisters
of their sons at home or at best in a screened garret above. In the
Conservative Synagogue a handful of American Jews sang uncertain distortions of the melodies and danced the Virginia Reel with
the scrolls of the Torah. A black-coated, black-bearded man, a spy
from Fire of the Torah Yeshiva for Men, perhaps, came in to
observe, and saw a woman holding the holy scrolls against her two
breasts. He stalked from the room, seething with the black foul
righteous smoke of the fire of the Torah. And Rachel too understood that this was incompetent, if not heretical, worship.

But there in the Revisionist Synagogue, in not the old but the new city of Jerusalem, on the following day, Rachel and Judy stood in the midst of the dancing which swept through the room like wind around and through Rachel, through even Rachel, almost against her will, and made them rise up and run and dance and the joy of the scrolls and of the child-bodies dancing and the deep voices chanting until Rachel had to go outside, and sat on the curb with her feet in the gutter under the vast and cold and silver Jerusalem sky and wept.

YOUR PAST IS WRITTEN IN OUR STONES

On Friday nights after Shabbat had set in, Rachel walked alone in the streets of Jerusalem. She could walk in the middle of the wide street in the luminous evening in the peace of the Sabbath because no cars were allowed to drive there. It was against God's rules for the peace of the day in the week that is the day of peace. Rachel didn't go to services, and Rachel didn't know how to pray, but she knew how to walk down the very center of the streets, and she did it as a ritual, an observance, an acknowledgement of and a yearning toward a time when cars did not shoot down the streets, when God's rules applied, when prayer might have been possible. She walked through the religious neighborhoods, where cars were fewest, where the light was most delicate, where the peace was richest. She could see families walking from evening services to the Friday night meal, lingering in the streets and talking or hurrying after the business of prayer in sacred disregard of the business of business. On one of these nights she saw a car driving where it should not. The religious generally put blockades in the streets against traffic, but these could be circumnavigated, pushed. At the noise of the motor, at the offense of the motorist, a group of men with clothes to pray, hair to pray, prayer shawls on their shoulders, scrambled for rocks on the ground and hurled them toward the car. But the car was gone, and some of the younger men, boys really, held unthrown rock in their hands, and Rachel suddenly understood that her hem wasn't low enough, her sleeve wasn't long enough, that her existence walking alone with breasts on the street was suspect, evil, and that the boys had turned to face her and were ready to throw their stones to strike her soulless flesh.

WHERE THE PAST MEETS THE FUTURE

In June Rachel descended from Jerusalem and returned to California. She found a summer job in an office which stood beside a church. On her way out every afternoon she passed under a sickly Christ and his four apostles, painted in the eerie, colored light of stained glass. She eyed Christ as coldly as she eyed the Americans who swarmed in the wide, wealthy streets. On an afternoon in July she went to the post office to buy stamps for the office. She had let her hair down; it fell in tight curls which looked, to Rachel, Israeli. She stood in line behind a black man, who was smoking a cigarette, whose body kept catching her eye until she had to look away. She listened to him arranging to rent a post office box. He looked at her for the duration of a long glance when the clerk looked down at the page, and then moved back toward her to touch the end of his cigarette to the lip of the ashcan at her knee. He looked at her again, gauging the curl of her hair, the width of her lips, the shade of her skin. When the second clerk dismissed a customer and called "next," the man stepped into her path and faced her and said, "Are you black?" She suddenly wanted to be as close to him as it is possible to get to the body of another human being. Then he knew; asked, as it slid away, "Half black?" "No," she said, glancing past him to the waiting clerk. It was so wide a question, and she wanted so hotly not to have given the answer she gave, the answer which had closed his face to her and made him turn away cold to take the slip of paper due him from the first clerk. He had never spoken to her. She saw nothing she could do other than step over to the second clerk and ask, emptied, for her rolls of stamps. He left the post office while she was waiting for her change: blind to her, inscrutable, a black man smoking.

EPPIE ZORE'A

Orchards

*I*magine if mango were forbidden.

Perhaps it wouldn't matter to someone who had never tasted mango. Someone born to a different mother, who didn't introduce her to this fruit, didn't teach her how fragrant a mango can be when it is ready, how to inhale its aroma before slicing it open, how to tell if it is ripe. It is the fruit my mother loved. She used to bring it home once a year, wrapped in soft tissue paper, and say, I brought you a surprise, meaning: this is between you and me; wait till your father takes his nap. Her eyes would be mischievous and bright. She would wait for the moment when the light softened and spilled through the kitchen window just so, and then set the rosy mango on ornate Passover china. She would bring out the thin, serrated knife I wasn't allowed to hold. And she would tell me about the tall mango trees she used to climb, how many different kinds there were, how laden with fruit free for the taking—greenies and tarts and spice and buxom—and how she used to puncture them and suck the juice out.

She would slice it very carefully, giving herself the smaller sections, and we would eat the fruit right to the skin. Nothing remained but the peel ridged with teeth marks and the yellow pit I didn't like to touch. Around mangos my mother abandoned decorum; she would put the large, oval pit in her mouth and get all sticky while I watched.

It was a faraway childhood she was remembering, a place she hadn't seen since she was abruptly sent away at thirteen. I believed she never talked about it except when she was eating mango with me. I believed I too was remembering her lost tropics, once a year. When we were finished we would go hunting for napkins, with me following her urgently although I'd kept my hands clean.

When I come home in the evening, you examine the traces the day has left on my face, and summarize them to me precisely. Then you pull me into your steamy study, where the temperature never drops below eighty so you won't remember it's winter in New England. You want me to recount the day's events, and you want me to listen to yours; I want to feel my hands on your cheeks and yours on mine. As a compromise we do both at the same time, which means turning off the lights and lying down a while. We taste each other's mouth, ears, jaws, nose. You seem so familiar, you say.

Perhaps, I answer. I don't want to disrupt our touching with language. But pretty soon you win, and the talking begins. We talk about the country we both come from, which I always refer to as yours, and everything that's wrong with it. About academic life, and everything wrong with it. My neuroses. Yours. Shouldn't we get up? Doesn't it seem that we've been in this bed forever? we ask each other. How *did* we wind up here?

We are used to thinking there was an apple in the beginning, but in the original text there is no apple, of course. For one thing, apples aren't native to that region. It seems they rolled down from the Lebanon mountains into our memories: if we go back to the text we don't even notice there's no apple there, and if we do, we're surprised. There are two trees, perhaps intertwined, and two versions of creation; but nowhere were there apples except in the Song of Songs.

Rapduni batapuchim ki cholat ahava ani, the lily of Jerusalem tells her flock of young friends. No translation can match this. Sustain me with raisins, refresh me with apples, the Revised Standard Version has it. Refresh me with apples: my my, is it the English or the writer who is tame. Because that's not what the poet says. Rather: lay me in a bed of apples, for I am sick with love. And like all those sick with love, I want nothing but to plunge deeper and deeper. Surround me with apples, wrap me, enrapture me. In this Song, there are apples everywhere—the lovers' breath is fresh as apples, they meet under the apple tree, apples roll like memories from the pure, crystalline North. To you and me, though, apples are nothing exotic. I often find them in my shopping cart, still rolling, where I never confine them in plastic. Granny apples, lemons, parsley, tangerines, all loose. On good days shopping is concentration and abundance. Goat camembert. Your favorite granola. Olive oil. A new kind of cauliflower that's blue. When I get to the counter I ask perfect strangers, do you think I've bought everything there is?

The scent of basil and coffee behind me in the back seat; I'm bringing all this to you. I carry the brown paper bags in, and wait until you come to admire and unpack them. You raise each fruit separately, slowly. Where did you find all this? you ask, though we both shop at the same place. You praise every item, pile the fruit on the table, and we leave it there for show.

Apple, in Hebrew *tapuach*. It's a big round word in our native tongue. From the root to exhale, blow, expand, in the sense that glass is blown and shaped at once. A word that comes from deep in the smithy's shop, but in the old texts it's not the human smithy that counts. Nor could human minds have forged the odd, intricate connections in this language, like the one between apple and blowing. *Tapuach* is a generic word for fruit. The Hebrew has earth apples for potatoes, and golden apples for oranges. When I was small, there were also Atalanta's golden apples. I thought they were the prizes of women who could run really fast and who knew exactly what they wanted. I planned to be that kind.

A story my mother loved to tell and I loved to hear: how Atalanta, the Olympic runner and excellent huntress, the woman with a name like a lost continent, upset her father's plans to marry her off. Instead of a contest among suitors, she arranged to compete with them herself. She declared she would have only the man who could run faster than she. But no man could.

In the end, though, she did marry. That's where the golden apples come in, and the tricky man who won her favor—Melodion, the honeyed man. Did she love him for his curly hair? When I'm listening to the story I never even see him. Instead, I see my mother's long fingers with the beautiful, delicate blue veins that show—as I explain to my young friends—whether a woman is compassionate and wise, and which I am worried I won't acquire. Some women have them, and some women don't. And I see blond Atalanta in her white pleated tunic, a breezy, invincible runner who will choose rather than be chosen by any man. I know that my mother and Atalanta are somehow related deep down, and that my mother ran very fast when she was young, although now she just walks to the bus in her high heels. When she leaves in the morning she looks elegant and busy and important, and when she returns in the afternoon she looks tired, but after her nap she's all mine. As the story continues, I still cannot see Melodion at all, only the golden apples he rolls towards Atalanta in mid-run. Something about their perfect gold surface, their weight, the way she can tell they will feel like fullness itself in her hands, a fullness as delicious as that endless flying run but more fascinating and strange. I see her stop to lift one up, and when it does indeed feel like fullness, exactly as she knew it would, she smiles. He gets ahead, but she could still win if she wanted. To stay on the safe side, he rolls her another. By the time he sends the third, she has conceded; they will become man and wife.

But was it his tricks that really decided things, or an amused Atalanta, pretending to be tricked? My mother says, think how she must have swept down to lift those apples and kept on running all the same. Woosh.

There was another story my mother told. Once upon a time the gods discovered an old man and woman who were very very good, and who loved each other very much. When a goddess came to visit, disguised as a beggar of course, and said she would grant them one wish, they asked to die at the same time. She liked them so much she devised something better. At death—they died arm in arm, kissing—they were turned into two trees, and as they grew side by side their branches intertwined. Isn't that touching, my mother says. She's so moved I think she might cry. But I am unconvinced this time, so I don't answer. No one in this story has any personality. I can see the trees very clearly, too, a set of mock orange trees whose carefully trimmed leaves form a gate over the entrance to our apartment house and the houses of all our neighbors. Orange trees or not, they never bear fruit.

The trees are still there to this day, the legend says. Here we are: my mother at twenty-eight, carefree and captivating; and myself, perhaps five, perhaps seven, equipped and complete with her images of love. But it's golden apples I want to know more about.

So I saunter into the world alone, looking, leaving my mother and her mangos behind. Not immediately, of course. By the time I'm thirteen, I too have been moved to a foreign country, this country, a process that can take up several years in an adolescent girl's life. But as early as possible, I go wandering through two continents, acquiring all the wrong lovers. They are sweet, they are alluring, and they're willing to be distracted: all wonderful qualities in a man. But their wrongness is easily recognizable long before I bring them home because whether my mother likes them or not (mostly the latter), they don't fit the pictures she and I etched in my mind.

Disappointed, I return to the country I was born in to live in a house surrounded by tangerine trees. The house is on a hill ringed by terraces and chicken houses, and underneath them heaps of chicken dung emit hot, redolent vapors. Further down there are mustard flowers and a failed reservoir. This is the village you have never yet left; these are the terraces you and your friends jumped, riding bareback with your mares when you were twelve. This is where you passed your childhood in such friendship with the animals that their personalities were much more interesting to you than those of the adults. But none of this explains why I see such a glow around your face when you first come to my door. We are introduced.

You speak so softly people have to strain to listen, although you stand very close, giving off a palpable warmth. And you look straight into everyone's eyes, as though nothing terrible could be exposed by doing so, nothing would be unraveled. It is impossible to lie in your presence, I realize early on. You shuffle. You would never embarrass anyone. You have been alone for a long while.

During our first meeting I tactfully mention another man in my life at least twenty times. But I find myself walking down to the abandoned reservoir hoping to see you, walking around the corner to the grocer's hoping to see you, beginning to walk by your house. And so, although we both have our reasons to deny it, we walk into the first chapter, where my mother's favorite Player—the Presence she insisted resembled her father, despite various clues to the contrary—has a leading role. And under our very eyes your village becomes His garden, the spiralling garden where you tame the animals and ride Breeza, the garden where He put both of us down just before the Sabbath, when all His work was done. That's the first chapter, before there were second thoughts, and the writer, or God, started over.

It's a story of a blessing. Later there will be a curse, too, and a prominent place for the large, single mango on a very young mango tree in the middle of the garden. But initially the creation is a love story. There's nobody there but us.

In fact, the world was made twice. The first time was gradual and perfect. Day by day He made trees and beasts and grasses, all according to their kind, and He saw that they were good. There were no dangers, and therefore no one was warned and nothing was forbidden. The sky was separated from the earth. Waters were gathered. There were greens and rivers, birds and sheep and leopards, and no one had wounded your dog, and your favorite mare had yet to go mad. The garden spiraled up from the river at the bottom, through the terraces of peonies that bloomed all year around and the rungs of goats, lambs and sheep, with their odd, beautiful habit of standing motionless to face the twilight. And above them those shiny black Arabian horses, and then the fruit trees all around: pomegranate and grapefruit and olive and aromatic lemon, and twenty kinds of citrus that can't even be named in English, and the cherry trees through which you rode, standing up, picking the ripe fruit with both hands, and plums; but no apple trees, of course. And no one had said this was a garden, as though there could be anything besides gardens in this world, and no one had said you or I would have to work. And nothing stood in the middle this time but ourselves, at the top of a knobby hill, with the honeysuckle and jasmine, which were naturally in flower. And everything was for us.

And He said: *Pru u'rvu. Pru u'rvu.* Be fruitful and multiply. That was when He blessed us. *Pru,* He said, meaning "Fruit," a verb, "Fruit," a command. Be as the fruit of these trees all around, fill and swell. Be sweet in one another's mouth.

Notice He didn't say be like these trees or these flowers. He didn't say we should be busy, like these bees. Nor fluttery and scented, like butterflies. Nor noble, like the stallions. There were only two models provided: Himself, inasmuch as it says we were made in His image that time, and the fruit, hanging luscious and precise. Which might give you some idea of what He was like. But then neither of us saw Him. There was only the effect of His sounds.

Not that you always admitted what you heard. When He whispered to us to come walk by the river, to search for each other there, and you wouldn't come. I knew well His whisper was all around you, and that the pull He exerted was powerful as reins. Wherever I looked I was sure you would appear, because the hush of His world on those afternoons before the Sabbath, with that warm breeze in the willows and the animals' slowed breath made Him impossible to refuse. And I would walk through the wadi at the rich, alluvial bottom of His garden, watching the miracle of this world, in which everything He spent the original six days separating so carefully—earth and sky, light and darkness, stars and roots, you and me—would regularly and repeatedly melt into one another at the end of the week, or the end of the day. And then, just as evening descended I would find you behind me on the terrace, focussed and glowing. You would laugh to catch me mumbling urgently to myself, and I would make futile attempts to disguise how much I enjoyed being caught.

So many ways His voice had of sounding through these meadows. When He played the fiddle at the top of the hill, and blew His damp evening winds through the honeysuckle and hyacinth, right after the regular evening rains you loved so much. When He puffed up the moon round like a fruit for the very first time and sent all the waters, over and under the ground, swelling towards it. And those inside us.

There was the silly, perfectly visible halo He put around your head at the start, like a naive Byzantine painter indicating the presence of goodness. After I saw your face, His voice became a yearning within me, something not heard, but felt. And there was no way to tell *His* thoughts from our flesh.

Or at least from mine. But you were cautious. You came to talk about poetry. I said the words are always at one remove from the world, longing to return. I was sitting with my feet up, my toes bare, and as we talked and you were listening, rapt, you raised your own feet and tried to match their soles with mine. You seemed surprised that yours were bigger, but you left them there, exerting only a tiny pressure. And so week after week we met, moving forward, holding back. Months later, with an infant's gesture, you would fumble with my bracelet and my buttons, not to open my shirt but just to touch. And I knew how thoroughly you must be hearing Him. You were ravenous, a hunger so intense it made you timid, although you're not a timid man. And still you waited, and wrapped yourself shyly in your plaid blanket when I came by late at night and didn't say yes, absolutely yes, but you constantly rolled me apples.

Sometimes, in fact, you said, no, perhaps not; we don't really know each other; this might be an illusion. At which times I said, go to hell. We sat very close. It's not that I don't feel for you, you'd qualify, and unconsciously begin rocking me a little, cradling to and fro. Then you'd look at me gently and say, you're hurt by all this. And I'd think, you might say so, yes, you might call it that, and loosen myself out of your arms, suspecting that your refusal gave you pleasure. But mostly I paid no attention, because I could recognize fullness immediately when I saw it, as I still can. I could tell well in advance what your face and your willingness would feel like in my hands.

It took us nine months. We understood different things, according to our kinds. You said love was endless curiosity; I thought it was already knowing. I felt I was the one calling the shots, you were sure it was you, and of course there was God's view. Each of us felt rather well connected to Him, but between us we didn't agree on many things. This is how it is in the first chapter, when He creates them, identical yet different, in a world the stuff of which is definition, boundary, and whose consequence is yearning: simple, potent, unitary. One. Before His second thoughts, His second chapter.

The second time He reverses it. We are no longer blessed by separateness and yearning across a boundary in the garden. No gulf of danger and difference concentrates our entire being, making desire the center of existence, making us, therefore, centered and whole. Together, we leave the warm country where both of us were born, and exchange it for New England. We trade the terraces of your village for the cement corridors of dark universities. We buy airline tickets and face immigration officers. It is we who have become one, gentle and familiar, contending with the shadowy world outside. A world He hasn't separated and sequenced methodically this time, by days and categories. A world where everything is mixed together, and we are left to our own arbitrary devices for naming or understanding things. On some days we have to stretch our imagination to see this world as a garden at all.

This time there's a prominent place in the center for the large, ripening mango on a very young mango tree in the middle of the garden. A single mango, leaf green with pale pink spreading, and confusing, beautiful leaves, like flowers. You might call this the story of a marriage. No one is made in His image any longer; things are not created and then separated at once. There is nothing but the continuous transformation of matter and its occasional residue. Adam is made out of dust, for instance. Eve is made of his rib. The humiliations begin.

And His commandment is precisely the opposite this time. Don't eat of the fruit, He says. And to help us forget He avoids using the word, lest the very sound, "fruit," act as a reminder. Don't eat of the tree at the center of the garden, He says, the tree of knowledge, good and bad. Don't eat, for you must not remember how the world, and the garden, once were.

You, who were the village's chosen son, its best rider and arbiter, are now the lonely man in the study who comes out to greet me every night. There are no horses with us here, none of their pungent, leathery scent, their pulsing, towering bodies with hypersensitive nerves making things so vivid for those near them. We have only cars, and long enclosed drives over hilly, monotonous landscapes. The garden, like that sultry *boostan* you took me to after love was finally declared and admitted between us, is shady, aromatic, and abandoned. It is littered with crab apples and ill-formed quinces. Fruit, rather than hanging gorgeously from trees, is lying on the ground. Always the possibility of corruption. This is the world of things already merged and merging with one another, like fruit and earth, like ripe and rot.

Like our bedroom Sunday mornings, the strewn jeans, newspapers, peach stones, used condoms, and a pile of clean shirts you'll have to walk through to get anywhere. Or like us waking up together on the couch on evenings we never meant to squander. After one of us made mashed potatoes, and drew the other into a long, meandering conversation on the unexpected benefits of eighteenth-century Russian serfdom, our latest idea of good dinner talk. Then becoming full and loose and tired, not remembering things we planned to read and think. Ending up on the couch soaking in one another's heat, as the shapless night deepens. We awaken to light, elusive necklaces of pain hanging down our backs, blankets falling all over the students' papers, the smell of each other on our fingers and the dinner remains on the plates and in our mouths. We lose all sense of what the hour might possibly be as these nights lengthen unbearably towards the foreign, icy winter you can't get used to.

We shop for one another, however irregularly, and when we finally fill the house with food again it sometimes takes days to unpack those paper bags, sort the oranges from the curry, according to their kinds. Things accrue in the wrong places or at least the wrong time frame, like tomato sauce behind the refrigerator, or old, hardened spaghetti from longer ago than last week or last month. In the cupboard by the phone we keep notes and bills and stray phone numbers, and crackers, and a hammer, and cereals and rice. Last month every time we opened it we were greeted by a flood of tiny butterflies.

Look, I said, something must be wrong here. You said it's just some moths and that I'm generally too suspicious. But I still thought it odd: tiny flying things fluttering out of falafel mix and Swedish crackers. Yet it was pleasant, too, somehow, a secret fount of life erupting from deep in our house, from those boxes of iron nails and biscuits. Besides, I trusted your judgment.

And then we had a warning: when I saw what I thought was a freshly trimmed finger nail of yours floating in my tea—I had seen you with the nail-cutter that morning—and spent several minutes fishing it out, thinking how elaborate the ancient Jewish law was, how it provided rules for everything including where and how to dispose of nail cuttings, and how I should tell you about that, and then discovered it wasn't a nail at all. It was extremely slippery. You were watching a movie with a friend in the living room, and I didn't utter a syllable. Fished it out, drank the tea down. In Mexico, I've heard, some drink tequila *with* the worm.

Then you found one on the counter. And another. The closet once inhabited by tiny moths seemed innocuous, until we looked into the bags holding cashews, flour, crackers, pistachio nuts, and found the perfectly drilled holes, the sticky threads of worm juice, the broken nuts. We could see the worms inside, working and slithering away. Nor were they confined to that cupboard. They had meanwhile colonized several drawers at the other end of the kitchen. We threw out bags and bags of dried food we had been keeping patiently for years. Still it wasn't over. There were worms everywhere. We found them escaping into our dishes and glass case, holed up under the wax paper, settled behind the food processor. On the phone your mother explained to us about worms, how to recognize the danger signs, and about their life cycle: butterfly, egg, larva, pupa. She said there's no particular season to any stage; all can happen simultaneously. When we returned to examine the kitchen's condition in the evening the cupboards were clean, but there were several large worms crawling slowly and securely on the ceiling. You were close to losing your hallmark containment. I was simply curious, examining the bags of nuts carefully, the busy undulations.

This is what it looks like when they bury a person in the ground, I reminded you. They always throw that metaphor at us, but it's not that bad, really.

Must you, you were practically begging. Do you actually *need* to say this, or are you doing it for pleasure?

You were disgusted and depressed all day.

For me it's the supermarket, not decay, that can grow dangerous. Times when I go early in the morning because we have friends coming and I want to save the day for reading about sugar plantations and slaves. And I think it will be a treat, walking between the potatoes and lettuce with the little sprinklers placed above it, and before I've done one aisle I find myself hysterical. I come home to beg you to hold me, and when you do I snap about the division of labor in this house, crying with terror that my life will be shrunk into supermarket aisles like my mother's life, because I have been taught about love by my mother's love. In the evening, after a day spent soothing away the argument, you will shut the windows tight. In the morning, the room, like our breath, will be heavy and ripe.

Everything is mixed together now. You take care of me when the shakes come in the morning; I support you when you choose outrageously stubborn stands. It takes no time to gauge one another's condition, and desire is no longer something stormy, but a steady current between us.

On what turned out to be the last Sunday of autumn we are dressing side by side, until you notice the stain on my silk pants. You suggest I iron them. There's agreement between us on ironing as a last-resort rescue for soiled clothing, although the level of desperation required is in dispute. I follow your guidance, and come upstairs to show you it was perfectly ineffectual. You can't go like that, you say and begin smoothing the folds in the fabric.

You're making it more noticeable, I say. I explain I've already tried it with hot water, that I've put in a fine effort, that I'm not to be blamed. The way I remember it, it's semen from last Sunday morning, but even so there's some confusion about how it got there. You come at me with a bristle brush we use to clean the bathtub. I'm trying gently to remind you that dried semen is very stubborn; it never does come off. Your preparations take longer. The first three shirts you try don't look right. Your favorite T-shirt is tight under the arm. I left your best sweater—the slate blue one your aunt knitted for you, the one you were wearing when we met on my stoop in a country where autumn is warm and balmy— somewhere in the university two weeks ago. As you iron the Indian shirt, I'm analyzing why you're anxious. In the car you force my seat belt on, and I chant my litany of annoyances: you forgot to buy toilet paper again, there's no gasoline in the gas tank, I still miss that tape of ballads you lost two years ago. But I have a surprise for you on the local radio station, something I've been planning for weeks. Not a tape; a regular Sunday morning show I found and was waiting for a chance to share: songs from home.

Later that afternoon finds us on the way to the train, entranced by the final yellow streaks over another depressed Northern city, driving through a gold world turned purple at an hour we aren't yet prepared to call evening. Driving back and forth on the same desolate stretch of highway, over and over, unable to find the right exit though we have been here so many times. Discovering, as the light fails, that this particular section of 787 has no lighting or signpost billboards. Keeping the car warm and funny for each other, knowing that a cold season is coming. And though we're together every day, even a two-day parting makes us cringe, so that when we finally do find the station, we agree that we *must* eat, which means waiting two more hours for your train, prolonging the uncertainty.

You have an omelette with feta. I read my book about slavery and complain about the style. Sure you won't change your mind? It's not that we're principally against these short partings, quite the contrary. But the chill suddenly in late October, the reminder that for months there will be winter, your sadness, your feelings about New York. Separating even briefly seems like a tearing, as though someone has sewn our bodies together invisibly. We feel small: the tentacles of winter just outside the car window, sharply palpable, my knowing you want to bury your face in my body, the compassion we're feeling for one another, how thick the loneliness that surrounds us. In honor of your return I will sweep the kitchen floor and do what I always do when you come home: shop.

We are deep in the second chapter, merged and merging. The chapter of cleaving to one another in foreign countries and becoming one flesh. Of your leaving your father and mother, who may well die in your absence without saying goodbye. Of a loneliness so great it cannot be assuaged by all the animals in the world, though this time He makes them expressly for this purpose. A loneliness unmitigated by their howls and murmurs and swishing, or by the act of naming and distinguishing them, which He generously delegates this time. Yes, He gives us work this round; our labor is cut out for us. But all the concentrated effort it requires can't relieve us of our solitude. Nor can love. It's the chapter in which He sees this loneliness, His handiwork, and says it is not good. But what He created even He cannot solve.

This round there are no blessings. We no longer have any doubts about who is calling the shots here, but the lines have been redrawn. It is not you against me in the subtle fencing of desire, but us against Him. Somewhere, not to be named, or touched, or looked at, hang the fruits He's revealed and then hidden.

And He says, don't even think of it; you can't have that blessing now. This is no longer a world in which some person, any person, can contain the other half. This is no longer a world which can be remedied by desire. You know better now. Furthermore, He tells us, there is nothing to be done with this memory you're carrying. Even if the fruit seems so close by, it is not to be had, now *or* later. It is your past. Don't you try to eat it, it was not made for your sustenance, let it hang.

As for the apple, its stubborn presence was no accident after all. It's not found on any tree in that second chapter but squarely on the ground: what was swollen, blown, and filled with breath but Adam? He's the one partaking of the root of "apple" in this story; he's the only thing engorged with life. When God saw him like that, made of earth, pathetic, destined to be lonely, He must have licked him all over very slowly like a tender mother cat. And then He gave him mouth to mouth. It was the initial ecstasy, and the last. For that moment Adam himself was the apple, of God's breath, of God's eye. And who is Adam if not the body of all our bodies, the source of our most subterranean knowledge, prior to language? Everything that followed his one moment of glory, and ours, would be losing and naming, losing and naming. What was left but reminders of God's kisses, hanging temptingly on trees? No wonder He said not to eat them.

After her children grew up, my mother liked to say that our task on this earth is to hold back corruption. She said if we worked hard enough we could stay in the first chapter. She thought homes should be kept clean. And in her later years she didn't eat mango anymore. Perhaps with her children gone she was too sad, or the sweetness was too much for someone who claimed there was nothing, nothing missing from her life. Myself, I sifted through her advice, threw out the bad. But I'll always align myself with Eve and the childlike, mango-loving woman, my first love, the one who knows she's cast out but still lingers, refusing to let go, remembering paradise in her mouth.

ABOUT THE AUTHORS

MAX APPLE's stories have appeared in various magazines since 1972. His books include: *The Oranging of America and Other Short Stories, Zip, Free Agents,* and *The Propheteers.* Apple grew up in Michigan, and for most of his career has lived in Houston, Texas, where he teaches writing at Rice University.

SAUL BELLOW was awarded the Nobel Prize for literature in 1976. He is a member of the Committee on Social Thought at the University of Chicago. His most recent works include *More Die of Heartbreak* and *Something to Remember Me By,* whose title story appears here.

MARSHA LEE BERKMAN lives and writes in the San Francisco Bay Area. Her fiction has been published in a wide variety of academic and literary magazines. Her novella, *The Persistence of Desire,* was awarded a prize in the 1991 *Quarterly West* Novella Competition. She has completed a collection of stories and is writing a novel.

MICHAEL CHABON was born in Washington, D.C., in 1963 and raised in Columbia, Maryland. He has written one novel, *The Mysteries of Pittsburgh,* and one collection of short stories, *A Model World,* most of which, including "S Angel," appeared first in *The New Yorker.* His second novel, *Fountain City,* will appear in 1993. Chabon's maternal grandfather's grandfather was the chief rabbi of Vilna. His father's first cousin was the great journalist Abraham Cahan.

E. L. DOCTOROW's novels include *The Book of Daniel, Ragtime, Loon Lake, World's Fair,* and *Billy Bathgate.* "The Writer in the Family" is taken from *Lives of the Poets: A Novella and Six Stories.*

ALLEGRA GOODMAN was born in Brooklyn in 1967 and raised in Honolulu, Hawaii. As a freshman at Harvard she published her first short story in *Commentary.* In her senior year in college, she saw the publication of her collection of short fiction, *Total Immersion.* Since then, she has published fiction in *The New Yorker* and has been writing a novel while studying for a Ph.D. in Renaissance Literature as a Mellon Fellow at Stanford.

MARK HELPRIN is the author of *A Dove of the East and Other Stories, Refiner's Fire, Ellis Island and Other Stories* (for which he received the National Jewish Book Award), *Winter's Tale, Swan Lake* (with illustrations by Chris Van Allsburg), and *A Soldier of the Great War.* Educated at Harvard and Oxford, he served in the Israeli infantry and Air Force.

ALLEN HOFFMAN was born and grew up in St. Louis, Missouri. After graduating from Harvard College, he studied the Talmud in yeshivas in Jerusalem and New York City. Currently he resides in Jerusalem with his family and teaches English at Bar Ilan University.

JOHANNA KAPLAN is the author of *Other People's Lives*, a collection of stories, and *O My America!*, a novel. Her books have been nominated for the National Book Award, the American Book Award, and the Ernest Hemingway–PEN Prize, and she has twice received the Jewish Book Award for fiction. She is a teacher of special education in the New York City public schools.

DEIRDRE LEVINSON was born in Wales and raised in the north of England. Her first novel, *Five Years: An Experience of South Africa*, was published in 1966, and her second novel, *Modus Vivendi*, was published in 1984. She teaches literature in New York City.

BERNARD MALAMUD, who died in 1986, was one of the pioneering figures in American Jewish fiction beginning with his novels, *The Natural* and *The Assistant*, and his collection of stories, *The Magic Barrel*, which won the National Book Award in 1958. Among the works that distinguished his subsequent career were *A New Life, The Fixer, Dubin's Lives*, and an edition of his collected stories which appeared in 1983.

DAPHNE MERKIN is a writer and critic living in New York City. She is the author of *Enchantment*, (the first chapter of which is included in this collection) which won the Edward Lewis Wallant award for best contemporary Jewish novel in 1986. Formerly the associate publisher of Harcourt Brace Jovanovich, she writes for *The New York Times, Mirabella*, and other publications. Her second novel, *The Discovery of Sex*, will be published in 1993.

LEONARD MICHAELS has published two collections of stories, a novel, and a work of autobiographical fiction: *Going Places, I Would Have Saved Them if I Could, The Men's Club*, and *Shuffle*. His stories have appeared in the O. Henry Prize collections, and *The Best American Stories*. He teaches at the University of California, Berkeley.

CYNTHIA OZICK, a novelist and essayist, is a four-time First Prize winner of the O. Henry Short Story Awards. Her books include *The Cannibal Galaxy, The Messiah of Stockholm*, *The Pagan Rabbi and Other Stories*, *The Shawl*, and a collection of essays, *Metaphor & Memory*. She has recently completed a play, which will be produced in 1993.

GRACE PALEY's stories have been collected in *Enormous Changes at the Last Minute*, *Later the Same Day*, and *The Little Disturbances of Man*. She lives in New York and Thetford Hills, Vermont, and teaches at Sarah Lawrence and City College.

NESSA RAPOPORT's first novel, *Preparing for Sabbath*, was published in 1981 and reissued in 1988. She has now completed her second, *The Perfection of the World*. A collection of her prose-poems, *A Woman's Book of Grieving*, is forthcoming in 1993. Her short stories, essays, and articles have been published widely.

ROBIN ROGER, who lives and works in Toronto, was educated at the University of Toronto, Columbia University, and the Jewish Theological Seminary of America. Her writing has appeared in several Canadian publications including *Quarry* and *Fireweed*. Her first novel, *Stamps*, was short-listed in the SEAL First Novel contest.

PHILIP ROTH was born in Newark, New Jersey, in 1933. He began his career with *Goodbye, Columbus*, winner of the National Book Award for Fiction in 1960; in 1987 he won the National Book Critics Circle Award for his novel *The Counterlife* and again in 1992 won the National Book Critics Circle Award for his autobiographical memoir, *Patrimony*. He has published nineteen books.

ADAM SCHWARTZ was educated at Macalester College and the University of Iowa Writer's Workshop. He teaches writing at Harvard, has been published in *The New Yorker* and *Wigwag*, and is presently working on a collection of stories.

LYNNE SHARON SCHWARTZ has written four novels, *Leaving Brooklyn* (nominated for a PEN/Faulkner Award), *Disturbances in the Field*, *Rough Strife*, and *Balancing Acts*; and two collections of stories, *Acquainted with the Night* and *The Melting Pot and Other Subversive Stories*. Her translation from the Italian of Liana Millu's *Smoke over Birkenau* won the 1991 PEN Renato Poggioli Translation Award. Her most recent book is *A Lynne Sharon Schwartz Reader*, published by the University Press of New England.

LORE SEGAL is a novelist, essayist, translator, and writer of children's books. Her recent work include *Her First American*, and *Other People's Houses*, and two Bible translations, *The Book of Adam to Moses* and *The Story of King Saul and King David*. She is currently completing a novel entitled *An Absence of Cousins*.

Isaac Bashevis Singer, the author of more than forty books, died in 1991. The leading writer of modern Yiddish fiction, he won the Nobel Prize for literature in 1978. His last published works include his *Collected Stories, Love and Exile: An Autobiographical Trilogy, The Death of Methuselah,* and *Scum.*

Joanna Spiro has published fiction in *Mademoiselle.* She is currently working on a Ph.D. in comparative literature at Yale.

Eppie Zore'a is a writer and student of the ancient Near East. Born in Jerusalem, she writes and teaches in Amherst, Massachusetts.